PERSISTENT GUILT

Also by Michael J. McCann

THE MARCH AND WALKER CRIME NOVEL SERIES

Sorrow Lake
Burn Country

THE DONAGHUE AND STAINER CRIME NOVEL SERIES

Blood Passage
Marcie's Murder
The Fregoli Delusion
The Rainy Day Killer

SUPERNATURAL FICTION

The Ghost Man

Persistent Guilt

A March and Walker Crime Novel

Michael J. McCann

The Plaid Raccoon Press
2018

Persistent Guilt is a work of fiction. Names, characters, institutions, places and events are either the product of the author's imagination or are used fictitiously. Any resemblance to actual persons, living or dead, events, or locales is entirely coincidental.

PERSISTENT GUILT
Copyright © 2018 by Michael J. McCann

All rights reserved, including the right to reproduce this book, or portions thereof, in any form.

ISBN: 978-1-927884-13-3
eBook ISBN: 978-1-927884-14-0

Cover image: imagoRB/Thinkstock
Author photo: Timothy D. McCann

www.theplaidraccoonpress.com
www.mjmccann.com

To the memory of my mother
Janet Irene Brook McCann

chapter
ONE

Detective Constable Kevin Walker of the Ontario Provincial Police looked up from his notebook in surprise. "He broke in where, again?"

Rony Haddad came out from behind his cash register and led the way through the store to an open door at the back. "Here. Through the window."

Kevin frowned at the tiny washroom which he'd used once, about a year ago, while passing through Rockport on his way to somewhere else. Sure enough, the window had been used to gain entry into the convenience store. Someone had broken the bottom pane, reached inside, unlocked the window, swung it in, and squeezed through an opening of about twenty-five inches by twenty.

"How high up is this window on the outside?"

"About seven feet. He dragged the trash bin from the front and got up on that."

"Have you been in here? Touched anything?"

"No, Kevin. I watch TV like everybody else, you know.

There might be fingerprints and DNA."

Kevin put his notebook in his jacket pocket and used his cellphone to take photographs of the window, the broken glass on the floor, and the smudged shoeprints on the toilet seat. "And it was just cigarettes? That's all they took?"

Haddad led the way up to the front of the store. "Six cartons. Everything that was left on this shelf." He pointed at a cabinet behind the cash register where his cigarettes were stored. Ontario regulations prohibited the open display of tobacco products, and like most merchants Haddad kept his stock in a metal storage unit with top-hinge flip-up covers. "It was like that when I got here this morning to open the store."

"Just the cigarettes," Kevin repeated, taking a few pictures of the cabinet and the empty shelf. Someone had used a crowbar or other similar tool to pry open the cover of one of the shelves, breaking the lock in the process.

"Yep, that's why I know it was the Lawson kid." Haddad had already explained his theory to Kevin. Last evening he'd turned away a thirteen-year-old boy who lived with his mother at the edge of the hamlet. The kid was constantly pestering him for cigarettes, which were illegal to sell in Ontario to anyone under the age of nineteen, and this time the confrontation had gotten a little loud. The kid stormed out of the store with an unpaid chocolate bar in his hand, but Haddad had waved it off, knowing he could get the money from the boy's mother, since it had happened before.

Kevin set his phone on the counter and jotted down a few more notes. He thought a thirteen-year-old might be able to make it through the small washroom window where a fully-grown adult might not, and so he wrote down the boy's name, the mother's name, and the street on which they lived.

"What time last night was he in?"

"Seven fifty, seven fifty-five. Right about then. Just before closing."

Kevin was writing this down when his cellphone began to buzz. He checked the call display and answered it. "Walker."

"A body on the Thousand Islands Parkway," said Detective Sergeant Tom Carty, commander of the Leeds County Crime Unit. "Probable homicide. What's your twenty?"

"I'm still in Rockport. The B-and-E at Willard's Convenience Store."

"Okay, that's good. You're the closest. First responders have secured the immediate scene, and EMS is on site. We're shutting down the Parkway, so make sure the west perimeter is set before you go in. I'll be there in about fifteen minutes."

"Where are you closing the Parkway?" Kevin asked.

"Between Larue Mills and Rockport."

"You don't need to close it this far down, do you? You could do it at Narrows Lane Road."

"You think?"

"Less disruptive. Fewer complaints."

"All right, Walker. That's fine. Now get your ass in gear."

"Uh, okay. Listen, Tom." Kevin hesitated, thinking quickly. Unlike the previous shoplifting incidents, which Rony Haddad had overlooked, the convenience store owner had called in this break-and-enter, so it couldn't be smoothed over with a warning. Kevin hated to see a young person's life derailed by a criminal conviction, but he knew of several cases in which this kind of trouble had become a life-changing occurrence for the better instead of for the worse. "Let's get a cruiser and a SOCO down here on the B-and-E. I think we know the kid who did it. I'd like something in my pocket before talking to him and his mother."

Having a scenes-of-crime officer come down to the convenience store to collect fingerprints and other physical evidence would hopefully give Kevin enough leverage to convince the boy that he should admit what he'd done and accept the consequences. It might be the first step in turning around his life before he travelled too much farther down this particular road.

"Okay," Carty said. "Leave it with me and get moving. Make sure the perimeter's set on the Parkway. Go."

"Yes, sir." Kevin ended the call. "I have to leave," he told Haddad, "but someone will be here shortly. I'm going to have to ask you to stay closed this morning."

"Shit. I was afraid of that."

"Don't touch the washroom or go around the side of the building before they get here. They'll look for shoeprints and whatever else. All right? We'll try to get you open before noon."

"Damn it, all right."

Fumbling for his car keys, Kevin hurried out.

chapter
TWO

The Thousand Islands Parkway was a forty-kilometre stretch of two-lane highway that ran along the north shore of the St. Lawrence River from Gananoque up to Butternut Bay, just west of Brockville. Bypassing the extremely busy Macdonald-Cartier Freeway, also known as Highway 401, the Parkway provided a scenic route along the river through the Frontenac Arch biosphere, which featured ancient granite ridges and a forest region that was home to a wide range of plant and animal life.

Just a few minutes west of the village of Rockport at Ivy Lea, the Thousand Islands Bridge connected Hill Island to Wellesley Island on the American side of the river. Proximity to an international border crossing in the middle of this picturesque stretch of the St. Lawrence meant that traffic on the Parkway was often a mixture of local and American travellers. Thankfully, however, it was only the third week in April and cottage season was still a month away, so tourists and visitors right now were at a minimum.

When Kevin arrived at the intersection of the Parkway and Narrows Lane Road, he found that OPP traffic units dispatched from nearby Lansdowne had already set up a barricade on the far side of the intersection, blocking eastbound access to the Parkway. A cruiser was parked sideways across the road. In front of the vehicle stood an eight-foot rail barricade on A-frame ends. A sign in the middle of the rail said:

EMERGENCY
ROAD CLOSED
By Police Order – Section 134 H.T.A.

Kevin pulled over onto the shoulder of the road and got out. Looking around, he spotted a uniformed officer with three stripes on his sleeves standing in a knot of constables next to the cruiser. The meeting broke up as Kevin walked across the intersection. Seeing him, the sergeant nodded and stepped forward.

"Kevin, what took you so long?" The sergeant, whose name was Melken, threw him a firm handshake. "How's the baby? A boy, right?"

"That's right, Sarge. He's fine."

"You won't get a good night's sleep for the rest of your life."

"Tell me about it." Kevin looked around. "Everything okay here?"

Melken nodded. "There was mist early this morning, coming off the river. It's pretty much all burned off now, so visibility's better."

"Yeah, it was foggy up my way, too." Kevin pointed across the intersection at a bait shop and convenience store on the northwest corner. The store had a giant replica of a smallmouth bass perched on its roof. "They have pizza by the slice in there, don't they?"

"Yeah, but it's shit."

Kevin squinted at the short dogleg that ran beside the

store up to Old River Road, which was a narrow gravel strip that paralleled the Parkway right past their crime scene. "What about up there? Should we block it off, too?"

Melken shook his head. "Houses. Local traffic. We need a bypass. We can't send everybody back to the 401."

"It gets pretty close to the Parkway at some points."

"Relax, Kevin. There's two hundred metres of brush between it and our crime scene. I've got a cruiser posted up there to make sure no one tries to get nosy."

Kevin thanked him and went back to his car. He eased around the barrier and the cruiser and accelerated up the empty highway.

A kilometre later he parked at the end of a line of vehicles and walked up to the barricade marking the inner perimeter of the crime scene. He showed the officer his badge and identification, signed the log, and approached Provincial Constable Nancy Wyndham, the first responder to the scene.

"EMS checked," she said, glancing over her shoulder, "but there's no doubt. You can see some of the stab wounds without even going down into the ditch. We're waiting for the coroner."

"Who called it in?"

She pointed at a nearby tan-coloured Subaru Outback. A bicycle was secured to the back of the vehicle on a trunk mount. The Subaru was parked inside the barrier, which meant that it was currently being treated as part of the crime scene. "Old guy was riding his bike on the path with his dog. Name of Garvey, Edward H. DOB twenty-eleven-forty-nine. He lives on Front Street in Rockport. The dog spotted the body and started to bark, so Garvey came over and found it."

Kevin glanced over at the paved bicycle trail that ran alongside the Parkway on its northern edge. At one time this stretch of road had been part of the four-lane 401 freeway, until a different route was constructed through Lansdowne and this portion was downgraded to a two-lane secondary highway. The unused westbound lane was eventually converted into a thirty-seven-kilometre-long bike path. The man, Garvey, would have been out getting his morning exercise when he came across the body.

"How'd the car get here?"

"He called his wife. She drove up to see what he was talking about. *Then* they called 911."

"Where's the dog?"

"In the vehicle, with them. It's registered to the wife. The vehicle, I mean. Patricia Mary Garvey."

Kevin turned around at the sound of someone arriving at the far barricade. He watched Tom Carty slide out of his OPP SUV and make his way into the crime scene. In the absence of Scott Patterson, who was currently filling in as operations manager at regional headquarters, Carty was acting as the supervisor of the Leeds County Crime Unit, which was mandated to investigate all criminal complaints within the detachment's jurisdiction.

"Tell them I'll be with them in a few minutes," Kevin said to Wyndham, nodding at the Subaru.

"Will do."

Kevin met Carty at a spot where a mixture of cedar trees and winterkilled bulrushes hid the view of the river. The shoulder was paved to a width of about four feet, a legacy of the old freeway, after which it dropped down into a ditch filled with the remnants of last year's Queen Anne's Lace and wild parsley. The body lay face down in the ditch, stiffened into an odd position with its knees pulled up under the torso and the arms partially extended, hands out, fingers spread wide.

It was female and nude. As Wyndham had said, Kevin could see several puncture wounds between the breast and hip bone facing him. The pale, bare flesh was marred by dark blood smears. The victim had been small, only a few inches more than five feet tall and about one hundred pounds. The straight, blond-brown hair was somewhat longer than shoulder length. The head was turned slightly away so that he couldn't see her face, but he had the general impression it was someone he might have seen before. Not someone he knew well, but someone he might have met once or twice.

It was the time of year when puddles were covered first thing in the morning by thin skins of ice that melted away before noon. The sun was warm in the blue sky as it shone on Kevin's exposed face and neck, but the air was cold when it stirred. The wind gusted off the nearby river, making him shiver as he studied the body from the top of the ditch. He glanced over his shoulder again at the bike path. It was maybe fifteen yards away. It was too cold for putrefaction to have gotten very far, but the odour of the body would have easily carried that far on the wind to the dog, with its powerful sense of smell, as it trotted past behind its owner.

"Is that a purse?" Carty said, pointing.

"Looks like it." Kevin had also noticed the large black handbag half-hidden in the rushes a few feet from the corpse's outstretched hand.

"No clothes, but a purse."

They both turned and took a step back as a large white cargo van pulled up to the barrier next to Carty's SUV. Kevin watched Identification Sergeant Dave Martin tumble out of the passenger seat and open up the back door of the van. Identification Constable Serge Landry got out on the driver's side and joined him as they grabbed large black kits and hurried over to the constable at the barricade to get signed in.

Kevin moved away, across the road to the far side, to give the forensic specialists plenty of room to do their work. Carty showed them the location of the body, pointed out tire marks he and Kevin had carefully avoided while having their own look, and then retreated in Kevin's direction, eyes down, hands shoved into the pockets of his OPP-issue parka.

"It's been at least three hours," Kevin said, thinking

about the rigor mortis.

Carty nodded, his eyes narrowing as he looked up and down the Parkway. "Where the hell did she come from?"

Kevin said nothing, trying to think of where he might have seen the victim before.

chapter
THREE

A few kilometres south of Smiths Falls, OPP Detective Inspector Ellie March pulled over at a gas bar to fill the tank of her grey motor pool Crown Victoria. When she hurried inside to pay, gritting her teeth against the frigid April wind, she grabbed a nutty cone from the freezer next to the counter and paid for it along with the gas. Outside, she pulled the Crown Vic over to the edge of the parking lot beside a garbage barrel and ate the nutty cone slowly, the car heater cranked up to its highest setting, trying to swallow her frustration with each bite of the vanilla ice cream, peanut bits, chocolate, and crispy cone.

She was on her way back to Sparrow Lake, where she worked out of an office in her four-season cottage. Earlier this morning she'd driven up to Smiths Falls to meet with Chief Superintendent Leanne Blair, East Region commander, and Inspector Todd Fisher, who was in charge of the Leeds County detachment within Leanne's region. The purpose of the meeting had been to give them a heads-up. An investigation for which she was responsible was about to be re-activated after a hiatus of nearly a year. Fisher was behind closed doors with Leanne when Ellie arrived, and while she waited she chatted with Fisher's operations manager, acting Staff Sergeant Scott Patterson, whose office was next door to Fisher's.

"I like what you've done with the place," Ellie said. She pretended to admire the many plaques, framed certificates of participation and recognition, and service awards that decorated the walls of Patterson's office.

"It looks exactly like my other office."

"Only a lot bigger."

Patterson laughed. "You got that right."

"Things going well with the crime unit?"

"Tom seems to have settled in," he said, referring to Carty, who was backfilling for him at the Elizabethtown-Kitley detachment office that also served as the administrative host for the detachment as a whole. "Of course, he doesn't have the same winning personality as the incumbent…"

"No one does, Scott."

"He seems to have come around on Walker," Patterson went on, "but it's a good job Sisson's gone, because she and Carty did *not* see eye to eye." He shook his head. "I still can't believe she placed on that sergeant's list. And ahead of him, at that. Oh, well. Now the only one he's got to contend with is Bishop. They don't like each other at all. Not at all."

Ellie leaned back from the door frame at the sound of a door opening. Down at the end of the corridor, Fisher emerged from Leanne's outer office. She took a step backward into the corridor. "Todd, do you have a minute?"

A short, fussy man with wavy grey hair and a brisk stride, Fisher stopped in his doorway and tapped the file folder in his hand against his leg. "Not really. Can't you just brief Patterson on whatever it is and he can let me know if it's something I need to be aware of?"

From the corner of her eye, Ellie saw Patterson deliver himself a mock punch in the head.

"You and Leanne need to be aware of it now, Todd," she said. "Just give me a minute and then I'll get out of your hair."

"Ellie, I thought I heard your voice." Leanne Blair came up the corridor toward them. "What's happening?"

"An FYI, Leanne." Ellie leaned back against the wall next to a framed black-and-white photograph, taken in the 1950s, of three uniformed officers standing next to an OPP cruiser. "I don't know if you saw the news item about Lambton, but we're resuming the investigation now that the court's handed down its ruling."

"I saw it in the clippings yesterday."

"It's ridiculous," Fisher said, tossing the file folder onto a chair inside his office door. "A waste of time and money."

"Ridiculous or not," Ellie said, "it's assigned to me and now I need a resource to work it."

"No problem," Scott Patterson said, easing around his desk to join the discussion.

"Yes, it *is* a problem." Fisher crossed his arms. "The mayor of a city we've been negotiating with for their policing contract. Terrible optics."

"Agreed," Ellie replied, "but it can't be helped."

Leanne stirred. "Let's take this out of the hallway, shall we?"

Ellie immediately stepped inside Scott Patterson's office so that the acting staff sergeant would not be excluded from the discussion. Taking the hint, Patterson went back around his desk and sat down again as Leanne joined them, settling into one of Patterson's visitors' chairs. "Todd?" she called out. "Come in and close the door, please."

As Fisher reluctantly complied, Ellie leaned against a filing cabinet and drew a pack of nicotine gum from the pocket of her suit jacket. She was not a heavy smoker, normally limiting herself to a single cigarette in the evening while trying to decompress before bedtime, but she'd discovered when she tried to quit altogether that the craving suddenly multiplied exponentially. It was her fourth day trying to use the gum as a way to get the whole thing back under control. So far, no luck.

"As you remember, Leanne," she said, a piece of gum in her hand, "this originated in a municipal complaint filed two years ago by a Brockville city executive against the mayor, Peter Lambton."

Leanne nodded. "The complaint alleged that Lambton had broken rules of ethical conduct by interfering in city contracts with a company owned by a friend of his."

"His nephew, actually." Ellie slipped the gum into her mouth and gave it a few quick chews. "A guy named Howie Burnside."

The complaint had been investigated by the city's integrity commissioner, an official appointed by the municipal council as a watchdog over the behaviour of city staff and elected members. The commissioner found that the mayor had in fact violated the city's code of ethical conduct. In his report to council, the commissioner explained that an additional allegation relating to criminal wrongdoing exceeded his jurisdiction. City council voted to turn that particular allegation over to the Brockville Police Service.

The police chief, however, took the position that he couldn't investigate Lambton because the mayor was directly connected to the committee responsible for the funding and administration of the police department. It would be a clear conflict of interest. As a result, he forwarded a request to the OPP that they conduct the investigation on his behalf. Senior management within the OPP decided to accept the hot potato, and Ellie was assigned to manage it.

Production orders for Lambton's financial and telecommunications records had been submitted and Ellie had just barely received the data almost a year ago when Lambton filed for a judicial review of the integrity commissioner's entire investigation. He asked the court to dismiss the original complaint and its allegations of wrongdoing, along with the ensuing report to city council. Ellie quietly put her investigation into neutral while the court deliberated.

A week ago, the judge hearing the request finally handed down her ruling, which dismissed Lambton's attempt to have the case thrown out. Two days ago, Lambton himself issued a statement maintaining his innocence but announcing he would not appeal the court decision. This public statement was Ellie's green light to reactivate the file and get on with it.

"As far as I'm concerned," Fisher said, "it's all smoke and no fire."

"That's what we're supposed to find out," Ellie replied patiently. "You know the drill, Todd." She looked at Leanne. "Section 122, *Criminal Code*, breach of trust by a public official, and section 123, influencing a municipal official. We're required to look at Lambton and his nephew for evidence that Lambton received free improvements to his cottage property in the Thousand Islands in exchange for making sure his nephew landed contracts with the city. End of story."

Fisher grimaced. "It's nonsense. Peter's a man of outstanding integrity. This has all the earmarks of a witch hunt by a disgruntled pissant trapped in a dead-end civil service job with an axe to grind. There's a personal element to this, I guarantee you."

Ellie looked at him. "Is this something you're saying from personal knowledge, Todd, or is it just your opinion?"

Fisher sighed. "All right, Ellie. What do you need?"

"I'd like Leung to work on it," Ellie said to Patterson, referring to Detective Constable Dennis Leung, a member of the crime unit.

Patterson nodded. "I'll pass the word to Carty."

"Thanks." Ellie turned back to Fisher, but he was

already opening the door and leaving the office. She looked at Leanne.

He's upset, Leanne mouthed.

Ellie raised an eyebrow.

Politics.

Huddled now behind the steering wheel of the Crown Vic, wishing it were summer already, Ellie finished her nutty cone and lowered the window to throw the wrapper into the garbage barrel. She thumbed the window back up, shivering, and shifted into drive just as her cellphone began to buzz. She shifted back into park and answered it, using the hands-free button on the steering wheel.

"Detective Inspector March?" As soon as Ellie heard the voice of the duty officer, who was calling from general headquarters in Orillia, she knew that her day was going to unfold much differently than she'd expected it would. As the duty officer recited a basic description of the call out and gave her the co-ordinates on the Thousand Islands Parkway, she realized that Scott Patterson's phone must have rung with the same notification while she was still leaving the building.

She shifted the Crown Vic into gear and swung out of the parking lot onto the highway, her irritation at Todd Fisher and the Lambton investigation already filed away in the back of her mind for future reference.

chapter

FOUR

"Mr. Garvey, I'm Detective Constable Kevin Walker. I'd like to ask you a few questions, if I may."

"Of course." Garvey pushed away from the back fender of his wife's Subaru. He was tall and thin, dressed in blue spandex leggings and a navy windbreaker. His white hair was thick and wavy. He wore an old pair of deck shoes instead of training sneakers; Dave Martin must have already claimed his footwear in order to compare their soles to the shoeprints he was currently lifting from the scene. "What would you like to know?"

"Maybe we could step over here, out of the way." Kevin walked across the road. Martin had set up cones and crime scene tape to create a wide semi-circle around the area within which he and Serge Landry were working, and Kevin gave it a wide berth as he led the way over the grass verge to the bike path. Kevin had actually never looked closely at the path before and was mildly surprised to find that it was very well kept, with a line dividing it down the middle into two lanes.

"How often do you use this path, Mr. Garvey?"

"Every day."

"Part of your morning routine, is it?"

"That's right. Who is she? How'd she get here?"

"That's what we're trying to find out, Mr. Garvey. You're saying you don't recognize her at all?"

"Never saw her before in my life. That's a pretty violent way to die, don't you think?"

Kevin understood that the man was upset. Finding a dead body, especially one that was a victim of violence, was something most people in this part of the world went through their entire lives without having to experience. Easy questions with simple answers might help him focus on providing information and maintain a grip on his emotions.

"So you and your wife live in Rockport? On Front Street?"

Garvey nodded, glancing at Kevin and looking away again.

"How long have you folks lived in the area?"

"Three years. Just over."

"And before that?"

"Ottawa." Garvey made eye contact with him again and held it this time. "I'm originally from Sarnia. Worked there for a number of years for the federal government, then transferred to Ottawa. Headquarters."

"Oh? What ministry?"

"Natural Resources. I'm a natural gas expert. Was, anyway."

"I see."

"When I retired, I was a DG."

"Director General? Is that right?"

"Economic Analysis Branch."

Kevin nodded. Having reached the senior management level before ending his career was obviously a point of pride for Garvey. Kevin took out his notebook and pen, opened to a fresh page, and jotted down the date and time.

"Rockport's your retirement home, is it?"

Garvey nodded.

"What brought you down here?"

"To the Thousand Islands?" Garvey raised an eyebrow, thinking that the answer should be obvious. "It's beautiful here. Plus, I'm a Chris-Craft enthusiast. I have four at the moment. The jewel is my twenty-six footer. Triple cockpit, built in 1928."

Kevin smiled. "Nice. Must be worth a few bucks."

"I've been offered one twenty-eight for it, but it's worth more than that."

"Impressive." One hundred and twenty-eight thousand dollars struck Kevin as quite a bit of money to pay for a toy, but he was vaguely aware of the value of high-end boats in general and Chris-Crafts in particular. "So you store them where?"

There were three marinas in the immediate area to choose from, and Garvey named the largest. Kevin wrote it down in his notebook. While still writing, he looked up and asked, "And you're sure you never saw this young woman around? At the marina, or maybe in a convenience store or somewhere?"

"No. Never."

"Did you go right down into the ditch when you found her?"

Garvey shook his head. "I know better than that. It was obvious there was nothing I could do for her."

"What about your dog?"

"Did she go down?" Garvey frowned. "I don't think so. When she left the bike path I called out to her without turning around. She's not supposed to go on the highway. She runs right beside me unless she stops for a pee, then she always catches right up again. When I realized she hadn't, I looked back and saw her across the road, barking at something down in the ditch."

"So what did you do then?"

"I stopped and called her, but she wouldn't come. She's usually very obedient. So I went back and stopped right across the road from ... well, right around here, actually. I was worried she'd get hit by a car. It gets busy along here. I called her again, but she still wouldn't come. She kept barking at whatever it was in the ditch." He closed his eyes and pinched his nose again.

"What did you do then?"

"I got off my bike." Garvey opened his eyes, looking across the road. "I put it on the kickstand and went across to see what Daisy was barking at. When I saw, when I, well, I, uh, I have a little pouch on my bike. You probably saw it. I keep a leash in there. I went and got it, and put it on her. I brought her back across the road. Then I called Patsy."

"Why did you call her before you called 911?"

Garvey frowned at him. "I wanted her to put Daisy in the car before anyone got here. So she wouldn't bother things or get hit by a car or something."

"Did Mrs. Garvey see the body, Mr. Garvey?"

He shook his head. "I told her to stay in the car. I put Daisy in the back and then called 911."

"Did anyone else stop while you were waiting? Any other cars?"

"No. Several went by, but no one stopped."

"Any of them slow down? Maybe behave a little oddly?"

Garvey shook his head. "They drive far too fast along here as it is."

"What about other cyclists?"

"No. No one else but me."

"Okay." Kevin made a quick note of the sequence of events as Garvey had described them. Then he closed the notebook and put it away. "Thanks for your help. Why don't you wait in the car with your wife for a bit? We'll let you know when you can leave."

"All right."

Kevin escorted him back around the taped-off area to

the Subaru and watched him get in the passenger side. Then he tapped on the driver's-side window. Mrs. Garvey, a small, sharp-faced woman with tinted red hair, lowered the glass.

"If you folks could stay here for a little bit longer, I'd appreciate it," Kevin said.

Mrs. Garvey nodded, eyes wide. "Did someone really kill her?"

"Looks like it. Thanks for your help; I appreciate it." Kevin glanced into the back seat at the golden retriever that was watching him with interest. He patted the roof of the car and walked away.

He met Carty on the far side of the road. A former military police officer, Carty still had the erect posture and humourless demeanour that Kevin associated with many veterans he'd known who'd deployed overseas, in Carty's case to Ethiopia and Afghanistan. "He's a little shook up."

Carty nodded, his eyes on Dave Martin, who was walking over to them.

Martin had pushed back the hood on his white coveralls and was running a hand through his hair. He was a small man, and as he stopped between the two of them to look up at Kevin he shielded his eyes against the glare of the mid-morning sun that was breaking directly over Kevin's shoulder.

"Okay, so we've processed the immediate surroundings around the body. We've got four sets of footprints. Two obviously belong to you guys, one to the witness, and one unaccounted for."

Kevin moved around closer to Carty so that the sun was no longer behind him, blinding Martin. "You want my boots now?"

Martin smiled. "Later is fine. Also, we have a very nice set of tire tread marks. We should be able to give you something definite on the vehicle that pulled over to dump her out."

"What about the purse?" Carty asked.

"Photographed, printed, and examined. Your victim's name is Andrea Matheson, DOB fifteen six eighty-nine. Address on the driver's licence is an apartment in Brockville. Credit cards, bank convenience cards, fitness club membership card, expired, all in the same name. We've already lifted the pic from her licence and uploaded it so you can use it for canvassing and whatever." He looked at Kevin. "What? You know her?"

"Yeah, the name's familiar. I can't place it just this second."

"Maybe this will help. She also had a bunch of business cards identifying her as director of fundraising for Clinics for Kenya."

"That's it." Kevin looked quickly at Carty. "Andie Matheson."

Carty frowned. "So you do know her?"

"Know *of* her. I know her boss, Kyle Baldwin. We went to high school together. I think I met Andie once or twice at fundraising events, but only to say 'hi, how are you.'"

"Anything between them?"

Kevin nodded. "They apparently met in Toronto, had a brief thing, and he offered her a job here. In Brockville, I mean. Then as soon as she moved, he broke it off." Kevin shrugged. "What I heard, anyway."

Carty raised his eyebrows, processing the information.

"Aha," Martin said, looking behind Carty at the far barrier. Just beyond it a grey Crown Vic had pulled up and parked on the shoulder of the highway. "Officer on deck."

Kevin looked over and saw Ellie March signing the clipboard held out to her by the constable controlling access to the crime scene.

Carty stepped closer to Kevin and spoke softly. "I'm going to want you to take primary on this, Kevin. Do you have a problem with that?"

Kevin shook his head, surprised. "No. No problem at all."

"Good. Bishop's nose will be out of joint yet again, but

he'll just have to deal with it." Carty looked at Ellie, walking briskly toward them. "He's canvassing on the next road right now. Call him down and go talk to this Kyle Baldwin right away. Let's see if he's the one who dumped his ex-girlfriend out here in the middle of nowhere."

"All right."

Kevin waved to Ellie as he headed off toward his car.

"How are you, Kevin?" she called out. "Getting any sleep yet?"

He smiled, shaking his head. As he ducked under the crime scene tape on his way to his car, he heard her greeting Carty and Martin.

"So gentlemen," she said, "what have you got?"

chapter FIVE

As Ellie listened to Dave Martin run through his preliminary findings, she turned up the collar on her trench coat and shoved her bare hands deeper into her pockets. Her gloves, she remembered belatedly, were on the back seat of the Crown Vic where she'd tossed them before eating her nutty cone. She hunched her shoulders and clenched her teeth to keep them from chattering as she focused on what Martin was saying.

Ellie hated cold weather. She should have been born in Arizona or some other place with a desert, someplace where it was warm all the time. It wasn't possible she was Canadian. Carty was watching her, his lightweight OPP-issue patrol jacket unzipped and only a navy tie and thin white shirt between himself and the frigid air. He and Martin were oblivious, enjoying the warmth of the late April sun while she shivered each time the wind found its way around the cedars across the road to assault her thin, sinewy frame.

"Because it dipped slightly below freezing last night," Martin was saying, "moisture in the air laid a thin layer of frost on the ground overnight, but by sunrise a warm front moved in and the frost started to melt. Made the surface of the road and the shoulder wet enough that the vehicle left nice tracks, and our dumper left very nice shoe prints. All of which dried quickly, thanks to the wind and sunshine. We're running them in our database."

"Good," she said, suppressing a shiver.

"You're cold? Ellie, it's plus seven degrees Celsius."

She looked at him. "Yeah, well, Dave, with the wind chill it's probably minus thirty. What else have you found?"

"Her purse was left with the body. The wallet contains eighty-five dollars in cash. The credit cards are still there as well, so it's not a robbery."

"What about clothing?"

Martin shook his head. "Nothing in the immediate vicinity."

"We've started the area search," Carty put in. "Because the vehicle was obviously eastbound, we're thinking we might find her stuff farther up the road in that direction."

"No signs of a turnaround?"

"No. We checked. The vehicle came this way from the direction of Rockport," he pointed to his right, "and after dumping her kept going eastbound. But we're checking the ditches and so on all the way along in both directions, don't worry."

Ellie nodded. It would now be the third homicide that the Leeds County Crime Unit had worked since she'd been assigned to major case management in the region, and by now she felt reasonably confident that they knew what to do. In the first investigation, involving the execution-style murder of a used-car trader in Yonge Township two and a half years ago, Carty had been a detective constable working as part of the team. No one in the crime unit had worked an active homicide investigation before other than Detective Sergeant Scott Patterson, but under Patterson's guidance and her experienced case management the offender had been identified and successfully brought to justice. In the second investigation, the brutal killing of a federal senator disguised as one of several barn fires that had occurred in the area last summer, Carty had taken the role of primary investigator, acquitting himself very well in the process.

Now, as acting detective sergeant backfilling for Patterson, he was the area crime supervisor whose job it was to make sure the investigation of Andie Matheson's murder was carried out to Ellie's satisfaction. If they needed more resources, Carty would be the one working the phone to find them. If an investigator wasn't doing his job to Ellie's satisfaction, Carty would need to address the problem or find a replacement. It was a test of his supervisory and administrative abilities more than his investigative skills this time around, and Ellie was curious to see how he'd perform.

"There are several houses behind us on Old River Road," Carty was telling her, "and Bishop was co-ordinating the canvass up there, but I sent him and Kevin up to Brockville to interview the victim's employer."

"You were saying she worked for a charity."

"Something called Clinics for Kenya. In Brockville. Kevin says he knows what it is, knows the guy who runs it. They went to high school together." He paused, staring at her. "I think he should be the primary on this one."

Ellie glanced at Dave Martin, who had cocked his head at the mention of Kevin's name. Although a sergeant in a completely different stovepipe of the organization, Martin was very familiar with personnel issues within the crime unit and was, she knew, a wicked gossip in his own right. He took an active interest in everyone else's business.

They were all aware that Kevin Walker had slipped into Scott Patterson's doghouse after the Hansen investigation revealed that Kevin had inadvertently provided inside information to the wrong person. His assignments during the Lane case had been much less important, but he'd managed to be in the right place at the right time when the barn fires and the murder of the senator were being solved. He had a knack for the job, if not the self-confidence to go along with it, and Ellie's partiality to Kevin as a young protégé in major case investigation was an open secret.

Without looking at Martin, she nodded at Carty. "Let's see how he does."

Carty's expression didn't change, but Ellie realized he'd been unconsciously holding his breath. He exhaled and was about to say something else when they were all distracted by the arrival of a vehicle at the barrier down at the west end of the inner perimeter.

"Thank God," Dave Martin said, "it's Nancy Drew. Now we can all go home."

Ellie watched Dr. Fiona Kearns, the coroner for Lanark-Leeds, breeze past the barricade with one of the EMS attendants. An experienced general physician in Perth with an extensive background in emergency medicine, Kearns was unpopular within law enforcement circles for her condescension, love of publicity, and know-it-all superiority.

"Play nice," Ellie said to Martin as he left their circle to escort the coroner to the body.

At that point Martin's cellphone began to emit a ringtone that sounded like something sampled from a Procol Harum song.

"Just a moment, Dr. Kearns," he called out. "I'll be right with you." As he thumbed his phone to answer the call, Kearns marched straight down into the ditch and crouched next to the corpse. Martin glanced at the sky and shook his head. Evidence be damned, apparently; the Great One was here. He moved off a few steps and put the phone to his ear. After a moment he hurried back to Ellie.

"That was one of my SOCOs, three kilometres east of us." His voice vibrated with excitement. Several of Martin's scenes-of-crime officers were with the Emergency

Response Team, which was co-ordinating the area search.

"They aced another set of tire tracks. Another pullover. In the bulrushes, guess what they found? A knife. Large, with blood traces. The guy got out where the road runs very close to the shore and tried to throw it in the river, but it fell short. Gotta be our murder weapon."

"What about clothing?" Ellie asked. "Did they find any clothing?"

Martin's shoulders dropped. "C'mon, Ellie. Isn't this big enough for you? One thing at a time, okay?"

"It is big," Carty said. "It's a miracle they found it."

Martin grinned at him, unable to resist the impulse to try out his Hans Gruber imitation: "You ask for a miracle? I give you the O...P...P."

chapter SIX

Clinics for Kenya was located in a Victorian brick duplex on King Street at the edge of downtown Brockville. The building sat in a sea of pavement with a four-pump gas bar on one side, a convenience store behind, and a parking area on the other side. Kevin backed into an empty space in the parking area and shut off the engine.

"Looks like we got here first." Detective Constable John Bishop snapped back his seat belt. He used the motor pool car's police radio to ask about the ETA of the cruiser they were expecting to join them and was told it would arrive in approximately five minutes. Grunting, he squinted at the late morning sun. "Sorry about the phone call. You started to tell me about this guy. Let's take a minute and go over it so I don't shoot him in the fucking head by mistake."

Bishop had spent most of the drive from the crime scene to Brockville on the phone with his wife. Jennifer suffered from severe anxiety and depression, and she relied heavily on her husband for support. She'd apparently agreed to go out to dinner tonight with friends from the hospital where she worked as a physiotherapist but was having second thoughts. She'd called Bishop half-hoping he'd agree with her decision to duck the commitment and half-hoping he'd encourage her to stick with it. He patiently listened to her list of misgivings, got her talking about her favourite co-worker, who was going, and at the end of nearly twenty minutes agreed with her decision to go after all. When he put away the phone and looked out the window, they were already on King Street and Kevin hadn't had a chance to discuss what they were about to do.

"No problem," Kevin said. "The victim, Andie Matheson, worked as director of fundraising for a charity called Clinics for Kenya. Basically, they raise money to pay for mobile clinics and medical supplies for the rural Maasi population in Kenya. She was responsible for organizing events, finding sponsors, collecting donations, that sort of thing."

"And you know this guy Baldwin, who runs the place?"

Kevin nodded. "Kyle Baldwin. We went to Brockville Collegiate together."

"High school buddies. Same year?"

"Yeah. Class of 2001. Not buddies, though. Kyle was in a different social circle."

Bishop rolled his eyes. "Hoity-toit."

"He hung around with kids whose parents also had a lot of money, put it that way. But he wasn't a jerk about it; he was a pretty good guy."

Kevin watched two young men get out of an unmarked white van and walk into the convenience store, hands in their pockets. One was tall and slim, the other short and stocky. "We were desk mates in Grade Eleven biology class. I couldn't stand cutting up the specimens, so he was the one who dissected the frogs and mice. I wrote up all the reports for us."

Bishop laughed. "A big jock like you, afraid of a little blood?"

Kevin ignored the jab, unwilling to admit he'd been too soft-hearted to do such horrible things to such small creatures, dead or not.

"He actually got into this charity the same year. It started out as a class project for geography, I think it was. He wrote an essay on the Maasi, and they got him to make a presentation on it at the next school assembly. After that he organized a fundraising event to raise money for medicine for them, a bake sale and yard sale thing at the school. People donated stuff, they ran it on a Saturday morning, and he raised a couple thousand dollars."

"Hnh."

"I remember him saying in a newspaper interview it was like a bug had bitten him. He couldn't get it out of his system. His father owned a farm equipment distribution company and apparently had business connections in Kenya. A lot of different countries in Africa, I guess. Kyle set up a charitable organization, and his mother and one of his dad's business partners helped run it while he was away at university. Then after Kyle graduated he came back and took it over as executive director."

"So who was the vic? His girlfriend?"

"That's what we'll have to find out, JB." Kevin watched the two young men come back out of the convenience store. The tall one, who'd been driving the white van, tossed an unopened pack of cigarettes to his companion and got in behind the wheel. "As I remember it, Kyle met her in Toronto at some event, and she came back here to work for him, I think on the assumption that they would be together, but it didn't work out. I'm fuzzy on the details. Just remembering something somebody told me, a while ago."

The white van slid out of the parking lot onto King Street and disappeared. A moment later, a black-and-white OPP cruiser circled around the gas bar and parked along the far side of the building, out of sight.

"Show time." Bishop pushed open his door and got

out.

Kevin led the way around the back of the building, giving the convenience store a long look. A bored cashier stared back at him through the tinted plate glass window, chin resting in his hand.

Kevin rounded the corner of the building and walked up on the driver's side of the cruiser, his badge in his hand in case the uniformed constable behind the wheel didn't know them. The man recognized him, however, and lowered his window.

Kevin squatted down to eye level. "Basically, this is a notification about the death of a co-worker, and then we'll transport them to the detachment office to interview them there."

"Sounds good." The constable, whose name was Dobbin, made an effort not to appear bored. "How many are we talking?"

"Not sure. It's a small non-profit, so maybe only a handful."

"Just thinking about additional transportation."

"We'll know shortly if it'll be necessary."

Dobbin's partner, whose name was Kline, leaned forward in her seat on the passenger side of the cruiser. "How's the baby, Kevin?"

"Fine."

"How's Janie doing?"

"Great, thanks."

"Glad to hear it."

Kevin shifted his eyes back to Dobbin. "All set?"

"Let's rock." Dobbin unsnapped his seat belt and raised his window as Kevin stood up.

Kevin led the way around to the front of the building. At that moment a Brockville Police Service cruiser pulled up to the curb and the passenger window slid down. Kevin crouched and looked in at the uniformed officer.

"Hey, Steve. Thanks for stopping by."

The cop's eyes slid from Bishop, who was waiting on

the sidewalk, to Kevin. "How's it going?"

"The usual." Kevin looked over at the driver, who was unfamiliar to him, and nodded. "We appreciate the assist."

"No problem. Who's the stiff?"

Kevin looked at the sergeant's stripes on the arm of the man's polyester patrol jacket. Steve Jackson was an eighteen-year veteran of the Brockville Police Service, and Kevin knew him from the local men's hockey league. They were friendly, and occasionally had a beer together after a game as part of a larger group, but Jackson tended to slash Kevin on the back of the leg when his attention was elsewhere, and was generally known for his foul disposition on and off the ice. On the other hand, when they went into a corner to fight for the puck, Kevin's elbow sometimes came up to catch Jackson on the side of the head. It was Kevin's way of reminding Jackson that he was much bigger and stronger, and that he wouldn't stand for bullshit.

"A woman named Andrea Matheson," he said, watching Jackson's eyes move back to Bishop with obvious dislike. "She worked for a charity in this building. We're taking all the co-workers in for interviews and should have the search warrant in a few hours."

"Meanwhile," Jackson said, "it's babysitting duty." He moved his eyes from Bishop to the building behind Kevin.

"We'll seal it up as soon as everyone's out, and we've got another patrol car en route to stay with it until the Ident team takes over, but like I say, we appreciate the help."

"Sure. Give my love to Curly." The window went up and the cruiser's engine shut off.

Kevin stood up and walked away. He had no idea why Jackson had a bug up his ass about Bishop, but there was obviously some history between them. It wasn't surprising, since they were alike in many ways—junkyard dogs with a grudge against the world beyond the chain-link fence that circumscribed their lives.

"Let's go." Kevin trotted up the cement stairs. There

were two front doors. On the wall beside the one on the left was a fancy oak-and-brass sign that said "Clinics for Kenya." He opened the door and walked in.

The hallway was decorated like a Victorian home. Kevin stepped through an inner door held open by a cast iron boot jack. Sunlight from outside sparkled through the stained glass transom above the door and painted the oak floor ahead of him with bright colours. On his left was a side table with a wicker basket containing brochures. Next to it was a walnut davenport displaying a collection of brass monkeys with trays holding business cards. On his right was a staircase with a heavy oak banister leading up to the second floor.

Kevin passed the monkeys and looked into the doorway on the left. A woman frowned up at him from behind a desk.

"May I help you?"

Kevin walked in, holding up his badge. Behind him, Bishop strolled past the doorway while Dobbin and Kline clattered into the hallway, closing the outer door with an authoritative thud.

"Detective Constable Kevin Walker, OPP. You are...?"

"Wilma Sutton." She pointed at a name plate on her desk. She was about sixty, lean and well-dressed, her frizzy short hair dyed an unconvincing blond. Her skin was tanned in a way that suggested a recent winter vacation somewhere far south of Brockville, perhaps in the Caribbean or Mexico.

"Is Kyle Baldwin here, Ms. Sutton? We need to speak to him right away."

She looked around Kevin, saw the distinctive OPP shoulder patches on the duty jackets of Dobbin and Kline, and reached for the phone. "He's just down the street, getting some take-out for lunch. I'll tell him you're here."

Kevin ran his eyes around the room while she called. It looked more like a modern office in here, with computers and laser printers, filing cabinets, a credenza littered with more pamphlets and brochures, bookcases holding three-ring binders, catalogues, and other reference books, and a paper shredder and recycling bin. An inner doorway on the far side led into the next office, which would have been the dining room back when the building was a residential duplex.

As Wilma Sutton murmured to her boss on the phone, Kevin went over to the inner doorway for a look. The next room was organized into two workspaces sectioned off by large grey office dividers. A laptop on the desk of the workstation he could see was turned on, the large bottom desk drawer was open a crack, and a woman's windbreaker hung on a coat rack in the corner.

"He's on his way." Wilma rose from her desk.

Kevin turned. "Thanks. How many people are here today?"

"Myself, Isabella, and Mr. Baldwin."

"Who works here?" Kevin asked, pointing at the workstation.

"Isabella. Isabella Tofalos. She's just upstairs right now, using the washroom. It's on the second floor."

"What's on the other side of that divider?"

"That's Andie's workstation. Andie Matheson." Wilma frowned. "She hasn't come in yet."

Kevin stepped through and stood in front of Isabella Tofalos's desk. On his right, Bishop arrived in another doorway from the hall behind them. Kevin joined Bishop at the opening to Andie Matheson's work space. A gap between the office dividers served as a makeshift doorway. Kevin looked in at a neat desk, a filing cabinet, a coat rack with a cardigan sweater and a shoe bag hanging on it, and not much else.

Bishop grabbed a chair from Isabella Tofalos's workstation and dropped it down where it would block access to Andie's office space.

They heard the front door open. There was movement in the hallway, and a man's voice said, "Hi there. What can I do for you?"

Kevin went back into Wilma's office. Standing next to her was a handsome, well-dressed man who was unbuttoning his trench coat as he stared around in mild confusion.

Kevin held out his hand. "Kyle, how are you?"

Kyle Baldwin shook hands. "Kevin. It's been a while. I've seen your picture in the paper." He frowned at the uniformed officers, who were staring at him. "What's going on?"

"We need to talk. With you and your staff." He paused at the sound of a toilet flushing overhead. "Where do you usually have your staff meetings?"

"In my office. Upstairs." Baldwin draped the trench coat over his arm. "What's this about? Is something wrong?"

"If we could have everyone together in your office, we'll explain."

"Okay." Baldwin looked at Bishop's badge and shook his hand, then led the way upstairs, Wilma on his heels, Bishop following close behind.

Kevin paused at the bottom of the staircase and looked at Kline, who was nearest. "One up and one down."

"Go ahead," Dobbin said, behind Kline.

She nodded and followed Baldwin upstairs. As they reached the top of the staircase, a door opened at the end of the hall. A young woman emerged, her head down, fiddling with something in her hand. She took a few steps before realizing there were people in front of her. Her head came up and her mouth opened. She stopped and pulled out a set of earbuds.

"What's going on? Is there a meeting?"

"Isabella Tofalos?" Kevin asked.

"Yes." She removed the other earbud and wrapped the cord around her cellphone. "What's going on?"

Kevin held up his badge. "Please come with us into Kyle's office."

She closed the washroom door behind her and pushed her long, straight black hair off her shoulder. "All right."

She edged past Kevin into Baldwin's office. Her perfume,

light and floral, trailed behind. She ran a hand over her hip, smoothing down her tight-fitting, knee-length black dress, and looked at him over her shoulder.

"Thanks," Kevin said.

She shrugged.

Baldwin's office was much larger than what Kevin had seen downstairs. The walls were decorated with a variety of African artwork, a large warrior's shield made of wood and leather, and framed displays of colourful bead necklaces.

Bishop wandered over to an antique side cabinet to admire a collection of wood carvings. He picked up a foot-tall warrior with a carefully painted leopard-spot headdress, a long spear, and a red-and-white shield. "Nice stuff."

"Thank you." Baldwin waved at the carving. "Feel free to take a close look. They're beautiful, aren't they? That one only cost me thirty dollars American at a bazaar in Nairobi."

"Doesn't sound like very much." Bishop put it down and picked up a mask with two black elephants on the forehead above the eyes. "This is pretty cool."

"They're all hand-carved by Maasi artists, so no two pieces are ever alike." Baldwin settled on the corner of his desk and folded his arms. "Now, what is it you need to talk to us about, Kevin? I'm getting a little worried."

Kevin moved to the centre of the office. Wilma Sutton had made herself comfortable in a leather chair opposite Baldwin's desk. Isabella Tofalos leaned against the back of a matching chair, closest to Baldwin, her arms folded and her legs crossed at the ankles.

"When was the last time any of you had contact with Andie Matheson? Kyle?"

Baldwin frowned. "Not since yesterday afternoon. Here, at the office. Wilma?"

"She didn't call in this morning. Everyone's supposed to let me know if they'll be away from the office. I didn't hear from her."

"So when was the last time you saw or spoke to her, Ms. Sutton?"

"Same as Kyle. She left the office shortly after four o'clock yesterday."

Kevin nodded and wrote it down in his notebook. "And how about you, Ms. Tofalos?"

"*Toh*-falos. Same thing. What's going on?"

"Did she leave with someone, or was she alone when she left for the day?"

"I was at my desk. On the phone." Isabella looked at Wilma, who shrugged.

"She was by herself. Just going home, like always. Is something wrong? Has something happened to Andie?"

"I'm afraid I have to tell you her body was found along the Thousand Islands Parkway earlier this morning, about two kilometres east of Rockport."

Wilma's hand flew to her mouth. Isabella stared at him in disbelief.

"I don't understand," Baldwin said. "Her body was found. Was she in a car accident? What happened?"

"She was murdered. I'm very sorry, I know this is difficult for all of you. Are you absolutely certain none of you received a text or voice message or anything else from her between the time she left this office yesterday and now?"

Baldwin moved to Isabella's side. His arm went around her shoulders. She turned her face into his chest and began to cry. Wilma Sutton covered her face with both hands.

"No, nothing," Baldwin said. "This is unbelievable. Murdered? How? I don't understand."

"Ms. Tofalos? No texts, voice mail, e-mail?"

Isabella shook her head.

"Ms. Sutton?"

"You must be mistaken," Wilma muttered from behind the mask of her fingers. "It must be someone else. It can't be Andie."

"I'm very sorry, folks. I know how incredibly hard this

is. There's no mistake, I'm afraid." Kevin put away his notebook. "Kyle, I'll need you to close up your office now. The three of you will come with us to the detachment office and we'll go over everything in detail. Anything you folks can tell us about Andie will be a really big help."

"All right." Baldwin slowly moved Isabella back so that he could make eye contact with her. "Are you okay?"

She nodded.

Bishop had quietly moved from his position at the side table to another table near the window, where he'd picked up a box of tissues in a brightly-painted wooden dispenser. He held out the box to Isabella, who pulled out six or seven of them and pressed them to her face. He took the box over to Wilma Sutton, who'd finally come out from behind her hands. He saw that her eyes were dry, but he held out the box anyway. She took it from him and placed it in her lap.

"Kyle," Kevin said, "does Andie have any family here?"

Baldwin shook his head. "Her parents are in Toronto. Ajax, actually. That's where she's from. I think she has a sister somewhere. Montreal?"

"What about a significant other?"

"She's single. I'm not sure if she's between boyfriends or what."

Isabella Tofalos murmured something behind her tissues.

"Pardon me?" Kevin looked at her closely.

She shook her head.

When he was certain she wasn't about to repeat what she'd said, Kevin turned back to Baldwin.

"Kyle, let me just explain how this will work. Andie's work area is now off-limits, and the office will be closed until further notice. We'll be getting a warrant to allow us to search her workstation and any other common areas she would've used in the building, okay? It often takes up to eight hours to get a warrant approved, but I can't really say at this point when you'll be able to come back here and get back to work. Do you understand?"

Baldwin nodded. "Yeah. I guess."

"Is there anyone else besides you folks who works here in this office?"

Baldwin shook his head. "The only other person on staff is Walter Jackson, our director of finance, but he has his own office a couple blocks from here. He's a chartered accountant."

"Okay. So Constable Kline and her partner will take you, Ms. Tofalos, and you, Ms. Sutton. Kyle, you'll come with me and Detective Constable Bishop."

"I don't understand," Wilma Sutton said, slowly getting to her feet. "Are we under arrest?"

Kevin shook his head. "Not at all. We just need to interview the three of you, and it may take a while to cover everything we'll need to ask you about. We'll do it at the detachment so we can record your statements on video. It's voluntary, of course, on your part, but the faster we can get this part of our investigation into the books the faster we can figure out who did this horrible thing and bring them to justice. Does that make sense to you?"

"I guess so," Wilma said.

"Of course," Baldwin said. "We'll do whatever needs to be done. Won't we, Belle?"

Isabella Tofalos nodded, aiming her wad of tissues at a waste paper basket next to Baldwin's desk. It banked off the side of the desk, hit the rim, and dropped in. "Let's go."

"Grab your coats and purses from your workstations," Constable Kline said, "but please leave everything else untouched. This way, please, ladies."

"I should turn off my computer," Wilma said, preceding Kline out the door.

"It'll be fine. Please leave it as is for now. Thank you."

As Isabella passed Kevin she paused, looking up at him. "Someone actually killed her? Andie?"

"I'm afraid so."

"You're going to find the fucker, right?"

"That's the idea."

She nodded and followed Wilma and Kline downstairs.

Bishop grunted in amusement and beckoned to Baldwin, who was retrieving his overcoat from a rack in the corner. "Let's go, Mr. Baldwin."

"There's a kitchenette in the back downstairs," Baldwin said to Kevin, "with a back door. We keep it locked ordinarily. I should double-check it."

"We'll do that for you, Kyle," Kevin said.

He nodded, frowning at Kevin and Bishop in turn. "I don't understand. Why would someone want to hurt Andie?"

"That's what we're going to find out," Kevin replied.

chapter
SEVEN

Ellie drove about two kilometres west from the crime scene on the Parkway, passing through the outer perimeter set up at the Narrows Lane Road intersection, and a kilometre or so later slowed down and turned under the wrought-iron gateway arch into Rockport.

The village could be seen more or less in its entirety by following Front Street as it ran in a crescent along the shore of the St. Lawrence River. It was little more than a narrow lane with no sidewalks or shoulders on either side. She coasted past a white frame church crowding in on the left and continued straight ahead, expecting to see water at any moment. On the right she passed the house belonging to their witness, Garvey, the man who'd found the body. It was a tidy little home with white siding, a dormer window on the upper storey, and a short picket fence out front.

Tall evergreen trees pressed in on either side of the lane, but once she was clear of them she reached the first bend in the crescent. The river glittered brilliant blue just ahead of her.

She passed the parking lot of a small marina. One or two cars shone in the late-morning sunshine, their owners likely walking down among the boat slips, sampling the spring weather. Up ahead on her left was a much larger parking lot. It was used by the buses that brought tourists in for the island cruises which were so popular in the summer. There were no buses today, but there were several cars at the far side of the lot, gathered around a food truck that was open for business. Prominent among these cars was a grey Ford Fusion that had apparently passed through a car wash some time in the past twenty-four hours, making it the only vehicle in the lot other than her Crown Vic that wasn't wearing a coat of road dust. Ellie swung into the lot and pulled up beside it.

As she got out, Dennis Leung was in the process of handing over his cellphone to someone inside the food truck. He stretched out his arm, pulled it back, touched something on the phone's screen, and held it out again. The middle-aged woman inside the food truck wiped her hands on her apron, took the phone, and looked at the screen.

"Sorry," she said, returning the cellphone as Ellie arrived. "Never seen her before."

"You're sure?" Leung frowned at the photograph on the screen of his phone. "Maybe with someone else? A man?"

"Sorry," the woman repeated, then looked at Ellie. "Help you? We're sold out of the mahi mahi tacos already."

"I'm with him," Ellie said, nodding at Leung.

"Oh." The woman walked away from the window. Utensils clattered as she went back to work.

"How's it going?" Ellie asked.

Leung dropped his cellphone into his pocket. "Slow. So far, nothing. Nobody knows her down here."

"Something will turn up."

As Leung checked his wrist watch, Ellie raised her eyebrows in amusement. The watch was large and flashy, probably new. It emerged from under the cuff of his neat charcoal car coat like a Ferrari rolling out of an underground parking garage. He frowned at it and looked up at her.

"I should get something to eat."

"We have some things to discuss," Ellie said, remembering that Leung was diabetic, "but we can talk and eat."

"This place is actually supposed to be good. According to Kevin, anyway."

Ellie took a step back, looking for a menu. "Do they have hamburgers, or just fries?"

"They sell seafood tacos, Ellie." He pointed at the side of the truck, where "Sandra's Off the Hook Fish Tacos" was painted in gaudy psychedelic lettering.

Ellie shrugged. "Okay. Fine. You order, and I'll get the same."

A few minutes later they carried their baja fish tacos with red cabbage, cilantro, and extra lime wedges over to Ellie's car. She got in behind the wheel and looked over at Leung as he settled in on the passenger side. "It smells good."

She shoved her bottle of water between her thigh and the centre console and pulled at the wrapping around the taco. "You're going to stay on this investigation, Dennis, but I've got something else for you to do for me at the same time. Scott's calling Tom about it, but I might as well give you the low-down right now while I have you here."

"Oh?" He swallowed and wiped at sauce at the corner of his mouth.

"Thirteen months ago we were asked to handle an investigation into criminal wrongdoing by the mayor of Brockville. This would have been right around the time you transferred from Toronto."

Leung raised his eyebrows over his taco. "I wasn't aware."

"It would have been in the news just before you got here. And we didn't spend much time on it because Peter

Lambton, the subject, filed a court challenge and everything got put on hold." She took a bite of the taco. "Christ, this is really good."

"So what's it all about?"

Between mouthfuls, Ellie ran through the basics of the case, from the complaint filed by the city's director of corporate services, a man named Warren Whitlock, through the investigation by the integrity commissioner and his findings of wrongdoing, to the referral of the criminal component of the investigation to the OPP.

By the time she was finished Leung had eaten his taco and was wiping his hands on a napkin. "What do you need me for, Ellie?"

"I caught it as the closest case manager in the region. I wish I'd been on vacation at the time. Anyway. I want you to follow up on the bank and phone data we got from our production orders, interview Lambton and his nephew, the contractor who supposedly did free work on his cottage"—she looked over her shoulder—"which is apparently around here somewhere, and whatever else we need to do to get this thing over with."

"All right, Ellie. Sounds good."

She wadded up the wrapping from her taco and tossed it into the footwell behind Leung's seat. One of the things she liked about Leung was that he never complained. He gave every appearance of enjoying his job and welcoming whatever work was handed to him. She also got a kick out of his penchant for flashy jewellery and nice-looking suits, which he'd explained to her once before were all bought on sale in the clearance sections of whatever stores he happened to find himself in while out shopping with his family. Bling on a budget—that was Leung.

"The homicide has top priority, it goes without saying," she said. "Kevin Walker is the primary, so stay on top of what he needs you to do. We'll fit this Lambton thing in on the side. If you're feeling pinched, let me know and I'll get some extra help on it."

"No problem." Leung adjusted his glasses, watching the woman in the truck serve another customer, a man who'd walked across the road from the marina.

Ellie took a long drink of water, then capped the bottle and tossed it after the wadded wrapper. "I'd better let you get back to work."

Leung nodded. "Nobody knows her. I don't think she spent any time here. She could have been killed anywhere and just dumped on the Parkway by someone on their way to literally anywhere else."

"At this point, yeah. But sometimes these things narrow down pretty quickly, Dennis."

"I know." He reached for the door handle. "I just hope it wasn't some guy from Alexandria Bay who dumped her on this side and went back across to the States. What a nightmare that would be."

"We'll cross that bridge when we get there, Dennis."

Leung got out and looked back in at her. "Kevin keeps saying you have a sense of humour. I still don't believe it."

"Beat it. Find someone who recognizes her."

Leung held up his thumb, then closed the door and walked over to the man at the food truck who was waiting for his taco.

Ellie watched him take out his cellphone and tap to the photograph of Andie Matheson. As she started the Crown Vic's engine and shifted into reverse, the man was already shaking his head.

chapter EIGHT

"Okay Kyle," Kevin said, entering the room and closing the door behind him, "sorry to keep you waiting."

"No problem." Kyle Baldwin sat with his hands folded between his thighs. His trench coat and suit jacket had been taken by a uniformed officer and hung up in a closet outside in the hallway. He nodded as Kevin set a paper cup of coffee down at the end of the desk, close to his elbow. "Thanks."

"It's black," Kevin said. "I've got some creamers and sugar here."

"No, it's fine. Thanks."

Kevin sat down at the desk and swivelled his chair around so that he was facing Baldwin. "We've got a number of things we need to cover, Kyle, so we should get right to it. The evidence we have so far tells us that Andie was killed some time early this morning, maybe six or seven o'clock, so the sooner we cover all the bases the sooner we'll find who did this and bring them to justice. Okay?"

"Of course."

"So right now it's a top priority for us to interview everyone who was closest to Andie in order to get a clear picture of what she might have been doing and where she might have been in the last twelve hours or so. Which is where you come in." Kevin reached for his own coffee and took a sip. "Although you and I know each other, Kyle, I want it to be clear this is an official interview, and I want you to understand what your rights are, just the same as everyone else we're going to talk to."

"Okay."

"You're not under arrest, Kyle, so any time you want to leave, you can. You're here voluntarily, which we appreciate. You have a lawyer, don't you?"

Baldwin nodded. "Casey, Hall and Walters."

Kevin smiled. "A whole law firm. All right. So, if anything comes up during the interview that you feel you want to talk about with your lawyer, please feel free to let me know, okay? There's a room next door where you can call them in private. Is there any reason why you might want to call them now, Kyle?"

Baldwin shook his head. "No, not at all. This is fine."

"Okay. As I said, you don't have to say anything to me, but since I *am* a police officer, a person in authority under the law, what you do say must be understood to be voluntary on your part. So you probably already noticed the microphone here on the desk and the camera up there," Kevin turned and pointed at the corner of the ceiling, "which are recording what we say during this interview. It's very important for everyone's benefit, yours and ours, that we have an accurate record. Okay?"

"Sure, of course."

"So what I want to do is start by asking you a few questions about Andie's routines, her work habits, that sort of thing. Did she have a regular work schedule she was expected to follow?"

Baldwin frowned. "Um, sort of. Wilma opens the office

at eight thirty every morning and closes it at four thirty."

"That's Monday to Friday?"

"Yes. Wilma works weekdays, but the rest of us do a lot of stuff on the weekends too, because many of our events are on a Saturday or Sunday. We all have keys, and we come and go as need be."

"Including Andie?"

Baldwin nodded. "I normally get to the office at nine in the morning, although I've been coming in earlier lately to get a head start on stuff. Andie comes in a few minutes after that. Nine-ish. Sometimes earlier, sometimes later. The understanding is that she contributes at least thirty-five hours a week, just like everyone else, and if she gets in later or stays later it doesn't matter to me. She's always been good about it."

"What about yesterday?"

"Yesterday?"

Kevin waited.

"Um, I'm not sure what time she got in. Around nine, I guess. I was on a conference call and had my office door closed. The call ended a few minutes before ten. I went downstairs to go out for a walk and she was there."

"What time did she leave?"

"Again, I'm not really sure. Wilma says about four, so I guess that's right."

"How much contact did you have with her during the day?"

"Uh, we had a staff meeting at eleven to talk about an event we have coming up soon. We do a May Day thing down at the waterfront that's sponsored by Jones Chemical and a few other companies. So it was a planning meeting."

"How did she seem during this meeting?"

"How did she seem?" Baldwin frowned, thinking. "Actually, a little distracted. A couple of times I had to repeat myself to her."

"Distracted in what way? Positively or negatively?"

"Uh, well, I'd say positively. She kept staring off into

space, you know, daydreaming. She had a little smile on her face."

"Like she was looking forward to something?"

"Yeah. I guess so. Yeah. I didn't give it much thought."

"Is that what she was like, generally? A little unfocused?"

"Andie? No. She's very efficient. She does a great job." He stared at Kevin, lips parted, and then grimaced. "Did a great job. Did. I can't believe it. I'm having a lot of trouble processing this, Kevin."

"I understand. Were you and she close?"

Baldwin picked up his coffee, took a sip, decided it was drinkable, and took a mouthful. He lowered the cup to his lap, both hands around it as though holding it for warmth, and looked at Kevin. "We were still friends. We got along well."

"You and she were in a relationship before, though, weren't you?"

"I still feel guilty about that." He nodded. "Yeah. It was very brief. We met in London, at a conference."

"London Ontario?"

"No, England. It was a huge NGO event. Non-government organizations. She was with Doctors Without Borders in Toronto at the time. This was, uh, six years ago. She was working as a fundraising co-ordinator for them. We met during an icebreaker, a cocktail thing, and we kind of clicked. We hung around together after that for the rest of the conference. She talked about her job and how she felt blocked by internal politics from any possibility of advancement. She was a real go-getter and wanted to make a difference. When it was time to come home, I gave her my card and told her to call if she ever wanted a change of scenery."

"You mean you offered her a job."

Baldwin nodded. "That's right."

"Just so I'm clear, Kyle, you had a sexual relationship with her at that time?"

"Yes," Baldwin replied, reddening.

"And what happened after that?"

"She called, about a month later. Wanted to know if the offer was still open. I said hell, yeah. So I met with her a week later and we did an interview. I had several meetings scheduled in Toronto that day, and it was easy to add her to the list. She said all the right things; I offered her the job, and she accepted."

"Did you continue to sleep with her?"

Baldwin put down his coffee cup. "That's why I feel so guilty. She wanted to start things up again, after she moved here from Toronto, but I had to say no. It had been a one-time thing for me. But I think it was one of the reasons why she took the job."

"To continue a romantic relationship."

"Yeah."

"How did she take it? When you told her it wouldn't happen?"

"She was pissed." Baldwin grimaced. "At first she thought I was kidding, but when I made it clear I wasn't she got really pissed off at me."

"Did you fight?"

"Yes." Baldwin raised a hand. "We *argued*. Nothing physical, Kevin. Christ. She yelled and screamed at me. But she got over it fairly quickly. She's a very intelligent person. She knew that the job I gave her was a lot better than the one she'd had before. It was a good move for her."

Kevin waited a beat before saying offhandedly, "I don't remember you with a broken nose."

Baldwin's hand flew up to his face. "Oh, yeah."

"How'd that happen?"

He flashed a quick smile. "I was helping to unload a truck at a clinic we were setting up out in the middle of nowhere. A wooden crate slipped and hit me square in the face. Knocked me right down on my ass. Everybody had a big laugh. Except for me, of course. It hurt like hell."

"Where was this?"

"South of Nairobi, a few kilometres from the Tanzanian border. About four years ago. Bled like a son of a bitch." He shrugged. "Last time I ever tried to show off and do the dirty work. I learned my lesson. Stand back and point to where you want it to go. That's what I do now."

"So when you and Andie fought, did it ever get physical?"

Baldwin sighed. "No, Kevin. Never." He closed his eyes. "I really liked her. A lot. We argued when she first got here, as I said, but from then on, we disagreed on stuff, yeah, but she'd moved on with things and we were cool. It was okay. Very good, actually. We were good friends."

"What can you tell me about her relationships after you broke up?"

Baldwin opened his eyes. "What? Sorry, her relationships?" He paused. "I don't know, she never talked to me about that. Belle might know more. They did lunch together every so often, stuff like that. She might have confided in her."

"You never saw her with anyone?"

"I saw her with a lot of people, Kevin. Being with people was her job. She had lunch dates and dinner dates and evening engagements with all sorts of people. You know, pitching our work to them, making them feel comfortable with fitting us into their budget, that sort of thing. But as far as serious dating, I have no idea." He shook his head. "I just don't know. I was careful to keep a space between us. Personal space. So I didn't keep track of that sort of stuff. Sorry."

"What about friends? You know, girlfriends, people she liked to spend her down time with."

"I'm not sure. I don't know of anyone."

Kevin frowned. "She didn't have friends here?"

"She could have, but I don't know. Maybe Belle knows."

"She never introduced you to anyone? A girlfriend picking her up after work, a friend she bumped into at one of your fundraisers? Anyone like that?"

"No. I really did stay out of her personal life, and she kept it very separate from her professional one."

Kevin leaned back in his chair and let a moment's silence settle between them. Baldwin watched him uncertainly. Kevin tapped a finger on the desktop and said, "A guy as good looking as you, Kyle. A young, attractive woman like her. You didn't keep an eye on her at all? Maybe reconsider your decision not to continue the relationship?"

"No." Baldwin looked down at his hands, blushing furiously.

"You're sure?"

"I'm sure."

"I'm surprised."

"Don't be."

Kevin frowned. "I don't understand."

"I don't—" Baldwin stopped. Bit his lip. "Go that way any more."

"You don't go that way any more." Kevin paused a beat, the phrase repeating itself in his head. Suddenly, he got it. "What are you saying, Kyle? Are you gay?"

Baldwin nodded.

"Is that why you broke it off with her in the first place?"

"Yes." Baldwin's eyes pleaded for understanding. "Look, Kevin, I was bisexual back then. But a week after I got back from London my friend, my male friend, proposed. We'd had sort of an open relationship up to then, but he wanted us to commit just to each other, and I agreed. We became partners. So when Andie moved here, things had already changed for me. I was committed to a relationship."

"Did you explain that to her?"

"Of course I did. She was furious. She felt betrayed, fooled, tricked. It took a while for me to convince her otherwise. Somehow I'd missed just how strong her feelings were for me when we interviewed. I thought she was pumped up about the career move, and that the sex had just been something on the side for her." He frowned. "At first she didn't want to meet Colin. Eventually she did. Everybody loves Colin. They became friends, sort of. It was cool. Eventually."

Kevin said nothing.

"I know you said this is being recorded," Baldwin went on, "and I understand that, but it's really important to me that this not become public. The fact that I'm gay."

"Why not? It's pretty much mainstream any more, isn't it?"

"Ha. Hardly. We're talking Brockville, Kevin. But much more importantly, it wouldn't fly well in Kenya. With the Maasi."

"Oh?"

"Male fertility still plays a large role in their culture. As the leader of Clinics for Kenya, I would … lose credibility with them if it became known. It would slow down the progress I've made with them over the years. They're somewhat resistant to modern medicine as opposed to more traditional remedies. They have a pretty extensive pharmacopoeia, actually, but it's not adequate any more in most rural areas and our clinics and medicine are badly needed. I can't do anything to jeopardise that. You understand, don't you?"

"What's your partner's full name, Kyle?"

"Oh God."

Kevin waited.

"Colin Davies. I guess you'll need to talk to him."

"Yes, we'll need his address, telephone number, place of work, all that."

"Okay." Baldwin recited the details to him. Apparently Colin Davies was a real estate agent who worked out of a brokerage office located in the north end of Brockville.

"So take me through the last twenty-four hours, Kyle. Where you've been and what you've been doing."

"Uh, sure. Okay." Baldwin leaned forward. "Let's see. I got to work yesterday morning at about eight forty-five or so. Is that what you want to know?"

"Yes. Keep going."

"Okay. Went up to my office, used the washroom down the hall, went downstairs again to go over the in-box stuff with Wilma. You know, incoming correspondence, e-mail, that sort of thing. She processes all of it and we go over who will deal with what. I take some, and the rest goes to either Belle or Andie, or Wilma handles it herself. That took about fifteen or twenty minutes. Then I had the conference call at ten, which went more than an hour. I met with Belle for about fifteen minutes right before lunch. She's our communications director, so I signed off on galleys for brochures. We talked about revamping our website. She wants to start a blog so we talked about that for a while. I had lunch with our local M.P., something I do a couple times a year to keep him interested in our work. That ran until one thirty. Back to the office, the usual routine, left about six forty, six forty-five."

"Oh? Why so late?"

Baldwin looked a little embarrassed. "I'm writing a book. About Kenya, and my experiences there. The charity. All that. My agent expects to see the manuscript next month, so I'm spending whatever extra time I can find on it. It's nearly done."

"I see. And then?"

"I went home. Got there about seven. Colin was there. He has a key. Actually, he'll be moving in next month, selling his place. But anyway. I fixed dinner, we ate at about eight, watched TV. That was it. I got up the next morning at seven, had breakfast with Colin, left at eight thirty, got to work about ten minutes later, and the same thing as yesterday morning. Until you showed up. And—"

Kevin watched him choke up and cover his face with his hands. He listened to Baldwin's heavy breathing for a few moments, then stood up and left the room.

chapter NINE

John Bishop was not a subtle man. Everyone had their own style, of course, and welcome to it, but Bishop preferred the direct approach. No finessing, no long silences, no bullshit. He was trained in various interviewing techniques, including the well-known Reid technique made famous in Canada by the OPP interrogator who used it to gain a confession from convicted serial killer Russell Williams; the less-confrontational PEACE technique commonly used in England; and other methods of questioning people sitting in the hot seat. However, Bishop disliked wasting time dancing around. Ask-and-answer was his ideal interviewing model.

"Okay, Mrs. Sutton," he said, rubbing his face after having gone through Andie Matheson's usual daily work routine for the third time. "Let's cut to the chase here. Do you know who killed her?"

"Oh God, no. Of course not." Wilma Sutton was weeping now, her eyes turned to the ceiling.

Bishop moved the box of tissues closer to her elbow. "But you've got a pretty good idea who might have done it, don't you?"

She shook her head, pulling out a wad of tissues and pressing them to her eyes.

"And you're sure you don't know who she was dating? Sleeping with? Having dinner and drinks with?"

"I don't," she insisted. "I have no idea. As I already said, I keep my business to myself." She sniffed. "And I stay out of other people's business."

"Yeah, but surely she was dating someone. A good-looking girl like her?"

Wilma blew her nose into the tissues, took a moment to collect herself, and sighed. "She was a lonely girl. Anyone could see that."

"She was lonely."

"Yes. Lonely, and sad. She didn't laugh very much. It was hard even to get her to smile sometimes."

"Was there something between her and Baldwin? Something that was upsetting her?"

"You've already asked me that twice, Detective, and the answer is still the same. As far as I know, Mr. Baldwin and Andrea got along just fine. Mr. Baldwin is extremely professional. For a young man. *Completely* professional." She looked at him pointedly.

Bishop held up a hand. "All right. Okay. I get it."

"Do I have to tell you again what I did over the last twenty-four hours, or is it on tape this time so I don't have to three-peat myself?"

Bishop stood up. Despite himself, he chuckled. "Nah, I think we're good, Mrs. Sutton. Sit tight for a bit longer, then we'll see if we can get you home."

chapter TEN

"Tell me a little bit about yourself," Kevin said to Isabella Tofalos, leaning his elbow on the little desk and cupping his head in his hand. "Where are you from?"

"Toronto." She patted her eyes with a carefully-folded tissue.

"Born and raised there?"

Isabella shook her head. She'd managed to collect herself during the long wait while Kevin interviewed Kyle Baldwin, and the look she gave him now was calm and controlled. "I was born in Greece. But I'm a Canadian citizen."

"Greece, is that right? Where in Greece?"

She tucked her long, straight black hair behind an ear. "Peristeri. Do you know where that is?"

Kevin smiled. "I don't have a clue. Where is it?"

"It's a suburb of Athens. In the northwest. Great shops, bars, Internet cafes. Very cosmopolitan."

"When did you come to Canada?"

"When I was four. But I've been back to visit a few times. We have family there."

"So you speak Greek as well as English?"

"I speak English, French, Greek, German, Spanish, Italian, some Turkish and some Russian."

"Holy cow. That's very impressive. No wonder Kyle says you're such a great communications director."

"He's nice. And of course, I've been picking up a bit of Maa, the Maasi language. Kyle speaks it too, did you know that?"

"I didn't. How did you come to work for him, Isabella?"

She shrugged. "It's a long story."

"I think we've got time."

She sighed and folded her hands on her lap. She seemed to take a moment to decide whether or not she wanted to talk or just get up and leave, since he'd already said she didn't have to stay. Then she nodded to herself.

"I was working at a print shop downtown. Not so far from my father's place in Greektown. He's a tobacconist. Anyway, Kyle was in the city for one of his conferences."

"This was where you met him?"

"Yes. I have a B.A. from York, but jobs are hard to find these days. For a while I was part-time at an ad agency, but when I met Kyle I was full-time at a printing company. He came in to pick up some brochures he'd gotten done for this conference. He'd supplied the artwork, and we were just running off the copies for him. I pointed out a couple of errors in the French translation."

"Oh?"

The corner of her mouth tipped up. "Kind of upset him. He had some other stuff, his speaking notes and that sort of thing, that he wanted copied too, and he asked me if I'd review the translations before we ran them. Said he'd pay for it. So I did. We cleaned them up and printed them out. When he picked them up, I said something about his foundation, that it looked like it was doing good work.

We talked a bit, then he asked if I wanted to come to the conference, hear a few speakers, see what it was all about. I said, sure.

"My pap didn't raise an idiot. I know an opportunity when I see one. So I went. He met me, showed me around, and was very nice."

Kevin smiled encouragingly. "Is that when he hired you and you came to Brockville?"

She shook her head. "No. Not right away. He said he was interested in hiring me, but couldn't right then. Additional travel expenses that year had screwed up his budget. Which was the truth. I checked it out later. So I stayed where I was for about eight months and did volunteer work on the side for his foundation."

"In Toronto."

"That's right. Then, when he did hire me, I worked out of Toronto for the next two years." She glanced at him. "My parents didn't want me moving away. I said, 'Mam, I'm twenty-six. I can take care of myself.' Anyway, I wish I'd stayed. Brockville sucks."

Kevin raised an eyebrow. "You don't like it here?"

She pursed her lips, staring at him.

"It's a harmless enough place, don't you think?"

She rolled her eyes. "It's a fucking gulag, excuse my language. I've tried to get him to move to a real city, Toronto preferably. Montreal would be fine. Even Ottawa would be tolerable. But he won't budge. End of story. So I'm here."

"Why won't he move?"

"You'll have to ask him that yourself. I'm not getting into it." She folded her arms.

"Okay. How do the two of you get along? You and Kyle?"

"Great."

"Across the board great, or here and there great?"

She put the tip of her tongue between her lips, stared at him for a moment, and then shook her head. "You've been practising your technique, haven't you?"

"In front of a mirror, every morning. Describe your relationship with Kyle, Isabella."

"We're friends. I like him. I admire him. He's very smart, very personable, very dedicated. How's that?"

"Keep going; you're doing fine."

"Am I sleeping with him? No. Did I ever sleep with him? No. Is that what you want me to say?"

"If it's the truth."

She stared at him. "It's the truth."

"Okay."

"My boyfriend, fiancé actually, is a sergeant major in the infantry. Overseas right now, but when his tour's up next year and he gets his discharge we're getting married and we're going to find a nice place to live, right on Danforth in the middle of Greektown. He's a cigar smoker, and Pap said he'd give him two fresh ones, his choice, every morning for the rest of his life if he brings me home." She managed a smile. "Kyle's already given me his blessing. So, no. I have no interest in Kyle other than as a really great boss, an incredible person, and a completely tireless worker for those people over there in Africa."

"How about Kyle's relationship with Andie?"

Isabella paused for a moment, studying him. "You talked to him already, obviously, so no doubt you would have gone over that with him in detail. So you already know she came to Brockville under what she later thought were false pretences. Then got over it and moved on with her life. You probably asked him how they were after that, if there was lingering tension or conflict or whatever. I'll just repeat what he's already told you. They were fine. No lingering tension. No hostility or conflict. They became friends, employer and employee. They had a lot of disagreements over sponsors and what events to do or to skip. Andie always wanted volume, but Kyle was a little picky about whom he would let the foundation be associated with. Yeah, they went at it from time to time. But Kyle's extremely professional. He's a great negotiator, and he knows when and how to compromise. They always worked things out between them. Satisfied?"

"How did Andie feel about being in Brockville?"

Isabella barked a short laugh. "Are you kidding? We were going to start a club. The *I Hate Brockville Club*. We would've made a fortune on membership fees alone."

"She wasn't happy here, then."

Isabella shook her head slowly, underlining the point.

"Was she seeing anyone, Isabella?"

"You mean, was she screwing anyone?"

Kevin waited.

Isabella looked at her hands and hesitated. "I don't gossip. It's a hard-and-fast rule."

"She's dead, Isabella. Someone brutally murdered her and left her in a ditch thirty kilometres from home. At this point it's not gossip, it's vitally important information. We need to know about everyone who was connected to her."

"I know." She squeezed the tissue in her hand. "I know, I know, I know."

Kevin waited.

"Look," she finally said, her eyes still down, "she tended to gravitate toward ... older men."

"Married men, you mean?"

She nodded.

"More than one?"

No response.

"Can you give me any names, Isabella?"

She looked at him. "We weren't very close, she and I. She was a flirty type, always buzzing around the guys and touching their arm, that kind of stuff. I don't do that sort of thing."

"You and she didn't get along?"

"Yeah, of course we did. We got along just fine. We didn't socialize after work, anything like that, though. We had lunch together now and then, but it was mostly me talking and her listening. She was pretty close-mouthed about her personal affairs."

"Can you give me any names?"

She shook her head. "There've been a couple of guys over the last few years. None of them apparently lasted very long. The only one I ever knew much of anything about was some guy at one of the big donors, in charge of their community relations division."

"Name?"

"Sorry. I never did know."

"Do you know what company he worked for?"

She shook her head again.

"How did you learn about him?"

"I heard her arguing with him on the phone in her cubicle. Normally I tune it out. I listen to music sometimes when I'm at my desk; it helps me concentrate. But this one time I overheard her. She started with business, shifted to personal, and got a little sharp with him."

"What did she say?"

Isabella frowned, searching her memory. "I don't know. Something like, 'I don't care if she finds out or not. You promised me.' Then she slammed the phone down and stormed out. I put my buds back in and looked busy."

"And that was it? You didn't find out anything else?"

She shrugged. "That was it."

"Isabella, what about her friends? Girlfriends, people she liked to spend her free time with."

"Hunph. You got me."

"You don't know of anyone she hung around with, as friends?"

"Not at all. She was really, really private, okay? It wouldn't surprise me if she didn't have any friends here. Maybe Kyle knows of someone, but I sure don't. Anyway, she came off as lonely, under all that pert flirtiness. There was a sadness, I guess you could say."

"All right." Kevin sat back, rubbing his chin. "We haven't been able to locate her cellphone yet. Do you know what kind it was? What carrier she subscribed to?"

"It was an iPhone. With a pink case. I don't know what

plan she was on."

"Do you know her number?"

Isabella rattled it off from memory.

"Any idea where the phone might be?"

"Nope."

"Did she use it much? Is it something she would always have around her, no matter where she was?"

Isabella gave him a look of mock astonishment. "Are you kidding me? What planet are you from? She never went anywhere without it. I never go anywhere without mine. I'm always using it. Aren't you?" She rolled her eyes. "Oh, wait. You're a square. You're probably still paying for a landline phone in your house."

"Yeah, it's a rotary-dial princess model sitting right next to my VCR and the black-and-white TV with the rabbit ears." Kevin sighed. "Tell me again where you were last night and early this morning, why don't you?"

chapter ELEVEN

Bishop drove, his black motor pool Crown Vic having been returned from the Parkway crime scene shortly after lunch by a uniformed officer, while Kevin leaned back against the headrest and closed his eyes.

The voice in Kevin's head prattled on about Kyle Baldwin and possible ways in which he might have had a conflict with Andie Matheson, but he really didn't want to think about it right now. He forced his mind to concentrate on blackness and the sound of the Crown Vic's engine and his own breathing, which he slowed down with a conscious effort.

"Still not sleeping, huh?"

Kevin's eyes popped open. They were at the edge of Brockville, about where County Road 29 became Stewart Boulevard. The speed limit here was sixty kilometres an hour. Bishop was tailgating a small red pickup truck that was trying its best to obey the law.

"Not really." Kevin sat up.

"Better you than me, brother." Bishop whipped around the pickup truck, mashing the accelerator with his boot. "How's Janie coping with it?"

Kevin's shoulder bumped against the doorframe as Bishop swung back into the right-hand lane. "She's used to it. But the break will do her good."

Bishop looked over at him. "Christ, that's right. You're on your own right now. How's that going?"

"Fine." Kevin looked out the window. Janie was in Toronto, attending the annual conference of a beauty association she'd joined last year. It had been a big decision to close her salon in Sparrow Lake for a week and leave the baby in Kevin's care, but she'd felt the opportunities to network and get new ideas for her business would be worth it. As well, she'd entered several competitions and hoped to show the hairstyling community what she could do on a big stage. Kevin understood how important her business was to her, and he whole-heartedly supported the trip.

"It's too early for him to be sleeping through, isn't it?"

Kevin grunted. "He's still waking up, but he's sleeping longer. He was only awake twice last night."

"How old is he now?"

"Two months. Nine weeks and three days, to be precise."

Janie's mother, Barb, was watching Joshua during the day, and arrangements had been made for Caitlyn and Brendan, Janie's two older children, to be dropped off at Barb's after school this afternoon. Tomorrow was a professional development day at school and Barb would take them again, as she also would on Saturday and Sunday. Janie was returning home Monday afternoon.

Bishop shook his head. "You've got your hands full, buddy."

"I signed up for it," Kevin said. "I can handle it." *Thank God for Barb*, he added silently.

Bishop rolled through the lights at Centennial Road and turned into the parking lot of Alton Villa Real Estate.

He stopped in front of the plain-looking little building and they got out. On the way to the front door, Bishop said, "I've never dealt with these guys before. Know anything about them?"

"Nothing." Kevin held the aluminum screen door open for Bishop and followed him inside. There was no one at the reception desk. Bishop strolled past it, looking around. A woman charged out of a side room, head down, a sheaf of papers in her hand. She sat down at a desk and punched a button on the telephone. "I've got them."

"Great, Delvia," a voice replied over the speaker. "Can I put you on hold for a second? Sorry."

"Sure." Delvia punched another button and looked up. "Hi, can I help you?"

Bishop put his hands on his hips, moving the edges of his jacket aside so that she could see the badge and sidearm on his belt. "We're looking for Colin Davies. Is he here?"

"He's out," she replied, frowning at the gun. "Showing a property. Can I help?"

The phone chirped. "Delvia, I—"

She cut the speaker and picked up the handset. "Jack, these look fine. Can I go over them and call you right back? You'll be there? All right. Ten minutes. Yeah. Bye." She hung up and frowned again at Bishop.

"You were going to tell me where we can find Davies," he prompted.

She rolled her chair backward and got up, striding to a large display board on the near wall. She searched the board for a moment, then pulled an eight-and-a-half by eleven photocopy from a holder next to one of the listings. "This one, I think."

"Twelve-sixty County Road Two," Bishop read aloud. "Off Maitland Road. That right?"

Delvia shrugged, waved dismissively at the paper in his hand, and went back to her desk.

Outside, Kevin took the photocopy from Bishop and glanced at it as he got in the Crown Vic. "Holy crap. Half a million bucks, for *this*?"

"It's got a pool." Bishop started the engine and backed out of the parking space.

"Big deal. So do we."

Bishop accelerated out onto Stewart Boulevard. "In-ground, Kev. Olympic-sized, not a plastic kiddie pool. Plus two acres. Four bedrooms. I'll bet it shows real nice."

"You sound like you might be interested."

Bishop concentrated on his driving for a moment, then said, "Might be, you never know."

"Oh?"

Bishop stopped for a red light at Stewart and Parkedale, then glanced over. "Jenn's thinking she might like to move to the country."

"I see." Kevin was aware that Bishop and his wife had had a rocky past and that he was working hard to mend their relationship. Bishop was the sort of man who normally kept his personal life private, and Kevin had no particular urge to pry, so he kept his eyes on the street ahead of them.

Once they were on the eastbound 401 Bishop said, "She wants a place where she can have big gardens in the back. Flowers, herbs, vegetables. The whole shootin' match." He pulled into the left-hand lane to pass a tractor trailer. "You've seen our backyard. Hardly enough room for a doghouse and a recycling bin."

He swung back into the right-hand lane and watched an OPP cruiser pass on the other side of the median, westbound, moving with the traffic. Its roof-rack lights were off, and the Crown Vic's police radio, which was turned down to a mutter, wasn't barking about anything in particular. "She wants a dog, too. For when I'm working and she's at home by herself."

Kevin thought about it. Bishop struck him as an unlikely dog owner, but then again, anything was possible. "Ever have a dog before?"

"Yeah. When I was a kid we had a rat terrier. Mean little

fucker, but I loved that dog."

"So if you lived in the country you'd get a dog, is that it?"

"Sure, Kev. Fine. Whatever she wants." He raised an eyebrow at him. "I personally don't give a fuck. I've been a city boy all my life, but hey, I'm spending all my time working rural. So why the hell not live out there, too?"

Kevin knew that Bishop had been born and raised in Chatham, a city of about a hundred thousand people in southwest Ontario. Bishop had talked once or twice about growing up as a street rat in the downtown core and living with his mother in an apartment above a drugstore, so Kevin understood what he meant about being a city boy. He wasn't sure that Bishop would be happy with a rural lifestyle. He said, "Are you looking at places?"

"Not yet. But anything's better than Brockville." Bishop grinned. "Sorry, kid. You're probably getting sick of people dumping on your hometown."

"That's all right." Although he now lived in the village of Sparrow Lake, a half-hour drive west in Yonge township, Kevin still considered himself a Brockville native. He was used to the city's poor reputation. "There are a few places for sale out near us," he said.

"Actually," Bishop said, "I was thinking more of something up around Smiths Falls. Closer to Ottawa. Besides, I wouldn't want to crowd you and March."

Ellie March's four-season cottage was located on Sparrow Lake, only a few minutes from the village itself. She and Kevin were practically neighbours, although they seldom saw each other.

Bishop took the Maitland Road exit and drove south to County Road 2, where he turned left. Kevin looked at a real estate sign that had been driven into the ground close to the intersection. It had a photograph of Colin Davies on it and a large red arrow on the top, pointing in the direction they were heading.

"At least if everybody runs when we get there," Bishop

quipped, looking at the sign, "we'll know which guy to shoot."

They soon reached the house they were looking for. Bishop followed a paved driveway up to a large brick split-level house. They parked behind a Range Rover and got out. The vehicle ahead of it, a late-model Ford Explorer, looked as though it had just gone through a car wash. The back seat was filled with real estate signs, boxes of brochures, and other junk. As they walked past it, the front door of the house opened. A man and a woman, dressed casually in jeans and windbreakers, stepped out onto the porch. They were followed by Colin Davies, who wore a trench coat over a sports jacket and trousers.

"Looks like someone else wants to see it," the woman said, directing an unfriendly look at Bishop, who was leading the way up the sidewalk.

"Hi there," Davies called out, stepping around her. "Do we have an appointment?"

"Nah," Bishop said. "It's more a spur-of-the-moment thing."

"Oh, sure. Okay. I'll be right with you."

"That's fine," Kevin said, following Bishop off the sidewalk onto the lawn so that Davies and his prospective clients could pass. "Nice property."

"Yes, it is. Thank you." Davies ushered the couple down to their Range Rover, where they stood for several minutes, talking things over. The man kept his eyes on the house while the woman kept hers on Davies, her mouth firm, her body language stiff.

"She ain't gonna pay half a mil for this place," Bishop said, admiring the flower bed along the front of the house, which had been cleaned up and was beginning to show signs of life. "I don't blame her. It doesn't look so shit-hot after all."

Kevin nodded, watching them. "Davies is in there pitching, though." When the woman finally turned away and opened the driver's side door, Kevin said, "Too bad.

There it goes." He watched Davies move out of the way as the Range Rover executed a K-turn and disappeared down the driveway.

"You want this?" Bishop asked as Davies trudged toward them. "Where you know Baldwin?"

"Okay." Kevin unclipped his badge and held it up. "Mr. Colin Davies?"

"Yes, I am. Are you here about the house? I have another appointment elsewhere in about an hour."

"Detective Constable Walker, OPP. This is Detective Constable Bishop. We need to ask you a few questions."

Davies stopped in front of him and squinted up, raising a hand to shield the sun from his eyes. He was a short, thick-chested man in his late thirties with a receding hairline and large, pale blue eyes. "Of course. What's this about?"

"We're investigating a homicide, Mr. Davies, and we need to ask you where you were over the last twenty-four hours."

He looked stunned. "A homicide. Oh my God. Who? Is Kyle okay?"

"Yes, Mr. Davies, Kyle's fine. Andrea Matheson, a woman who worked for Kyle, was found dead this morning."

"Oh my God. Andie. What happened? What's going on?"

"Mr. Davies, is there somewhere we can talk? Can we go inside?"

"Sure, sure, of course. No one's home. They're still in Florida. Come on." Davies led the way inside, removing his boots in the vestibule and putting on a pair of slip-on shoes. "Don't worry about your boots. I keep these here for myself. I've been trying to sell this place all winter."

"You ask me," Bishop said, making a token effort to wipe his feet on the mat, "it's priced way too high for folks around here for what you get."

"You may be right." Davies led the way into the kitchen, pointing at high stools around a kitchen island. "Please, sit down. Oh my God, I need a moment. Do you want coffee? I made a pot, but it seems the Dillaboughs only drink fair trade and this is just regular off-the-shelf Arabica, so there's lots."

"Thank you," Kevin said, unbuttoning his jacket. "Just a bit of sugar."

"Black." Bishop slid onto a stool.

"I'm sorry," Davies said, busying himself at the counter, "I need a moment to handle this. Andie's dead? I don't believe it. It's horrible."

Kevin waited for Davies to come around the island, two coffee mugs in his hand. He accepted one and glanced at the elaborate logo of Alton Villa Real Estate that festooned the side of the cup. "Thanks. When was the last time you saw Andie Matheson, Mr. Davies?"

Davies sat down next to Bishop and gave him the other cup of coffee. "I don't know, a couple days ago? Not yesterday. The day before, I guess."

"How well did you know her, Mr. Davies?"

"Colin. Just Colin, please. I knew her fairly well, I suppose." He gestured with a hand. "I'm assuming you know that Kyle and I are in a relationship."

Kevin nodded.

"Well, I knew Andie through him. I'd see her at the office and at some of their fundraisers and other things like that. We'd talk. She's a nice kid." He made a face and lowered his eyes. "*Was* a nice kid. Young and pretty. Very innocent. But smart. Really smart. She had a future. Shit. *Damn* it."

"Colin, we need you to account for your whereabouts over the last twenty-four hours. Tell us where you've been and what you've done."

His eyes flew up. "What? You must be kidding."

"We're very serious," Bishop said quietly.

"But it's ridic—" He stopped, took a breath, and looked from Bishop to Kevin. "No. You're right. I understand. You want to know where I was yesterday?"

"Yes," Kevin said. "Start at noon. Where did you have lunch?"

"Here," Davies replied, an edge coming into his voice. "I was supposed to meet the Dillaboughs here at one yesterday. I brought a sandwich and came early, to make sure everything was ship-shape. They didn't show. I called at one thirty and left a message on her voice mail. She called back at two fifteen, for Christ's sake. 'Oh, we had other things to take care of,' she said."

"What time did you leave here yesterday?"

"About two thirty. I went back to the office and worked there until five. Then I went over to Kyle's. He got home around seven. We had dinner, watched TV, and called it a night around eleven or so."

"You had dinner about what time?"

"About, uh, eight o'clock, I guess."

"Who cooked, you or Kyle?"

Davies smiled. "Kyle's the chef, not me. I stay out of the kitchen, for everyone's safety."

"Did you stay there all night?"

"At Kyle's place? Yes." Davies glanced at Bishop, who had shifted his weight, then said to Kevin, "We're planning to move in together. I'm putting my house up for sale. But first we wanted to make sure we wouldn't drive each other completely insane."

Kevin smiled. "How's it going?"

"Actually, just fine. We'll be fine. So, yes, I got up at six, Kyle got up about seven, and he fixed us breakfast. We watched the morning news, then he left for work at eight thirty and I left about a half hour later."

"Did either you or Kyle leave the apartment during the night?"

"No. I sure as hell didn't, and Kyle never got up at all. I'm a very light sleeper. I wake up whenever he gets up, whether it's to use the toilet or go to the kitchen or whatever. He never stirred all night."

"Okay," Kevin said, "thanks. Tell me something, what

happened to his nose?"

"His nose? What do you mean?"

"Well, it's obvious he broke it at some point. It wasn't like that in high school. Was he in a fight with someone?"

Davies blinked, a little confused. "No, he doesn't get into fights. It happened in Africa. Some kind of accident when he was helping unload a truck. A crate fell on him or something. It was several years ago. You should ask him about it."

"How would you describe his relationship with Andie Matheson?"

Davies pushed out his lips, thinking. "Good. Professional. He liked her. He respected her for the job she was doing for him. She was excellent."

"How was she around you?"

"Mmm, not so good, at first. She said a few things. But I'm an adult, I've dealt with it before, and I kept things cordial at my end. She came around after a while, and she was fine. We became friendly. Not friends, because we never socialized or anything like that, but friendly."

"What's Kyle's temper like? Does he get angry a lot?"

Davies snorted. "No. Why?"

"Does he often lose his temper?"

"No! Look, I've seen him frustrated, I've seen him irritated, annoyed, and I've seen him cross at someone, but I've never seen him lose his temper."

"Surely once or twice," Kevin said, sounding skeptical.

"Never. Not the way you're thinking, that's for damned sure."

"When he's frustrated or irritated, as you describe it, does he express himself physically? You know, punch a wall or throw something across the room or slam his fist down?"

"No. He's a pacifist, Detective Walker. He doesn't believe in war or physical violence in any form. I keep teasing him that he should become a Buddhist and just get it over with. You know, *Ahimsa*? 'Do no harm'? That's him to a T."

Kevin glanced over Davies's shoulder at Bishop, who shrugged microscopically.

"Look," Davies added, "if you think Kyle had some kind of lover's quarrel with Andie and did something to her, you're off base. Way off base."

"Can anyone else corroborate your statement that you and Kyle spent all your time between seven last night and seven this morning together at his condo?"

"Uh, I don't know." Davies thought about it. "We didn't have visitors. I turned my phone off. Oh, I tell you what." He nodded to himself. "That building has an extensive security system. Trust me, I checked it out before I agreed to move in there with Kyle. I'm a big believer in home security. They have video surveillance that records everyone who enters and leaves, and I'm sure it'll back up what I'm saying. You should get hold of that. Then you'll know I'm telling the truth."

"We'll look into it," Kevin said, standing up and shaking Davies's hand. "Thanks for your help."

chapter

TWELVE

Ellie walked into the meeting room and sat down at the head of the table. According to the clock on the wall it was still six minutes before four in the afternoon, but as she scanned the faces gathered around the table she saw that everyone was already present. Coffee had been poured and bottles of water opened, tablets and laptops were powered up, notebooks and files were open and ready. Ident had uploaded crime scene photos two hours ago, and the file co-ordinator, Leo Forsythe, had incorporated them into the online case file. Ellie sensed that everyone on the team had already seen them and was anxious to get started.

"Dave," she said, "why don't you start off by filling us in on what you've got so far."

Down at the far end of the table, Dave Martin glanced at his tablet. "Okay, folks, first things first. Our crime scene on the Parkway is definitely a dump site, so our primary scene is still unknown. The victim was transported by car and dumped, nude, along with her purse. The offender then drove one-point-four kilometres east, pulled over again, and got rid of the knife. Footprints at the first scene tell us the body was in the trunk, but the second time around they're just at the front of the vehicle, suggesting the knife was inside with the offender."

"So he unloaded the body and the purse from the trunk at the first stop," Kevin said, "but forgot the knife was in the car with him. When he realized he still had it, he pulled over the second time, walked around the front of his car, and threw it away."

"Yes. He *or* she. A reasonable hypothesis, Kevin. Extrapolate from it what you will about our offender's state of mind at that point." Martin's eyes flicked again to his tablet. "According to our coroner, the esteemed Dr. Kearns, the victim was stabbed fifteen times with a large knife. The chef's knife found at the second location appears to be a match size-wise, and the blood traces retrieved from it will no doubt ring all the bells, so I'd say it's safe to proceed on the assumption that it is, in fact, the murder weapon.

"Dr. Kearns said she found evidence of recent sexual activity that would have occurred shortly before death," he continued, "but no overt evidence of sexual assault. In an uncharacteristic outburst of modesty, false or otherwise, she cautioned it'll have to be verified by the forensic pathologist at autopsy, and it was just her *opinion* that sex prior to death had been consensual. Finally, she estimates that time of death was approximately seven o'clock this morning."

Ellie brushed a strand of hair from her eyes. Consensual sex followed by extremely violent and repeated stabbing, followed by a disorganized dump job.

She stared down the table at Martin. State of mind, indeed. He was probably thinking what she was thinking right now, that the multiple stab wounds suggested a highly-emotional mindset, the knife was likely a weapon of opportunity, grabbed without much forethought, and the bungled dump job suggested a disorganized killer still struggling with panic or extreme stress. A common profile in domestic homicide, certainly, where a family member or lover acted spontaneously out of jealousy or in response to abuse of some kind.

She leaned forward. "Dr. Kearns tells me the autopsy will be done by Dr. Burton Saturday morning at Kingston General."

"Kevin," Carty said, "you and I will be there."

Kevin nodded, saying nothing.

Ellie watched Kevin control his expression as he wrote in his notebook, eyes down. She was aware that it would be his second autopsy and that the first, which he'd attended with her, had not gone particularly well for him, stomach-wise. She hoped he'd do better this time. They took some getting used to, as she knew from personal experience, and they weren't for everyone. Kevin would have to find a way to handle it.

She got up and walked around to the side table for a bottle of water.

"I've uploaded a list of the contents of the victim's purse," Martin continued, "which was pretty much your typical female paraphernalia. However, notable for its absence is a cellphone. It wasn't in her purse, it wasn't nearby, and it wasn't at the secondary site either. We're extending the ground search, so we'll see if it turns up."

"You think it was tossed out, like the knife?" asked Leung.

"We don't know what happened to it. It may still be at the murder site, it may still be in the offender's possession, or it may be anywhere between point A and infinity."

"Along with her clothing," Kevin said, glancing at Ellie as she walked behind Leung on her way back to her seat.

"Right. Also still AWOL." Martin swiped his tablet. "We lifted a great set of footprints, apart from those belonging to the witness Garvey and you two." He looked at Kevin and Carty. "We're running them now in our database. I'll let you know if something specific pops. They measured ten inches, which is in that grey area where they could have been made by either a female or a male. For example, my shoes leave a ten-inch print."

"Yeah, but you're a pipsqueak," Bishop said.

"I am, yes, but I'm a brainy pipsqueak." He shrugged at Kevin. "I'll have a lot more specifics for you the next time we meet."

"Thanks," Ellie said, sitting down again and opening the bottle of water. "Tom, where are we on the warrants?"

"Wiltse's working on them," Carty replied. "We'll have ones for the office, her apartment, and her car, which is parked in the lot behind her building. They should be ready by early evening."

Detective Constable Ben Wiltse was the crime unit's warrant co-ordinator. He was responsible for writing and submitting requests for search authorizations on behalf of the team, and he did so by preparing what was known as an ITO, an Information To Obtain a Search Warrant. An ITO was supposed to provide a judge with all the relevant facts and evidence contributing to the police's reasonable grounds to believe that further evidence relating to the crime in question could be found at the location specified in the ITO.

Because the ITO must make a "full, frank and fair" disclosure of all the information available at that point with respect to the search request, Wiltse was always sequestered during major case investigations such as this one. He disappeared from the detachment office and worked out of a cubbyhole at regional headquarters, meeting only with Kevin or whoever else was requesting the warrant. Their meetings focused only on what Wiltse needed to know in order to write up an ITO a judge would approve. Anything else, anything extraneous to the request, was kept from him so that he could focus only on the material facts. In this way, he could truthfully swear that he was providing everything the judge needed to know, and only what they needed to know, in order to make a neutral and impartial decision on the application.

Ellie had actually only met Wiltse once, at a softball game in Westport more than a year ago. She remembered him as young and slender, with straight brown hair, a quick laugh, and green eyes that never stopped moving. He made a joke about being known as the Leper of Leeds County, shook her hand, and ran out to his position in the outfield. If not for this encounter, she might have wondered if Ben Wiltse was a figment of her imagination.

"Production orders have been submitted for the victim's phone and bank records," said Bill Merkley, the regional intelligence co-ordinator working with the team on the case. "I should have information for you tomorrow."

"Thanks." Ellie turned back to Kevin. "Are your search teams set?"

"John will handle the office with you," Kevin said, glancing down at Martin. "Correct?"

"Yes, and Jamieson," Martin confirmed, referring to Forensic Constable Bill Jamieson, who was part of his Ident team. "Landry will do the apartment and car with you, Mark. Right?"

Detective Constable Mark Allore nodded, his expression neutral.

"I understand the victim had family in Ajax," Ellie said, changing the subject. "What about notifications?"

"Carried out late this morning by Durham Regional Police," Kevin reported. "Her father, Dr. Bob Matheson, is a dentist with a small office in Ajax, and her mother, Anneke, is his receptionist. According to the mother, she kept contact with her daughter on Facebook but hadn't been in touch with her for the past three days. Apparently this wasn't unusual."

"Other family?"

"She has an older sister in Montreal, married. We're waiting to hear back on her."

Ellie nodded. "I've spoken to Rachel," she told the team, referring to Constable Rachel Townsend, a media liaison officer based at regional headquarters in Smiths Falls. Rachel was always her first choice when it came to major cases, and she was happy to have her on board once again. "She has other commitments this afternoon, but I'll bring you up to speed on where we're at with communications. We've included the victim's name in her afternoon media briefing and press releases, now that next of kin have been notified. It'll be out there on the evening news. Rachel's also preparing Crime Stoppers spots for radio and TV."

Ellie looked down the table at Kevin. "She mentioned you two had been discussing another strategy."

Kevin nodded. "We talked about trying a cellphone canvass," he told the table. "Rachel ran it by Staff Sergeant Patterson, and he was okay with the idea."

Ellie had given the matter some thought before the meeting. The OPP had used the technique before in a homicide investigation in this region. It would involve serving production orders on cellphone companies to obtain lists of all cellphones identified to have been in use in the area of their dump site on the Thousand Islands Parkway in the hours leading up to the discovery of the body. Once they had the lists, they would send a text message to each phone number asking the cellphone owners to visit a website so that they could answer a few questions which might help the investigation. It was generally considered a "Hail Mary" attempt to find witnesses when leads in a case were drying up and the investigation needed a transfusion of new information.

"We'll see," she said. "I'm not against it. In fact, it could be very useful. Let's give things a few days, though, before we run it upstairs."

Kevin nodded, understanding. It was still a sensitive issue with the public. Although the production order asked only for phone numbers and not the names and addresses of subscribers, some people felt it was the thin edge of the wedge in terms of an encroaching police state where Big Brother could reach out and touch them whenever He felt like it. Reactions to receiving such a text message had been mixed in the past, and Ellie preferred to keep the idea in her back pocket for the time being.

"What about our more conventional canvassing? Any luck?"

"Nothing," Kevin said, looking at Leung.

"That's right," Leung said. "No one I talked to recognized the picture of her, and no one saw anything unusual on the Parkway during our time frame when she would have been dumped. Nothing."

"I got the same," Bishop said. "Mark?"

"Zip," Allore agreed. "You didn't miss anything after you left, JB."

Kevin asked, "You covered all the residences on Old River Road above the dump site, correct?"

"Seven in a three-kilometre stretch," Allore confirmed. "Two were non-responsive, but we did a telephone follow-up and spoke to householders in both cases. One was down at the western end of our canvass. The resident drove west to get on the 401 for Kingston, so she didn't pass the dump site en route and didn't see or hear anything unusual before she left."

"And the other one?"

"In Ottawa. Staying with her daughter and son-in-law. Hasn't been home in four days."

"We also covered the whole length of Tar Island on that side of the bay," Kevin told Ellie. "Absolutely nothing. No odd lights, no noise. A few people told us there was fog at sunrise, and they couldn't see across to the Parkway anyway."

"What time was sunrise this morning?" Ellie asked.

"Just after six," Kevin said.

"Six ten," Martin chipped in. "The body would have been dumped between seven and nine fifty, when Garvey called 911, and it would have been daylight, yes, but visibility would have been limited by the early fog you're referring to, Kevin."

Kevin nodded, remembering that when he'd reached the traffic barrier this morning Sergeant Melken had said something about the visibility being a little difficult in the area after sunrise.

Ellie's cellphone, sitting on the table in front of her, vibrated twice. It was the signal that she'd received a text message. She glanced at the screen and said to Kevin, "take us through your early list of possible suspects."

"As far as family goes," Kevin began, "once we know where the sister was we can rule her out. The biggest question still remains whether the victim had an active boyfriend."

"What about Kyle Baldwin?"

Kevin looked at Bishop.

"He's a possibility," Bishop conceded, "but I'm pretty sure the girlfriend angle's out. His relationship with this Colin Davies guy is definitely solid. Baldwin could have killed her for some other reason, something we don't see yet, but not because she was banging someone else and he was jealous. It doesn't work for me at all."

Ellie raised an eyebrow. "Have you verified his story for last night and this morning?"

"Everything Baldwin said checked out with what Davies told us," Bishop acknowledged, "but we're going to make a request for surveillance video from Baldwin's condo building and see what it tells us."

"All right." Ellie glanced down as her cellphone screen went dark. "Anyone else?"

"The two other employees of Clinics for Kenya," Kevin said, "Isabella Tofalos and Wilma Sutton, both check out in terms of their whereabouts between estimated time of death and discovery of the body. They're in the clear." He frowned at his notes. "Tofalos reported the victim had a possible relationship with someone working for a local company she did fundraising with. We're hoping the searches tonight will turn up a lead there."

"All right, that's fine for now." Ellie gathered up her

things and stood up. "Keep it moving. Momentum's very important, as you well know."

In the corridor, as the team filed out of the meeting room, Ellie paused beside the door. When Leung came out, she tapped him on the arm. "Can you be available around eight tonight?"

"Sure. What for?"

"I want to talk to Peter Lambton. City council's meeting tonight, and I want to get this thing moving."

"Sounds good, Ellie." Leung smiled. "I'm always open to a little overtime."

"Talk to your sergeant about that one," she said. As Leung headed off to his cubicle, Ellie checked her text message. It was from Deputy Commissioner Cecil Dart, provincial commander of Investigations and Organized Crime at GHQ in Orillia:

Will be at Nepean Sportsplex Sun AM. *Can you meet me there?*

Ellie sighed. She made her way down the hall to the cubbyhole Carty had made available for her use while the Matheson case was being investigated. Cecil Dart was a politically ambitious senior manager who made no effort to hide the fact that he considered himself Ellie's rabbi within the force.

In the winter of 2015, Dart's son Craig, a detective constable in the Leeds County Crime Unit at the time, had fallen through the ice on Sparrow Lake while being pursued by an armed suspect. Ellie had risked her own life to pull him to safety. Dart remained grateful for what Ellie had done, but the sentiment made her feel distinctly uncomfortable. She didn't want a rabbi. She was happy doing what she was doing right now and wasn't ambitious for higher office. She didn't like internal politics and was uneasy benefiting from it in any way.

Yes sir, she replied. *Any particular time?*

Dart was her boss's boss, and normally she wouldn't meet with him without the knowledge or presence of

Superintendent Tony Agosta, the director of the Criminal Investigation Branch, who was her immediate supervisor. She wondered if Tony knew what this was about.

As she sat down at her tiny desk, her phone buzzed with another text message.

I'll be there from 7 AM on, so whatever suits. Arena 2. See you then.

Yes sir, she replied. She backed out of Messenger, thumbed the phone into sleep mode, and dropped it into her jacket pocket.

She stared at a calendar that was tacked to the wall, still showing the month of February. The photograph on the top page featured grinning young people snowboarding down an alpine slope under a bright blue sky. She felt cold just looking at it.

Whatever Dart wanted, she had a very strong feeling she wasn't going to like it.

chapter THIRTEEN

Still a little put out by Isabella Tofalos's suggestion that he was a technological square, Kevin used his cellphone to check the time as he walked up the sidewalk to the Clinics for Kenya office. It was 6:23 PM, still about an hour and a half before sunset. Clouds had moved in over the course of the afternoon, and although there was still some light in the sky there was little warmth left in the air. Kevin rolled his shoulders under his sports jacket, pulled his open car coat together, and trotted up the stairs.

After signing himself in with the constable who was controlling access to the building, he found Bishop in Wilma Sutton's office, cellphone pressed to his ear. The stocky detective winked at Kevin, held up a finger, and said, "I think that'll be great. Yeah, for sure. You bet."

Kevin stepped back out into the hallway, gathering from Bishop's tone that he was talking to his wife. He looked at the collection of brass monkeys and ran his eyes over the business cards they held. The second monkey from the left still offered cards that had been printed for Andrea Matheson. Her name, office address, and cellphone number were listed in an African-looking font, with the Clinics for Kenya logo on the right. They were identical to the cards found in her purse.

"Okay, Jenn," Bishop said, "I'll call you when I'm leaving. Okay? Love you."

Kevin stepped back into the office as Bishop was putting away his phone. "How's it going, JB?"

Bishop parked his haunch on the corner of Wilma's desk and shrugged. "Slow. Nothing spectacular so far."

A camera flash winked from beyond the doorway, where the Ident team was processing Andie Matheson's cubicle. "Anything odd or out of place?"

"Naw. Desktop computer bagged and tagged, plus an old laptop. Baldwin says it was issued to her when she first started working here, but she didn't use it any more."

"Oh?"

"Worked almost exclusively on her cellphone. Most people do, these days."

Kevin looked up as footsteps creaked across the ceiling.

"He and his lawyer are hanging out upstairs in his office," Bishop said.

"Any problems?"

"The usual whining and bitching and carping, but nothing too serious."

"Okay. Keep me posted."

Bishop grinned at him.

Upstairs, Kevin looked down the hall at the washroom, where a scenes-of-crime officer was down on his hands and knees in the open doorway, examining the floor. He knocked on the doorframe of Baldwin's office and walked in. A uniformed constable lounged inside the door, studying a Maasi mask hanging on the wall in an attempt to stave off maddening boredom. Kevin nodded and crossed the room.

"Kyle, how are you doing?"

"All right, considering." Baldwin shook his hand. "This is Richard Hall, our attorney. Rich, this is Detective Kevin Walker."

"Detective Constable Walker," Kevin said, shaking hands with a frowning, middle-aged man in a black chalk-stripe suit. "Do you represent the clinic, Mr. Hall?"

"I do. I'm also Kyle's attorney, but I'm here right now to protect the interests of the organization." He waved a copy of the search warrant, which he held in his left hand. "This is completely over-reaching, as far as I'm concerned."

"You should take it up with the judge, Mr. Hall. We're here to investigate a homicide."

"Oh, I intend to."

Baldwin fidgeted. "Rich, it's all right. I don't have a problem with them searching the common areas, as I already said."

"Well, I do. I—"

"Do I have to stay?" Baldwin interrupted.

"Are you all right, Kyle?" Kevin asked.

"I have a horrible migraine." Baldwin closed his eyes and pressed his knuckles against his temples.

"No, you don't have to," Hall said. "I'll stay here until they're done."

Baldwin opened his eyes. "Thanks. I just need to take my medication and lie down for an hour."

"Can I give you a lift?" Kevin asked. Since Bishop was the searching officer for the purposes of the warrant, Kevin's presence was not necessary. Giving Baldwin a ride back to his condo would give him a chance to ask him a few more questions in a less formal setting. It might also get him a look inside his apartment, which he'd never seen before.

"Thanks," Baldwin replied. "I came over with Rich, and I don't feel up to walking home."

Baldwin said very little in the car other than to give Kevin the address of his building, which Kevin already knew was down on the waterfront, and to suggest that he park in one of the visitors' spaces close to the front entrance.

As they crossed the front lobby to the elevators, Kevin glanced over at the large glass doors of the building's administrative offices. He and Bishop planned to stop in tomorrow morning to talk to the manager about access to their video surveillance records.

Since neither Baldwin nor Colin Davies was an actual suspect at this point due to a lack of evidence, Kevin knew they didn't have enough juice to convince a judge to issue a warrant for the recordings. However, if the manager agreed to provide them with access on a voluntary basis, Kevin and Bishop might possibly be able to verify the story the two men had given them about being at home when Andie Matheson was murdered.

The condominium, which was on the eighteenth floor, was nothing short of stunning. After explaining that Colin was out shopping and wouldn't be back for more than an hour, Baldwin hung up Kevin's trench coat in the hall closet and led the way into a sitting room just off the dining area.

There was a leather couch and two armchairs, a glass coffee table with magazines strategically arranged for maximum aesthetic effect, and windows—three bay windows looking out onto the St. Lawrence River. The condo was on the southwest corner of the building, so the windows afforded a spectacular view of the river and the shoreline on the American side.

Kevin stared down at the steel-grey water, burred with whitecaps which foretold the bad weather that was moving in.

"Wow, this is incredible, Kyle."

"Thanks. Would you like a coffee or something?"

"You said you were going to lie down."

Baldwin smiled faintly. "It takes my medication about twenty minutes to kick in, and the caffeine helps. I'm going to have a cup, so you're welcome to join me. I'll stretch out when I feel it starting to take effect."

"All right, thanks."

While he waited for Baldwin to return with the coffee, Kevin looked at a small bookcase on the far wall. There were a couple of books on African politics, biographies of Warren Buffett and Nelson Mandela, a few cookbooks, and other assorted volumes which suggested that while Baldwin's interests might be eclectic and wide ranging, he wasn't much of a reader. The collection had the look of an accumulation of Christmas and birthday gifts.

He picked out an encyclopedia of famous T-shirts and found the spine was so stiff it was obvious that the book had never been opened. He flipped through a few pages and put it back again.

"Here we go." Baldwin came in with a tray holding two cups on saucers, spoons, a pitcher of cream, and a sugar bowl. "I used the Tassimo; I hope that's all right. It's too late for a whole pot." He set the tray down on the coffee table and dropped onto the couch.

"That's fine. Thanks." Kevin took one of the cups and eased into an armchair. "Pardon me for asking, Kyle, but how do you afford a place like this?"

"Nice, eh?" Baldwin leaned forward with an effort and spooned sugar into the remaining cup of coffee. "It cost a fortune. The building's only a few years old, you know."

"I know." The project had taken nearly a decade to complete due to zoning and permit issues that constantly seemed to delay construction. At several points Kevin had believed, like most people in Brockville, that it would never be completed.

"I bought it using an inheritance." Baldwin sipped cautiously and frowned. "You met my mom, didn't you?"

Kevin shook his head.

"I thought you might have, somewhere along the way. Anyway, her father, my grandpa, was a Molson. A cousin of Senator Hartland Molson. He sat on the brewery's board of directors and owned a healthy chunk of stock, et cetera et cetera. When he passed away, I was mentioned in the will. I was in Grade Eleven at the time, the year I started the Clinics for Kenya charity."

"The same year we were in biology together," Kevin said.

"Yeah, that's right." Baldwin looked surprised. "I guess it was. Did we have any other classes together? I can't remember."

Kevin shook his head.

"Anyway, my mother put the money in trust for me until I graduated from Ryerson. I used some of it to buy this place." His eyes moved around the room and settled on Kevin. "It was part of the deal I made with her."

"Deal?"

"Yeah." Baldwin put down the cup and saucer. "We've always been very close. My dad, he was always away somewhere, Africa, the Middle East, brokering his farm equipment, living out of hotel rooms. Off in his own world. But my mother was always here, always the centre of *my* world."

Kevin waited, watching him.

"When I chose Ryerson, she wanted to know what my plans were once I got my degree. The charity was already up and running, and it was making its demands. She offered to help look after it while I was at school, keeping it here in Brockville, on the understanding I'd come back and take over after graduation. I thought about it for a while and then said okay. I've never had a problem with living in Brockville. So after graduation I came back and stayed with her until they started building this place. I'd made a promise to her to come back here for good, or at least for as long as she was alive, and I intended to keep it. I figured sinking this kind of money into my own condo would let her know I'd stick around." He smiled apologetically. "A rather long answer to a simple question."

Kevin nodded, thinking about how different their lives had been. When he was sixteen, his mother had already been battling stomach cancer for two years in their wartime bungalow on Hubbell Street while his father, a foreman at the detergent factory, was living with his girlfriend across town. Meanwhile, the kid sitting next to him for an hour each day in biology class was, unbeknownst to him, a Molson heir worth millions of dollars.

Life was a very bizarre trip. To say the least.

"There's something I need to ask you about," Kevin said.

"Okay." Baldwin massaged his temples.

"Are you all right?"

"Yeah. The medication should kick in pretty soon."

"Isabella Tofalos mentioned that Andie had a relationship at one point with a sponsor. A guy who was in charge of his company's community relations division. Do you have any idea who that might have been?"

Baldwin lifted his eyes to the ceiling, pursing his lips. "No, I don't think so. As I said before, I stayed out of her personal life."

"She never mentioned the name of anyone she was seeing?"

"No. Sorry."

Kevin sipped his coffee. "That's all right. We expect to find a list of sponsors in her files, so we'll go through them and follow up on each one. It's part of the legwork we have to do in cases like this." He set down the cup and saucer.

"Wait." Baldwin suddenly stood up. "I have that information right here. You say it was a local company? Brockville?"

"That's our understanding."

"Okay, just a minute." Baldwin left the room.

While he waited, Kevin took out his cellphone and checked the time. He looked to see if he'd received any texts or other messages. All was quiet. Everything was apparently progressing just fine without him.

It was silent in the apartment. Eighteen floors up, there was no sound of traffic coming from outside. There were no voices leaking through the walls from next door, no footsteps across the ceiling. It was like sitting in a capsule in the vacuum of deep space, halfway between the Earth and the moon, close enough to sensory deprivation to make him feel slightly uncomfortable.

Kevin had grown up in a neighbourhood sandwiched between the freeway and the freight rail main lines running through the city, and he'd gone to sleep each night listening to the white noise made by the constant flow of cars, trucks, and trains. He found background sounds somehow comforting, and he was still adjusting to the relative silence that descended on the village of Sparrow Lake each evening after darkness fell.

After a few moments he heard Baldwin returning. He slipped his cellphone back into his pocket.

"Here." Baldwin sat down and passed across a manila file folder. "That's a copy of our sponsor list for local companies. It's got the contact names, as well. The guy you want may be one of them."

"Thanks." Kevin glanced through the pages, which contained a list of companies, contacts, and notes on events sponsored in each case. "You had this here?"

"I keep backup files," Baldwin shrugged. "You know, off site, in case of fire. Electronic and hard copy."

Kevin stood up. "I should go. Let you get some rest."

"I can feel the meds starting to work. I'll lie down for an hour and it'll be fine. Colin should be home by then."

As Baldwin retrieved his car coat from the hall closet, Kevin said, "What can you tell me about your building manager. Gerberson?"

"Gerverson." Baldwin passed over the coat. "What about him?"

"We have a meeting with him tomorrow about the security footage for the building. Colin suggested we take a look at it, and we thought it sounded like a good idea."

Baldwin nodded.

"It's going to have to be on a voluntary basis," Kevin

explained. "I was hoping to get a heads-up on what kind of guy Gerverson was, whether he'd be co-operative."

"I'll give my mother a call."

Kevin frowned. "Pardon?"

Baldwin laughed. "She's the COO of this place. I guess I didn't mention that. George Gerverson works for her. She'll call him tonight, and he'll have what you need ready for you in the morning."

"Uh, no, that's okay. We'd rather approach him ourselves first, if you don't mind. If he calls your mother about it when we make the request, fine, that's up to him. But I'd rather do it this way."

"Sure, no problem."

On the way down in the elevator, Kevin leaned against the back wall and thought about his own mother, and how insistent she'd been that he never allow himself to become bitter about how their lives had gone. No matter how sick she'd been and how difficult it was for Kevin to look after her all by himself with no father around and no other family or friends to turn to for support, she'd demanded that he remain positive and cheerful.

He'd promised that he would, and although it had been a hell of a struggle, it was a promise he believed he'd been able to keep.

The promises we make to our mothers.

It was one thing, he supposed, that he and Kyle Baldwin had in common.

chapter FOURTEEN

Faye's Coffee Shop was a narrow hole-in-the-wall across the street from city hall on King Street in downtown Brockville. Although it was past eight o'clock in the evening on a Thursday, the place was packed. Two servers edged up and down the narrow centre aisle between the booths, their upheld trays loaded with plates of food and ceramic mugs of steaming coffee.

Peter Lambton occupied a booth two-thirds of the way down, sitting with his back to the street. As Ellie dodged an extra-large all-dressed pizza on a tray, she saw that the mayor was eating a late dinner with two other people.

"Mr. Lambton?" Ellie held up the wallet containing her identification and badge. "I'm Detective Inspector March, OPP. This is Detective Constable Leung. They told us across the street you were here. We need to talk to you."

Lambton slowly looked up, half-smiling. His eyes caught on her badge. "I'm getting something to eat. Can it wait?"

Ellie made eye contact with the young man sitting directly across from Lambton. Like the mayor, he wore a city hall identification card on a lanyard around his neck. Unlike the mayor, he'd already finished his meal and was nursing a half-empty glass of cola. "You won't mind if I sit down there, will you?"

"No, no, not at all." He quickly slide out of the booth and stood up.

The young woman sitting beside him, another city hall employee, followed him out into the aisle. Her smile flashed and faltered. "We're already done eating," she said.

"Good. You can catch up to His Honour later." Ellie waited until they'd squeezed by Leung, then she motioned for him to sit down ahead of her. Leung scooched over on the bench seat and she settled down next to him.

"It's council night, and we were having a post-meeting meeting," Lambton said, using a linen napkin to wipe salad dressing from the corner of his mouth. "We weren't finished yet. What do you want?"

Ellie watched him pick up his fork and resume his attack on the food in front of him. She figured it was a Cobb salad, judging by the chunks of hardboiled egg still on the plate. "You were informed in writing on March 26, 2017, that the Ontario Provincial Police was launching an investigation of allegations of criminal wrongdoing involving yourself. I'm here to inform you that we're resuming that investigation now that your request for a judicial review has been turned down by the court."

Eyes on his plate, Lambton swallowed and said, "Okay." He worked the fork briskly, loading up another mouthful.

"Detective Constable Leung will conduct a more formal interview at a later time," Ellie said, "but if there's anything you'd like to tell us now, we'd be more than happy to listen."

Lambton chewed and swallowed, set down his fork, and used the napkin on his mouth again. He was a handsome man, only fifty-two years old, his blond hair parted in the middle and combed back in careless waves that were fading to white at the temples. He wore a tan leather jacket over a white turtleneck sweater, and the watch on his left wrist was large and expensive looking. He was slim and fit, known to be a jogger and a workout fanatic, and the salad for dinner suggested he watched his diet and avoided unhealthy food.

"What am I supposed to say?" He tossed the napkin down and picked up his bottle of spring water. "The whole thing's ridiculous."

"According to the allegation, you accepted personal favours from your nephew Howie Burnside and his landscaping company in return for influence on city contracts."

"Wait, don't forget bullying and intimidating city staff, throwing rocks through their living room windows, sabotaging their cars, and stalking their kids at school." Lambton shook his head. "I think we need to institute drug testing at city hall, starting with the director of corporate services and working down to his dubious, so-called witnesses."

"Are you saying the allegations are baseless, Mayor Lambton?"

He stared at her over his bottle of water as he swished a mouthful and swallowed it. "Yes. And as for the landscaping job at my cottage, I have a proper invoice at home, with a receipt that'll prove I paid for it. You're welcome to copies."

"Please make the originals available to Detective Constable Leung when he contacts you tomorrow."

"I'll be happy to." His eyes shifted to Leung. "Call my secretary and make an appointment. She'll try to fit you in somewhere."

"I'll be there at ten o'clock tomorrow morning," Leung replied. "You can let her know, if you like."

Lambton stared at him. Leung calmly stared back.

Ellie slid out of the booth and stood up. "We appreciate

your co-operation, Mayor Lambton. Enjoy the rest of your meal."

He smiled sourly at her as Leung got out from behind the table. "Thanks. Don't let the door hit you on the ass on your way out."

As she left the restaurant, Ellie glanced over her shoulder at Leung. He narrowed his eyes, his lips thinning as he declined to say what he was thinking.

She gave him a little nod and led the way to the Crown Vic, which was parked around the corner.

They were going to come after Peter Lambton hard and fast.

chapter FIFTEEN

The apartment building in which Andie Matheson had lived was located in the north end of town. Although not much older than Kyle Baldwin's place, it was considerably more modest in terms of lifestyle and amenities. Kevin rode up a small elevator to the fourth floor and stepped out into a strong odour of cannabis that filled the hallway.

The Brockville city cop leaning against the wall next to the open apartment door rolled his eyes. "I know. I'm not sure which unit it's coming from. The whole floor reeks of it."

Kevin pulled on a pair of latex gloves and disposable shoe covers from an open box outside the door. He stuck his head in and spotted Detective Constable Mark Allore in the living room, on his hands and knees, peering under the couch. "How's it going?" Kevin called out.

Allore started, bumping his head. He straightened and turned. "Oh, hi, Kev. Come on in. Serge has already vacuumed the floor."

Identification Constable Serge Landry came out of the bathroom and pulled back the hood on his white jumpsuit. "Hey Kev. Just did the shower drain. Check it out." He held up an evidence bag filled with scummy hair and other unidentified particles.

"Lovely, Serge. You're the best."

Landry smiled. "Don't touch any surfaces because I haven't dusted for prints everywhere yet, okay?"

"Sure. No problem."

"Not our primary crime scene," Landry added. "No bloodstains or signs of a clean-up."

"Good to know." Kevin looked around. The furniture was plain and not new. There were a few framed prints of famous paintings on the wall, but the apartment didn't look or feel personalized.

"I talked to the super," Allore said, as though reading his mind. "She rented it furnished, so I'm not sure yet exactly what belonged to her."

"Okay." Kevin looked at Landry, who shrugged.

They were all thinking the same thing. While Andie had been living in Brockville for six years, she'd occupied this apartment for only the last fourteen months. Consequently, the hair, fibre, and trace evidence collected from the furniture could have come from any number of sources predating her arrival. It was little better than a hotel room on that account, as far as forensic evidence was concerned.

"I bagged dirty laundry from the hamper," Landry went on, "trash from the kitchen, this stuff"—he waved the evidence bag—"and there's dirty dishes in the sink that may be good for something. But no—"

"Cellphone," Kevin finished.

"Correctimundo." Landry put the evidence bag containing the drain hair into his metal carrying case. "It ain't here. But we haven't done her car yet. You never know."

Kevin nodded. Andie Matheson's vehicle, a 2011

Honda Civic, was parked in the lot behind the building. It was possible she'd left her cellphone there, but Kevin was doubtful, unless she'd been in such a hurry to get somewhere that she'd forgotten it.

"By the way," Landry said, "I haven't had a chance yet to look at the stuff from your convenience store."

"You've been kind of busy."

"Yeah. Anyway, Wainwright brought in great fingerprints and shoe prints, so I'll look at them tomorrow and get back to you. Ça va?"

"Sure, thanks, Serge." Kevin nodded. Paul Wainwright was the scenes-of-crime officer who'd attended Willard's Convenience Store in Rockport this morning after Kevin had left for the call out on the Parkway.

He took a slow tour around the living room, trying to get a feel for the victim and the life she'd lived in private. There was an armchair and a rocking chair in addition to the couch, a modest-sized flat screen television on a stand with a DVD player, and a small shelving unit with a handful of movies, mostly box sets of television comedy series and reality TV shows, along with a few popular superhero feature films.

He took out his pen and used the blunt end to tap the Eject button. The disc in the tray was *Friends: The Complete Third Season*, disc two. He tapped the button again, reloading the disc.

He crouched in front of an end table to look at a framed photograph of four people sitting on the front steps of a modest-looking brick house. Appearing to be in her late teens, Andie sat between a middle-aged couple who must have been her parents. An older version of Andie sat on the far side, hands clasped between her knees, her smile wide and infectious. The sister, presumably, whose name was Mary Anne. Not quite as pretty as Andie, she had the same blond-brown hair and clear, pale complexion. Along with an obviously sunny disposition.

Andie's expression was more serious, Kevin thought,

almost bewildered, as though she didn't know quite what was expected of her in that moment. Her father, sitting between the two girls, was short and stocky, his thinning hair combed across his scalp and his eyes squinting behind wire-frame glasses. The dentist, Dr. Bob Matheson.

Kevin thought he looked friendly, benign, easy-going. Anneke, Andie's mother, sat at the end with her hands in her lap, staring at the camera with obvious discomfort. Her husband's office receptionist, Kevin remembered. The source of Andie's girlish beauty, and also perhaps her serious disposition.

He peeked into the kitchen, where Landry was dusting the open fridge door. "Can I come in?"

"Don't touch anything."

Kevin looked over his shoulder at a half-empty refrigerator. There were a few bottles of water, condiments, an unopened block of cheese, jars of pickles and olives, a carton of milk, and not very much else. No leftover meals, and no alcohol products at all.

"What about the cupboards?"

"Not done yet, sorry. Pictures at eleven."

"Okay."

"There were a lot of take-out containers and packaging from microwaveable stuff in the trash. This woman wasn't much of a cook."

Kevin wandered out into the hallway, edging past Allore, who was searching a linen closet in the hall. He went into the bathroom.

Shower stall, commode sink, toilet, mirror, medicine cabinet. No bath tub. Tooth brush and a tube of toothpaste in a plastic cup on the sink. He slipped his pen under the door of the medicine cabinet and pulled it open. Assorted makeup, an open box of tampons, a bottle of Pepto-Bismol, ibuprofen, hand lotion, face cream, other various items. A half-empty prescription bottle, the label conveniently facing out. Kevin recognized the name of a common anti-depressant, prescribed by a local doctor and filled at a pharmacy a block from her office downtown.

On the top shelf he saw an open box of condoms. Apparently she'd been sexually active. Kevin closed the door and went back into the hallway. Who was her boyfriend?

The last room on the tour was the bedroom. It was about ten feet by twelve, small and cluttered. The unmade bed was double sized. The pillowcases and sheets were purple and green, and the comforter was navy blue with light blue stripes. Landry clearly had not processed in here yet, as the bedclothes would be bagged up for examination in the laboratory, so Kevin contented himself with a look around.

The walls were decorated with posters stuck up with variously coloured push pins—the Tragically Hip, Good Charlotte, and, surprisingly, Leonard Cohen. One of the dresser drawers was partially open; white panties were caught in the crack. On top of the dresser he looked at a woven basket filled with inexpensive costume jewellery, a ceramic lamb, a framed studio portrait of Andie's parents, a stack of music CDs that included two Leonard Cohen albums and the Good Charlotte record that was in everyone's collection, a saucer holding six dollars and thirty cents in change, and a small giveaway flashlight with the Jones Chemical logo and Brockville address printed on it, which she had probably picked up at one of their fundraising events.

On the side table next to her bed he saw a paperback copy of *The Hunger Games* with a bookmark sticking out about a third of the way in, a half-empty bottle of water, and another prescription bottle, this one two-thirds empty. He bent down for a look. It was a common sleeping aid, prescribed by the same doctor and filled at the same pharmacy as the anti-depressant in the bathroom.

Back in the living room, he nodded at Allore and headed out, dropping his booties into the bag next to the open box of fresh ones. On his way down in the elevator, he thought about what he'd seen and how it fit with what he knew about her.

She was twenty-nine, pretty, and still single. From out of town, and she didn't seem to have settled in. On the way over from Kyle Baldwin's condo, Kevin had spoken to the officer with Durham Regional Police who'd notified Andie Matheson's parents of their daughter's death. According to her, neither Bob nor Anneke Matheson had any idea whom their daughter might have been dating up here. Andie kept such things to herself, apparently. The sister in Montreal, Mary Anne, had said the same thing. Andie kept her private life private, even from her family.

Kevin got into his car and started the engine. Overall, it would seem that Andie had left a very small footprint. Her apartment showed few personal touches. It had the look and feel of a student dorm room or a motel room. A place to eat take-out meals, binge-watch old television programs, and sleep. She seemed to have had few personal possessions; perhaps they were back home in Ajax, preserved in a bedroom in her parents' house.

She'd been very good at her job. Efficient, Kyle had said, and intelligent. She'd had enough self-confidence, it would seem, to glad-hand and sweet-talk corporate executives while working them for financial support, as well as to stand up to Baldwin when her opinion on business decisions differed from his. A capable, effective fundraiser.

So why was she still here, in Brockville? She'd had no friends here. She kept to herself after hours as far as girlfriends went, but had carried on more than one affair with married men. Was it her job that kept her here, as Kyle Baldwin had suggested, or was it the affairs?

Kevin drove across town, trying to puzzle it out. He passed the hospital and worked his way over to Bartholomew Street. A block and a half before King Street, he turned into the driveway of a one-and-a-half storey frame house and parked behind a Honda CR-V with a bumper sticker on the back that said "Proud Grandma!"

He shut off the engine and closed his eyes for a moment.

He sat there until the thoughts buzzing around in his head leaked away, leaving in their place a quiet sense of calm. He opened his eyes, took out his cellphone, and called Janie.

"Hey Kev." Her voice sounded tired. "How are the kids?"

"I'm just about to go into your mom's now. I'm sitting in the driveway."

"Oh? What's going on?"

"Tough day." He let it ride for a moment before adding, "We caught another homicide."

"Oh, no. Not again." Her long, drawn-out sigh rustled in his ear. "Are you okay?"

"Sure. I'm primary again, so it's going to be busy." He shifted in the seat, pulling the keys from the ignition. "Never mind that. How are you doing? How'd it go today?"

"The first one, I aced. Absolutely. The second one, not so much. The guy's hair was way too straight, and I just couldn't get it going."

Kevin closed his eyes again. At the convention today she'd participated in two competitive events, and tomorrow she'd be in the big one for women's hairstyling. It was her first time competing against other professional hairdressers, and when she'd left she'd been half-nervous and half-cocky about the whole thing.

"Sorry, remind me again. Which ones were today?"

"Men's trend cut and style this morning and creative technical blowdry this afternoon. Are you going to be able to handle the kids with this new case?"

"Yeah, don't worry. Were you able to sleep last night?"

She laughed. "I went up to my room after dinner and conked out. Slept around the clock. I haven't gotten that much sleep since before Josh was born."

"You need it. It's a good idea for you to get away, get a break."

"That's what you keep saying, Kev. You may be right."

"I know I'm right." He heard a lot of noise in the background. "What's going on now?"

"Oh, I'm just outside the banquet room, next to a little bar they've got set up. People are going back in for a bunch of speeches and presentations and stuff."

"How was dinner?"

"Real nice. I had roast beef and baked potatoes and a plate of vegetables. Ate like a pig."

"Good for you. Do you have enough steam left to sit through the speeches?"

"Yeah, for a while. I've met a few people here, big shots from Toronto, and I'm trying to network."

Kevin laughed.

"Hey, don't laugh, you mutt. These guys publish a magazine. I might be able to get in it."

"That'd be outstanding." He listened to her speak to someone nearby, a woman whose loud laughter brayed in his ear through the cellphone. "I should let you go."

"Yeah. Look, I'm gonna call Mom and get her to keep the kids until I get back."

"No, don't, Janie. I can handle it."

"I know you can, but she can look after them while you're out tracking the bad guy. Who got killed, Kev?"

"A woman named Andrea Matheson. Works for a guy I knew in high school, Kyle Baldwin."

"The charity guy."

"Yeah."

"Sounds bad." She lowered the phone, said something, and raised it again. "I gotta go. Give my love to the three little bunnies, okay? Tell them mommy's got a buncha cool giveaways for them."

"I will."

"Love to you, too, big guy. I miss the hell out of you."

"Me too. Go kick some hairstylin' ass."

He ended the call and got out of the car, his mind back to exactly where he wanted it to be. He opened the trunk and secured his firearm in a portable gun safe tethered by a steel cable to a strut, then walked up the sidewalk and let himself into the house.

chapter SIXTEEN

The smell of food hit his nostrils as soon as he stepped into the hallway and shut the front door behind him. Roast chicken, gravy, and—he sniffed—French fries. He pulled off his cowboy boots and followed the sound of the television into the living room.

Caitlyn sat in the Laz-y-Boy, her feet tucked up beneath her, a bowl of popcorn in her lap. She grinned at him, showing a mouthful of half-chewed popcorn, and crooked her little finger in greeting.

Barb was sitting on the couch, Brendan's head in her lap. The boy was sound asleep, his mouth open. Barb smiled up at him. "You look tired."

"I am. How's Joshua?"

"Sleeping. He was good today. No problems at all."

Kevin crept upstairs and eased open the bedroom door on the right. Once Janie's bedroom before she'd moved out, it was now furnished with bunk beds for Caitlyn and Brendan when they stayed over, and a new addition, a white swivel bassinet, the portable kind that was easy to store in the car. Joshua slept soundly, wrapped in a white blanket with a blue stripe around it.

"Hello there, Toughie," Kevin whispered. "Are they treating you all right here?"

The baby breathed quietly and slowly. At peace.

He'd been born three weeks prematurely, and everyone had been worried about his immune system and other side effects that were possible when entering the world a little earlier than expected. Joshua had proven to be quite healthy, however, and now at nine weeks and three days old, he was well into a normal infancy.

"Love you, Josh." Kevin tiptoed from the room and went back downstairs. In the living room, he sat down at the far end of the couch, next to Brendan's bare feet.

"Are you hungry?" Barb asked. "Can I get you something to eat?"

"I'm starved. I don't remember eating lunch."

"I'll bring you a plate." She eased Brendan up off her lap and passed him over to Kevin, who gently swung the boy around. He grabbed a throw cushion from behind him and lowered Brendan's head onto it, next to his thigh. Barb stood up and patted the top of Kevin's head. "I'll just be a minute."

"Did you catch the bad guy today, Kevin?" Caitlyn asked, licking butter from her fingertips.

"Not today, Cait, but we will. What're you watching?"

"A cartoon. Her name's Peg. That's her cat. His name's Cat. They're helping these pirates put a puzzle together so they can find a treasure."

"That sounds interesting."

"It's okay." She dug out another handful of popcorn. "It helps kids learn arithmetic. They have to add and subtract stuff to solve the problems."

"That sounds very good." Kevin stared at the television, watching a commercial. He had no idea what they were selling. His brain had slipped slightly out of gear as soon as his backside hit the couch.

"Kevin, can I ask you a question?"

"Sure, Caitbug."

"Do you think Mommy would let me get a cat?"

"Why not?" He blinked at the TV and then looked at her, the nature of her question having just sunk in. "Uh, I'm not sure, Cait. I don't think your mom likes cats, does she?"

"Sure she does. She just doesn't like all the poop stuff, but I told Nanna I'd look after that. I *promise*, I would." When she saw the look on his face, she added, "Mom and I talked about it once before."

"You did? When was that?"

"Oh, a long time ago. In the before-Kevin time."

"I see. In the awful B-K time, when the earth was dark and no one was allowed to have even a tiny little kitten."

"Are you pestering this poor man about cats now, Caitlyn?" Barb came into the room and set up a TV tray in front of Kevin.

"We're just talking about it, Nanna. That's all."

Barb laughed, going back into the dining room to fetch Kevin's plate of food and glass of milk.

"You said Mommy had a cat once, didn't you, Nanna?"

"She did." Barb arranged Kevin's meal on the TV tray and stepped back. "Do you need anything else?"

"No, this is great."

"Your mom had a cat when she was a girl," Barb said, sitting down again on the couch. "Her name was Badger."

"Badger?" Caitlyn frowned at the name.

"Your mom named it that because it was black and white, like a badger. Anyway, when Badger passed away, as all cats do in the end, your mom was heartbroken. She said she'd never have another pet."

"Maybe she's changed her mind. It was a long time ago."

"You'll have to ask her, darling."

They watched television as Kevin ate his chicken and fries. Brendan began to snore, a low, clotted sound.

"I think he's getting a bit of a cold." Barb looked at Kevin's empty plate. "Would you like anything else? I have some cherry pie."

"That sounds good. Maybe later, Barb. Thanks."

Barb picked up the TV tray, waited for Kevin to drain his glass, then carried everything out into the dining room.

"What's on after this?" Kevin sank back in the couch and crossed his legs, feeling even more tired now that his stomach was full.

"Another Peg cartoon."

"Oh. Okay."

Out in the kitchen, the telephone rang. Kevin heard Barb answer it, her voice a distant scratching as she talked.

"Would *you* like a cat, Kevin?"

"Huh?" He opened his eyes and looked at her. "Sure, I like cats. I had a cat when I was in high school."

"What was her name?"

It took a moment for her question to register. "Pepper. He was a boy."

"I'd like to call my cat Boo Boo."

"That sounds cute."

The next Peg cartoon was well underway when Barb returned to the living room. "That was—" she stopped short when she saw that Kevin was asleep, legs splayed, his head lolling to one side, his mouth open like Brendan's.

Caitlyn shook her head at her grandmother. "He's just *exhausted*."

"Yes, he is. That was your mother on the phone, Cait. You and Brendan and Joshua are going to stay here with me over the weekend. Sound okay?"

Caitlyn nodded. "There's no school tomorrow, Nanna. It's a PD day for the teachers. Can we stay here all day?"

"Sure. You can help me look after Joshua."

Caitlyn looked at Kevin, who had closed his mouth and rolled his head to the other side. "I'll be glad when Mommy's home, though."

She sighed. "He needs *her* to look after *him*."

chapter SEVENTEEN

It was late when Ellie finally got home to her cottage on Sparrow Lake. She let herself in through the kitchen door and turned on the light. According to the clock over the sink, it was 11:34 PM. She tossed her keys on the counter and grabbed a can of beer from the refrigerator. Leaning against the doorframe of her office, formerly the spare bedroom when she'd bought the place, she opened the beer and took a long drink.

The searches of Andie Matheson's work cubicle, apartment, and car had wrapped up earlier in the evening. Processing of the physical evidence collected at the three scenes would begin immediately, and if something popped Dave Martin would let her know right away. Her cellphone had remained silent over the past ninety minutes or so, however, with no new calls or texts, so it was possible she'd be able to gear down and get a few hours of sleep without being disturbed.

Other than the purring of the refrigerator motor, the

cottage was quiet. She took another mouthful of beer, swished it around to feel the carbonation buzzing against the insides of her cheeks, and slowly swallowed. It had been a long day, and she was tired.

Her irritation at Todd Fisher had largely passed, but she was still not impressed with his attitude toward the Peter Lambton investigation. As the detachment commander, Fisher was obligated to treat all important cases occurring within his jurisdiction with appropriate diligence. Was it preachy of her to think that? The political aspects of the investigation were admittedly unpleasant. She wasn't exactly champing at the bit to take down a politician of Lambton's prominence. She didn't see it as another chance to advance her career; she was simply carrying out an assignment.

Lambton's attitude this evening, though, had certainly amped up her desire to find out whether there was fire somewhere within all the smoke. His smug self-confidence and dismissiveness had rubbed her the wrong way. However, Leung was the dogged, unwavering kind of detective who would persevere throughout and wouldn't let a suspect's attitude slow him down.

She drained the can and tossed it into the recycling bin next to the kitchen door. She opened the fridge door, realizing she was hungry, and suddenly remembered the bag of hamburgers she'd left in the car. She must be tired, to have left her supper behind.

She went out and retrieved the bag from the passenger seat of the Crown Vic. Back inside, she opened another can of beer and tore open the paper bag, spreading its contents on the kitchen table: two double bacon cheeseburgers with extra sauce; a large order of French fries; and an apple turnover for dessert.

In her defence, she'd known that the Silver Kettle, a dump of a restaurant in the village of Sparrow Lake that happened to produce exceptional food, would be closed at this hour, so she'd stopped in Brockville for take-out before coming home. Her body never seemed to care what it received for fuel, though. Most times she crammed into her mouth whatever was in front of her without really noticing what it was. She was blessed with a metabolism that burned off however many calories she happened to consume and left her the same size, no matter how old she was getting.

She took a huge bite out of one of the burgers and stood up, grabbing a napkin from the torn-up bag. It was delicious. Wiping her mouth, burger held up to keep its component parts from falling onto the floor, she took a step toward the office. There was probably unread e-mail she should look at before turning in for the night. Colleagues such as Gavin Elliott, who was also an OPP detective inspector working for Tony Agosta, or Tom Faust, now retired and working in the private sector, were always good for a last-minute message.

She knew that although she lived in solitude in a two-bedroom cottage on a lake in the middle of nowhere, she wasn't alone. She was estranged from her family, yes. Her ex-husband had remarried and her two daughters despised her, but she had friends. Work friends, granted. But they liked her. And Ridge Ballantyne, the elderly pop musician who lived next door, also seemed to like her.

She wasn't alone in the world. Not really.

She turned away from the office, too tired to turn on the computer and go through all the rest of the motions involved in reading her e-mail and responding to it. Time for that tomorrow. They knew what she was like. They didn't expect anything different from her. It was all fine.

She took another big bite of the hamburger. She wandered over to the table and grabbed her beer, took a swig, and crossed the living room floor. She felt good. She felt fine, actually.

There was residual guilt, yes. Persistent guilt was a way of life with her, as it was with most other people. There were feelings of guilt about her elderly adoptive parents,

Paul and Mary, and the fact that she no longer stayed in touch with them. Guilt about her failed marriage to Gareth, a failure that was not entirely her fault but mostly her fault. Guilt about her two girls, who couldn't stand the sight of her. Guilt at having screwed up her only chance in life to have an actual, real family.

Feelings of guilt, yes. But at the end of the day, she felt no regret whatsoever about the decisions she'd made and the life she was now living. She'd made the correct choices for herself, and that was what counted. Other people could, and would, take care of themselves.

That's what she was doing, after all. Taking care of herself.

She looked at her reflection in the sliding patio doors that led out onto the back deck. Her shoulder-length hair was a bit tousled; apparently she'd run her hand through it a few times not very long ago while thinking about something or other. Her long-sleeved, pale blue blouse was a little wrinkled. She should probably iron stuff before putting it on in the morning. Her jeans looked a little loose. Was she losing weight, despite the junk she ate?

She made eye contact with herself. Ellie March: failed mother, friend of prime ministers and highly-placed Mounties, hermit, hard ass. The corner of her mouth tipped up and she raised the can of beer.

Happy birthday, Ellie.

Forty-three didn't feel the slightest bit different than forty-two.

chapter
EIGHTEEN

As Kevin jumped into the passenger side of the black motor pool Crown Vic the following morning, Bishop was just turning off the morning news report on the radio. Kevin slammed the door and held up his notebook.

"Sorry, JB. Forgot this." He dropped the notebook into the pocket of his sports jacket and reached for the seat belt.

"No problem." Bishop shifted the transmission into reverse and lurched out of the parking space alongside the detachment office. He peeled out of the parking lot and turned left, heading south toward Brockville.

Kevin watched Bishop tap his fingers on the steering wheel in time to music playing in his head. The clouds that had moved into the area yesterday afternoon had moved out again overnight, and the temperature had stayed above zero. Today was shaping up to be another sunny day.

"Nice morning."

"You betcha." Bishop slowed and turned left onto

Centennial Road. "So, Kev, I've been thinking. I'm going to take the lead on this guy. I'm tired of pussy-footing around. Maybe a little neck squeeze will loosen up some useful information."

"Mmm."

They were on their way to the campus of Jones Chemical, located in the heart of the industrial park on the northern edge of town. Headquartered in Frisco, Texas, Jones employed over four hundred people here in a large plant that manufactured various detergent products instantly recognizable on grocery store shelves across North America. It was, in fact, the company for which Kevin's father had worked as a shop foreman for nearly three decades until his retirement six years ago. Despite that connection, Kevin had never been out here. There'd never been a need, until now.

Bishop parked in the visitors' lot. They walked into the administration building at the south end of the campus. Bishop waved his badge at one of the receptionists sitting behind a long, curving counter.

We're here to see a dude named Derek Colter, and yes, he knows we're coming."

First thing this morning, Kevin and Bishop had gone over the file Kyle Baldwin had provided last night on local sponsors, and they'd put together a short list of men who would have had contact with Andie Matheson and also might have stretched it into a personal relationship. At the top of their list was Derek Colter, director of community relations for Jones Chemical.

As they waited for the receptionist to summon Colter up front, Kevin wandered around, looking through the big plate glass window at the parking lot beyond. He knew a few people who worked here—it was impossible not to, since they were the second-largest employer in town—but they were all on the plant side, not over here on the administration side. A few of them knew his father but most, thankfully, did not.

Turning, he glanced at Bishop, who winked at him.

A door opened and a man emerged, hand extended to Bishop. "Hi, I'm Derek Colter. Detective Walker?"

"Detective Constable Bishop. This is Detective Constable Walker."

"Oh, of course, Detective Bishop. Hi." Colter shook hands and turned to Kevin. "You're the one who called, am I right? Detective Walker?"

"Yes, I did." Kevin shook hands with him. The man's grip was firm and businesslike.

"How about we go to your office?" Bishop asked, feigning politeness. "We've got a few questions for you."

"Oh, sure. This way."

They signed the visitors' log, accepted stickers with a large V on them which they promptly shoved in their pockets, and followed Colter through a door behind the reception area.

He was short, medium-sized, and somewhere in his late forties or early fifties. He wore a grey glen plaid suit that had a few miles on it. His sandy-coloured hair was thinning rapidly and his stomach didn't quite tuck in under his belt, but Kevin decided Colter would still qualify as a reasonably handsome man.

They trooped down a corridor in a typical office environment. Colter led them around a corner and through a fire door into another corridor. His office was three doors down, on the left. He waved them in and followed, closing the door behind him.

"Please, have a seat." Colter circled around his desk and sat down. He reached a hand tentatively toward the phone on his desk. "Would you like coffee or anything?"

"Naw, we're good." Bishop dropped into a chair and unbuttoned his suit jacket. "Let's get right to the point. How well did you know Andie Matheson?"

Kevin was still on his feet, giving the office a once-over. It was about twelve feet by sixteen, large enough not to feel crowded by its furnishings. There was a small window in the back corner that looked out onto a courtyard. Framed photographs hung on the walls that featured some tropical vacation spot Colter had apparently visited with a woman, presumably his wife. There was another large studio photograph of the same woman on his desk, angled so that it could be seen both by Colter and his visitors. She was a handsome-looking mature woman with auburn hair, blue eyes, and a square chin. Her smile was faint, and it failed to reach her eyes.

Kevin watched Colter's face as he hesitated over Bishop's question. It was immediately obvious they'd put the right man at the top of their list.

"It's terrible, what happened to her." Colter folded his hands in front of him. "I couldn't believe it, when I heard it on the news."

Bishop stared at him. "You saw her a lot, right? From what I can tell, this place is a big contributor to the clinic thing she worked for."

"Yes, that's right." Colter glanced anxiously at Kevin, who was settling into the chair next to Bishop, notebook and pen out. "Jones Chemical is a proud sponsor of their largest fundraising events, and we donate generously every year."

"Sure, sure. Which means you and the Matheson woman knew each other well, correct?"

Colter nodded. "We did. I did, I mean. I knew her well." He swallowed. "Which makes what happened even more upsetting."

"She's not so crazy about it either, pal." Bishop shifted his weight. "So how long were you screwing her?"

Colter blanched. He looked at Kevin. "Really, I..."

"Did you have a sexual relationship with Andrea Matheson, Mr. Colter?" Kevin asked, his tone stern.

Colter swallowed again. "Yes, I ... we did."

"When?" Bishop demanded.

"It was a while ago. We ended it. I did, actually. A while ago."

"When?" Bishop repeated, annoyed. "A year ago? A month ago?"

"Two years ago. During the summer. Look." Colter straightened in his chair, making a visible attempt to rally. "Look. As soon as I heard she'd been killed, I knew I'd be talking to you people. I won't hide anything from you, I promise. It's just ... very difficult. It was a huge mistake that could have cost me my marriage." He glanced at the photograph. "She never found out, but if she did, I'd be finished. Kaput. Done."

"Well, I'm sympathetic about your marital situation," Bishop lied, "but the fact of the matter is that somebody stabbed this woman to death early yesterday morning and dumped her body like a used piece of meat on the side of the road with no clothes, no dignity, no respect, no nothing."

He leaned forward. "There was sex involved, and you just told us you'd had sex with her before." His eyes flicked to Kevin. "I think we need to take him in."

Before Kevin could say anything, Colter shot up out of his chair. "No, wait! It's not like that! Let me explain!"

Bishop cocked his head.

Colter paced over to the window and stared out at the courtyard without seeing it. "Andie was a great person, full of life, easy to deal with. She had a way of making you feel like you *wanted* to hand over half of your community relations budget to her clinic, just to see her smile. I don't normally show up at a lot of the stuff we sponsor, I mean, I have staffers who do that sort of thing, but it got to the point where I'd personally attend the Clinics for Kenya events just so I could spend a few minutes with Andie. One thing led to another. We had a few dinners, just the two of us. Then it started."

Bishop yawned.

"This was two summers ago, do I have that right?" Kevin asked.

"Yes." Colter returned to his desk but stayed on his feet.

"Did anyone else know about it?"

"Christ, I hope not. As I say, Connie still doesn't know. Andie wouldn't have told anyone, I don't think. How did you find out? Did someone tell you?"

"Sit down, buddy," Bishop said.

Colter sat.

Bishop crossed his legs. "So where did you two rendezvous?"

"Motels."

"Her apartment?"

Colter shook his head. "She never let me go in. I picked her up outside a couple times, and dropped her off, but I never went inside."

"So where were these places you took her?"

"The Motel Eight on Highway 2, mostly."

"The one just east of town?"

"Yes."

"What about the other direction? Down toward Gan, the Islands?"

Colter shook his head. "No, that would be too far. Too much driving."

"And not enough banging," Bishop finished. "Okay. Let's shift gears a little. Tell us where you were Wednesday night and yesterday morning."

After some hesitation, Colter explained he'd worked in his office until six in the evening before driving home. He and his wife got dressed up and went out for dinner at the home of friends who live in Maitland, east of the city. After being prodded by Bishop, he provided their names and cellphone numbers. At around 11:30 PM on the way home, his car, a two-year-old Mercedes 4Matic, blew a tire. He had a chronic back condition, he explained, so he called CAA and they sent a tow truck. The driver removed the flat tire and put on the emergency spare tire from the trunk.

"So what time did you get home?" Bishop asked.

"It was almost one o'clock. I was exhausted. Connie was asleep when we pulled into the driveway." Colter looked at

Kevin. "I have the CAA receipt in my car, if you want to see it."

Kevin nodded, writing in his notebook.

"Did you go back out?" Bishop snapped.

"God, no. We fell into bed and it seemed like only an hour later the alarm went off. It was six." He frowned. "Connie kept the car yesterday, and I took a taxi to work. She got the tire fixed at Canadian Tire. I was here at the office all day. Wait."

He eased over onto one haunch and removed his wallet from his back pocket. He dug out a business card and put it on the desk in front of Kevin. "This is the receipt I got from the cab driver. I'm going to claim it as an expense. Does that help?"

Kevin leaned forward. It was a card from a taxi service in town. The driver had helpfully written down the date and time, presumably to legitimize Colter's expense claim, and had initialled it at the bottom. He glanced at Bishop, who shrugged.

Kevin took out his cellphone and took a picture of the card. "Thanks."

"Okay," Bishop said, "let's get back to your affair. Who called it off, and when?"

"I did. It was, uh, the last week of September." Colter shook his head. "We'd had another close call. We'd gone to the motel in the afternoon, after some kind of school thing in the morning, and I was waiting to pull out of the parking lot when one of Connie's friends drove by. I was sure she'd seen me. It wasn't the first time I'd had a close scrape, but I really panicked this time. I was sure the woman would tell Connie. I went around like a madman for three days, waiting for the axe to fall, then decided this was it. The next time we had lunch together, I told Andie it was all over."

"She was upset, right?"

Colter stared at his hands, an odd look on his face. "She was relieved. I could tell."

"Relieved."

He nodded. "At first she'd talked about a long-term thing between us, but I would never get into that kind of a conversation with her, and I knew after a while she was just going through the motions because, well, because she was lonely. I was company for her. Sort of."

Bishop grunted. "She was a little bit young for you, don't you think?"

"I suppose. I'd just turned fifty, and I was struggling with the mid-life thing. For three and a half months it was the most exciting time I'd had in years, but I knew I had to call it off."

"So your wife wouldn't find out and ditch you."

"Yes, and because I love her. I really do."

Bishop shrugged.

Kevin asked, "Do you know of anyone else Andie was involved with? Any other men in her life, either before or after your affair?"

Colter made a face. "Well, she sort of mentioned she was on the rebound from some guy she'd been involved with before me."

"Name?"

"It was the guy who owns the Pine Glens Golf and Country Club. I forget his name. She said it was a one-night thing, that the guy was into rough stuff and she steered clear of him after that."

Kevin and Bishop exchanged glances. Kevin made a note of it while Bishop asked, "Anyone else?"

Colter shook his head. "Sorry. She didn't talk about herself hardly at all. I'm afraid I did most of the talking for both of us. She was like that. She was a very good listener but didn't say much herself."

"Okay." Bishop looked at Kevin, who shook his head. "All right, Colter, thanks." Bishop hauled himself to his feet. "How about you take us out to that expensive ride of yours and show us the CAA receipt?"

They went back to reception. Kevin and Bishop signed

out, returned their unworn visitors' badges, and followed Colter to the employee parking area where he unlocked his Mercedes and rooted around in the glove compartment until he found the receipt.

Kevin told him to hold it flat on the hood of the car as he took a picture of it with his cellphone. Bishop amused himself by gawking through the window at the interior, which was as neat as a pin.

They thanked Colter for his time, shook his hand, and watched him slouch back into the building.

"Fucking goober," Bishop said.

Kevin walked around the Mercedes and used his phone to take pictures of all four tires. He got back into the Crown Vic and immediately sent the photos to Dave Martin for comparison to the tire tread marks found at the crime scene.

Bishop started the engine. "Okay, kid. How's about we go see if there's anybody out hitting little balls with skinny sticks?"

"Sounds good to me," Kevin replied, fastening his seat belt.

chapter
NINETEEN

Ellie looked at Leung as they were walking into city hall and said, "That's new, isn't it?"

"Yes, it is." He led the way to a side door and up the staircase that would take them to the second floor. His new suit was wool, royal blue, and to complement it he wore a light blue shirt, dark blue striped tie, and brown suede penny loafers.

"My wife won twelve hundred bucks on a lottery ticket last week." He turned a corner on the stairs and smiled down at her. "New clothes for everyone."

Ellie watched him shoot his cuff and glance at his watch. It was another gaudy knock-off from his collection, large and silver, but above it on his wrist he also wore a slender bracelet of blue, white, and maroon plastic tube beads, no doubt made for him by one of his daughters. Ellie wasn't so crazy about the brown loafers, preferring the look of black lace-up shoes with blue suits, but she liked the plastic bracelet just fine.

At the top of the stairs Leung hesitated, looking left and right, and then figured out how the room numbers worked. He led the way to the right, down three doors to a meeting room. They walked in through the open door.

A man sat at the far end of a long table, file folders piled in front of him. He stood as they entered and held out his hand.

"I'm Warren Whitlock. You must be Detective Inspector March. Pleased to meet you."

Ellie shook his hand. "Mr. Whitlock. Thanks for meeting with us this morning."

"My pleasure." His grip was soft, tentative. He was very tall and thin, and he was casually dressed in a black cardigan sweater over a blue dress shirt, black denim jeans, and black slip-ons without socks. He shut the door and shook hands with Leung. "Please, have a seat."

"As Detective Constable Leung explained when he called," Ellie said, "we're conducting the investigation into alleged criminal wrongdoings by Mayor Lambton stemming from the complaint you filed. We have a few questions we need to ask—"

"Look," Whitlock blurted out, "I was able to convince the integrity commissioner not to release the names of the witnesses, and I'm sorry, but that's the way I want it to stay. Surely you have more than enough to make your case without disrupting their lives any more than they already have been."

Ellie glanced at Leung, who was opening his notebook. "Is there a question of privilege, Mr. Whitlock, that I'm not getting?"

He passed a hand over his short red hair. "No, there isn't. I'm not a lawyer, and the information they gave me or the commissioner was not protected in any way. I'm just thinking of the human element, that's all."

"The human element?"

Whitlock struggled to make eye contact. "The commissioner understood there was a risk in making their names public, given Lambton's behaviour toward them."

His eyes finally settled on his hands, which were clasped together in front of him. "I think we need to continue to safeguard them and their families."

"I can appreciate all that," Ellie said, "but I'm sure you understand that we're now conducting a criminal investigation. Withholding evidence, including the names of important witnesses, is not a very good idea."

"I know." Whitlock picked up a file folder and put it down again. "It's not my intention to withhold anything."

Leung shifted in his seat. "Why don't you start by explaining what you do here?"

He was following the script he and Ellie had worked out in the car on the way downtown. He would lead the interview, and she would rap the hammer if and when it became necessary. "You're director of corporate services for the city, is that correct?"

Whitlock nodded. "I'm also the city's chief financial officer."

"I see. I thought maybe you were, like, the city clerk."

"Actually, he works for me." Whitlock smiled faintly. "The Department of Corporate Services includes Finance, Human Resources, IT, and the Clerk's office. I'm responsible for the city budget and financial plans, our annual audited financial statements and reports, labour relations, hiring and firing of city employees, and a lot of other stuff. I'm very busy."

"I can imagine. How long have you had this job?"

"I've worked for the city for twelve years altogether, the last five as director." He watched Leung jot this down and added, "I'm a CGA and a CPA. I hold an Honours Bachelor of Social Sciences in Public Administration and a Master of Arts in Public Administration, both from Carleton University. When I was first hired by the city as an administrative assistant, I was hugely over-qualified. So I guess it's not surprising I've been able to climb the ladder fairly quickly."

He flashed a quick smile. "I should be able to make city manager in the next five years, although probably not here. Brenda seems locked into that job for life."

"You must like this kind of work," Leung said.

"Yes, I do."

""But you don't get along very well with Peter Lambton."

A cloud passed over Whitlock's features. "Not at all. I don't like arrogant bullies. I was never the kind of person to get into schoolyard fights, but I don't back down, either."

"Is that why you filed the complaint against him? Because you don't like him?"

"No, of course not. Didn't you read the report?" He grabbed a file folder, pulled out a photocopy of the integrity commissioner's report, and spun it across the table.

"Yes, I've read it," Leung replied, ignoring the document. "How did it start? Tell us about what led you to file a complaint in the first place."

"Because he and his nephew harassed and intimidated city employees, *my* employees, he colluded with said nephew to influence contracting in exchange for personal favours, and he treated the whole thing with a disgusting sense of self-entitlement that made me want to puke."

Ellie caught Leung glancing at her. There was no mistaking Whitlock's visceral dislike of Peter Lambton.

"You stated in your complaint," Leung continued, "that someone came to you with information that Mayor Lambton ordered members of your staff to disclose bidding information to him on competitive tenders. Tenders that his nephew's company, Grass Wizards, ended up winning as the lowest bidder."

"That's correct."

"Who was your informant, Mr. Whitlock? Who told you this was happening?"

"No comment."

"We're not journalists," Ellie reminded him. " 'No comment' doesn't work for us."

Whitlock said nothing. He chewed on a fingernail, eyes down. Ellie noticed that all his fingernails were bitten down to the quick.

Leung cleared his throat. "What can you tell us about the company, Grass Wizards? I understand they now have a number of city contracts."

"Yes, that was the first year they'd submitted bids to us. Grass Wizards Landscaping, a sole proprietorship company owned by Howie Burnside. Before that, apparently, they'd contracted with homeowners to cut their grass in the summer and plow out their driveways in the winter." Whitlock examined his ravaged fingernail. "Apparently they don't do snow any more."

"What city contracts do they have?"

"Four different grass cutting and tree trimming contracts. One for parks, greenbelts, and cemeteries; one for environmental services, police, and fire halls; one for roadsides and community parks; and one for athletic fields. Each time they were the lowest bidder and won easily." Whitlock spread his hands. "The city's policy is to award to the lowest bidder."

"How much are they worth?"

"The contracts? The four of them, together, add up to about four hundred and seventy-five thousand dollars."

Leung pursed his lips. "I see. A decent amount of money, I suppose."

"You could say that."

"You don't really think so?"

Whitlock bit his lip. "Burnside's into other stuff as well."

"Oh? What kind of stuff?"

"I'd rather not get into that." Whitlock folded his arms and glanced at the clock on the wall behind Ellie.

"Walk us through the complaints," Leung prompted. "Tell us what your employees reported to you."

"It's all there," Whitlock said, gesturing at the report in front of Leung.

"I know," Leung replied patiently, "I read it. We'd like to hear about it from you verbally. Sometimes a fresh retelling brings out details that were considered less important initially but might kind of jump out at us now."

"I don't see how—" Whitlock interrupted himself, frowned at his knuckle, and then nodded. "All right. I'm sorry. I understand. I first heard that Lambton was trying to interfere with our bidding processes in early June 2015."

"Who told you that?"

"I'd rather not say. Anyway, it was just hearsay. 'Something's going on, you need to look into it.' That kind of thing."

"This was an employee of yours? Someone else in city hall? Or a friend, maybe?"

"I'd rather not say. It's too late now, anyway." Whitlock shook his head. "I would have discussed it right away with Mark McGuinness, my city clerk, but he was on vacation at the time, so I called Marian in and talked to her about it." Seeing Leung frown, he added, "Marian Applewood. She supervises our procurement unit."

"How many people work in the unit?"

"There are four clerks who report to Marian."

"Okay. Does Marian have first-hand knowledge of the mayor's contacts with her staff regarding his nephew's bids?"

Whitlock hesitated, unhappy that the names were beginning to come out. "No. Not according to her."

"So then the two of you, yourself and Applewood, interviewed the clerks. Tell us about that."

"As the commissioner states in his report, two of them reported contact with the mayor regarding contracts open for tender. One clerk told us Lambton wanted to look through the four grass-cutting files, but she refused. The other one stated that he wanted to give her 'confidential information on an anonymous basis' regarding one of the other bidders that would disqualify them from the process. She wouldn't accept the document he was trying to unload on her. She told him to talk to either Marian Applewood or Mark McGuinness."

"Did he?"

"Not according to either one of them."

"Did the other bidder stay in the race?"

Whitlock shook his head. "They withdrew before the closing date. After I started looking into all this, I called them to talk about it, but they refused to comment. They haven't bid on any other city contracts since."

"Which company was this?"

"Oleander Landscape Services."

Leung leaned back. "According to the integrity commissioner's report, the clerk who was approached for access to the files reported incidents away from work that were construed as possible intimidation. I'm paraphrasing. The commissioner didn't provide specifics. What can you tell us about that?"

"She said that the same night she'd refused to give him access to the files, a rock was thrown through the living room window of her family's home. Her husband called the police, but of course there wasn't anything they could do about it."

"I see." Leung glanced at Ellie, who raised an eyebrow.

"Later in the week," Whitlock went on, "their daughter reported being stalked at school. Two days in a row some man was across the street, taking her photograph during recess. The girl also reported being followed by a grey van with tinted windows while she was walking with friends to a corner store during lunch period. Again, they called the police but it didn't go anywhere."

"This clerk believed the mayor was behind these incidents?" Ellie put a healthy dose of skepticism into her voice to see how he'd respond.

"Lambton was very annoyed when she turned him down for a look at the files," Whitlock retorted. "Very annoyed. He threatened to get her fired."

"Is that a fact?" Leung said.

"Yes. And he said the same thing to me, when I confronted him."

"That was after your interviews with the staff?"

Whitlock nodded. "I told him that staff had been approached and even threatened, and that I was considering lodging a complaint against him. He laughed it off. When I told him I was dead serious about it, he threatened to have a talk with Brenda about having me fired for incompetence."

"You're referring to Brenda Morton, the city manager?" Leung asked.

"Yes. My boss."

"To your knowledge, did such a conversation take place?"

"Not according to Brenda. I asked her, and she said she'd never heard a word from Lambton about any of it. Not until after the complaint was filed. Then he apparently had plenty to say to her."

"Oh?"

"It was a pretty thorough character assassination."

"Oh?" Leung prompted again, raising his eyebrows.

"It's not important. What's important is seeing this through to the end. Now that he's declined to appeal the court decision to quash the commissioner's report, he'll have to pay his fine. But what he did deserves a lot more than just that."

Ellie stirred. "So who are the witnesses, Warren? If they're willing to provide us with information that'll help our investigation, it may make the difference in being able to make a solid case for criminal wrongdoing."

Whitlock shook his head. "Sorry." He glanced again at the clock on the wall behind her. "I really need to get back to work now."

Ellie stood up as Leung slid a business card across the table. "Call us when you think of anything else we should know."

Outside in the hallway, after Whitlock had gathered up

his files and disappeared to his office, Ellie retraced her steps and looked in at a woman sitting at a desk in a small office.

"I'm looking for Marian Applewood," she said. "Is her office around here?"

The woman nodded, pointing behind her at an inner doorway. "But she's not in today."

"Oh?"

"She's on a compressed work week," the woman explained, "and takes every other Friday off. Today's her day."

"Okay, thanks."

In the hallway, Ellie looked at Leung and said, "Let's get an address on this Applewood woman and go have a chat with her."

Leung smiled. "Sounds like a good idea."

Ellie pointed at the door of a washroom a few feet away. "Give me a few minutes. Why don't you go down to the mayor's office while I'm otherwise occupied and get the Grass Wizards receipt he promised us?"

Leung nodded and headed off for the staircase.

When Ellie emerged from the washroom, she found Leung lounging in the corridor, his eyes on his cellphone. When he saw her, he slipped the phone into his jacket pocket and pushed away from the wall.

"No luck," he said. "His assistant said he's in Kingston this morning and she didn't know anything about an invoice and receipt for us."

Ellie narrowed her eyes.

"On the other hand," Leung added, "I did manage to get a home address for Marian Applewood."

"Fine." Ellie led the way to the staircase. "Let's go see what she has to say, Dennis."

chapter TWENTY

Ellie pounded the edge of her fist on the screen door of the bungalow on Dewar Crescent. Somewhere inside the house a small dog began to bark. She glanced over her shoulder at Leung as they listened to a man's voice calling the dog in a rough baritone.

"Skipper! Come here! In here. Good boy."

Ellie waited. After a few moments the inner door opened and a heavy-set, balding man looked out at them.

"Help you?"

Ellie held up the wallet containing her badge and identification. "OPP. Is this where Marian Applewood lives?"

"She's out in the backyard. What d'you want her for?"

Ellie took a step back and looked to her left, where the driveway extended along the side of the house toward the rear of the property. "Can we get to the backyard through there?"

"Yep. Feel free."

"Thank you. Are you her husband?"

The man launched into a coughing fit that ended with a choking sound and a deep swallow. Through the screen door Ellie could smell the sudden odour of hard liquor, bourbon or rye. Mr. Applewood managed to nod before stepping back and closing the door.

Ellie followed Leung down the cement steps and around the corner of the house. It was a modest war bungalow just a stone's throw from the freeway on a short crescent one block north of the YMCA. They passed a small metal tool shed at the edge of the back lawn, the door of which appeared as though it hadn't been closed for at least a decade. Ellie looked in at garden implements, tangled water hoses, empty hanging plant pots, and other miscellaneous yard items piled up in a tumbled mess.

Ahead of her, Leung held up his badge to a woman who was raking the lawn along the back fence.

"Detective Constable Leung, OPP. Are you Marian Applewood?"

The woman leaned on the rake and ran the back of her gloved hand across her forehead. "Yes, I am. Who did you say you were?"

"Detective Constable Leung, ma'am. Ontario Provincial Police. This is Detective Inspector Ellie March. May we ask you a few questions?"

The woman broke into a sudden smile. She leaned the rake against a water barrel and stripped off the glove of her right hand as she approached Ellie. "Detective Inspector March! I've seen your name in the news. It's a pleasure to have a chance to meet you."

Ellie nodded, shaking hands. "Thanks. We're investigating possible criminal wrongdoing on the part of Mayor Peter Lambton. As you probably know—"

"Yes, I'm aware of your investigation." Applewood moved over to a white plastic patio table and brushed off a scattering of last year's dead leaves. "I've got some chairs. Let's sit down." She disappeared around the far side of the house and came back with three plastic chairs, which she unstacked and arranged around the table. "Please, sit down."

"We're sorry to disturb you on your day off," Ellie said.

"I'm glad to take a break." Applewood sat down. "I have a bottle of water around here somewhere. Can I get you folks something? Coffee, a cold drink?"

"No, thanks. We're fine."

"It's no trouble. Danny can bring it out to us." She removed her other garden glove. "He's just inside."

"No, we're fine."

Something in Ellie's voice made Applewood frown. "You saw my husband?"

"We spoke to him at the front door. He told us you were around here."

The woman sighed. "He's a truck mechanic, but the company he worked for went out of business, so there's just my salary right now to pay the bills. It's not a good time to be job hunting, especially at his age."

"We understand. We want to talk to you about the investigation involving Mayor Lambton. We've just come from an interview with Warren Whitlock. We'd like to get your insight into how this all came to light."

"All right." Applewood touched her hair, which was coloured a light auburn. She turned to look at Leung. Her profile was sharp, her nose a little hooked and her jaw tucked back, creating a slight overbite, but her eyes were bright and intelligent as they studied the detective. "I suppose he explained to you that this all started with him. Warren and his mysterious 'anonymous informant' who tipped him off that something was going on."

Leung nodded.

Ellie said, "Do you know the identity of this informant?"

Applewood shook her head. "All I know is that Warren was convinced, right from the start. He was like a dog trying to get at a rat in the woodwork; he just kept scratching and digging."

"You and he interviewed support personnel in your unit, is that correct?" Ellie asked.

"Yes. I'm supervisor of procurement. We handle the tendering process; we have the bids assessed by an independent third party; and we issue the contracts and do the follow-up maintenance to ensure the terms of the contracts are being met by the contractor, all that sort of thing."

"Do you report directly to Whitlock?"

"No, to the city clerk, Mark McGuinness. Mr. McGuinness reports to Mr. Whitlock."

"I see." Ellie crossed her legs. "Was McGuinness involved in this process at all? The initial investigation, the interviewing of your staff?"

"No. This originally came to our attention in August, two years ago. Mr. McGuinness was on vacation with his family in the Maritimes. He had no idea what was going on. By the time he got back, Mr. Whitlock had already filed his complaint." She chuckled sadly. "Mr. McGuinness was pretty confused by the whole thing."

"We'll want to talk to him anyway," Leung said. "Is his office on the same floor as yours?"

"No, he's downstairs, at the back of the building. But you won't be able to talk to him for a while, I'm afraid."

Leung's eyebrows shot up. "Oh? Why not?"

"He's down in Florida right now, at his timeshare. He's not due back for another week."

"Okay," Ellie said, "we'll catch up with him later. How many are there in your unit, Marian?"

"I have a staff of four clerks and a part-time receptionist. I share the receptionist with the supervisor of accounting."

"You interviewed all of them with Whitlock at the time he voiced his concerns about the mayor, is that correct?"

"Yes, Ellie. That's correct." Applewood frowned. "Sorry. Detective Inspector March."

Ellie waved it off. "Call me Ellie. Don't worry about it.

Who did you start with?"

Applewood hesitated. "Did Mr. Whitlock give you their names?"

Ellie said nothing.

"It doesn't surprise me. He told me to keep their identities confidential when the police got around to interviewing me, once Mayor Lambton's court challenge was done. He's worried that they might be threatened, but it's ridiculous."

"What makes you say that?" Ellie asked.

"Well, Mayor Lambton is a royal pain in the you-know-what, but he's not stupid by any means. I think he knows full well this particular bus has already left the station. Now that the police are involved, it would do him absolutely no good to threaten these women with reprisals if they come forward to you as witnesses. He knows that."

"But if I understand correctly, there were several incidents while the tendering process was underway that led your employees to believe they and their families might be at risk."

"Yes, it's true."

"Who did you start with?"

"There were two that Mayor Lambton approached directly, Patsy Williams and Sabrina Arliss. Mr. Whitlock and I interviewed Patsy first."

"Describe how that went."

"We brought her into Mr. Whitlock's office. She was very upset. She cried through most of it." Applewood shook her head. "We had issued our four main grass-cutting tenders all at the same time, and about a week before they closed the mayor came in late one afternoon, just before the end of the day. I'd already left for a dental appointment, and Patsy was the only one there. I think he planned it that way, waiting until there was only one person in the office. He asked to see the files on the four tenders."

Ellie glanced at Leung, who was taking notes, his notebook balanced on his knee.

"That doesn't happen," Applewood said. "We take a lot of pride in our procurement process being completely airtight. Patsy says she refused to show him the files, and I believe her."

"What else did she tell you?"

Applewood went on to repeat essentially the same story that Whitlock had told them, that the same night someone threw a rock through the living room window of her family home, and that later in the week her daughter reported being stalked while at school and while walking to a nearby convenience store with friends during lunch hour. She went on to confirm that a second procurement clerk in her office, Sabrina Arliss, was approached by the mayor under similar circumstances, late in the day, with no witnesses present. He tried to give her information on an anonymous basis about a landscaping company competing with his nephew for the grass-cutting contracts, but Arliss refused to accept it. In her case, there was no subsequent intimidation and no follow-up from the mayor.

Ellie glanced at Leung again. He was dutifully taking notes on everything Applewood was telling them, but they both knew it was nothing more than background information. The criminal wrongdoing they were investigating didn't include these attempts by Lambton to interfere in the bidding process, which fell under the jurisdiction of the municipality as a breach of their code of ethical conduct.

"Are you aware of any work that Grass Wizards did for the mayor at his personal cottage?" she asked.

"I'm afraid not. I know that's why you're here, I understand that's where the criminality might come in, but I just don't have anything to offer you. I've heard the talk about it, of course, but I don't have any first-hand personal knowledge about it at all. If it wasn't something that passed through our office, it's not something I know anything about."

"All right." Ellie looked at Leung, who shook his head

and closed his notebook. "We appreciate you taking the time to talk to us."

As they walked up the driveway along the side of the house, Applewood said, "I feel sorry for his wife."

Ellie stopped. "Who?"

"Kathryn Lambton. His wife. I feel sorry for her."

"Why do you feel sorry for her?"

"Well, she hasn't had an easy life with him, that's for sure. He's certainly a favourite with the ladies. There was talk he had an affair several years ago." Applewood stopped, embarrassed. "I admit, I don't like him on a personal level, but I should just keep things professional."

"How well do you know his wife?"

"Fairly well, although we don't socialize." Applewood glanced behind Ellie at her house. "Different social circle, obviously. She's Brenda's cousin, did you know that?"

Ellie looked blankly at her.

"Brenda Morton, the city manager. Kathryn's a Morton; their fathers were brothers. It was very uncomfortable for both of them when Mr. Whitlock filed his complaint against the mayor. It put Ms. Morton in an impossible position, the top civil servant reporting directly to the mayor and council on everything, and being the mayor's wife's cousin at the same time. Kathryn was mortified. It's a mess."

"Warren Whitlock reports directly to Brenda Morton," Leung reminded Ellie.

"Yes," Applewood said, "that's correct. He filed his complaint without briefing her first. On any of it. She was blindsided, to say the least."

"I'm surprised her family connection to the mayor didn't cause problems before," Ellie said. "It sounds like a conflict of interest waiting to happen."

"It never came up," Applewood said. "You have to know Ms. Morton to understand. She's the straightest, most honest and decent person you ever met in your life. Everyone respects her through the roof."

"What about her cousin, Mrs. Lambton?" Ellie asked.

"Kathryn's a lot quieter than Ms. Morton. She doesn't work, but she volunteers at the library and does a lot of things with her friends. She paints, and her best friends are artists."

Ellie started back down the driveway, then stopped again. "Do you know who it was that Lambton was supposed to have had the affair with several years ago?"

Applewood shook her head. "All I heard was that it was a young blonde. Typical."

Ellie handed her a business card. "If you think of anything else we should know, please call."

"Thank you." Applewood took the card, hesitated, and handed it back. "I'm embarrassed to ask, but would you mind autographing it for me?"

Ellie stared at her, at a loss for words.

Grinning, Leung held out his pen.

Ellie took the card and pen, signed her name on the blank back of the card, and gave it to Applewood a second time.

"Call us if you think of anything we should know," she repeated.

"Absolutely," Applewood promised, beaming.

chapter TWENTY-ONE

Kevin didn't care much for golf courses. Their exclusive country club atmosphere always struck him as elitist and antagonistic toward outsiders. Besides, he didn't like golf. Many of his hockey-playing friends switched to golf during the summer to stay in shape, but as far as Kevin was concerned, golf wasn't a sport, it was a recreation. Like bowling. Which, to his mind, was a lot more fun. When you went bowling you could take the kids, make noise, and generally have a blast without people looking down their noses at you.

Apparently it was still too early in the year to play at the Pine Glens Golf and Country Club, but the clubhouse was open. As Kevin followed Bishop across the parking lot to the glassed-in entrance, he was thinking about the CCTV footage they'd picked up from Kyle Baldwin's condominium building on the way over. George Gerverson, the building manager, had called Mrs. Baldwin to pass on their request, as Kevin had thought he might. The conversation between the two of them was short and to the point. Gerverson hung up and said, "Give me about twenty minutes."

"We'll wait," Bishop said.

They dropped off the USB drive containing the surveillance video at the detachment office, making arrangements for it to be couriered immediately to the lab at Smiths Falls for analysis, before heading off to Pine Glens. Kevin doubted it would reveal anything that would strengthen the case against Kyle Baldwin. His gut was telling him Baldwin wasn't involved in Andie Matheson's murder.

At the front entrance of the clubhouse, Kevin followed Bishop through automatic sliding glass doors into a reception atrium. Straight ahead was a dining room, on the right was a lounge overlooking the eighteenth green, and to the left was a counter behind which a young man looked up at Bishop with an expectant smile.

"Looking for Leon Gracz." Bishop held up his badge. "Where's he at?"

"I'm very sorry, sir, he's not here at the moment." The young man's gold name plate identified him as Brad, a customer service associate.

"When'll he be back?"

Brad's smile faltered. "I'm not sure. Would you like to talk to the general manager? She's here today."

"Where do we find her?"

Brad led the way through a plate glass door and down a short corridor to an open office door. He knocked on the doorframe. "Mrs. Fournier? Do you have a minute?"

Bishop nudged Brad out of the way and moved in, badge up. "Detective Constable Bishop, OPP. We're looking for Leon Gracz."

"I'm Mary Lou Fournier," the woman said, standing up. "I'm the general manager. May I help you with something?"

"Gracz. Is he here?"

Fournier folded her arms. She was a short, no-nonsense

brunette. Her green golf shirt and khaki trousers were a little loose, as though she'd lost a few inches over the winter and hadn't yet caught up on the wardrobe side of things. "He's out of the country. What do you want to see him for?"

As Bishop dropped into a chair and unbuttoned his suit jacket, Kevin said, "We understand that your club sponsors a benefit golf tournament every year for Clinics for Kenya. Is that right?"

Fournier swung her gaze over to him. It was like a machine gun on a tripod pivoting to take aim at the bridge of his nose. "Yes, that's right."

"We're investigating the murder of Andrea Matheson. She was the director of fundraising for Clinics for Kenya, and it's our understanding she worked with you folks on the golf tournament."

"I'm sorry," Fournier said, "you are—?"

"Detective Constable Walker." Kevin opened his jacket so that she could see his badge, which was clipped onto his belt. "Did you work with Andie on the tournament, Ms. Fournier?"

"Mrs. Fournier. And yes, I did." Fournier sat down. "I heard what happened to her. It's absolutely terrible. Violence against women is endemic in modern society, and it has to stop. Do you know who did it?"

"That's why we're here," Bishop said. "We understand that Leon Gracz owns this place."

"Yes, he does. He's in Arizona. He goes down there in January and doesn't come back until after May Day."

"To your knowledge, has he been down there all the time this past week?"

Fournier grinned. "You betcha. I've called him on their landline the past four days in a row. It's tax time, boys, and we're up to our necks in it. He's in Goodyear, by the way."

"Landline. Okay. What about his cellphone?"

"He doesn't use it when he's down there," she said. "'A holiday's a holiday,' he always says. He hates it when I call and disturb his peace and quiet."

"Yeah, but I can see you get a big kick out of it," Bishop said.

Kevin sat down and took out his notebook. "What was the nature of the relationship between Leon Gracz and Andie Matheson?"

Fournier rolled her eyes. "She avoided him like the plague. The only time she'd stay in the same area code as him was when we did publicity photos together. Otherwise, I handled everything. It's part of my job anyway."

"She didn't like him?"

"Are you kidding me? He made a move on her a couple years ago. It lasted one night and that was it. He's not the kind of guy you get cozy with. Trust me."

Kevin raised his eyebrows.

"Correct," Fournier said. "Once. My husband and I were separated at the time. I was working late and he came in. I was pretty down, we got talking, one thing led to another. I went down the hall to his office with him and bada-boom. It went bad right away and I had to get a little harsh with him, let him know it wasn't going to happen again."

Kevin said nothing.

"He's into rough sex," Fournier said with exasperation, as though Kevin were too dense to get the point. "Slapping and biting and punching and all that shit. I got out of there and he followed me down here, to my office. We were the only ones in the building. It was pretty late. He wanted to take up where he left off, but I studied self-defence with a former U.S. Marine across the river, and I dislocated his thumb for him. Grabbed his wrist"—she pantomimed with her left hand—"grabbed his thumb"—she reached out with her right hand—"and twisted the fucking thing right out of joint."

"Ouch," Bishop murmured.

"The candyass fainted. When he came to, I gave him a glass of water and explained to him what the rules were going to be from that point on. No sex, no sexual advances at all, or else the thumb twister comes out again for another visit." She held up her right hand and wiggled the fingers. "And if you try to fire me I'll bring your wife and kids into it, *plus* I'll catch you alone one night in the parking lot and tear your fucking thumb right off your hand and shove it down your throat." She bared her teeth in a predatory grin. "It did the trick."

Bishop shook his head.

Fournier looked at him but said nothing, as though sizing him up as another potential candidate for pain compliance.

"What about Andie Matheson?" Kevin asked. "Do you know for certain she had the same experience with him?"

"Yeah."

"What happened?"

"She came around to my place one night. He'd done the same thing to her that he'd tried on me. She was crying and upset and she wanted to know if I thought she should go to the police. I said, 'Fuck the police.' No offence."

"None taken," Bishop said promptly.

"I put her in my car and drove her out to Leon's place. He'd gone to her apartment, see, and she'd let him in, but he was back home now and that's where I wanted to do this. His wife was out watering the lawn and his boy was shooting baskets in the driveway. I pulled up behind his Mercedes and got out, dragged Andie to the front door and pounded on it like I was insane. The wife and kid stopped what they were doing and stared at us. When he came to the door I said, 'Give me your hand. Give me your fucking hand.' Needless to say, he just stood there. I said, 'If you ever bother this woman again, the pain you experience is going to scramble your brains so bad you'll think you're a fucking chimpanzee. Do I have your fucking attention now?' He didn't say a word, just nodded and shut the door again. So that's how she was able to get out from under."

"Just out of curiosity," Bishop ventured, "why do you keep working for a guy who's such a prick?"

Fournier laughed. "I run this place. Front to back. You'd crap your pants if you knew how much this club's worth. That's why I'm so careful at tax time. Everything bulletproof and above board. Plus, Leon's happy to pay me an extremely generous salary. When the time comes, though, I'll move on to a big-league club and I won't look back."

"Do you know anyone else Andie might have been involved with?" Kevin asked. "After Leon Gracz?"

Fournier thought about it. "We weren't buddies. We didn't hang out together, but I know she had a fling with some married guy at one of the big companies in town. I'm not a gossip, you understand. I don't really give a shit. But it was my impression it was that Colter goof, at Jones Chemical."

Kevin nodded. He made a show of writing down Derek Colter's name. "Anyone else?"

Fournier paused, looking up at the ceiling. She exhaled noisily and dropped her eyes down to Kevin's. "A couple of weeks ago my husband and I were having dinner in Kingston. Our anniversary."

"Congratulations," Bishop murmured.

"Anyway," she went on, ignoring him, "who do we see at a table near the back but His Honour the mayor and Andie Matheson, nose to nose and holding hands."

Bishop sat up as though she'd grabbed his wrist and latched onto his thumb. "You said *what* now?"

"I'd heard," she went on, "there might have been a thing between them three or four years ago. Just a rumour that went around, you understand?"

"Who did you hear this rumour from?" Kevin asked, his pen frozen just above the page of his notebook.

"Who the hell knows? People talk. But as I heard it, a couple of his wife's friends saw them out together back then, like I did a couple of weeks ago, and went to his wife with it. Kathryn's her name. Apparently she confronted Lambton with it and he broke it off. Until recently, apparently." She spread her hands. "That's the way I heard it. Take it however you like."

Kevin caught Bishop's eye. The detective dropped his jaw in mock astonishment.

"Poor Andie," Fournier said, her voice uncharacteristically soft. "She had zero luck when it came to men."

chapter
TWENTY-TWO

Dennis Leung was in a bit of a hurry, and he didn't like it. It was now 12:43 PM and Ellie March had called a team meeting on the Matheson case for 1:30 PM. There was something else he needed to do first, and he was running late.

Mayor Lambton's executive assistant had kept him waiting nearly an hour at city hall while His Honour participated in some kind of *in camera* meeting that couldn't be interrupted. When Leung reminded her that the mayor had agreed to provide documents relating to their criminal investigation, that they were supposed to have been provided yesterday, and that they'd been promised to him by 11:00 AM this morning, the executive assistant shook her head and pleaded ignorance. She knew nothing about any documents for the OPP, and Lambton had said nothing to her about it before going into his meeting.

Leung was by nature a calm and patient man, and so he settled into a chair in the outer office and waited. He checked his cellphone for e-mails and texts, responded to a couple of unrelated messages, and then put the phone away and closed his eyes.

His mind was always active, and he spent the next block of time exploring his thoughts and feelings about Lambton. Since Leung had only been in the area for a year and a half after his transfer from Toronto, where he'd been assigned as an OPP liaison to the Alcohol and Gaming Commission, his personal knowledge of local politics in general and Mayor Lambton in particular was not extensive. Their encounter last night with Lambton in the restaurant had gone a long way toward filling in some of the blanks, however.

The mayor was clearly self-confident and arrogant, and he made no effort to hide his condescension toward the OPP as an organization and its members as individuals.

Leung had done a little online reading this morning over his breakfast tea. Several years ago, city council had voted to request a proposal from the OPP to provide policing services to the municipality. The cost of maintaining the Brockville Police Service had gone up, and several councillors believed there might be significant savings if they contracted out their municipal policing to the OPP. The mayor had opposed the idea, arguing that the city was better off with their current police force.

The OPP, for their part, prepared and submitted a proposal to Brockville city council in January. It came in at a higher cost than the proposed new BPS budget, and council voted to reject it.

Leung was somewhat surprised to see that Lambton had downplayed his victory. His public statement on the outcome was limited to the observation that it had been an important exercise to go through and that it was gratifying to see that the BPS was, after all, a cost-efficient and effective solution to municipal policing. As he'd maintained all along.

An interesting aspect to the whole thing, Leung mused,

was that the proposal would have seen Brockville integrated into the Leeds County detachment, and Inspector Todd Fisher would have then become, in effect, Brockville's chief of police. Leung wondered how The Fish had felt about that possibility.

He opened his eyes as someone entered the outer office, but it was not the mayor. A middle-aged man in jeans and a T-shirt handed the executive assistant a fistful of mail and disappeared, rolling his cart on down the corridor.

Leung spent the next block of time checking his cellphone again, answering another unrelated text message, and mentally re-organizing his itinerary between now and this afternoon's team meeting.

At 11:56 AM the executive assistant took a phone call. She listened, acknowledged what she'd heard, and hung up. She got up from her desk and went into the inner office. A moment later she returned with a legal size white envelope, which she handed to Leung.

"Mayor Lambton said this is what you're looking for."

Leung thanked her and left. There was no point in complaining about what had just happened. No matter how irritated he might feel, the mayor had been determined to play his little game, and there was nothing Leung could have reasonably done to prevent it.

Despite the loss of time, Leung remained determined to pay a visit to the Grass Wizards business and interview Howie Burnside before the team meeting. First, however, he needed to stop for lunch. As a diabetic, he couldn't afford to skip a meal, so he picked up a six-inch submarine sandwich on the way to Burnside's place and found a parking spot along the waterfront to wolf it down.

The Seaway was now open for the season and Leung watched a container ship pass as he ate. He liked living in Brockville, and he liked policing the rural area surrounding the city. He didn't really miss the fast pace and intensity of Toronto, and he and Lily didn't really miss their extended families all that much. They drove back there to participate in the major holiday celebrations, alternating between her family and his, but they were always relieved to return home afterward.

They'd settled in here. Lily had finally moved back up to management level in the bank where she worked, and their three daughters loved their school. Things were good for them right now. He hoped he'd be able to stay in his current assignment for a long time.

He finished the sub and wiped his hands and face on the napkin. He started the engine of the Fusion, but before pulling back out into traffic he opened the glove compartment and found a pair of latex gloves. Putting them on, he opened the white envelope and took a look.

It was an invoice, all right, complete with the Grass Wizards letterhead, a detailed explanation of services provided to landscape Lambton's cottage property along with their costs, and the all-important "Paid in Full" stamp near the bottom. Stapled to the invoice was a receipt showing that payment had been made with a credit card for the full amount.

There was little doubt in Leung's mind that it was the original invoice, as it was extensively creased from having been folded multiple times, and it bore numerous smudges and stains, including several fingerprints.

He dug around in the glove compartment some more and pulled out an evidence bag. He dropped in the invoice and receipt, along with the envelope, sealed the bag, and filled out the blanks on the outside of the bag.

He pulled out into traffic and headed east until he passed the city limits. Just before reaching the invisible boundary that separated the jurisdiction of the Leeds County OPP detachment from that of the Grenville detachment to the east, Leung turned into the large dirt parking lot of Howie Burnside's landscaping business.

A high chain link fence ran around the property, with a metal gate on wheels that was swung open and held in place by a concrete block. A small office building lay straight ahead, at the back of the lot. To the right, close to the road, Leung saw unattached snow plows and backhoe buckets arranged in a line. In front of the building were several parked vehicles. He rolled over and found a parking spot between a black smart car without licence plates and a green pickup truck with the Grass Wizards logo on the door.

Getting out, he paused for a moment to look at the smart car. It struck him as small and fragile, like an enclosed golf cart. He couldn't imagine himself driving one. He preferred large sedans, like the Crown Vic, and had been a little disappointed when he'd been assigned a Fusion by the detachment motor pool. Thank goodness, he thought, that they hadn't gone to something like these little sewing machines in an attempt to economize and protect the environment.

He walked into the office building. He found himself in a small reception area. A young man sat with his feet up on the corner of a battered metal desk. Dried mud was trapped under the heels of his cowboy boots. He was eating pizza from an open box next to his elbow. Grease dripped into the palm of his hand and trickled down his wrist.

Leung held up his badge. "I'm looking for Howie Burnside. Is he here?"

The man tossed his unfinished piece back into the box and ran his hand through his dirty blond hair to get rid of the grease. He picked up the telephone and punched a button. When the call was picked up at the other end he said, "Want a laugh? Come up front and check this out."

He hung up the phone and watched Leung with amused blue eyes until there was movement in a hallway on the left. A middle-aged man stood there, staring at Leung.

Leung held up his badge. "Detective Constable Leung, OPP. Are you Howie Burnside?"

The man looked at the blond. "What the fuck, Paul? I'm trying to eat lunch."

Paul laughed, picking up a fresh piece of pizza. "C'mon,

where's your sense of humour? When's the last time a cop walked in here? Let alone a chink cop."

"I'm looking for Howie Burnside," Leung tried again, "the owner of this business. Is he here?"

"No, he ain't." The man turned around and started back down the hallway. "Whatever you're selling we ain't buying, so take a walk."

Leung followed. "Can you tell me where I can find him? I need to ask him questions about an active criminal investigation."

The man turned into a small, cluttered office and sat down behind a desk. As Leung followed him in, the man turned his attention to a half-finished popcorn chicken box meal.

Leung looked at a name plaque on the desk that identified the man as Robert Nolan, office manager. He repeated, "Where can I find Mr. Burnside?"

"I don't fucking know." Nolan picked up a chicken ball and tossed it down again. "He's at one of our work sites. I don't know which one. Have a good day."

"Look, Mr. Nolan, we're investigating possible criminal wrongdoing by Mr. Burnside's uncle, the mayor of Brockville, and we need to interview Mr. Burnside to give him a chance to provide any information he thinks might help clear things up. Why don't you give me his cellphone number and I'll get in touch with him right now?"

Nolan sighed, leaning back in his chair. He looked over Leung's shoulder and called out, "Paul! Get the fuck in here!"

Leung thought about telling him they were preparing a warrant for all of the business's records as a way to apply pressure on the man to co-operate, but he decided instead to say nothing further.

The situation was deteriorating rapidly, and he realized he'd made a mistake coming on his own. There was a level of antagonism toward law enforcement here that he'd failed to anticipate. The best thing to do right now was to withdraw and come back later in force.

As he made this decision, Paul's cowboy boots thumped down the hall and into the office. Leung felt a hand grip his elbow.

"C'mon, Ching Chong, let's go."

Leung moved his arm forward, trying to free his elbow, but Paul held on, using his other hand to grab the fabric of Leung's suit jacket just below the right shoulder for additional purchase. Leung took a quick step forward, trying to break free, but Paul jerked him backward.

Leung heard the seam of his jacket rip.

He immediately swung his left elbow backward. It wasn't a forceful blow, but it was carefully aimed. It connected solidly with Paul's solar plexus.

Paul coughed and let go, but Nolan was up out of his chair and around the desk. He stopped short when Leung held up a hand.

"You don't want to do this."

"Get off our fucking property, and don't come back without a warrant." Nolan's breath, puffing in Leung's face, was heavy with the smell of masticated chicken and stale coffee.

"Assaulting a law enforcement officer in the execution of his duty is a serious criminal offence," Leung said. "You really don't want to go down that road, do you?"

Paul, recovering his wind, put a hand on Leung's shoulder.

Nolan looked past Leung's ear. "Get him the fuck out of here. Now."

Paul tugged on Leung's shoulder. "C'mon, Charlie Chan. Easy way or the hard way, right?"

Leung turned and stared at him. When Paul got the hint and removed his hand, Leung brushed past him and left the building.

chapter TWENTY-THREE

After having poured herself a cup of coffee from the urn at the back of the room, Ellie was walking up toward her seat at the head of the table when Dennis Leung hurried in and dropped into an empty chair in front of her.

"Hi, Dennis," she said as she passed behind him. "I think you're the last one we were waiting for."

"Sorry about that." Head down, Leung fumbled for the tablet in his briefcase.

"Your new jacket's torn," Ellie remarked. "Did you know that?"

Leung nodded, eyes on his tablet. "Long story. I'll tell you later."

"All right." Ellie closed the door and took her seat. "Let's get started. Dave, you're up."

From his place at the far end of the meeting table, Dave Martin waited until the chatter died down before beginning. A twenty-two-year veteran with sixteen years in as a forensic specialist, Martin hardly looked the part.

His boyish features and mischievous personality gave the impression that he might be more leprechaun than scientist, but his expertise in fingerprint analysis was well known. He'd published several articles on the subject which were included in reading lists at the Canadian Police College, and he was often called upon as a Crown witness to give expert testimony in criminal prosecutions. All in addition to his work as commander of the Forensic Identification Unit for East Region.

He started them off with a report on the murder weapon, explaining that it was an eight-inch Pott Sarah Wiener chef's knife that came from a very expensive set not readily available in stores.

"What the hell's a Pott Sarah Wiener?" Bishop grumbled.

Martin explained that Pott was a German company that manufactured high-end, hand-made cutlery, and that Sarah Wiener was a celebrity chef who not only endorsed the products sold under her name but also tested them in her own kitchen before they were put into production. These knives were hand-made, he told them, from high-quality Solingen steel with plum wood handles in a process that comprised ninety distinct steps.

"My point being," he concluded, "the rest of this set is most likely sitting in the kitchen of an expensive house belonging to people who like to own the finest things. This knife isn't something you'd toss into your cart at the Walmart while you're out grabbing a few odds and ends."

"That helps," Ellie remarked.

"It does." Martin swiped his tablet and told them that they'd also recovered a blood-stained tissue snagged on a dead weed in the ditch only a few meters from the knife itself. Apparently, he explained, the offender had taken a moment to wipe the knife before throwing it away.

"This removed fingerprints and also possibly hair, skin tissue or other items of interest," he said, "but it was a hasty job and a lot of blood was left where the blade joins the handle."

Blood from the knife, the tissue, hairs, fabric, and other related evidence had been sent to the Centre of Forensic Science in Toronto for analysis.

"How long until we hear back?" Carty asked.

Martin reflexively glanced at the clock on the wall. "We've submitted to the CFS as an urgent case, which by default means anywhere from ten to forty-five days turnaround time." He shrugged. "I talked to my special friend down there, and she thinks she might be able to run the swab from the knife this weekend. If we can get samples from the autopsy to her on Saturday, we might be in luck."

Ellie nodded. The CFS was the largest forensic laboratory in Canada, and she was aware that they routinely received well over ten thousand service requests a year, a third of which involved biological samples. While Martin's lab in Smiths Falls was well equipped and his staff handled a lot of the forensic testing load in regional cases, DNA evidence was always sent to the CFS for analysis.

Leung leaned forward. "Why are you so sure it's the murder weapon?"

"Oh, I don't know. A lifetime's experience, maybe?" He laughed. "Let me walk you through what we've done on it so far. For the evidence wonks in the room, and you know who you are," he looked at Kevin significantly, "we swabbed for a Kastle-Meyer test and it came up positive for blood. We then swabbed for an ABAcard HemaTrace test which rang the bells on human blood, so the knife wasn't just used to carve a raw roast beef or to kill a chicken or whatever."

"Doesn't the HemaTrace test give a false positive for ferrets?" Kevin asked.

Martin began to laugh. It took him a moment to catch his breath, and because it was Dave Martin, they all waited patiently for him to continue.

Kevin felt his face grow warm. He subscribed to an

online service providing academic articles in the fields of criminology, forensics, and other law enforcement subject areas, and he'd recently read an article about this particular test. Unfortunately, he realized belatedly, he'd chosen a poor time to pick the identification sergeant's brain on the subject.

"You're right," Martin finally managed, "there's a possibility, however small, that someone used this knife to kill a ferret. Sneaky little bastards. However, I'm a betting man, so I'm gonna roll with our victim."

"Getting back to where it came from," Kevin said quickly, looking down the table at Mark Allore, "we need to know if it's mail order only or if it's sold retail, who bought the set and where, anything at all we can find out about them. If the knife can lead us to the primary crime scene where the murder was committed, that would be huge."

As Allore scribbled it down in his notebook, Martin told the team what had been learned from the tire tread marks collected at both dump sites. Judging from the measurements and the pattern of grooves and ribs, the tires were P235s, a common type. Further measurement determined that the wheelbase of the vehicle was 286 centimetres, while its front track width was 163.332 centimetres and its rear track width was 162.306 centimetres.

Bishop grunted, bored.

"Put these three specs together," Martin continued, "and they only match either a Volvo XC Ninety SUV or a Ford Five Hundred between 2003 and 2015. There are twenty-five total possibilities, but you're only looking at two kinds of car, either a Volvo or a Ford."

"What about the victim's car?" Carty asked.

"She drove a Honda Civic. Which yielded all kinds of physical evidence, I might add, but nothing so far that rocks my world."

"And no cellphone," Kevin said.

"Correct. No cellphone."

"We received her phone records just before lunch," Bill Merkley said, speaking for the first time. "I'll be working on them this afternoon."

"Thanks," Kevin said. He looked down at Ellie. "John and I had a couple of very interesting interviews this morning." He turned back to Martin, interrupting himself. "You received the USB drive, I assume, with the Baldwin condo security video?"

Martin nodded. "It's being reviewed. I'm not usually comfortable trying to prove a negative, which I gather is what you're expecting."

"I just want to know if and when either Kyle Baldwin or Colin Davies appears on the video, that's all."

"If they do, I'll let you know. And speaking of negatives, the photos of the tires you sent me from the Mercedes in the Jones Chemical parking lot are not a match to anything found at the crime scenes on the Parkway."

Kevin glanced again in Ellie's direction. "John and I interviewed two people this morning, one of them connected to the tire treads Dave just mentioned."

Bishop cleared his throat. "We found out that the victim had an affair with a boob named Derek Colter, director of community relations for Jones Chemical. Which means he orchestrates the donations to Baldwin's charity, which also means he took advantage of his face time with Matheson to get physical with her. According to him, it was only for the summer two years ago. He broke it off because he was scared his wife was going to find out. His alibi checks out so he's not our guy"—he nodded at Martin—"which the thumbs-down on his tires would also confirm. However, he told us that Matheson said she was on the rebound from some one-night stand that had really shaken her up."

Bishop took a drink from his bottle of water before continuing. "Turns out to be a guy named Leon Gracz. Owns the Pine Glen Golf and Country Club."

Carty grunted. "I know Gracz."

Bishop looked up at him. "And...?"

"Nasty piece of work."

"Apparently," Bishop agreed, "but out of the country at present, so also not our guy. Kev and I interviewed his general manager, name of Fournier, comma, Mary Lou, period. Tongue on her like a chainsaw. She had lots to say about her boss, but none of it helped us. Then she dropped a little bombshell."

"Don't keep us in suspense," Martin said.

"Sure, Sarge, sure. Anything you say. According to Fournier, she and her husband—and I pity the poor bastard just on general principles—were having dinner two weeks ago in a restaurant in Kingston when they saw our vic at a table near the back holding hands with Hizzoner the Mayor."

Carty abruptly sat back. "What?"

"Gets better. According to her, Matheson and Lambton had a thing three or four years ago but he got busted by some of his wife's friends and broke it off. But it looks like he couldn't stay away from the honey pot forever."

Ellie and Leung exchanged looks. She leaned forward. "Are you sure about this, John?"

"I'm sure that's what she told us," Bishop replied. "Am I sure Lambton's the mysterious boyfriend she was seeing when she was killed?" He shrugged. "We're not there yet, but I like the sound of it."

"The next step," Kevin put in, "will be to interview Lambton's wife and these friends of hers about the past alleged affair. And Lambton himself, of course."

Ellie held up a hand. "Let's proceed carefully with this. We're looking at a potential minefield. Tom, we need a new set of warrants so that we can look at his phone and bank records again."

Carty nodded. Although they were already in possession of Lambton's telephone and financial records, that information had been obtained through a warrant connected to the criminal wrongdoing case only. If they wanted to look at the records again for a possible connection between Lambton and the murder of Andie Matheson, they would have to apply to a judge for authorization to search them a second time for this new purpose. The system worked this way in order to prevent police from conducting generalized fishing expeditions in a subject's personal information.

Ellie looked down the table at Merkley. "Bill, you'll work with John on the analysis?"

The regional intelligence co-ordinator nodded.

"I can't believe where this is going," Carty said.

"I agree," Ellie said. "I want this corroborated every step of the way. John, you and Bill get busy, all right?"

"Got a few minutes when we're done here?" Merkley asked Bishop.

"Sure, Billy. Rock 'n' roll."

Ellie caught Kevin's eye. "Are you comfortable taking the investigation down this road?"

"Completely."

Ellie nodded. "Let's see where it goes, then."

As the meeting broke up and the room cleared, Ellie remained in her seat for a moment. She closed her eyes and rubbed her forehead. She felt as though she were about to stick her hand into a hornet's nest, but one thing was certain—the Andie Matheson murder case had apparently just turned a corner.

chapter TWENTY-FOUR

It felt a little odd, Dennis Leung thought, to be still working on the Lambton breach of trust investigation while the rest of the team was haring off on the Matheson homicide angle.

He was coming from a longish meeting with Ben Wiltse, in which they had gone over everything Wiltse would need to draft an information to obtain a search warrant for the cottage owned by Peter Lambton. They wanted access to the property and the cottage itself so they could not only assess the landscaping as it currently stood, but also search for evidence relating to what Grass Wizards had done for Lambton three summers ago, including paperwork, photographs, or video recordings that might be kept in the cottage. Leung was hoping to be able to get the search done tomorrow afternoon, and Wiltse was confident the paperwork would be ready for him when he wanted it.

On his way downtown to meet Lily on her coffee break, Leung navigated the mid-afternoon Brockville traffic with his mind on other things.

When he and Ellie had met with Warren Whitlock, the city corporate services director had offered the opinion that Howie Burnside was known to be involved in other activities besides landscaping. Given the tone with which he'd said it, and Leung's treatment when he'd shown up at Grass Wizards looking for Howie, it seemed likely that the company name had been chosen as a play on words and that Burnside and his employees moonlighted in cannabis production or distribution, or both. The two boneheads he'd met at the office had come across as bikers, for sure.

Leung prided himself on his ability to handle stressful situations with calmness and a clear head. He was an excellent marksman, although he'd never drawn his weapon while on duty, and while a student at the University of Toronto he'd been a member of the varsity Graeco-Roman wrestling team in the 75-kilo weight class. His weight had since gone up from 163 pounds to 176, but he was still in good shape and felt he could handle himself.

As a law enforcement officer with a reasonable expectation of a long career, he wouldn't be able to succeed if physical encounters such as the one he'd experienced today upset or frightened him. So far they hadn't. Just the same, the rough handling Paul had given him still rankled.

It wasn't something he was prepared to let ride.

Lily was waiting for him at a table in a restaurant two doors down from her bank on King Street East. There were two take-out cups of tea in front of her, one for him and one for her. Reflexively he glanced at his watch and saw that he was only two minutes late. Her break ran from 2:45 to 3:00 in the afternoon, and she'd gone ahead and ordered knowing that he would be more or less on time. He always was.

He bent over and kissed her cheek. "How's your day going?"

"Oh, very busy. And you?"

Leung sat down, his back to the restaurant, and removed the top on his cup of tea. "The same." He sipped. "Mmm, good. It's still hot."

"I just got here. You changed your suit."

"Just the jacket. I got something on it and dropped it off at the dry cleaners."

"Are you sure it's okay for you to take time off right now?"

He smiled. Although they'd been married for fourteen years, he was still crazy about her. Her long, straight black hair, which she wore pinned up at work but reached to the small of her back when she let it down in the evening, was beginning to show traces of grey, and lines were beginning to show at the corners of her eyes and on her forehead, but to him she was still the delightful young woman he'd met as a university senior while finishing his degree in economics. The sound of her voice still made his heart skip, and the touch of her hand still made his pulse jump.

His life was good, as long as Lily was in it.

"Yes, it's okay," he said. "You said you wanted to talk to me about May."

On his way out the door this morning, while Lily was getting the children ready to go to their sitter, since there was no school today, she'd intercepted him with a little tug on the arm. "Coffee break, this afternoon? At the usual place?"

He'd nodded.

"May has something she wants to ask you, but we need to talk about it first."

"Okay." At twelve years old, May was the eldest. Lucy was ten, Lan was eight, and Meilin was six. Leung never failed to marvel at how wonderful an experience it was for him to live in a house with five females, despite the fact that May and Lucy constantly fought, Lan seldom spoke to anyone, and Meilin only pretended to be a perfect little angel.

"What's going on with her?" he asked, wondering

if it had anything to do with the fact that the onset of puberty had recently begun to affect May physically and emotionally.

"She wants a summer job." Lily wrapped her hands around her tea cup. "She floated the idea to me last night, and I said I'd run it by you."

"She's only twelve. She's too young to have a job."

"I know, but it's something her teacher wants to organize for several of the children in her class."

"I don't understand." Leung didn't particularly like May's teacher, Mrs. Schultz. He wouldn't go quite so far as to say she didn't like children who were not Caucasian, but he'd definitely not gotten positive vibes from her during their parent-teacher meetings earlier in the year. May was a model student who always received high marks in all her subjects and had never shown any behavioural problems, so he wasn't really sure what the issue was. "What does she want May to do?"

"She's organizing a tutoring arrangement for the summer. She wants her best students who will be going into Grade Eight next year to tutor some of the children who will be coming into her grade in the fall in subjects where they need a little extra help. She asked May if she'd like to tutor in math. Apparently she has two other children already lined up, one for science and another for language."

"I don't understand," Leung repeated, feeling a little dense and frustrated, as he usually did when Mrs. Schultz's name entered the conversation. "How is it supposed to work?"

"Mrs. Schultz gave May her home phone number and suggested we call, so I did. The idea is that children whose parents sign them up will get an hour tutoring twice a week during the summer, every Tuesday and Thursday. The charge is ten dollars for the hour, and the tutors get to keep the money. She said May is so brilliant in math, and such a good communicator with the other children, that she'd be a natural."

"Where is this supposed to be happening?"

"At her house. Apparently she's cleared it with the principal."

Leung was wondering what a quiet little background check would turn up on Mrs. Schultz when a heavy hand clapped him on the shoulder. Startled, he turned around and looked up at Paul, the dirty blond from Grass Wizards.

"Saw you coming in here, Charlie! Thought I'd stop in and say hi." Paul gave his shoulder an extra squeeze, as hard as he could, while looking around. "Never been in this dump before. How's the coffee?"

Leung twisted in his seat, pulling his shoulder free.

"This must be the little lady," Paul went on, reaching his hand across the table to Lily. "Nice to meet you. Are you guys married, or is this one of them little secret things nobody's supposed to know about?"

Lily didn't move. She kept her eyes on Leung.

"Move along," Leung growled. "Right *now*."

Paul lowered his hand. "Sure thing, Charlie. No problem. Just trying to be friendly. And I just wanted to remind you, like I said before," he stared meaningfully at Lily, "there's an easy way and a hard way to do shit, so just remember that."

Leung got to his feet, but Paul was already back-pedalling away from him.

"Keep your nose clean, Ching Chong!" He gave a little wave and left the restaurant.

Leung took a step, intending to follow him, but Lily stopped him with a word.

"No."

He slowly unclenched his fists and sat down again.

"Should I be worried?" she asked.

"No." Leung forced a tight little smile. "Just some punk. I'll take care of it."

She glanced at her watch. "I need to get back. What

about May?"

Leung sighed. Despite the stress he was feeling, he was still able to appreciate Lily's coolness and her willingness to trust him. "We'll talk to her tonight. After dinner."

"All right. But on first blush? What do you think?"

"If it's something she wants to do," he said, realizing he sounded grouchier than he'd prefer, "then it might be good for her. Good experience."

"I think so, too. We'll talk to her tonight."

Leung got up from the table, trying to decide what to do if he found Paul waiting for them outside.

He preceded Lily out of the restaurant, violating his normal custom of holding the door open for her. He scanned the street.

Paul was nowhere in sight.

Just to be sure, he walked her back to the bank and saw her through the lobby to her office before returning to his car.

chapter TWENTY-FIVE

Early evening. Back in the meeting room of the detachment office, Ellie sat on the corner of the long cherry wood table watching an IT person put the finishing touches on the video recording set-up she'd requested. Showtime was only a few minutes away, and she was mentally rehearsing the interview she was about to conduct.

The team had spent a very busy afternoon bringing in witnesses and getting statements signed. Mary Lou Fournier, the general manager of the Pine Glens Golf and Country Club, had confirmed her statement to Kevin and Bishop that she'd seen Peter Lambton holding hands with Andie Matheson at a restaurant in Kingston two weeks ago, and that she'd heard rumours they'd also had an affair several years ago.

She also provided the names of two women from whom she'd heard the story. One, whose name was Wanda Macfarlane, signed a statement in which she said she'd seen Lambton and Andie in a passionate embrace behind a media truck at a Canada Day event three years ago, while the other, Shirley Freeland, had not yet been contacted.

Fournier's husband, Marc-Andre Fournier, also signed a statement confirming his wife's story about seeing the pair in the restaurant in Kingston. Fournier was the deputy fire chief of the Brockville Fire Department, and to Bishop's skeptical eye he certainly seemed to be tough enough to give his wife a run for her money as a scrappy hardass. It was a relief not to have to feel sorry for the poor bastard after all.

Repeated efforts to locate Lambton's wife Kathryn were unsuccessful.

When Ellie felt reasonably confident that the information linking Lambton and Andie Matheson had been confirmed by other sources, she sent a car to Lambton's house, a two-storey brick home down on the waterfront, to bring him up to the detachment office for questioning.

Lambton called his lawyer before agreeing to leave his house. The lawyer, whose name was Joseph Paoli, promptly called Inspector Todd Fisher to complain. Minutes later, Fisher called Ellie to complain. Ellie kept this call short, acknowledging Fisher's "deep concern" and assuring him that Lambton would be handled with "courtesy and professionalism."

Minutes later her phone rang again, and this time it was Paoli himself. Ellie patiently explained to the lawyer, who was a partner in the largest firm in the county, that his client was not under arrest but was now considered a person of interest in the Andrea Matheson homicide investigation.

"That's what your officers told my client, but frankly we can't believe it. It's pure lunacy."

"I assure you," Ellie replied, "it's not. But any help your client can give us in clearing up certain aspects of this case would be greatly appreciated."

"I need to be there with him."

"You're welcome to come up to the detachment office

any time, but I understand Mr. Lambton has already consulted with you on this specific matter."

"He has, yes."

"Then I expect you're comfortable his rights have been protected."

"Yes. But I still want to be there."

Ellie sighed. Unlike in the United States with its Miranda rule of criminal procedure, in which someone brought in for questioning can immediately put the brakes on the interview process by demanding to consult a lawyer, the rights of individuals to retain and instruct counsel in Canada have been interpreted differently by the courts.

While the *Charter of Rights and Freedoms* guarantees "the right on arrest or detention to retain and instruct counsel without delay and to be informed of that right," the 2010 Supreme Court of Canada decision in *R. v. Sinclair* ruled that this Charter right "does not mandate the presence of defence counsel through a custodial interrogation."

As a result, if Paoli wanted to be present in the building he was certainly welcome to show up, but he would get no further than the outer lobby unless Ellie decided that Lambton's legal position had changed during the interview to the point that he needed to consult his lawyer again.

Ten minutes after the IT person had put the finishing touches on the video setup and disappeared, Kevin ushered Lambton into the room and sat him down opposite the camera.

"This is an outrage," the mayor blurted, eyeing the recording equipment, which included three microphones strategically located on the table. "I'm going to talk to my lawyer about filing harassment charges."

Ellie took her seat, and Kevin settled in next to her. "Detective Inspector Ellie March," she said, pulling the microphone closer, "April twenty-first at"—she glanced at the clock on the wall—"nineteen thirty-four, with Detective Constable Kevin Walker also present. Mr. Lambton, I believe the officers who brought you up here this evening explained to you that your presence is entirely voluntary, is that correct?"

"Yes they did," Lambton groused, "but the entire thing is harassment and I won't put up with it."

"You're completely free to leave at any time. Do you wish to do so?"

The mayor shifted his weight and bit his lip. "I should."

Ellie waited.

He pushed his chair back and crossed his legs. Once again he was wearing the tan brown leather jacket that was apparently his trademark, this time over a pale blue cotton shirt with a button-down collar, brown jeans, and brown Reebok sneakers designed to look like bowling shoes. "What the hell," he said, running a hand through his blond hair, "let's get this settled. Ask your questions."

Ellie indicated the camera and explained that the interview would be recorded to ensure an accurate accounting of everything said by Lambton himself and also by Ellie and Kevin.

She reminded him of his *Charter* rights and confirmed he'd consulted his lawyer and did not feel a need to consult him again at the current time. She added a secondary caution, to the effect that anything he'd previously said to police, specifically when informed of the reason for this interview by the officers sent to bring him in, should not influence him or make him feel compelled to say anything at this time.

"Yes yes yes, I get it."

Ellie rested her elbows on the arms of her chair and steepled her fingers. "You are now considered a person of interest in the investigation of the Andrea Matheson homicide. Do you understand what that means?"

"Why don't you tell me?" Lambton invited.

"Good idea. We define a person of interest as someone whose background or relationship to the victim, or opportunity to commit the offense in question, warrants further investigation. I'll tell you right now that no evidence currently exists that suggests you should be arrested and charged, but we do have information that connects you to the victim, Andrea Matheson, and that's why we need to speak to you tonight."

"Oh, wait. Let me guess. Someone saw me talking to her at a horseshoe tournament, or maybe it was the Santa Claus parade."

"How would you describe your relationship with Ms. Matheson?"

"Acquaintances."

"What does that mean?"

"It means," Lambton rolled his eyes, "I knew who she was, she knew who I was, and when we saw each other at some event we'd say hello, talk for a few minutes, that sort of thing."

"Did you ever see her socially at any time? On occasions not connected to business?"

"No."

"Are you saying that the only time you saw her was while you were acting in your capacity as mayor?"

"That's what I'm saying."

"When you interact with females, do you generally make physical contact with them?"

Lambton made a face. "What the hell kind of question is that?"

Ellie waited, watching him.

"What the hell do you mean by physical contact?" He frowned. "I shake their hands, if they offer first. If they're Quebeckers and they want to do the double-cheek-kiss thing, I go along with it. Other than that..."

"Is it your practice to hug women in public?"

"Sure, my mom when I'm in Kingston, my wife sometimes, although she doesn't like it."

"Did you ever hug Andrea Matheson in public?"

"Why the hell would I do that?"

Ellie leaned forward. "We have a signed statement

from a witness who saw you embracing and kissing Ms. Matheson behind a CTV media vehicle on July the first three years ago during a Canada Day event at Hardy Park, down at the waterfront. The kiss was described as 'passionate.'"

"Someone must have been smoking up back there."

"Are you saying you never embraced or kissed her?"

"That's what I'm saying."

"What about hand-holding? Did you ever hold her hand in public?"

"This is ridiculous. Is this what you brought me up here for?"

"Witnesses have stated to us that they saw you in the Limestone Grill in Kingston on the evening of April seventh of this year at a table with Ms. Matheson in an intimate setting. You were holding hands and leaning close together in conversation."

Lambton's jaw clenched. He glanced at Kevin and forced a humourless smile. "Not true. It must have been someone else and they mistakenly thought it was me."

"You're the mayor of Brockville," Ellie said. "You're a public figure. Hard to mistake you for someone else."

"And yet," he replied, "they did. Imagine that."

"Did you have a sexual relationship with Ms. Matheson?"

"Of course not. I'm a married man." Lambton narrowed his eyes. "Wait a minute. It's that fucking weasel Whitlock, isn't it? He's the one feeding you all this bullshit."

"Why would he do that?"

"What? Are you kidding me? The guy's had a hard-on for me ever since—" he broke off, glancing up at the camera, "well, for a while now. The little prick."

Ellie leaned forward. "Ever since when, Mr. Lambton?"

"Ever since I made it clear to him that he's a loser. A whiner, a weasel, and a loser. Brenda should fire his ass and get someone competent in there."

Ellie took a few moments to think about what she was hearing. The animosity toward Lambton that Warren Whitlock had shown this morning when she and Leung had interviewed him was certainly reciprocated by the mayor, but Ellie sensed she was picking up on something else from Lambton, a defensiveness that she felt was connected to something other than the trouble Whitlock and his complaint had caused.

"Where were you on Wednesday evening?"

Lambton's eyes went up and to the right, as though trying to recall. "Let me see. Night before last. I went down to the cottage."

"This is a cottage you own?"

"Yes."

"Where is it located?"

"Down near Ivy Lea. On Hill Island."

Ellie raised her eyebrows. This was the island on which the Lansdowne international border crossing was located, in the St. Lawrence archipelago between Ivy Lea and Rockport. It was fairly close to the spot on the Parkway where Andie Matheson's body had been dumped. "Must have cost quite a bit to buy."

"It's been in the family for several generations."

"I see. Did you go by yourself, or did your wife go with you?"

"I went by myself. I wanted some away-time. It's very quiet down there. I sat on the deck and watched the sunset."

"Was Andie Matheson there with you?"

Lambton screwed up his face. "No. Don't be absurd."

"When did you leave?"

"I ended up staying overnight. I drove back to the city the next morning."

"At what time?"

"I left at right around seven thirty, I guess."

"Did you take the 401 or the Parkway?"

"The 401. It's faster."

"Where did you go?"

"What do you mean, where did I go? I went home. Showered and got dressed for work."

"Mmm." Ellie looked at him for a moment. "Your wife's name is Kathryn, isn't it?"

Lambton nodded.

"Was she at home when you got there?"

"No, she wasn't."

"Where was she?"

"I don't really know, to tell you the truth."

"How are you two getting along these days?"

For the first time in the interview, Lambton appeared uncertain of himself. Then he quickly smiled and said, "Fine."

"Things are okay between you?"

"Why wouldn't they be?"

"Any recent fights or arguments?"

Lambton glanced at her left hand. "Are you married?"

"Please answer the question, Mr. Lambton."

"*Mayor* Lambton, please. And the answer is, 'What the hell do you expect?' All marriages have their disagreements from time to time. It's natural."

"Where's your wife right now?"

"I don't know. Maybe at home now. I'm not sure. She keeps her own schedule."

"We've been calling the landline number at your residence all afternoon," Kevin said, "and there's no answer. Does she have a cellphone?"

"Of course. Doesn't everyone?"

"What's the number?"

Lambton hesitated before reciting it. Kevin wrote it down.

"Do you have any idea at all," Ellie asked, "where we might be able to reach her?"

Lambton made a face and snapped his fingers. "Shit. I forgot. She said she was going up to Collingwood to visit her sister. I was thinking that was tomorrow. Today's

Friday, right?"

"Yes."

"I lost track of the days. I keep thinking it's Thursday. Anyway, she said she was going to take the day and drive up there."

"What's her sister's name, address, and telephone number?" Kevin asked.

"Her name's Mary Beth. Her husband's Ted Weston. He's a lawyer." He rattled off a street address in Collingwood and a telephone number. "That's their home phone. I don't know their cell numbers."

"Do you call them often?" Ellie asked.

Lambton shrugged. "No. Pretty much never. Can't stand them, to be honest with you."

"And yet you're able to remember their telephone number just like that."

"It just popped into my head. Is there anything else?"

Ellie looked at Kevin. "Make sure he has a ride home."

Kevin nodded, standing up, as Ellie reached behind her to switch off the recording.

Lambton got to his feet and tugged at his jacket. "Aren't you going to say it?"

Still sitting, her face blank, Ellie asked, "Say what?"

"You know, 'don't leave town'? Isn't that what the cops always say when they don't get anywhere but they still want to throw their goddamned weight around?"

Ellie shrugged. "Why would you want to leave? It's your town, Mr. Mayor."

Lambton leaned across the table. "Exactly. *My* town."

He followed Kevin out the door.

chapter TWENTY-SIX

On her way through the parking lot to her car, Ellie popped a fresh piece of nicotine gum into her mouth and gave it a vigorous chew. The night air was cool. She flipped up the collar of her overcoat, clamped her briefcase-cum-handbag under her arm, and pulled out her gloves. As she passed through the halo of the spotlight on the corner of the building, she thought she could see figures waiting for her at her car.

Kevin leaned against the rear fender, his hands shoved into his jacket pockets, and Bishop was draped over the hood, hands folded in front of him. They straightened as she approached, expressions expectant.

"I thought you guys had gone home," she said, unlocking the Crown Vic with her remote key fob. She opened the door and tossed her bag onto the passenger seat.

"We got talking," Kevin explained, "and JB made a few phone calls. We thought we'd fill you in before we leave."

"Okay." Ellie shut the door and leaned back against it.

"What's up?"

Bishop hesitated, eyes down. Ellie waited, aware that of all the detectives in the crime unit, Bishop was the one who still did not seem to trust her. She was certain it was not because she was female but rather because she was from general headquarters. It was the same barrier she encountered with Bishop's detachment commander, Todd Fisher, and a number of other field resources in the region to which she provided major case management. It was an attitude, somewhat parochial in her opinion, that often blended with strong union sentiment into an us-versus-them, headquarters-versus-field operations mentality that was difficult to overcome.

It didn't matter that Ellie had earned the crowns on the epaulettes of her uniform the hard way, working her way up from a greenhorn provincial constable driving a patrol cruiser on the back roads north of Brampton to detective constable and detective sergeant before moving to GHQ after thirteen years of service in the field. All that mattered to folks with this mindset was that she was on the other side of the fence now: "them" instead of "us."

Or perhaps she was misreading Bishop. Perhaps he felt intimidated by her, detective constable to detective inspector. Perhaps it was a rank thing more than anything else, and a suspicion that she secretly looked down on him and didn't approve of what she saw. Weighed in the balance and found wanting.

"Two things," he said, meeting her eyes, "after we cut Lambton loose. First, I finally got a voice message from Shirley Freeland, the other friend of Kathryn Lambton that Mary Lou Fournier mentioned. I'll interview her tomorrow morning while Kev's in Kingston."

Ellie nodded, remembering that Kevin would attend the Matheson autopsy in the morning. "Okay, good."

"Second, I talked to Mary Beth Weston, in Collingwood. Mrs. Lambton's sister. She had no idea Kathryn was coming up to see her. She said she hasn't heard from her for at least a week."

Ellie frowned. Lambton had been very emphatic that she'd set aside the day today to make the four-and-a-half-hour drive to her sister's home. "What else did you get from her?"

"Mostly confusion," Bishop replied, "but a couple of tidbits. Their maiden name's Morton. Their father was Edward Morton, owned a big sawmill in the Collingwood area, got into real estate specializing in hunting lodges and luxury cottages, that sort of thing. Worth a ton of dough."

"Blue Mountain country," Ellie said. She was familiar with the area, which was located on the southern tip of Georgian Bay.

"You betcha. When the old man died, the two girls split the estate. Kathryn got the lumber business, which she sold, and the sister got the real estate stuff, which *she* hung onto. According to her, the whole thing was worth over forty million each."

"That's a lot of money." Ellie tilted her head. "She didn't seem to have much hesitation in talking to you."

"Yakked my frigging ear off, excuse the language. Anyway, she has no use for Lambton whatsoever. Called him a slimy sleazebag, or words to that effect." He glanced at Kevin. "By the end of the call, she was a little worried about where her sister was."

"Has Kathryn Lambton ever done this sort of thing before? Driven up to visit her without prior notice? Or disappeared without telling anyone where she was going?"

Bishop shook his head. "She says not. It's out of character. You want my opinion, if this Freeland woman can't help us find her, I'm all for declaring her a missing person and taking it from there."

"I agree," Kevin said.

Ellie thought she knew where they were going. Officially categorizing Kathryn Lambton as a missing person would open the judicial door for them to file production orders for her cellphone records and GPS data, which might help determine her whereabouts. In Ellie's opinion, it might quickly come to that if Kathryn wasn't located very soon.

"Let's see what tomorrow brings," she said, shivering, "and then we'll take it from there. Good work, John."

"Thanks." He grinned at her. "You look like you're freezing. Get in the damned car and go home, will ya?"

"Sounds like a real good idea." She opened the door and slid in behind the wheel.

"Good night, Ellie," Kevin said.

"Good night, Kevin. John." She shut the door and started the engine as the two detectives moved back into the shadows.

chapter TWENTY-SEVEN

Dennis Leung was one of those guys who preferred chewing gum instead of candy or other types of junk food while putting in the hours on a surveillance detail. He always made sure he had several packs of sugar-free gum in the car with him before setting up, and he routinely went through most of it before the stakeout was finished.

He'd opened up his first pack and had chewed and discarded about half of it when Paul, whose full name was Paul Whiteman, emerged from his mobile home a few kilometres outside of Brockville. It was just after nightfall, and Paul's tail lights led him down Halleck's Road to Highway 2, where he turned left and drove a few kilometres to a dumpy roadhouse called Larabie's.

Leung cruised by, giving Paul a chance to get out of his truck and walk inside, then he U-turned and went back. The big parking lot out front was poorly lighted, and Leung found an inconspicuous spot on the far edge between a derelict tow truck and a passenger van. Satisfied that the floodlights in the lot weren't reaching his hiding spot, he pulled out his camera, a thermos of cold tea, his notebook and pen, and his stash of gum.

For this kind of work, he used his own equipment. His camera was a two-year-old Nikon digital SLR model to which he had added a night-vision module that allowed him to shoot still images or video recordings under low-light conditions. He set the camera's exposure and focus modes to manual, dialled the ISO up to 6400, and moved the shutter speed to one-thirtieth of a second. After a few test shots and adjustments he was satisfied with the results. He settled down to wait.

He'd finished the first pack of gum and started on the second when a black BMW sedan pulled in. By this time Leung had photographed all the licensed vehicles in the lot, which were mostly pickup trucks and motorcycles, and he'd written down all the plate numbers in his notebook. As he eased his camera up over the steering wheel, he saw Howie Burnside get out of the BMW. He was a small guy, dressed in a dark windbreaker, jeans, and cowboy boots, and he was carrying a small black tote bag. Leung hadn't seen him before in person but recognized him from the driver's licence photograph in the file he was maintaining for Ellie on the Lambton case.

Leung shot a few frames as Burnside entered the roadhouse, then he put the camera down and made a note of the arrival in his notebook.

A few minutes later, some guy with a motorcycle helmet in his hand came out of the roadhouse and rode off on one of the Harleys parked near the front entrance. Leung shot pictures and wrote it down, uncertain if it meant anything. It might just be some random guy going home after a few quick beers. Once the guy had roared out onto the highway and disappeared into the darkness, silence settled back down around Leung.

When he was a young detective assigned to the Brant County detachment east of Hamilton, Leung had learned about surveillance from an old hand named Gerry Conlin. Conlin's nickname was Skittles, after the popular candy that was his preferred oral distraction during the long hours involved on a stake-out. Skittles had taught him how to use isometric exercises to reduce physical stress and fatigue while sitting still for hours at a time, and he'd also encouraged him to come up with mental exercises to counteract the boredom that inevitably settled in.

Leung liked numbers. Tonight he'd memorized all the license plates and played around with the numerical values of the letters in terms of where they ranked in the alphabet. He'd added all the numbers together and calculated the mean, median, and the square root of their total, and then he'd assigned the vehicles in the parking lot a rank in terms of the total number they represented once the letters and digits were added up, first in descending order and then in ascending order.

He was starting to wonder whether he was going to have to use his urine bottle to relieve his distressed bladder when Howie Burnside came out of the roadhouse and sauntered across the lot to his BMW. He was empty handed.

Leung photographed his departure. The black tote bag had apparently remained inside.

Leung had just finished updating his notes when another Harley rumbled into the lot and parked under the spotlight near the front door.

It was a different guy than the one who'd left earlier. He dismounted, took off his helmet, and looped the chin strap over the handlebar of his bike before heading inside.

Leung dutifully shot his portrait and noted the bike's plate number, which was new to his list. This Harley wasn't a Sportster like the earlier one. It was a Fat Boy that looked identical to the bike Arnold Schwarzenegger drove in the movie *Terminator 2: Judgment Day*. Leung wasn't an aficionado of motorcycles by any stretch of the imagination, but he knew a cool-looking bike when he saw one.

Only a minute or so passed before the biker came back out and sat sideways on the seat of his Fat Boy. He lit a cigarette and casually gave the parking lot a slow, sweeping examination. Leung eased down, the top of his head just below the horizon of the dashboard. He gave it a few moments, holding his breath, and then gradually slid back up for a peek.

The biker was leaning forward, forearms on his thighs, staring at the ground between his boots. He spat and drew on his cigarette, running a hand through his hair.

As Leung switched to video recording, the front door opened and Paul came out. He was carrying the black tote bag in his hand, and after a cursory survey that missed Leung's darkened section of the parking lot, he walked over and handed the bag to the biker.

Sticking his cigarette into the corner of his mouth, the biker unzipped the bag and poked around inside. He zipped it up again and set it on the back fender of his bike. He leaned back, reaching behind him for something.

Watching, Leung realized there must be a saddlebag back there, the soft leather kind that sat just above the exhaust pipe. Sure enough, the biker produced a tightly-wrapped package and handed it to Paul. He lengthened the strap on the tote bag and slung it crossways over his shoulder so that it rested on his back.

Paul hotfooted it over to his truck. The biker donned his helmet, kick-started the Fat Boy, and rumbled off. Leung continued to video record until Paul rolled past him and out onto the highway, then he thumbed the camera's controls and tossed it onto the passenger seat with a tight grin.

Exercising due caution, he followed Paul back to his mobile home and waited for an hour until the interior lights went off. Then he quietly drove away, thinking that payback was going to be a sharp-toothed bitch for Paul Whiteman and his asshole boss, Howie Burnside.

chapter
TWENTY-EIGHT

The following morning while driving eastbound on Highway 401, Kevin passed under the Detective Constable Richard G. Robinson Memorial Bridge, which was dedicated to the memory of the twenty-four-year OPP veteran who had passed away in 2013 while representing the Kingston field unit of the Intelligence Bureau at a conference in Buffalo, New York.

With about forty-five minutes of driving ahead of him, Kevin had plenty of time to think. While stark images of vital organs and viscera continued to fill his head, he was able to force his mind down more productive channels as he drove. At the same time, he felt a little pleased that he'd survived the morning without making a fool of himself this time.

The autopsy of Andie Matheson had been performed by Dr. Carey Burton, director of the forensic pathology unit at Kingston General Hospital. Kevin attended along with Carty and Dave Martin, who'd travelled together for the event.

As upsetting as it had been to watch Andie's lifeless body systematically taken apart, photographed, examined, weighed, and otherwise manipulated during the long, painstaking post-mortem process, Kevin had managed to make it all the way through without getting sick. He took careful notes, listened to Dr. Burton's running commentary and his conversations with his assistants, and successfully held his stomach in check.

In his book, a definite victory.

The first autopsy he'd attended had been performed on the body of a murdered man he knew from Sparrow Lake, a used car broker who'd lived a few blocks away from him in the village. He'd endured everything up to the moment when the stomach was removed and opened, revealing the remains of a meal that Kevin had often ordered himself from the Silver Kettle restaurant—a bacon cheeseburger and home-cooked fries. His gorge had involuntarily risen and he'd barely made it out of the building before throwing up into a snowbank. He could still remember Detective Sergeant Patterson's laughter as he'd fled the room.

Afterward, knowing he'd have to face the ordeal again at some point in his career, he'd done what he always did in situations like this—he read everything he could get his hands on about it.

A trip to a used book store in Kingston had turned up a copy of Mallory and Wright's *Pathological Techniques*, and he'd plowed through it dutifully, memorizing terms and techniques and studying the illustrations with the gravity of a medical student facing dreaded examinations.

Although it had once been a standard textbook on the subject, *Pathological Techniques* was one hundred and twenty years old, so he went looking for another reference book that was a little more up to date. Another trip to Kingston yielded *Post Mortem Technique Handbook* by Sheaff and Hopster, published in 2005. In addition to illustrations, this one also featured very graphic photographs. He forced himself to study them carefully as he worked his way through the textbook, chapter by grim chapter, until he finally reached the bitter end.

The books went into a cardboard box in the basement when he was done, where the kids wouldn't stumble across them, but the information remained in his head, along with a sense that he understood the post-mortem process at an intellectual level that might prove helpful in the future.

In fact, it had. After the external examination of the body was completed and samples of blood, tissue, and fluids had been collected for later analysis, Kevin watched without flinching as Dr. Burton's diener cut a Y-shaped incision to begin the dissection.

Forcing himself to see the body not as a person, not the pretty and vulnerable Andie Matheson, but as a cadaver under scientific study, he was able to identify the evisceration technique being used by the pathologist as the one known as *en masse*, or the Letulle technique, in which most of the internal organs were removed at the same time and organized for systematic, individual examination later in the procedure.

As the thing wore on, he mentally compared what he was seeing to what he'd read. It helped him get through it. It also helped him focus on Dr. Burton's findings, one of which proved especially surprising and significant.

The external examination confirmed the coroner's observation at the scene that the victim had been stabbed fifteen times, twelve times on the torso, twice on the left thigh, and once on the palm of the left hand. The hand injury was likely a defensive wound sustained when the victim had attempted to protect herself from the attack.

The wounds differed in appearance and depth, but Dr. Burton assured Kevin that this kind of variation was common given the degree of force used in each blow, the movement of the victim during the attack, and the twisting of the weapon as the assailant repeatedly struck.

Two of the blows to the torso had severed major arteries,

and cause of death was determined to have been loss of blood. Dr. Burton believed the bleeding that resulted from these two particular blows would have been brisk. Death must have followed fairly quickly.

A small mercy, Dr. Burton allowed.

Time of death, given the observations of the coroner at the scene and evidence gathered during the post-mortem examination, was estimated to have been between 6:30 AM and 8:00 AM on Thursday, April 20.

Food was still present in the stomach. Dr. Burton explained to Kevin that emptying time usually ranged anywhere from two to four hours. The victim's last meal had probably been consumed, in his opinion, about an hour before death. To all appearances it had been a chicken salad of some kind.

Carty pointed out, somewhat skeptically, that chicken salad hardly constituted a typical breakfast, assuming the victim had eaten it between five thirty and seven in the morning.

"I'd say not," Dr. Burton agreed, "but there it is, nevertheless."

Dr. Burton also confirmed Dr. Kearns's observation that the victim had experienced sexual activity not very long before death. The presence of semen was not detected, suggesting the use of a condom. Detailed examination did not reveal injuries that would be consistent with sexual assault, and Dr. Burton agreed with the coroner's belief that the sex had been consensual.

In addition, Dr. Burton discovered that the victim was nine weeks pregnant when she died. The finding was a surprise to everyone in the room.

Dr. Burton would order an analysis of the fetus's DNA to help identify the father, if an opportunity to do so should arise.

Kevin thought about this unexpected discovery as he drove along. Did the fact that Andie Matheson was going to have a baby factor into her murder? Who was the father? Kyle Baldwin? Peter Lambton? Someone else not yet on their radar? Was she killed by the father to hide the pregnancy, or by someone who was jealous that the child was not theirs? Or by another woman jealous of Andie and furious that her husband or lover was the father?

Or had Andie kept her pregnancy a secret, since she was barely two months into her term, and it hadn't played a role in her murder at all?

As he passed the Mallorytown Road exit his cellphone buzzed. Using the hands-free device, he answered it. "Kevin Walker."

"Kevin, Detective Constable Perry Ladouceur, BPS." Ladouceur was one of the few detectives on staff with the Brockville Police Service that Kevin didn't know particularly well. He'd transferred in from Thunder Bay two years ago, if Kevin remembered correctly. He had a reputation as a lunch bucket kind of cop, not afraid of hard work and long hours. Kevin's kind of guy.

"Hey, Perry. How's it going?"

"Busy day. I'm at the Thousand Islands Mall. We're talking to some guy who's been doing a bit of dumpster diving out the back."

"Sounds like fun."

"Yeah, well, not for him. He tore open a garbage bag and started puking his guts out."

"Oh?"

"We've got bedding and a shower curtain covered with dried blood, a lot of it, some women's clothing, men's clothing with a lot of blood soaked into it, and a pair of women's boots. I thought of your homicide and figured you might want to take a look."

Andie's missing clothing, and evidence from the elusive primary crime scene!

"I'll be there in twenty minutes," he said, glancing at the dashboard clock.

"I'll be here," Ladouceur replied, ending the call.

Kevin pulled over onto the shoulder of the highway and

found Dave Martin's number in his contact list. Knowing that Carty was driving, he called the identification sergeant and asked to be put on speaker.

"What's up?" Carty demanded from behind the wheel.

Kevin filled them in on the discovery.

"We're about fifteen minutes behind you," Carty said. "We'll meet you there."

"I'll call Serge," Martin said, excitement in his voice. "He'll bring the van. This is great!"

"Easy, Dave," Forensic Constable Bill Jamieson said, his voice reaching Kevin faintly from the back seat of the SUV. "Remember your blood pressure."

Martin laughed.

Kevin ended the call and pulled back out onto the highway, thinking that he belonged to a very strange breed, indeed, that could get this pumped up at the prospect of fingering through blood-soaked bedding and clothing.

He listened for a moment to the white noise of the car's engine and its tires on the pavement and thought of the hermetic silence of Kyle Baldwin's luxury condominium. A separate world. Protected by money, family, and privilege.

A very, very different place to be than the one in which Kevin had chosen to live his own life.

chapter TWENTY-NINE

Shirley Freeland lived in a nineteenth-century stone house on Flint Street down near the waterfront in Brockville. A glassblower who specialized in lampworking, she used the downstairs rooms of the house for her shop and studio while living upstairs in four small bedrooms. She met Bishop and Mark Allore at the front door and showed them back through the workshop into a sun room. They sat down after refusing an offer of coffee.

"I'll just finish mine, then," she said, settling into a large wicker chair.

"Feel free." Bishop unbuttoned his jacket and looked around. "Nice place."

Freeland sipped her coffee and smiled. "Thanks. I bought it after I divorced my second husband."

"Glad to hear it. You said on the phone you're friends with Kathryn Lambton. When was the last time you saw her?"

"Thursday morning. She stopped in for breakfast.

She didn't seem very well." Freeland put her coffee down and crossed her legs. She wore an untucked white dress shirt with the sleeves rolled up, black capris, black canvas slip-ons, and a red scarf tied around her long blond hair. Her hands and wrists were peppered with multiple small scars from pops, drips, and accidental burns from the blow torches and molten glass she'd worked with over the years. She was small, composed, and a little disdainful of their authority as police officers. She reminded Bishop of a cousin of his he'd grown up with in Chatham, all business and no nonsense. He decided he was going to like her.

"What do you mean, she didn't seem very well?"

"She was moody, lost in thought. Not really there."

"Did she explain why?"

Freeland shook her head. "She usually confides in me, because she knows I'll hold in confidence whatever she says." She gave Bishop a meaningful look.

He glanced at Allore, whose notebook and pen were out. "Okay, Ms. Freeland, let's cut to the chase, shall we? We've been told you were aware that Mrs. Lambton's husband had an affair several years ago with a woman named Andrea Matheson, who was found murdered Thursday morning. As you no doubt heard on the news. Care to confirm this and explain how you knew about it?"

Freeland sighed. "Sure, since it's not betraying a confidence. This was back when I was still on city council. I was working late one evening and walked into his office to see him about something or other. I don't remember what it was now. He and the Matheson girl were doing it on the desk. I caught them *in flagrante delicto*, you might say."

"When was this, exactly?"

"August, three years ago. Don't ask me the specific date, because I don't remember. Just before the Labour Day weekend; that's all I can tell you."

"Okay, so three years ago. Did you tell his wife about it?"

She shrugged. "Not right away. You said on the phone

you've already talked to Wanda? Well, she talked to Kathryn before I did. She'd seen them smooching at a Canada Day thing that summer, and she blabbed about it without really considering whether or not it was a good idea. Kathryn said she wasn't the first person to tell her that sort of thing. So I came forward as well. I figured at that point she needed to hear it all. To be able to make an informed decision on what to do about it."

"You mean whether or not to divorce the bum."

"Basically."

"Did she confront him? Is that what happened?"

"Yeah." Freeland took a drink of coffee before continuing. "He promised to break it off and behave himself, and she took him at his word. As far as I know, that's what he did."

"Until recently?" Bishop prompted.

"I don't know." She frowned. "I'm not sure."

"But you heard stuff."

"That he'd started up again with her? Yes. But I don't know for sure if any of it's true. *Was* true."

"You hadn't seen them together again recently, is that what you're saying?"

"That's what I'm saying."

"How well did you know Andrea Matheson?"

"Not really at all," Freeland replied. "I knew her to see her around, but as far as I can remember we never even had a conversation."

"Okay." Bishop glanced again at Allore, who seemed to be getting it all down in his notebook. "Tell me more about Lambton."

"Professionally or personally?"

"I don't know; how about both?"

"Professionally, he's a very good mayor. He represents us well with the AMO—"

"The what now?"

"The Association of Municipalities of Ontario. Brockville's a member. As I was saying, he represents our interests well as a smaller city going up against the giant municipalities, he does his best to bring investment and jobs in, he's aggressive in council and—"

"So aggressive he got a big-ass complaint lodged against him, right?"

Freeland paused for a moment. "You know what really bothers me?"

"No. What really bothers you?"

"When people don't let me finish my sentences; that's what really bothers me."

Eyes down, Allore coughed.

"Sorry," Bishop said. "Won't happen again. Bad habit. What about Lambton personally?"

She considered the question. "Almost impossible to like. An annoying know-it-all, for one thing. Arrogant and obviously used to getting his way on everything. A sense of privilege that doesn't really go with his background. His family was working class, and he got his start as a customs officer at Lansdowne. Did you know that?"

Bishop shrugged.

"Got himself elected to the township council down there twenty years ago, and that's how he got into politics. Quit the customs job, worked as a broker for a while, quit that job, got married and divorced within a two-year span, moved up here and got elected to council in 2006, then married Kathryn in 2008 and was elected mayor two years after that."

When he was certain she was finished speaking, Bishop said, "As I understand it, she's worth some serious coin."

Freeland nodded.

"Which is his motivation for staying on her good side, right?"

"Yes."

He saw her hesitate, and pounced. "What? What else is there? Abuse? Did he knock her around?"

"No, not like that." She glanced at Allore. "He has a very bad temper. He shouts and screams. He's verbally abused her for years. He doesn't hit her, but I've seen bruises on her arms from where he's grabbed her. I've asked her about it, and she insists he doesn't hit her. Grabs her and pushes her, apparently, but that's the extent of it."

"That's bad enough," Bishop said.

"Yes, it certainly is."

"It's very important that we contact her."

"Just a minute." She stood up and walked out of the room.

Bishop looked over at Allore. "Was it something I said?"

Allore shrugged.

Freeland returned with a tablet in her hand. "She hasn't been on Facebook for at least a day. I messaged her yesterday and she hasn't seen it."

Allore sat forward. "May I?"

She handed him the tablet. Allore studied it for a moment before setting it down on the coffee table. He wrote down the name associated with her Facebook account and glanced up, holding his finger above the screen.

"Go ahead," she told him.

Allore checked out Kathryn's "About" page, which contained almost no information, and switched to "Friends," where he found only nine connections. Jotting down the names, he said, "She doesn't seem very active here."

"She's not a big fan of social media, but we use Messenger almost every day."

Allore turned the tablet around until it was facing Freeland. "Could you show me?"

She picked it up and tapped her way to Messenger and the link with Kathryn Lambton. She opened the thread and showed it to him. Her last message to Lambton had been delivered at 3.46 PM on Thursday but had not been viewed.

"Thanks," Allore said.

Standing up, Bishop handed her a card. "When you

hear from her, call us right away. It's very important."

"I understand."

As they were walking back through the workshop to the front door, Freeland said, "You're aware, I take it, that Andie Matheson was in a relationship with Warren Whitlock as well, a couple of years ago?"

Bishop stopped, his hand on the doorknob. "Who?"

"Whitlock. The city director of corporate services. This was after Peter Lambton broke it off with her the first time around. The next year, I think it was."

Bishop glanced at Allore, who was hauling his notebook back out to write down the name. "So who's this guy, exactly?"

Freeland folded her scarred arms and leaned back against the wall. "The city clerk reports to him. He's the one who filed the complaint against Peter Lambton to begin with."

"Oh ho. Okay."

"Most people don't like him," Freeland said, "but I always felt sorry for him. A policy wonk like him married to a bitch like Erica Burnside and caught up with that family? He didn't stand a chance."

"I'm not tracking you here," Bishop said. "Who're you talking about now?"

"Warren Whitlock was married to Erica Burnside," Freeland said to Allore, since he seemed to be the less confused of the two. "Erica Burnside's the sister of Howie Burnside. The mayor's nephew? Grass Wizards Landscaping?"

"Okay," Allore said, nodding as he made notes, "I know. When were they married?"

"Oh, I'm not sure. Some time after he moved here from Ottawa. Warren was already separated from her when he and Matheson had their fling. He would have been on the rebound, though. Christ." She shook her head. "They were pretty awful to him."

Allore raised his eyebrows. "In what way?"

"The old man's name is Robert Burnside. He's a psychiatrist with a long history of selling prescriptions on the side and molesting his patients. A real piece of work. Dear little Howie's a chip off the old block." She stared at Allore. "Grass Wizards? It's a play on words, right?"

"Okay." Allore looked at Bishop, who shrugged.

"Anyway," Freeland went on, "the daughter's probably the worst of the bunch. She beat up a girl when she was in high school and that was a big mess. Drug busts, you name it. Really beautiful thing, though, which I imagine is what attracted Whitlock to begin with." She sighed. "The stories I heard."

"Enlighten us," Bishop invited. When she hesitated, he rolled his eyes. "Oh, wait. You don't gossip or betray confidences or whatever it was you said there."

"You've got a smart mouth, detective."

"It's true," he admitted.

"She used to beat him up. That's what we heard. With her fists, with a belt buckle, that sort of thing."

"The girl did? To this Whitlock? And he went along with it?"

"Not willingly. It was abuse, pure and simple. He left her after a year, but the entire family continued to persecute him long after that, apparently. A family of bullies, sick bullies."

"Sounds like it." As Bishop opened the door, he looked over her shoulder into the room that she used as a shop. He could see displays of glass pendants and beads, vases, figures, and other works of art created by Freeland in her workshop. "Can I ask you one more question?"

"Sure, detective. Ask away."

"Um, do you give lessons?"

"Lessons?"

"You know, in the stuff you do." He nodded with his chin toward her shop.

"You mean in lampworking? Sure, I have in the past. Not lately. Why do you ask?"

"Dunno. Just thinking. Actually, my wife Jenn really digs that stuff. She has a collection of it. Not a lot, but a few things. Candy trays or whatever. Anyway, I think she might be interested in learning how to do it, if you give lessons."

Freeland smiled at him. It was a friendly smile, with only a little amusement at the edges. "Well, Detective Bishop, you've got my number. If she wants to call me, maybe we can set something up."

"Thanks," Bishop said, going out the door, "I appreciate it. I'll mention it to her."

"You do that."

Outside on the sidewalk, he turned to Allore and said, "This could be the best idea I've had in the last six months."

"What, you mean the Whitlock angle?"

"No no no, not that. The glass lessons. I think maybe Jenn'll go for it, big time."

Allore shook his head and followed him down the street to the car.

chapter THIRTY

The Thousand Islands Mall on Parkedale Avenue was at one time Brockville's primary shopping venue, but the economy that once drew large-chain retailers away from the downtowns of Canadian communities to decentralized shopping centres along busy strips had now yielded to an economy in which consumers shopped online and no longer bothered wasting the gas and time to drive to brick-and-mortar stores. Empty storefronts and sparse crowds in the Thousand Islands Mall in particular testified to the fact that Brockville, like many smaller communities in eastern Ontario, was experiencing the unpleasant side effects of this modern economic evolution.

Brockville Police had barricaded the rear of the mall, and when Kevin arrived he waited for several minutes for Detective Constable Ladouceur to appear. When Ladouceur showed up and Kevin was logged in, they walked the length of the building to a dumpster not far from one of the rear entrances. Kevin stopped a few metres away and said,

"What a mess."

"Yeah. The guy who found it is down there." Ladouceur pointed at a BPS cruiser beyond the far strip of yellow tape. "He picks cans and bottles for the deposit."

"I'll talk to him in a minute." Kevin stared at the bags of garbage that had been pulled from the dumpster and torn open. Most were obviously from the mall units selling food, judging from the discarded wrappings, paper cups, and wadded napkins. The prize, however, was a large green bag that had been split down the side. The gleaner had pulled out a mass of bloody bedding and several items of women's clothing before realizing what he was getting into. There were several puddles of vomit nearby. The man's half-filled shopping cart stood where he'd left it, behind a parked car a metre away on the far side of the dumpster.

"He said it was about halfway down into the garbage," Ladouceur said, "so it was probably there for a couple of days."

Kevin nodded. They would have to canvass store employees and managers, find out who'd been working since Thursday morning, and determine whether or not they'd seen anyone toss the bag into the dumpster. As he thought it through, he looked at the back wall of the building and noticed a security camera above the rear entrance about twenty metres from the dumpster.

"Tell me that works," he said.

Ladouceur laughed without humour. "It does. The problem is, this place is run from an office in Toronto, and they're a bitch to deal with. They'll sit on your warrant for as long as they can before releasing it to you, and whine and complain the whole time."

"But that shouldn't be a problem for you boys," Sergeant Steve Jackson said, joining them.

Kevin nodded. "Hopefully not."

"Where's your sidekick, Curly?"

"Busy." Kevin glanced at Ladouceur. The city detective's

face was carefully neutral. "I really appreciate the call. Ident's on the way, and we'll try to get this worked as fast as possible."

"Yeah, don't get your balls in a twist." Jackson waved his hand as though granting a special favour. "If it was out front it'd be different, but nobody comes back here anyway except store employees. These are all their cars."

Kevin nodded. "You've still got the guy down there?"

Jackson grunted. "We let him sit in the car, but only after he'd finished puking. Nobody wants to clean up that kind of a fucking mess."

Kevin chuckled as though he appreciated the humour and started down toward the far end. Ladouceur said something to the sergeant and followed.

"If I can help with the interviews inside, Kevin, just say the word."

"Thanks." Kevin was passing the rear entrance of the mall, which consisted of a small concrete porch, metal railings, and a recessed glass-and-steel door. He glanced at the door and was shocked to see Caitlyn on the other side, waving at him.

"I'll be right there," he told Ladouceur, hastily changing course.

A uniformed police officer stood inside, with his back to the door, posted there to prevent access to the crime scene. He was looking down at Caitlyn, who was chattering away to him and pointing outside. As Kevin trotted up the stairs, the cop turned around and looked at him.

Kevin unclipped his badge and held it up. The cop nodded and opened the door.

"Kevin!" Caitlyn exclaimed. "What're *you* doing here?"

Kevin slipped through the opening and put his hands on her shoulders. "I'm working, Cait. What are you doing here?" Gently but firmly he moved her back a pace and turned her around.

"Shopping at the drug store!" She grinned at him over her shoulder. "Nanna brought us, and we're going to get

Mickey Dee for lunch."

"Sounds good." Kevin moved her a few steps down the corridor. "Where is Nanna, anyway?"

At that moment the door of the women's washroom opened and Barb emerged with Brendan in tow. "There you are, Caitlyn!" she exclaimed, her voice stressed. "I thought I asked you to wait for us!"

"I was bored. Look! Kevin's here!"

Barb noticed him for the first time. "Oh my god, she almost gave me a heart attack."

"There's police!" Caitlyn informed her, pointing to the cop behind them, who was watching with amusement. "And outside, too. That's why Kevin's here."

"What's going on? Is something wrong?"

"Just something found in the garbage we need to take with us for one of our cases," Kevin said, moving Caitlyn forward. "This little lady doesn't need to see it, though."

"I'm so sorry," Barb said.

"I want to see!" Brendan announced, trying to shed his grandmother's hand.

"Nanna's going to take you to McDonald's for lunch now," Kevin said.

"Come on, Caitlyn." Barb grabbed her hand. "I'm really sorry, Kevin. She was right there behind me."

"I couldn't see anyway," Caitlyn said. "The policeman was in the way."

"Just boring stuff," Kevin assured her. "Go with Nanna now and I'll tell you about it when I get home. Deal?"

"Deal."

"I'm really sorry," Barb repeated.

"No harm done. I'll probably be late tonight again. See you then." He watched them hurry up the corridor and disappear into the mall.

He was still adjusting to the concept that they were going to be his children as well as Janie's. Right after their marriage last October, Kevin had discussed with Janie the possibility of adopting them. She'd been pleased with the idea, so he'd gone ahead with the application.

In Ontario, children seven years of age and older must give written consent to the adoption, and because Brendan was still only six at the time, Caitlyn's consent was the only one required in writing. She'd presented the court with a document so sweet and touching it had brought tears to Kevin's eyes. There was absolutely no doubt in his mind that she would be the perfect daughter for him.

Unfortunately, the law also required that both birth parents also provide written consent to the adoption, and Janie's ex-husband had refused. Although Doug Warrick was currently serving a prison term in British Columbia for armed robbery and had no desire to see his children ever again, he'd balked at the idea of another man taking his offspring away from him.

As a result, Kevin was now required, through his lawyer, to convince the court that it was in the best interest of the children to dispense with their birth father's consent and proceed with an order of adoption.

It was a process that took time. It was necessary for Kevin to demonstrate that he would provide the children with the security and stability of a family unit, the benefit of inheritance laws which, given Kevin's prospects for a good pension and his predilection for life insurance, would result in a decent legacy should something fatal happen to him, and that he would be a positive role model for them. Although Warrick was a certified bag of dog shit, the court was nonetheless compelled to weigh Kevin's positive points against the disadvantages of severing the legal connection between the children and their natural father.

Allowing them to witness an active crime scene, Kevin realized in sudden frustration, would definitely not work in his favour.

On his way back outside, he looked at the cop and raised his index finger to his lips. "Shh."

The cop gave him a wink as he held the door open for him.

chapter THIRTY-ONE

On his way out of town to execute a search warrant at the Hill Island cottage property belonging to Peter Lambton, Dennis Leung made a quick detour to an abandoned gas station on County Road 29 just before the Brockville city limits. Pulling into the lot, he found an unmarked black Crown Vic waiting for him behind the pumps.

He pulled up on the driver's side and lowered his window. "How's it going, Beth?"

OPP Detective Constable Beth Sanderson nodded. "Good. What's happening?"

"Not much." Leung passed over a USB drive, which Sanderson slipped into the pocket of her leather jacket. "I hope you can use it. That's three hours out of my life that I'll never get back."

She laughed. "Wuss. I'll take a look."

The USB drive contained the photographs and video sequences Leung had gathered last night during his surveillance of Paul Whiteman, along with a typed copy of his notes. Sanderson, a member of the Drug Enforcement Unit, would be able to use the information as a starting point for her own evidence collection against Whiteman, Howie Burnside, and the bikers with whom they apparently did business on an ongoing basis.

"I'll keep you posted." Sanderson raised her window and rolled out of the lot onto the highway.

Satisfied, Leung pulled out in the opposite direction and turned his thoughts to Peter Lambton and the landscaping of his rather valuable Thousand Islands cottage property.

chapter THIRTY-TWO

The St. Lawrence River looked spectacular from where Leung stood, on top of the seawall at the edge of Peter Lambton's cottage. Located on the eastern tip of Hill Island, on the south shore across from Wellesley Island on the American side, the well-treed lot was an acre in size, and the waterfront portion of the property ran for two hundred feet.

A stone staircase descended to a boathouse next to which a forty-two-foot cabin cruiser was tethered to a long dock. The water was reasonably calm this afternoon, and Leung watched the boat gently move up and down and back and forth in a corkscrewing motion that was almost hypnotic.

"I left a voice message again," Joseph Paoli said, coming up behind him.

Leung turned, almost reluctantly. "You have no idea where he is?"

Peter Lambton's attorney shook his head. "His cellphone's either off or the battery's dead. It goes right to voicemail. There's no answer at his home or office numbers."

Search warrants were being executed this morning in an attempt to cover all their bases in an investigation which, to Leung's mind, was likely going to produce no criminal charges against either Peter Lambton or his nephew.

Howie Burnside's home and the Grass Wizards business location were also being searched right now. Leung had heard that Paul Whiteman and another biker friend had attempted to prevent entry by chaining the big gate across the Grass Wizards entrance. When officers removed the chain with bolt cutters and moved inside, Paul's friend had pulled a handgun and waved it around. They were both in custody and the search was ongoing.

Leung had smiled grimly at this last little piece of news. While Howie Burnside and Peter Lambton might squeak through without being charged, Paul Whiteman's adventures with the judicial system were just beginning to ramp up. There would be much, much more to follow.

Couldn't happen to a better guy.

Leung gave the river a last, wistful glance and preceded Paoli up the stone pathway toward the cottage. "As I said, the warrant includes the interior. I'll need you to open it up now."

Paoli produced a set of keys from his pocket and sorted through them as they mounted the steps of the long, enclosed verandah that ran the length of the cottage. A uniformed constable held the screen door open for them, but Leung stopped and touched Paoli on the arm. "If you don't mind?"

Paoli nodded and gave the keys to Leung.

The scenes-of-crime officer who had been photographing the grounds joined them on the steps.

"Not much to see at this time of year," she said, removing the lens on her camera and digging in her bag for a replacement. "In terms of the landscaping, I mean."

Leung nodded. Someone had started on the spring cleanup, but there was still a great deal to do. Only a portion of the lawns surrounding the cottage had been raked so far, and much of the debris that had been trapped under the snow all winter still lay on the grass, which was beginning to show some green amidst the brown. The lawns also needed to be rolled, as moles had busily tunnelled beneath the surface during the winter, creating bumpy little eskers that ran all over the place.

A few of the gardens had been cleared of their winter mulch, and while some bulbs had already produced flowers—Leung thought they were crocuses and hyacinths, but he wasn't an expert on the subject—others were showing green shoots that promised a spectacular display of daffodils and tulips in the weeks to come. Some of the shoots had dead leaves impaled on their tips, having penetrated right through them as they forced themselves upward toward the sun.

"Still two weeks before last frost," the SOCO added, zipping up her camera bag.

The invoice from Grass Wizards provided by Lambton had itemized the type and number of shrubs and perennials planted as well as the quantities of bagged mulch, interlocking paving stones, and other materials used in the job. Leung and the SOCO had toured the grounds and photographed what they thought represented the work, three years after the fact, but to Leung's mind it was a relatively useless exercise. There was little doubt the work had actually been done; the issue was whether or not Lambton had paid for it.

Leung crossed to the inner door and fumbled with the keys, trying several before finding the correct one. He unlocked the door and swung it open.

"Hello? Anyone here? OPP, Detective Constable Leung. Anyone home?"

Silence, punctuated by the ticking of a grandfather clock in the entry.

Leung looked over his shoulder. A second uniformed constable had joined his partner on the verandah steps. Leung directed the man holding the screen door to remain outside while his partner would accompany the detective and the SOCO inside.

His first concern was to ensure that there was no one in the cottage. He paused in the entry. Other than the clock, he could hear no sounds of anyone present. No voices, no footsteps, no floorboards creaking, no music playing, no television audio, no doors opening or closing.

His nostrils dilated, picking up the odour of cleaning liquids and aerosol spray. Air freshener, floor polish, and ... bleach?

He turned around. Joseph Paoli stood behind him, eyes down as he composed a text message on his cellphone, presumably to his client. "Mr. Paoli, please step back out onto the porch and remain with the constable until I ask you to come in."

Grunting, Paoli retreated, still working on his text message.

Leung walked through the entry. On the left was a sitting room, on the right a large dining room, and straight ahead a staircase leading up to the second floor. He caught the uniformed officer's eye and gestured to the left, then signalled the SOCO to take the dining room on the right.

Slipping his hand under his jacket until his palm touched the butt of his holstered sidearm, Leung slowly made his way upstairs.

The carpet beneath his boots looked new. It occurred to him he'd forgotten to wipe his feet on the mat inside the door before treading all over the place, but that was the way it went. He took a second look; the carpeting *was* new. He was sure of it. It smelled new.

As his eyes reached the level of the upper landing, he stopped for a brief survey. There was a bedroom door at the top of the stairs on the left. It was closed. Straight ahead from the top of the stairs was an open door leading into the bathroom. The hallway ran around to the right, where Leung saw a closed door halfway down and another one, as he twisted for a look, at the end of the hall. Three bedrooms altogether.

No sounds. No movement. But a strong odour of cleaning products and ... paint.

He reached the top of the stairs and approached the door on the left. He took out a pair of latex gloves from his jacket pocket, pulled them on, and knocked on the door.

"Hello, police. Anyone here?"

Silence.

He opened the door and looked in at what appeared to be a guest room. It was furnished with a double-sized antique bed, a tall wardrobe and chest of drawers, a bedding box, and other assorted pieces of bedroom furniture that probably would have cost Leung four months' salary if he tried to buy them in an antique store. The air in the room was still and stale, as though the door hadn't been opened in some time.

He went into the bathroom. The smell of cleaning products was extremely strong in here. The sink and tub were sparkling clean, as was the ceramic tile on the floor. Nothing seemed out of place—soap dispensers, folded towels and facecloths, the usual bathroom accoutrements one would expect to see.

The tub had a shower head, but there was no shower curtain on the rod.

The first door down the hall to the right was another guest room. Like the first, it also gave the impression of not having been entered in a while.

The door at the end opened into the master bedroom, and here Leung was confronted by a different prospect altogether.

The room was lighted by four large windows facing the river. The curtains were tied back, allowing the sunlight to flood in. The bed was another antique four-poster, but the mattress and box spring were new, still in their plastic sheaths. There was no bedding and no pillows.

The rest of the furniture in the room all seemed to be slightly out of position, as though every piece had been moved recently and not put back into its proper spot afterward. The walls were freshly painted in royal blue. The pine flooring looked new. The boards had been recently waxed and polished to a high shine.

Leung went back to the nearest guest room and looked again at the floor. It was also made of wide pine planks, but the finish on them couldn't hide the age of the boards that showed in subtle grooves, dents, and marks.

He went back into the master bedroom.

Definitely new flooring.

He went back downstairs where the SOCO and constable were waiting for him.

"We're clear," the SOCO told him. "Shall we get started?"

"In a minute. Where's the kitchen?"

"This way." She led him through the dining room into the kitchen. It was large and equipped with expensive appliances, including the largest refrigerator Leung had ever seen in a private home. He walked across the room to an island that was set up for food preparation.

Prominently displayed on the island was a set of Pott Sarah Wiener kitchen knives in a tall walnut block. It was a type of knife block that opened like a book into three sections. The middle section had been removed for use as a cutting board. There were seven knifes held by magnetic strips in the interior of the block, ranging in size from a small paring knife to a nine-inch bread knife.

Leung stared at an empty space between the bread knife and the six-inch chef's knife. It was a space that would have held another long knife, perhaps an eight-inch chef's knife. His eyes swept the island. The knife wasn't lying loose where someone might have carelessly set it down. He wandered around the kitchen.

It wasn't in the sink. It wasn't in the dishwasher. It

wasn't in the silverware drawer.

Stop, Leung told himself. Stop. Stop. Right now. Stop.

"Out," he said to the SOCO. "Turn around, right now. Go outside."

She frowned at him. "What? I don't understand."

"Out, out, out." He shooed her back through the dining room to the front entry, where the uniform was still waiting for them. "Outside," he said, "right now. Everyone out."

"I don't understand," the SOCO repeated. "What the hell's going on?"

"Right place," Leung said, herding them out onto the verandah, "wrong warrant."

Paoli looked up. "What's going on? What's wrong?"

"Please go back to your car, Mr. Paoli, and stay there until further notice."

"What? What are you talking about?"

Leung puffed out his cheeks as the adrenaline surged through him. "I have to make a call. We just walked into a whole new ball game."

chapter
THIRTY-THREE

The only place to get coffee on the Canadian side of Hill Island was a little café between the NEXUS enrollment centre and the duty free shop. This late on a Saturday night in April it was closed, but Kevin knew the owner, a retired Peel Regional Police staff sergeant named Chadd who lived with his wife Serena and a Doberman Pinscher upstairs. He knocked on the side door, and when Chadd came downstairs and saw who it was, he unlocked the café and let them in.

Ellie had run out of nicotine gum and was dying for a smoke, but when she saw that the café specialized in ice cream cones, she had a better idea. While Chadd put on pots of coffee to accommodate Kevin's take-out order for the crew processing Lambton's cottage, Serena waited patiently as Ellie debated the wide range of flavour choices. Finally she settled on Watermelon Wonder, three scoops, no sprinkles.

They sat at a table to wait for the coffee. Forever a cop,

Chadd asked a few questions about what was going on. When it quickly became obvious they weren't going to tell him anything, he nodded and slipped into the back room to give them their space.

"The tourists love this place in summer," Kevin said, handing Ellie a wad of napkins. "Chadd made a hell of a retirement investment."

"Mmm." The ice cream was giving her a headache, but it was damned good. She wiped her lips and dabbed at the drips on the bottom of her fist. The smell of brewing coffee filled the place.

Now that they had found the primary crime scene where Andie Matheson had been stabbed to death, Kevin felt they were a lot closer to being able to charge Peter Lambton with her murder without needing a confession from him.

Dave Martin had already collected blood evidence from the hardwood floor in the front entry and from the underside of the banister leading upstairs, places missed by the killer during his cleanup. He'd also found the victim's fingerprints almost everywhere downstairs, further proving she'd been present in the cottage while still alive. In the refrigerator he found a plastic clamshell container of half-consumed chicken caesar salad from which he'd also lifted her prints.

According to the label on the container, the salad had been packaged on Tuesday, April 18, with a best-before date of Friday, April 21. Kevin remembered that the remains of a chicken salad had been found in the victim's stomach by Dr. Burton during the post-mortem. There seemed to be little doubt that Andie Matheson had eaten part of this particular salad about an hour before her murder.

Watching Ellie work on her ice cream cone, Kevin said, "I'm starting to worry about Kathryn Lambton. I don't have a good feeling about it."

Ellie nodded. To her, it was a toss-up at this point as to whether Kathryn had run away from her husband in fear of her own life or had run away because she'd killed Andie Matheson herself and hoped to get away with it. Lambton was their primary suspect at the moment, but Ellie wasn't about to rule out the jealous wife theory just yet.

There was a knocking at the front door, which Chadd had locked again after letting them in. Someone put their face to the glass, cupping their eyes to stare inside.

Kevin stood up. "It's Dennis."

"I better finish this," Ellie said.

Kevin wound his way through the tables and unlocked the door as Serena came out from the back to check on the knocking.

"One of ours," Ellie said, swallowing the last of her cone.

Serena waved and disappeared again.

Ellie wiped her fingers as Leung sat down. "How's it going?"

"Still underway." Leung was overseeing the area canvass of properties along the road on which the cottage was located. Most of them were still closed up, but a few were four-season homes with residents who might have witnessed something of importance last Wednesday night or Thursday morning, or might have been aware of the impromptu renovation work that had occurred shortly thereafter.

"Nothing yet?" Kevin asked.

Leung shook his head. "Something weird, though. Something to keep among the three of us for now."

"What have you got?" Ellie asked.

"The place next door to Lambton's cottage, on this side. Really nice property. No one home."

Ellie waited. She'd driven by the cottage he was referring to without having given it more than a cursory look.

"The name on the mailbox kind of threw me. I thought, No. Can't be. But it bugged me, so I decided to chase down the ownership on it."

"And?"

"You'll never guess whose place it is."

"Haven't a clue," Kevin said.

"Todd Fisher," Leung said. "Inspector Todd Fisher, if you can believe that."

chapter THIRTY-FOUR

When Todd Fisher answered his front door, he was wearing pyjamas and a housecoat. He'd taken the time to comb his hair and wash his face after Ellie had called ahead, but it was obvious he intended to go right back to bed just as soon as she got through with whatever it was she wanted from him.

As a career cop, Fisher had long since grown used to calls in the middle of the night. He was the type of person who could get back to sleep without much effort, so being awakened on police business didn't particularly bother him.

It didn't mean he had to like it, though.

"What is it, March?" He reluctantly held the door open for her.

"We need to talk."

Fisher's house was a sprawling bungalow on an acre lot in a very nice neighbourhood in Smiths Falls. The ceilings were ten feet high, the walls were painted in soothing pastel colours, and the ceramic flooring included a hydronic radiant heating system, which explained Fisher's bare feet. He led her into the living room, where he'd already turned on matching table lamps at either end of a monstrous sofa. He motioned her to an armchair and sat down on the sofa, moving a pillow out of his way.

"Doris is asleep. Her door's closed. What's so important it can't wait until tomorrow?"

"As you know, we've issued an arrest warrant for Peter Lambton." Ellie shunted out onto the edge of the chair cushion. "Do you have any idea where he might be?"

"No, of course not. Why on earth would I?"

"We're also looking for his wife, Kathryn. Do you know where she is?"

Fisher stared at her for a moment before rubbing his forehead, eyes closed. "I'm very tired, March. Please get to the point."

Ellie studied him for a moment. Normally she'd afford a colleague the courtesy of not disturbing him late at night for something that could possibly wait until the next morning, but her exasperation with Todd Fisher had reached its limit. At the same time, she actually *did* consider it a courtesy to give Fisher the rest of the night to prepare for what would take place tomorrow morning at regional headquarters.

"How well do you know Peter Lambton?"

Fisher opened his eyes. "What? I know him. What about it?"

"Imagine how unpleasantly surprised I was," Ellie said, "to learn that the cottage on Hill Island next door to Peter Lambton's, which is now our primary crime scene in the Andrea Matheson homicide investigation, belongs to you."

"Yes? So?"

"Todd," she said, her voice betraying exasperation with his stubborn obtuseness, "you're on the spot. You need to tell me, straight up, whether Lambton's nephew's company has done any work for you, either here or at your cottage."

"Well, yes. As a matter of fact, they have."

Ellie sighed, looking at a fireplace beyond the far end of the couch on which Fisher sat. Embers glowed beneath a layer of ash. Their warmth was too faint to reach her. "Tomorrow morning you're going to sit down with Leanne and make a full disclosure. You're going to bring invoices, proof of payment, whatever you have for this work, and you're going to walk her completely through it."

"I don't understand, March."

"Jesus!" She thumped the arm of her chair. "Wake up, Todd! On more than one occasion you've declared, in front of witnesses, that you believe the breach of trust investigation of Peter Lambton is a witch hunt. You've gone out of your way to defend him."

Her eyes widened. "Christ, don't tell me you've put it in writing."

Fisher said nothing, his eyes lowering.

"E-mail to Leanne?" Ellie guessed. "Surely not a memo."

"E-mail."

"Ah, shit, Todd."

It had gone from a basic corruption complaint to a homicide investigation, the victim had been stabbed to death in a cottage next door to Fisher's, and here he was with personal ties to the subject and his sketchy nephew. And on top of that, he'd sent an e-mail to his supervisor, the regional commander. "In which you—no, don't tell me, let me guess—insist the investigation against Peter Lambton should be dropped."

"I can see where it might look bad." Fisher pinched the bridge of his nose. "When Patterson called about the new warrants, I knew I'd made a mistake. Surely..."

"Tomorrow morning," Ellie repeated, "you're going to meet with Leanne and put everything on the table. Everything."

Fisher nodded.

Watching him, Ellie suspected he'd nursed a faint hope that nothing would come of his connection to Peter Lambton and Howie Burnside, but now that the proverbial shit had hit the fan he would have to defend himself from a potentially career-damaging situation. Departmental policy required that any real, potential, or perceived conflict of interest be immediately reported by a member to their supervisor. In Fisher's case, that was Chief Superintendent Leanne Blair, the regional commander.

The code of conduct went to great lengths to define conflict of interest and to set out the process for reporting and responding to situations of potential conflict. In Fisher's situation, if he'd been dimwitted enough to have accepted work done on his property or properties by Grass Wizards for less than the normal cost or, heaven forbid, at no cost at all, his subsequent insistence that the investigation against Lambton be dropped would be perceived as evidence that he'd accepted an unfair benefit in exchange for influence. His career would very quickly go off the rails.

In Ellie's case, her knowledge and awareness of Fisher's poor judgment required her to report it to *her* immediate supervisor. By giving Fisher a chance to start the process himself right away, however, she was hoping her own report would be nothing more than an administrative addition to the file, after the fact.

"I suppose Leanne won't be able to keep the PSB out of it," he said.

"You know she won't, Todd. Can't, and won't."

Notification of the Professional Standards Bureau was mandatory in a situation like this one. The PSB would review and evaluate the complaint to determine if it needed to be assigned to an investigator. Ellie hated to think where it might go from there.

"Look," she said, standing up, "it's none of my business, and you don't have to answer because I'm only asking on a personal level, but did you pay for the work Burnside's company did?"

Fisher nodded, slowly getting to his feet.

"Full price? No discounts for a pal, no free labour, no corners cut?"

"No. No corners cut. I paid the going rate, full price, and the work was good."

"Glad to hear it."

At the front door, she turned around. "I take it you have someone competent for legal representation."

"Don't worry about it, Ellie." He held the door open for her. "I know a few people."

"Fine." On the porch, she turned around before he could close the door. "One more thing."

"Yes?"

"You didn't answer one question I asked you earlier. Do you have any idea where we can find Kathryn Lambton?"

"I haven't a clue, Ellie. Sorry."

Nodding, she hurried down the steps to her car.

chapter THIRTY-FIVE

Ellie was dozing on the back seat of the Crown Vic, wrapped in a duty jacket she kept in the trunk, when someone knocked on the window. She sat up, blinking, and saw Kevin peering in at her. She nodded, pushing the jacket aside.

He opened the driver's side door.

"He's here."

"I'll be right in." She ran a hand through her hair to remove some of the sleep kinks as Kevin closed the door and disappeared back inside. Yawning, she glanced at her watch. The phosphorescent hands told her it was nearly ten minutes past four in the morning. She'd gotten about two hours. It would have to do.

She went inside the detachment office and stopped first in the washroom before heading down the hall to the interview room.

Five hours ago, a witness on Hill Island had described watching vehicles come and go at the Lambton cottage on

Thursday afternoon while drifting in her kayak a few dozen metres from shore. She'd recognized Lambton, of course, since he was a neighbour on the island and frequently in the news. She'd also seen a large truck with the Grass Wizards logo on the side, a similarly-marked van, and several men who seemed to be following Lambton's instructions like a harried, out-of-breath work crew.

When shown a series of photographs, she identified Howie Burnside as one of the men. The others, who'd carried rolls of carpeting, cans of paint, and lengths of flooring in and out of the cottage, were not recognizable to her from any of the other photographs.

Apparently she'd lingered for some time, occasionally paddling against the current to stay in visual range. She watched the show with a pair of opera glasses hung around her neck that she said she always took out onto the water with her.

"In case something interesting happens," she explained.

It took a few hours to process an arrest warrant for Howie Burnside, but as soon as the paperwork was in their hands they dragged him out of bed and into the back seat of a cruiser for the brisk ride to the detachment office. Kevin looked up now and smiled as Ellie stepped into the observation room.

"He's asleep."

Ellie stared at the monitor for a moment before dropping into a chair that Carty had politely left unoccupied for her. "Has he talked to a lawyer?"

Kevin glanced at the monitor. Howie sat with his legs extended and crossed at the ankles, his arms folded, and his head down. A faint snoring sound was coming through the audio feed. "Yes. Joseph Paoli, as it turns out."

Ellie accepted a cup of coffee from Carty. It tasted good; black with a teaspoon of honey, not sugar. She nodded her thanks, but Carty's attention was on the monitor. "Has he made any statements yet?"

"No," Carty replied.

"All right, let's wake him up and see what he gives us."

Howie stirred as Kevin walked into the interview room and sat down. He pulled his feet in and covered a yawn, opening his eyes to give Kevin a quick once-over.

Kevin opened his file folder and clicked his pen, pretending to read as he gathered his first impressions.

He'd never seen Howie before in person, and the man wasn't at all what he'd expected. Leung had summarized Howie's business dealings and suspected drug-related activities, emphasizing the obvious connections to a local chapter of an outlaw motorcycle gang, and Kevin had formed an impression in his mind of a stereotypic biker, a hardcase with tattoos and an attitude.

In reality, Howie was much different. He was small, about five ten and one hundred and sixty pounds. His sandy brown hair was straight and carefully barbered. He was clean-shaven, neat, and tidy. His black frame glasses perched halfway down his nose, giving him an almost nerdish look. His high forehead and thin lips gave him the appearance of someone Kevin would expect to see on television providing analysis on the politics of environmental change or some similarly esoteric subject.

As Kevin walked him through the preliminaries, Howie listened carefully and provided polite answers at the proper times. Yes, he understood the reason for his arrest. Yes, he'd spoken to his lawyer and no, he didn't feel a need to speak to him again at the moment. Yes, he understood he didn't need to say anything and that anything he did say might be used as evidence against him. No, he didn't want water or coffee. Yes, he understood they were being videotaped and audio-recorded.

Kevin then asked a series of basic questions establishing Howie's spot in the food chain. Yes, he was Peter Lambton's nephew. His mother, Alice, was three years younger than Lambton. She was bipolar and had taken medication for her condition for as long as Howie could remember. No, the affliction apparently hadn't been passed down to him. Yes, his father, Robert Burnside, had been his mother's psychiatrist when they married. Yes, Robert had been in trouble off and on since Howie was a kid, but Howie had made it a personal policy to stay out of his father's business, legitimate or otherwise.

There was only one sibling, his younger sister Erica. Yes, Erica was a bit of a hellion. Yes, she'd been married for a couple of years to a guy who worked at city hall by the name of Warren Whitlock. Regrettably, Whitlock was a doofus that nobody in the family could stand, and Erica had walked out on him. Yes, she should probably seek professional help because Howie believed she'd inherited their mother's condition.

"Tell me about your business," Kevin suggested.

"Grass Wizards?" Howie smiled. "Catchy name, huh? Some people think it suggests a bunch of stoned-out gamers tooling around on riding lawnmowers, but guess what? There's a whole generation of stoned-out gamers who got old and bought houses and started businesses with factories and shops or whatever that need landscaping maintenance, and those dudes dig the name a lot more than 'Howie's Property Maintenance' or 'Four Seasons Landscaping' or some stupid, hackneyed thing. Know what I mean?"

"Okay." Kevin turned over a piece of paper in the file folder. "Does your Uncle Peter help you out with your business? Use his position as mayor to get you an edge?"

"I'd rather not talk about that, if you don't mind."

"What about house renovations? Ever do much of that?"

"From time to time, I guess. We're not really into that, though. We do exterior work. That's our area of expertise."

"What about for your uncle? Ever do any interior work for him? Say, at his cottage on Hill Island? You did landscaping for him, I know that, but have you ever done any interior renovations for him there?"

Howie opened his mouth to say something and then closed it again. His eyes studied Kevin for a moment and seemed to sense where the questions were going. "Yeah."

"When was that, Howie?"

"Recently."

"How recently?"

"I guess it was last Thursday."

"What did the work involve, Howie?"

"Oh, painting. Some flooring and carpeting. That kind of thing." Still watching Kevin closely, he added, "He wants to get the place ready for the summer. Big plans on the social front, apparently."

"I see. Did he pay you for the work?"

Howie grinned apologetically. "Yeah, cash. But don't tell the CRA, okay? They won't like it."

"Just you, or was your crew with you?"

Howie compressed his lips and looked at his hands.

Kevin waited until it was obvious an answer wasn't forthcoming. "That's okay. We know the current locations of Paul Whiteman and Peter Goodwin, since they were arrested for extremely bad behaviour yesterday afternoon, so we'll ask them about it. We've also picked up Robert Nolan," Kevin glanced at the file, "uh, Ronald Chumley, and Daniel Quinn. I believe they're all on your payroll as well, right? We'll ask them if they helped you fix up Uncle Peter's cottage. But even better, our witnesses will be able to identify everyone they saw there that afternoon." Kevin smiled. "So don't worry, we'll get it all straightened out. Let me ask you something else."

Howie removed his glasses, polished the lenses on the shirt tail that was sticking out from under his navy sleeveless sweater, and put them on again.

"What did you do with the old stuff you removed during your renovation at the cottage?"

"I beg your pardon?"

"Come on, Howie. You put in new flooring and carpeting.

What happened to the old flooring and carpeting?"

"Got taken to the dump."

"Which one?"

"The closest one, of course."

"You took it there yourself, personally?"

Howie said nothing.

"One of your guys made the run for you, is that it?"

Howie adjusted his glasses so that they sat higher on the bridge of his nose.

"That's okay," Kevin said, "I understand. We'll find it. There's a dump just the far side of Lansdowne, out King Street, but you guys probably went to the other one, above Rockport, because it would have been more or less on the way home. We'll check them both." When Howie didn't react, he added, "I imagine the stink must have been pretty bad. I wouldn't want to be driving around with all that mess in the van. Enough to turn your stomach."

Howie looked at his hands.

"We'll talk to whoever was working at the landfill site when you guys came through and find out who was with you in the vehicle. They'll tell us. Although it'd be better if you told us yourself, right now." He paused. "Did you pay cash for the load?"

Howie glanced at the camera in the corner of the ceiling, looked at his knuckles, opened his mouth wide to stretch his jaw muscles, and poked his glasses back up on his nose. "Obviously."

"You paid cash when you dumped the carpeting and flooring and the rest of it at the dump?"

"Yes."

"Which dump?"

"Escott-Rockport Road."

"You were there?"

"I handle the cash."

"Were there blood stains on the material you tore up and hauled away?"

Howie sighed.

Kevin waited.

"Blood, shit, you name it."

Kevin said nothing.

"Danny—one of the guys—fucking hurled, so there was that. It was a damned mess; you were right."

"Whose blood was it?"

"I have no idea. None whatsoever."

Now that Howie had decided to talk, Kevin began to press for details. "How did you get the job? Did Peter Lambton call you down?"

"Yes."

"What time was that?"

"I don't know. Around noon."

"What did he say in this phone call?"

"That there'd been a bad accident at the cottage, upstairs in the master bedroom, and he needed a quick reno job. I said, 'Can't it wait?' and he said, 'No. Get your ass down here right now, and bring your crew. I want it done this afternoon, all of it, and I'll pay three times what the job's worth.' So we drove down and took a look. After Danny got done tossing his cookies, we went and bought the materials and got busy."

"Where'd you buy them?"

"The Building Centre in Lansdowne."

"Do you know where Peter Lambton is right now, Howie?"

He hesitated. "A buddy of his, they were both with customs back in the day, he has a camp on Loughborough Lake. They get together from time to time. Did you check down there?"

"Thanks for the tip."

"No problem."

Kevin sat back. He'd been jotting a few notes in the file folder as Howie spoke, but now he put down the pen and leaned on his elbow. "You need to think very carefully, Howie, about how you're going to answer the next few questions. These are important questions, and how you answer them will have a big bearing on what happens to you in the future."

Howie said nothing.

"You were informed when you were taken into custody that you were being arrested under section 240 of the *Criminal Code* for being an accessory after the fact to the murder of Andrea Matheson. Were you aware that this was Andrea Matheson's blood you were cleaning up for your uncle?"

Howie pursed his lips.

Kevin waited. When it was obvious that the question wasn't going to be answered, he said, "Did you know Andrea Matheson?"

Howie hesitated, shrugged, and said, "Yeah. I knew her."

"You'd met her before? Talked to her?"

"Yeah."

"Were you there Thursday morning when she was killed?"

"No. Definitely not."

"You seem to be your uncle's janitor, Howie. Did you take her body out on the Parkway and dump it in the ditch for the dogs to find?"

"No! Jesus Christ! Absolutely not."

"You're sure of that? Even if I told you we had tire track prints that put you there?"

"No fucking way, man. I wasn't there. None of my trucks were there. I had nothing to do with it. None of my guys had anything to do with it."

"What about your uncle? Did he kill Andie and dump her on the Parkway?"

"No. I don't know. No. He had a thing for her. She was special to him."

"Did he tell you he'd killed Andie that morning?"

"No. No way."

"Did you know it was Andie's blood you were cleaning up?"

"Yeah yeah yeah, I figured it out. I'm not stupid. What the hell else could it have been? What else would have left that kind of an awful fucking mess?"

"Do you think Peter Lambton killed her?"

"No, I don't! He couldn't have."

"Why not?"

"Like I said, he had a thing for her. He was different around her. He was ... gentle. Kind. His usual sarcasm and condescension just seemed to disappear. I don't know how to explain it."

"What about your Aunt Kathryn? Could she have killed Andie Matheson?"

Howie stared at him. Apparently the thought had occurred to him before, but he wasn't ready to put his speculation into words.

"Is she the kind of person, Howie, who would kill someone? A younger woman screwing her husband?"

"I can't see it." Howie averted his eyes. "I just don't see it happening that way."

"Did you kill her, Howie?"

"Shit!"

Kevin waited.

"No! Christ, no. Of course not."

"But you knew her. Did you have sex with her at any time?"

"No, man. Not a chance. She was Uncle Pete's girl. Strictly hands off."

"Yeah, but there were a couple of years where they had broken up. That gave you an opportunity to check her out, right?"

"Wrong. No way. She was still his girl. End of story."

"You mean they continued their relationship?"

"I don't know. That's not what I meant. I heard she went with other guys before they got back together. But he always had a thing for her, and no way was I going to get in the middle of that."

"Your Aunt Kathryn knew about all this?"

Howie shrugged. "I guess so. She knew the first time, sure. I don't know if she knew about them hooking up again."

"Do you know where Kathryn Lambton is right now, Howie?"

He shook his head. "Haven't seen her for a while."

"Any idea where she might have gone?"

"No. We're not that close. She doesn't particularly like me, so I keep my distance. You know how it is."

"Does that piss you off, that she doesn't like you?"

Howie flashed an ironic smile. "Nah. It goes with the territory."

"What territory is that?"

"I think I've run out of answers for you. Sorry."

"No problem." Kevin stood up. "Some other folks will be coming in with questions for you, Howie, on a few other topics of interest. See how you make out answering them."

chapter
THIRTY-SIX

Six hours later, Ellie spotted Cecil Dart sitting on a bench outside one of the indoor skating rinks at the Nepean Sportsplex in Ottawa. The hallway was filled with people, mostly parents and grandparents, milling about as though waiting for something to start, eyes down on their smartphones, seemingly unaware of their surroundings.

Dart's cellphone was pressed to his ear, and he was listening intently to whatever the person at the other end was saying to him. When he caught sight of Ellie he nodded and held up an index finger.

She changed course and wandered over to an observation window. The ice surface down below was deserted except for a Zamboni machine. She watched it circle around the rink a few times, converting scratched and scuffed ice into a smooth, glistening surface. When she glanced back at Dart, he was poking at his phone, presumably to end the call, so she strolled over in his direction.

"Did you find a place to park?" he asked, putting his

phone away.

"It was a challenge. Some guy over in the back lot was pulling out, so I got lucky."

"It's a madhouse. We've never been here before. She usually competes somewhere in the GTA. How's your case?" He patted the bench beside him.

"Good." Ellie sat down on the edge of the bench and clasped her hands tightly between her knees. "We finally picked up our primary suspect, at a camp on Loughborough Lake. He's being transported now."

"Christ." Dart rubbed his bulbous nose, watching her with small, dark eyes. "The mayor of Brockville. You've got nerve, Ellie."

"He's looking good for it at the moment. We'll see what he has to say this afternoon. How's Alice doing?"

"Not bad. She skated well enough in the preliminaries to advance. She's nervous, but she's good. I'm biased, of course."

"How old is she now?"

"Nine." Dart shook his head at a middle-aged woman who was walking toward them.

Ellie looked up. It was Eugenia Dart, the deputy commissioner's wife. Alice was their granddaughter, the oldest child of their son, Craig, who'd divorced his wife Norma and accepted a transfer to the Sudbury detachment. Norma and the children had moved to Orillia at Cecil's and Gene's invitation, so that they could help in the raising of their grandchildren.

Not that Ellie was comfortable knowing all this stuff about the Dart family. There was a certain inevitability to it, though, that she'd given up trying to avoid.

Ellie gave Gene a small wave. Gene waved back, winked at her husband, and headed for the door into the rink.

"This thing with Fisher," Dart said. A chime sounded. He glanced at his cellphone, thumbed the power button on the side to send it into sleep mode, and dropped it into his shirt pocket. "The way you handled it was fine."

"Thank you, sir. I don't feel very good about it. On several levels."

"I'll bet you don't." Dart watched the crowd around them. "Leanne feels worse, believe me."

Ellie said nothing. The matter of Todd Fisher's behaviour was no longer her immediate concern and wasn't something she felt comfortable talking about. On the other hand, since the Professional Standards Bureau which would conduct the investigation fell under Dart's command, it had moved from the regional stovepipe into his, and as a result Dart had a very serious interest in its outcome.

"Have you talked to Tony recently?"

Ellie blinked at the abrupt change of subject. "This morning, briefly."

She'd called her supervisor, Tony Agosta, to bring him up to speed on the Peter Lambton situation. It had been a somewhat tight-lipped conversation on both sides, given the potential public relations nightmare involved in arresting the mayor of a city of just over twenty thousand people.

"Be careful," had been his final words on the subject. "Be very, very careful."

Dart studied her for a moment. "He hasn't been informed yet that a decision has been made, so I need you to keep this strictly under your hat. Do you know what I'm talking about?"

"No, sir. I don't."

"Tony applied last winter for an international assignment beginning in June. For some strange reason he has a burning desire to spend nine months in Africa."

"Oh." Ellie thought she remembered the poster that had gone out on it. Some United Nations mission to set up police training academies in the Sudan or one of those countries. She didn't have the background for it herself and wasn't interested in international postings, but she remembered that Tony had an extensive training background and had been excited about applying for it.

"He's going," Dart said, "but he won't find out until next week."

Ellie nodded, pleased. "He'll be thrilled."

"He'll need a replacement." Dart looked at her meaningfully.

Ellie said nothing.

"You have a little time to think about it. The news will probably break next Wednesday. Since I was going to be here this weekend, I decided to broach the subject with you now, in person, beforehand. Understand? I want to look you in the eye, right here on this bench, and tell you the job's yours if you want it."

"I appreciate that, sir." Ellie kept her face expressionless. Dart was offering her a very desirable temporary promotion ahead of the rest of her colleagues in the Criminal Investigation Branch, and the political significance of it was not lost on her. It would give her invaluable experience at the senior management level, and it would go a long way toward greasing the skids to an appointment at the rank of superintendent when a permanent opening became available.

She was still getting used to the fact that she no longer had to apply for jobs in a competitive process now that she was a commissioned officer. Senior management positions were staffed by appointment only.

A good résumé needed good politics behind it.

Ellie hated politics, but she kept her mouth shut.

"Of course," Dart went on after a moment, "you're going to have a similar conversation with Leanne very soon, am I right?"

"I don't—" Ellie stopped, suddenly understanding what he was saying. With Todd Fisher looking at a reassignment or paid leave while his situation remained under investigation, the Leeds County detachment would need a replacement commander. Since Ellie already held the appropriate rank, it would be fairly easy for Leanne

Blair to facilitate a lateral transfer should Ellie express an interest in the job.

It was a possibility that had never occurred to Ellie, and one that she viewed with spontaneous revulsion.

Back to the field?

Never.

Dart smiled, watching the expressions flicker across her face. "Call me by next Wednesday morning, will you, Ellie?"

She sighed. "Yes, sir."

chapter THIRTY-SEVEN

Ellie was still in the Sportsplex when a call came in from Kevin. She walked into an empty alcove and sat down on a bench before answering. "March."

"Lambton's here now," Kevin said. "He's being processed."

"Good." She glanced at her watch. "I'll be there in about an hour."

"He'll keep. We found the stuff from the cottage at the dump. Hardwood flooring, carpeting from the stairs. It's on the way to the lab."

"All right." Ellie felt around in her jacket pocket before remembering that she was still out of nicotine gum.

"It's getting interesting, Ellie. Merkley got the GPS data on Kathryn Lambton's cellphone."

Ellie straightened. "I'm listening."

"He tells me that she was at her home all night Wednesday night. She stayed in town all day Thursday, until late Thursday evening."

"I see." Ellie watched a small group of people move past the alcove. They were staring down at programmes, trying to figure out which rink they wanted. They didn't see her and were quickly gone. "She's probably in the clear on Matheson, then."

"Her cellphone is, anyway," Kevin joked. If Kathryn Lambton could show that she'd had her phone with her during this time period, when Andie was murdered, it would essentially clear her of suspicion.

"What about after that?"

"Here's where it gets weird," Kevin said. "Shortly after ten o'clock Thursday night the phone's picked up on a tower at Mallorytown and shortly after that the tower off Hill Island Road between the 401 and the Parkway. Then it's gone just before eleven thirty."

"Gone?"

"Contact lost. No other traces of it anywhere. Either the phone was turned off or it was destroyed."

"So her last known location is most likely the cottage."

"Yes. About sixteen hours after Andie Matheson was killed, and about six hours after it was given an emergency renovation by Howie Burnside and his crew, she was apparently there, at that cottage."

Ellie grimaced, scratching the top of her head. "Damn. Where is she, Kevin?"

"I definitely wish I could answer that question."

Ellie looked up as another group of people passed her alcove. They were trailed by a woman with her head down as she talked to someone on her cellphone. A shock of recognition passed through Ellie. As if by telepathy, the woman looked up at Ellie and quickly looked away again.

"All right," Ellie said quickly, "stay on it. I'll be there in an hour." She put the phone away and strode out of the alcove. The woman was a few metres ahead of her, walking briskly. Ellie caught up and touched her arm. "Suzie, hi."

The woman reluctantly stopped and turned around. "Oh, hi."

"What are you doing here?"

Suzie turned away. "I'll call you back." She ended her call and put the phone into her handbag. "I didn't expect to see you here."

"Me neither." Ellie looked around. "Is everyone here?"

"No. Just me and Meg." She looked around, by turns puzzled and annoyed. "Are you with—"

"I just came up here to meet a colleague," Ellie said. "His granddaughter's competing. It's a Skate Canada event."

"I know."

Ellie heard that tone she was so very familiar with, the condescending and patronizing tone this woman always took with her. Suzie was everything Ellie wasn't—blonde, cute, tall, sexy, young, and Ellie's children's mother in every sense except the biological one. They hadn't seen or spoken to each other since Ellie's ill-advised attempt to attend Megan's eleventh birthday party in Toronto two years ago, but it could have been yesterday given Suzie's instant assumption of precisely the same attitude she'd displayed on that unhappy day.

"Where's Mel?"

"She's with Gareth. He's in Brussels right now, on party business."

"I see." Ellie's ex-husband, Gareth Bowen, was an economic advisor for the Conservative Party of Canada. "That'll be great for Mel."

"She's been there before. We all have." Suzie glanced at her watch.

It was a Longines, Ellie noticed, similar to ones she'd seen while having the battery replaced in her Hamilton Field Quartz wristwatch in Nordstrom's last month.

Ellie had paid six hundred bucks for the Hamilton as a birthday present to herself a few years ago, and she'd noticed the Longines cost twice as much as hers. Not nearly as durable as a Hamilton, though, which was a popular choice for law enforcement and military personnel.

"I have to go, Ellie. Meg's going to be on soon." Suzie

began to turn away.

"Wait. Is she skating? In the competition?"

"Yes, of course." She barely refrained from rolling her eyes. "That's why we're here."

"I didn't know she was into it. In tournaments, I mean." Ellie knew that Megan liked to skate, much more so than her older sister Melanie, who was a book reader, but she had no idea her daughter had gotten this serious about it.

"This is her fourth year. Her coach is connected to the women's Olympic team." Suzie backed away. "I really have to go now, Ellie. She's about to go on."

"I'll come with you," Ellie said, a little thrilled to learn that her girl was doing something this bold and adventurous with her life.

Suzie stopped. "I'd rather you didn't. She might see you in the crowd and get upset."

Ellie stared at her, pleasure evaporating into consternation. "What?"

"She's very nervous. It's the semi-finals. She needs total concentration. If she sees you, she'll get thrown off. It'll affect her progress."

Unable to move, Ellie watched Suzie turn away to follow the crowd through the big doors into the arena gallery.

Should she just go on in, anyway? And to hell with Suzie and her patronizing exclusionism? It was *her* daughter, after all. A human being she'd carried in her body for nine months and given birth to, had nursed and fussed over, and had always loved as deeply as she was capable of loving anyone. Didn't she have the right to be there in the crowd, cheering her own daughter as she competed in a strange city far from home?

Someone bumped into her from behind and murmured an apology as they pressed forward toward the doors. Ellie realized she was in the way.

She moved off to the left and found herself in front of an observation window that looked down onto the ice surface, just like the one she'd stood before earlier while waiting for Deputy Commissioner Dart to finish his phone call. She looked down at skaters this time, a few girls coasting around the boards, getting a feel for the resurfaced ice. Cameras flashed in the crowd, people made their way to their seats, and the scoreboard flickered as an advertisement crossed the screen.

Ellie frowned at the girls on the ice. Was one of them Megan?

She'd be a lot different than the last time she'd seen her, Ellie knew. The physical difference between eleven and thirteen would be significant. She'd be taller, more athletic looking, bonier than before. The baby fat would be long gone. Instead of jeans and a T-shirt she'd be wearing a costume like the ones the other girls were wearing. Her hair would be different, probably pulled up into a bun on top of her head. She'd always had Gareth's looks, his sandy hair, blue eyes and narrow face, but what would she look like now? An adolescent; no longer a child. Would she have breasts already? A young woman's hips?

Was that her?

Ellie focused on one of the girls, watching her drift past the penalty box, her hand on the boards, pulling herself slowly forward.

It might be Megan. It could be her. It was hard to tell for sure.

Ellie found it difficult to breathe. She couldn't go inside the gallery. Suzie was right. Even if she hid right at the top, in the standing-room-only section, there was a slim chance Megan would spot her. Ellie knew her daughter hated her and knew the sight of her would be upsetting. It *would* have a negative effect on her performance.

Trying to catch her breath, Ellie reasoned that they would show the names of the competitors on the scoreboard. When it was Megan's turn to skate, they would put her name on the board and Ellie would know it was her. She could wait here at the window and watch her daughter skate when her turn came around.

As she stood there, the first competitor's name appeared on the scoreboard. *Elizabeth Allison.* A stranger. Someone else's daughter.

Ellie looked at her watch, her Hamilton, that popular choice of cops like her.

It was impossible to know how long it would be before it was Megan's turn. How long would each girl's routine take? How long would it be in between each one? If they were taking them in alphabetical order, Megan might be next after this first girl. Bowen after Allison. She should hang around.

She looked at her watch again. She couldn't stay. Peter Lambton was waiting. The case was moving very quickly, and she needed to be there. She could sense the finish line approaching. She'd promised Kevin she'd be there in an hour, and it would take that long to make the drive down to Brockville. She was already running a little late, in fact. She couldn't stay.

It was the same as it had always been, wasn't it? Her professional life always took precedence over personal things. No matter what.

The girls were right to expect nothing from her. To want nothing from her. They were right. She was nothing to them now. A stranger.

Determined not to cry, she turned away from the window and left the building.

chapter THIRTY-EIGHT

"We're going to have a different kind of conversation this afternoon," Kevin said, opening his file folder. "I've explained your rights to you, you've talked to your lawyer, and now I'm going to ask you some very specific questions about Andie Matheson."

Peter Lambton said nothing. His trademark tan leather jacket had been removed and hung up somewhere, and his trademark smirk was likewise gone, replaced with a clenched jaw that betrayed tension and fatigue. His legs were crossed at the ankles and his hands were clasped together in his lap.

"First, though. Where's your wife? Where's Mrs. Lambton? Can you tell me where she is right now?"

Lambton shook his head, a small, tight movement.

"Please answer verbally," Kevin prodded. He was aware that the camera would capture his non-verbals, and that a head shake or nod could count as a response for forensic purposes, but he wanted him talking. If Lambton felt pressured to speak, to verbalize his responses, then he might be more forthcoming in his answers. "Where's your wife? Where's Kathryn?"

"I don't know."

"All right. As you know, we've conducted a very thorough search of your Hill Island cottage, and we're confident it's the location where Andie Matheson was murdered. The last time we spoke, you said that you spent last Wednesday night and Thursday morning at the cottage. Do you still maintain that this is where you were during that time?"

Lambton said nothing.

"Let me ask you the question again. Where were you last Wednesday night and early Thursday morning?"

They listened to the overhead fluorescent lights hum for a few moments before Lambton stirred. "I was there. At the cottage, like I said."

"Was Andie Matheson there with you?"

"Yes. She was."

"Did you kill her?"

"No. I didn't."

"Do you know who did?"

"No."

Kevin sorted through the documents in the file folder and took out a photograph. "This is material that was removed from your cottage and taken to the landfill site on the Escott-Rockport Road. We've spoken to your nephew, Howie Burnside, and a couple of the guys who work for him. They've told us they removed it from your cottage and took it to the dump. This was on your instructions, isn't that correct?"

"Yes."

"We've already matched the blood on the carpeting and flooring to Andie Matheson's blood type," Kevin said, showing him another photo, "and we're confident that the DNA test will give us a match as well. Were you aware that this was Andie's blood when you ordered your nephew to clean everything up at the cottage and get rid of it?"

"Yes."

"How did you know it was hers?"

"I put two and two together."

"You put two and two together." Kevin frowned, as though confused. "What do you mean by that?"

Lambton shrugged. "I figured out it was her, that's what I mean. That it had happened ... there."

Kevin put the photographs back into the file folder. "Let's take a step back for a minute. You've admitted to me now that you spent last Wednesday night at the cottage with Andie Matheson. Take me through things so I'll have a clearer picture of what happened. What time did you get to the cottage on Wednesday?"

"I'm not sure, exactly. Around seven, I guess."

"Seven in the evening?"

"Yes."

"Was Andie Matheson with you?"

Lambton nodded. "I picked her up at her apartment before six. We stopped for a few things along the way."

"So you got there around seven. Tell me about the evening. How it went."

Lambton took a moment. Finally he cleared his throat and sat up a little. "It was good. It went well. We had dinner. I cooked. She's, she was, a terrible cook." He made brief eye contact with Kevin. "I like to cook."

"So you had dinner. No one else there, is that correct?"

"Yeah. It was very quiet. We watched a movie and then went to bed."

"You had sexual intercourse with her, correct?"

"Yes."

"Was it consensual?"

"Of course it was!" Lambton straightened up, as though prodded. "What the hell's the matter with you? Look, I know how this appears. I know she's dead, I know someone caught her in that bedroom and killed her, murdered her, but we were in love."

He leaned over the corner of the table toward Kevin.

"I've never felt that way toward anyone in my life. We'd been involved once before and Kathryn found out, and I wasn't in a position at that time to go through a divorce, you know, given Kathryn's social standing and, yes, her money. So I tried to break it off. I told Andie we couldn't continue. She had a few relationships afterward, I'm aware of that, and I tried to forget her, but I couldn't. I couldn't."

Kevin jotted a few quick notes. There were several points he wanted to expand on, but he was reluctant to disturb the rhythm of the interrogation. "So you went to bed and had sex. What happened after that?"

"We went to sleep."

"Did either of you get out of bed during the night?"

Lambton nodded. "Around four or five. I got up and went to the bathroom. She went downstairs, I guess for something to eat."

"How long was she downstairs?"

"I don't know. I went back to bed. I fell asleep. I didn't hear her come back up." He ran a hand through his hair.

"Did you hear anything at all during the night that was unusual?"

"What do you mean?"

"Voices, as though she might be talking to someone, or footsteps, doors opening, anything unusual like that?"

"No. Nothing. I'm a heavy sleeper. Once I'm out, I'm out."

"What time did you get up?"

"Six thirty. I always wake up right around then."

"Was she there with you? In bed?"

"Yeah."

"So describe to me what happened after you woke up."

Lambton pursed his lips and then closed his eyes for a moment, breathing deeply. "She was asleep. I kissed her but she just wanted to sleep, so I got up."

Kevin waited.

"I showered, got dressed, and checked on her again. She was still asleep, so I left. I left her like that. I left, and

I drove into town."

"Into Brockville?"

"Yes. I left her—" he choked. "Never, I never, uh, saw her again." He covered his eyes with his hand.

"What about breakfast? Didn't you have breakfast before you left?"

Lambton shook his head.

"Did you skip breakfast?"

He shook his head again. "No."

"Where did you have breakfast?"

"In town."

"Where?"

"Faye's." Lambton removed his hand. "It was a breakfast meeting with Johnson. The president of the Rotary Club."

"How long did it last?"

"An hour. He's a slow eater, unfortunately."

"And then?"

Lambton straightened, uttering a long sigh. "And then I went home. Changed clothes, called Andie, got no answer, texted, got no answer, and started to drive back down to the island."

"What time was this?"

"Uh, I left the house about ten forty-five, eleven o'clock. Is that what you mean?"

"What about your wife? Did you talk to her while you were home?"

He shook his head. "She wasn't there."

"Oh? Where was she?"

"I don't know. Maybe she'd left already for her sister's."

Kevin paused, pretending to be confused. "I don't understand. We're talking about Thursday right now. The last time you were here you told us she was driving up to her sister's on Friday. Which was it?"

"You're right." He waved a hand in the air. "Sorry. I keep getting the days confused. She drove up on Friday."

"And yet we've spoken to her sister," Kevin said, his

voice stern, "and she had no idea Kathryn was coming up to see her. She still hasn't heard from her. How do you explain that?"

"I can't. I've told you what she told me she was going to do." He added, "I hope everything's all right."

"She told you she was driving to Collingwood to see her sister?"

"Yes."

"When did she tell you this, exactly?"

"Well, I can't say exactly. It would have been the night before."

"Thursday night, is that what you're saying?"

"Yes."

"When? At dinner? After dinner? In bed that night?"

He shook his head. "We sleep in separate rooms. She goes to bed at ten, so I don't say bugger all to her after that."

"I see. So, at dinner?"

"I had dinner in town."

"After dinner. That's when you spoke to her and she told you she was driving up to see her sister the next day?"

"Yes."

Kevin paused. He could sense that Lambton was lying, but he wasn't exactly sure what he was lying about. He insisted Andie was alive when he left the cottage, and he'd described a plausible timeline for how he'd spent Thursday morning, including the early breakfast meeting that could easily be verified. It was still entirely possible, however, that he'd killed her before leaving the cottage for his Brockville breakfast meeting.

Was he lying about the conversation with his wife? Kevin was bothered by Kathryn's continued absence. He was even more bothered that their GPS evidence indicated she was in the vicinity of the cottage as late as ten o'clock in the evening on Thursday. If she'd left the cottage after that, either to go to her sister's place or somewhere else, she'd apparently done so without her cellphone, or with it turned off or otherwise disabled.

"What time was it when your wife told you she was driving to Collingwood the next day?"

"I don't know. Before she went to bed."

"What time did she go to bed?"

"Ten, like I said. As always."

There it was, Kevin thought. A definite lie. "That's not true, is it? You know it, and we know it."

"Of course it's true."

Kevin took a piece of paper from the file folder and put it down where Lambton could see it. "Her cellphone GPS records. She was picked up by this tower," he pointed, "and passed through this cell, between nine fifty-five and ten fourteen. She was heading westbound on the 401, because she was then picked up by this tower," he pointed again, "and passed through this cell between ten fourteen and ten twenty-five. At that time the data terminates. Either her phone was turned off, the GPS function was switched off, or the phone was destroyed. Which was it?"

"I have no idea. Was her phone stolen, is that what you're telling me?"

"We're obtaining your cellphone GPS data as well. The production order's been approved by the judge, and your service provider's processing it now. It's going to tell us that you were also there, at the cottage, on Thursday night, isn't it?"

Lambton leaned back, folding his arms across his chest.

"Did you and your wife have a fight? Is that what happened?"

Lambton said nothing, staring at a spot on the opposite wall.

"Did you know Andie Matheson was pregnant when she died?"

Kevin watched Lambton's eyes widen. The man grunted. His jaw slowly unclenched and his lips parted. He slowly turned his head to look at him.

"No."
"It was your child, wasn't it?"
"Oh no. Oh no."
"Did you know she was pregnant?"
"No. No. No. It can't be."

Kevin waited for a moment, watching him. It was obvious he hadn't known. The news was like a sucker punch to his solar plexus, knocking the wind out of him. He was struggling to process it.

"What about—oh God, what about, what about the, the baby. Is it...?"

Kevin shook his head.

Tears welled in Lambton's eyes. He shook his head, turning away. "God. God damn it. She didn't know. She would have said. She would have held it over me."

Kevin kept his expression neutral. He was a little confused. Andie Matheson had been nine weeks pregnant, and she would have known about it. Would she have used the information against Lambton as some kind of leverage?

"The bitch. The fucking bitch. She would have known I'd want it. What if she did know? Is that why she did it?"

"Did what?" Kevin's confusion deepened.

Lambton wiped his eyes with the back of his hand. "Nothing. Nothing at all."

"Who are you talking about? What do you think they did?"

"No one. Nothing. I'm done talking."

"Are you talking about Andie Matheson? Did she try to use her pregnancy as some kind of leverage over you?"

No response.

"Your wife? Are you talking about her?"

Nothing.

"Where is your wife? Where is she?"

Lambton curled his lip. "I have no fucking idea. And that's the last word you'll get out of me. I'm done. Fuck. This is *done*."

chapter THIRTY-NINE

Dennis Leung followed a stone path that trailed around the side of the Lambton cottage, his eyes down. Some kind of plant had grown between the stones and along the side of the path, something with tiny flowers that had turned brown beneath the winter snow and would soon be thriving again. Leung thought it might be creeping thyme, but he wasn't sure. It was thick in spots, but not thick enough to hide what he was looking for.

Last night an exhaustive search of the cottage and exterior grounds had been conducted, and while Dave Martin and his forensic identification unit had done their usual thorough job, darkness had limited them outside, despite their large spotlights on tripods and hand-held flashlights. Leung had come down this afternoon to take another look around under better visual conditions.

In particular, he was hoping to find Andie Matheson's cellphone, which was still missing. An iPhone in a pink case might elude searchers working after dark, but Leung thought it might jump out at him from its hiding spot amid the debris of a winter-killed garden if he persisted. It was true that he and SOCO Constable Jayne Witten had examined the grounds yesterday while executing the search warrant for evidence relating to the Lambton breach of trust investigation without spotting the phone, but on that occasion the search had been rather high level, a general survey of the landscaping in order to assess what had been done to the place by Grass Wizards. This morning he and Witten had gone over her photographs with a fine tooth comb, hoping for a miracle, but none had been forthcoming.

Leung stopped at the corner of the building and stooped down to sift through a pile of leaves that had been heaped around a crop of perennials as mulch to protect the roots over winter. The flowers had been cut back, but Leung thought they might be peonies, judging from the thickness of the truncated stems and the shoots that were beginning to show on the crowns of the root clusters. He passed a gloved hand through the leaves and patted down to the soil around the plants. Nothing.

Straightening, he looked around. It was a nice spring afternoon. The sky above was blue and the sun was strong enough to have warmed the air to a temperature of about 10 degrees Celsius. He wore a navy windbreaker over a sleeveless grey sweater and a blue dress shirt, but had donned a pair of navy cargo pants for the occasion and had swapped his shoes for a pair of green Wellington boots from the trunk of his car before starting his search.

It wasn't a particularly bad way to spend a Sunday afternoon. His eyes trailed across the lawn to the river beyond. Apparently a few of the locals agreed with him. He spotted the woman in the kayak who'd been their eyewitness yesterday, the person who'd watched Howie Burnside and his crew clean up last Thursday after Andie's murder. She seemed to be watching him now through her opera glasses, so he waved. She lowered the glasses and waved back.

East of the kayak, a fishing boat crept slowly along, about thirty metres from shore. It was an eighteen-foot aluminum boat with a canvas canopy and a big outboard motor. A man was fishing out of the back of the boat with a cane pole and heavy black line. Leung thought he was probably trawling for brown bullhead, a common catfish which were most popular when taken out of cold water at this time of year. Leung had eaten bullhead many times, and particularly enjoyed the way his father had grilled it on their backyard barbecue when he was a boy.

The stone walkway branched at the corner of the cottage where Leung stood. One branch led around the back, while the other crossed the lawn through a series of raised flower beds on its way to the stairs leading down to Lambton's dock. Leung followed the latter pathway, searching carefully between the mulched-in perennials and around the bases of ornamental shrubs strategically positioned between the raised beds.

If he wasn't able to find Andie Matheson's missing iPhone, then perhaps Kathryn Lambton's cellphone would be a consolation prize. Her disappearance was still a mystery that bothered everyone on the team. Since her phone's last known location was here on the island at around 11:30 PM Thursday night, Leung wondered if she'd come to the cottage knowing that Andie Matheson had been killed here.

They were waiting for Peter Lambton's most recent phone records to see whether or not he'd been back here Thursday night as well, and in the meantime they were trying to figure out what he'd been talking about when Kevin had interrogated him yesterday afternoon.

John Bishop felt strongly that Lambton had killed Andie and was spreading a smoke screen to confuse the issue. However, they'd already checked out Lambton's nearly-new Lexus SUV, and there was no way it was the vehicle that had dumped the body and the knife on Thursday morning.

Ellie agreed that Lambton was acting in a very guilty manner and that he definitely had something on his mind that was weighing him down. They would have to wait for the evidence, however, to clear up the mayor's role in things.

Leung slowly worked his way along the path, his head down, crouching now and then to probe possible spots that would conceal a cellphone. His mind flashed on May's cellphone, also an iPhone. As the oldest, she was the only one of the girls currently allowed to keep one, and she guarded it closely.

He and Lily had spoken to May on Friday night about the possible tutoring job. May's enthusiasm had been contagious, and on Saturday Leung and Lily dropped in on Mrs. Schultz to talk about it. The teacher had praised May's intelligence and willingness to help other children, and Leung had reluctantly decided to go along with the idea. Sitting in the woman's living room, drinking her tea and listening to her plans for May and the other tutors, he hadn't picked up any negative vibrations from her this time. Perhaps he'd been wrong that she tended not to like Asian children—

He straightened at the sound of shouting down on the water.

A man's voice, exclaiming something inarticulate.

Leung began walking along the path, coming out from behind a large bush that blocked his view of the river.

He heard the voice of the woman in the kayak, asking a question.

The man responded loudly as Leung reached a point where he could see both crafts. The kayak was moving swiftly toward the fishing boat, which was stationary.

As Leung reached the top of the stone staircase leading down to the dock where Peter Lambton's forty-two-foot cabin cruiser was still tethered, he saw the man leaning over the hull of his boat, struggling with something in the water. It was very large, and he'd apparently snagged it with his hook while trawling slowly through the water.

Leung hurried down the stairs. The woman in the kayak reached the fishing boat, circling around to the side to give the man a hand unsnagging his hook.

Suddenly, she screamed and pushed away, frantically paddling backward.

Leung stopped on the dock and watched as the man pulled the head and shoulders of a human body up out of the water.

chapter FORTY

Kevin was bone-tired, dead on his feet. He stumbled along the side of the road in the dark, wishing it hadn't been necessary to park his car so far down from the cottage.

After interrogating Howie Burnside at four o'clock this morning he'd driven home to Sparrow Lake and crashed for a few hours in an empty house. Barb was looking after the kids today at her place, so he didn't really need to feel as guilty as he did about fobbing off his responsibilities onto her. They were fine. They loved being there, and she was taking good care of them. He dozed fitfully, then abruptly dropped into black, dreamless sleep.

When he awoke two hours later, his head was filled with congestion. He was worried that he was picking up Brendan's cold, which had worsened yesterday. After drinking a glass of orange juice in the kitchen, he called the school at Mallorytown and left a message that Caitlyn and Brendan would be absent tomorrow due to illness but would probably be back on Tuesday. That done, he'd showered and dressed and returned to the detachment office for his interrogation of Lambton, thankful that the congestion had cleared up on its own somewhere between his house and the office.

The fatigue, however, had not. Two months of interrupted sleep and short nights were beginning to catch up to him.

It had been a long day, culminating in Leung's discovery and the call out that brought them all back to the cottage at Hill Island. Thank goodness he kept himself physically fit. Otherwise, he'd probably just lie down on the side of the road he was walking along and pass out from sheer exhaustion.

At least his confusion over Lambton's statements this afternoon had been resolved. The man's obviously guilty behaviour had been connected to the death of his wife, Kathryn Lambton, and not to his lover, Andie Matheson.

Kevin made his way slowly down the long line of parked vehicles, eyes down, watching for potholes and loose rocks. Somewhere behind him he heard voices. A vehicle engine started. Tires crunched and headlights suddenly illuminated the way ahead of him.

He stepped between two parked cars as the Forensic Identification Unit's big white van passed, with Dave Martin at the wheel. Kevin lifted his hand but Martin didn't see him, staring straight ahead, concentrating on not clipping off someone's side mirror as he eased down the road.

Kevin followed the red tail lights for a few car lengths until they disappeared around a bend and he was immersed once more in darkness. If he remembered correctly, his car wasn't too much farther along.

As he reached the front of the grey Crown Vic, he saw a cigarette tip glow in the dark on the passenger side, toward the rear of the car. He smelled the smoke and knew it was Ellie.

He stopped at the gap between the Crown Vic and his

Fusion, which was indeed the next one in line, and looked through an opening in the trees at the river. The moon was up, and its light was fractured across the tips of countless peaks as the wind rolled the surface into wave after wave.

"Thought you'd quit."

"Yeah, well, so did I."

He waited, not sure if she wanted privacy.

"It looks so damned cold," she said.

"It is." He edged between the back bumper of the Crown Vic and the front bumper of his car.

Her duty jacket made a rustling sound as she turned to look at him. "Damned shame."

"Yeah." He and Ellie had both viewed the body of Kathryn Lambton after the recovery crew had pulled it from the river. Shocked and horrified, the man in the fishing boat who'd found the corpse had dropped it back into the water. It had taken a while to find it again, bring it back up to the surface, and convey it back to shore. The operation was supervised by Dr. Kearns, the coroner, and as always she'd chafed everyone's nerves with her bossy excitement. Every time Kevin had looked over at Ellie, her jaw was clenched and her eyes were narrowed, and he knew it wasn't just because she was freezing.

The coldness of the water had delayed bloating and decomposition somewhat, but after more than sixty hours under water the corpse had inevitably shown the expected effects of submersion. Soft tissue at the ears, lips, and eyelids had been nibbled at by scavenging fish, marbling was visible on the face, and the hands showed significant washer woman wrinkling.

Everyone's attention, though, went very quickly to the clear signs of manual strangulation at the neck, and the remnants of the rope wrapped around her ankles.

When they questioned him again after Leung's discovery, Lambton had described to them with surprisingly little coaxing how he'd confronted his wife outside the cottage near her car on Thursday night.

They'd argued about his resumption of the affair with Andie Matheson, and he hadn't bothered to lie about it. She'd accused him of killing Andie, he'd levelled a counter-accusation, she'd called him several vile names and had begun hitting him, and he'd fought back with lethal force.

Afterward, he'd used his cabin cruiser to take her body out about thirty meters from shore. He tied the boat's anchor to her ankles and dumped her overboard.

The rope he'd used had been old and worn, however, and it had parted while the fisherman had struggled to free his hook from Kathryn's body.

As he'd walked the mayor through his confession, Kevin quickly realized that Lambton believed his wife had murdered Andie Matheson. Kevin hadn't bothered pointing out that the GPS data obtained from Kathryn's phone had placed her in Brockville during the time when Andie's murder had occurred. Even if he had, Lambton would have dismissed it as false or mistaken information. The man was thoroughly convinced he had killed the murderer of the woman he truly loved.

Kevin leaned against the back fender of the Crown Vic next to Ellie. "I could tell he was lying but I thought he was lying about having killed Andie. I thought it was unlikely at that point he was hiding the fact he'd killed his wife instead."

Ellie raised the cigarette to her lips and inhaled. The glowing tip cast a pale red light on her face. Her eyes stared straight ahead, unblinking.

"We're back at square one with Matheson," Kevin said. "We still don't know who killed her, if he didn't."

Ellie said nothing, turning her head at the sound of someone trudging down the road toward them. There was a dull thud and the footsteps became irregular for a moment as the person stumbled over something in the dark.

"Fuck," a voice muttered. It was Bishop, on his way down to his car.

"Careful, JB," Kevin called out.

"Christ, it's darker than the inside of a fucking cow." Bishop stopped beside Ellie's Crown Vic and put his hand on the roof. "Great. Now I've got a stone in my shoe. Jesus."

"Did you know," Kevin said, "scientists have discovered a colour darker than black? They call it Vantablack. It's so dark our eyes can't even see it."

"Give it a fucking rest, will you, Walker?" Bishop tipped the stone out of his shoe and wrestled it back on. "I thought you guys would be long gone already."

"About to head out," Ellie said.

Bishop walked between the cars and stood next to Kevin. "I'm glad I didn't have to go out on the damned boat. Cold as hell out there."

"Yeah." Kevin put his hands in his jacket pockets. Mark Allore had gone out with Identification Constable Landry and the recovery team, and when he'd come back his ears and cheeks had been bright red from exposure to the cold wind crossing the surface of the river.

After Dr. Kearns had completed her examination of the body, Allore had accompanied the transportation unit to Kingston to maintain chain of custody of Kathryn Lambton's remains until they were signed over to the forensic pathology unit at Kingston General Hospital. As Allore got into the vehicle, Kevin had heard him asking the driver to boost the heat. It was the type of work that could chill you to the bone.

"Well," Bishop said, thumping Kevin on the shoulder with a gloved fist, "maybe tomorrow morning you and I should go have a word with that Whitlock guy. I'd say he's probably next up on our hit list, since Hizzoner apparently didn't do it."

Kevin frowned. "Who?"

"Are you talking about Warren Whitlock?" Ellie asked, leaning forward to look at Bishop.

"Yeah yeah. Some city hall guy." He rolled his eyes at Kevin, who obviously didn't know the person they were talking about. "He was married to Lambton's niece or something, then after he got out from under that little piece of work, he had a thing with the vic. With Matheson, I mean."

Ellie stared at him. "When did you learn this?"

Bishop shrugged. "Yesterday, I guess it was. Allore and I talked to the friend, what's her name? Freeland? The friend of this one?" He jerked his head toward the water, indicating Kathryn Lambton. "She just kind of threw it out there as we were leaving."

"Did you file on it?" Kevin asked. If Bishop had filed an interview report in their system after talking to Shirley Freeland, Kevin was sure he would have seen it. The fact that Bishop had discovered another former lover of Andie Matheson would not have escaped his notice.

"I thought Allore was going to," Bishop replied. "He was taking all the notes."

"Shit, JB, he must have thought you were going to. You're the senior officer in that situation; you should have made it clear who was going to file the report."

"Cool your jets, Kev. I'm not the senior fuck-all around here. You're the guy supposed to be giving all the fucking orders, not me."

"Kevin's right," Ellie said, throwing away her cigarette, "but we'll talk about procedure later. What time is it?"

Kevin lifted his arm and pushed a button to illuminate the dial on his watch. "Ten forty-two."

Ellie pulled her cellphone out of her jacket pocket. She tapped to her contact list and punched a number. "Dave, it's Ellie. Listen, is there someone at the lab right now?"

Kevin watched her profile in the glow from her cellphone screen.

"Okay, that's fine," she said. "Let him know that Kevin will be contacting him shortly. We have a new suspect—yes, the Matheson homicide, back to that one again—and Kevin will send him all the tombstone info as soon as he's got it. We need fingerprint comparisons right off the bat, and then DNA as soon as it's feasible. How's it going with the stuff from the dumpster? Good. Any word from CFS? Okay. Call me if anything pops. Thanks."

She ended the call. "Kevin, I want to be able to connect Warren Whitlock to the cottage, the stuff pulled from the dumpster, or to anywhere else we can. I want to know how he got down here, what car he used, everything. Make it happen."

"Will do."

"Bill Jamieson's at the lab. Get Whitlock's address, DOB, everything to him ASAP. Maybe we'll get lucky and his fingerprints are already on file."

Kevin nodded. He would need to return to the detachment office right now to run the appropriate systems checks. Barb knew he was going to be running late, so it would just be a matter of not waking them up when he finally got to her place.

Ellie leaned forward again to look at Bishop. "File that damned interview report and everything else that's still pending, will you?"

"Yes, ma'am."

Kevin motioned with his chin for Bishop to move through the gap between the cars ahead of him. At this point he was so frustrated that he didn't dare speak to him.

chapter FORTY-ONE

Kevin found himself sitting at his mother-in-law's kitchen table with a half-eaten sandwich in his hand.

"You were snoring," Caitlyn said, leaning over in her chair to look into his eyes. "Are you all right?"

"You were sleeping at the table," Brendan observed around a mouthful of white bread, peanut butter, and grape jelly. "You were sleeping sitting up."

"I was?" Kevin took a bite of his sandwich and chewed slowly. Tuna fish.

"Hush now," Barb said, refilling Brendan's glass of milk. "Kevin had to work late last night. He didn't get nearly as much sleep as you two snoozers."

"Did you stay up late watching TV?" Brendan asked, picking up his milk. He coughed before drinking. There was still some congestion in his throat, but his cold seemed much better this morning.

"Nanna just said he was working late," Caitlyn said. "He wasn't home."

"Well, sometimes he watches TV way late at night."

"He falls asleep watching TV," Caitlyn explained.

"That's different."

"Probably misses all the good stuff."

Barb sat down with Joshua in her arms. She offered him a bottle and the baby began to feed. "Don't talk about Kevin like he's not here. It's not polite."

"Sorry, Kevin." Caitlyn said.

"That's all right. I was snoring?"

Both children laughed. "It sounded like a baby pig," Brendan said. He made a snorkelling sound, and Caitlyn laughed.

"Finish your lunch," Barb said, catching a drip at the corner of Joshua's mouth with the nipple of the bottle. "You have to pack your things and get ready to go home."

Brendan groaned. "I like staying here."

"Your mother will be so happy to see you." Barb looked down as Joshua gurgled. He seemed to smile up at her.

Kevin looked at his watch and saw that it was a few minutes past noon. Last night he'd driven directly from Hill Island to the detachment office and called Jamieson at the lab in Smiths Falls. Setting his cellphone on speaker, he'd run Warren Whitlock's name in the Canadian Police Information Centre database and found his driver's licence, which provided an address and date of birth, but a further check revealed no vehicle registered in his name. Kevin had been hoping for a Volvo or Ford between 2003 and 2015, of course, which would match the vehicle Dave Martin said the killer had used to dump the body and the knife, but no such luck.

Jamieson searched in the Automated Fingerprint Identification System but also came up empty. Whitlock had apparently never been fingerprinted before. Kevin was a little surprised, thinking that as an employee of the city he would have gone through a criminal background check, but further research showed that at the time Whitlock had been hired, in 2005, it hadn't been a requirement for the kind of position he'd accepted.

Kevin ran further checks in CPIC but came back with no criminal record, no outstanding warrants, and no prohibitions against driving or owning a firearm. Generalized Internet searches yielded a few news articles, most of them related to his complaint against Lambton, but nothing useful.

Warren Whitlock had a relatively small electronic footprint, it seemed. It was as far as they could go without a warrant, and Kevin believed they were far short of sufficient probable cause to get them that warrant.

When lunch was finished, Kevin helped the children pack their things. Once they'd worked through all the fussing and scrapping and fruitless searches for lost items that had already been tucked into their knapsacks, Kevin put Joshua into his car seat and the other two settled into their places on either side.

They waved goodbye to Nanna, and Kevin backed out of the driveway onto the street It was 1:34 PM, according to the dashboard clock.

Kevin expected Janie to be home at around 2:30. She'd gotten a ride with a couple of women from Ottawa who'd picked her up on their way to Toronto and were dropping her off on their way back. She'd sent Kevin a text right after lunch telling him they were en route and on schedule, so he knew he had about an hour.

He caught Caitlyn's eye in the rear-view mirror. "We're going to make a quick stop, Cait. Only a few minutes. All right?"

"Sure, Kevin. What for?"

"There's someone I want Joshua to meet. We'll just say hello and then get going."

"Okay."

Kevin drove up Bartholomew Street and worked his way over to Stewart Boulevard. After crossing the bridge over the train tracks he turned left and drove along Front Avenue until he reached Perth Street. He looked across the intersection at the eastern end of Hubbell Street. He hesitated until someone behind him tooted their horn. Reluctantly he crossed Perth Street and headed down Hubbell, a one-way street running west. He drove a couple of blocks and then pulled over to the curb.

"Why are we here?" Brendan asked, lowering his window.

"This is where I grew up," Kevin said, shutting off the engine.

Caitlyn leaned forward. "On this street?"

"Yes." He looked across the street at a two-storey stucco house with a small covered front porch. "That was our house."

"It looks nice."

In fact, it didn't. The stucco was weather-stained and crumbling, the white window sills and trim needed painting, and the porch roof looked unsafe. The paved driveway running along the side was cracked and stained. The backyard, from what Kevin could see, was overgrown and untended.

Behind the houses on that side of the street, a narrow, wooded green space ran between the fenced backyards and the railroad tracks beyond. When Kevin was a kid he'd spent countless hours down there with his friends, playing catch on the foot path, exploring the undergrowth, and watching the freight trains from the safety of the tree line. It had been a place of refuge, a way to escape an unhappy home into a happy alternative world.

Not long ago the city had converted the old foot path into a segment of the Brock Trail, a six-kilometre bike path running from the waterfront downtown up through the city. Along this stretch behind Hubbell Street it paralleled Butler's Creek, in which Kevin had often waded barefoot to catch crawfish and search for interesting-looking stones.

Brock Trail was now considered part of the Frontenac Arch Biosphere Reserve Trail System. As a result, it connected to the bike path along the Thousand Islands

Parkway where Andie Matheson's body had been found five days ago.

As Kevin sat there, trying to breathe through the stress and convince himself that he needed to go through with this thing, regardless of how it might turn out, he realized that time, in a way, had led him in a gigantic circle from his childhood to this moment as an adult.

He was not a believer in fate or destiny. He believed that time was linear. Yet here he was, convinced he'd travelled in a circle after all, one that connected him as a child playing on the foot path behind this house to himself as an adult, responsible for a murder investigation many kilometres down that same path. A circle that connected Kevin the son to Kevin the father, the man sitting here, trying to find the courage to get out of the car and walk across the street.

"Wait here, you two." Kevin unbuckled and got out. Opening the back door, he reached over Brendan, freed Joshua from his car seat, and lifted him out.

"Where you going?" Brendan asked.

"Just across the street."

"Can I come, too?"

"No. I'll only be a minute." Kevin looked at Caitlyn. "You both stay buckled up, all right?"

She nodded.

Kevin checked for traffic. With Joshua cradled in his left arm, he crossed the street and walked up the driveway that was so familiar to him. He opened the aluminum screen door, held it with his foot, and knocked on the inside door.

Silence. There was no window in the door, so he couldn't see inside.

Kevin glanced back at the car. Caitlyn and Brendan were motionless in the back seat, staring at him.

Kevin knocked again, using the edge of his fist this time, and was rewarded with a faint clatter from somewhere inside. In a moment footsteps approached and the door opened.

"I'm not buying what you're selling," the man said, opening the door, "unless it's free food or liquor, in which case I'll take whatever you got."

"It's me," Kevin said.

His father stared at him for a moment, lips parted, eyes narrowed. He was smaller and thinner than Kevin remembered. His wavy hair was dyed shoe polish black, and his handsome face was deeply lined. The cleft in his chin and the dimples in his cheeks were more pronounced, and his forehead was corrugated with wrinkles.

"Well, well, if it isn't Sir Kevin the Steadfast. What brings you home on such a lovely spring day?" The smell of alcohol was strong, and the slight burriness of his speech betrayed the fact that he was already well into his daily allotment. Kevin remembered that he liked to have a shot of his namesake, Johnnie Walker, with his toast and coffee for breakfast, and then take it from there. Nothing, apparently, had changed.

"Hi, Dad. How are you?"

Johnnie leaned against the doorframe. "How am I? Is that why you come here after, what, ten years? To ask me how I am?"

In fact it had been sixteen years since they'd last seen each other, on the day when Kevin had moved to Kingston to attend St. Lawrence College a few weeks after his mother's funeral. It had been a ragged, unpleasant parting.

"I didn't come to fight, Dad. You look like you've been losing weight."

"Yeah, well, that's what prostate cancer'll do for you, but they tell me it's beatable, so that's what I intend to do."

"I'm sorry," Kevin said.

"Think nothing of it. But that's what you should do, too."

Kevin frowned, not following him.

"Beat it."

"I will," Kevin said, "but I wanted you to meet your grandson. This is Joshua Kevin Walker. He was born on Valentine's Day, February 14."

"Ain't that sweet." Johnnie kept his eyes on Kevin's, like a challenge. He refused to acknowledge the baby resting quietly in the crook of Kevin's arm. "Tough for me to have a grandson when I don't have a son, don't you think?"

"I'm sorry you feel that way. I wanted you to see him."

"What the fuck for?" Johnnie's voice rose. "What the *fuck for*? Who the hell do you think y'are, coming around after all these years like Mister La-de-dah? Better than your old man? Huh? Is that what you still think, after all this time? Mister Fucking Superiority! With your college degree and your kid and your cop career and your fucking picture in the paper!"

"I don't think that, Dad. I never did. I'm sorry you feel that way."

"You're sorry, all right. A sorry, worthless, snivelling little snot-nosed shit. Always were; always will be."

"Goodbye, Dad." Kevin stepped back, took hold of the edge of the screen door, and let it close toward his father.

"Goodbye don't come close to it." Johnnie grabbed the screen door and slammed it shut. "Get lost, and don't fucking come back."

Kevin somehow made it across the street and returned Joshua to his car seat without seeing anything through the haze in front of his eyes. Behind the wheel, he started the car, drove down to the next intersection, turned right, pulled over to the curb, shut off the engine, and gripped the steering wheel tightly.

"Wow," Brendan said, "that man was really mad at you, Kevin."

Kevin said nothing, concentrating on his breathing.

"Who was he?"

Kevin watched a black squirrel cross the street in front of the car.

Caitlyn shushed her brother, but Brendan said, "I just

want to know who he was. He was really swearing bad."

Kevin said nothing, fighting a furious battle to regain control of his emotions. He'd made a mistake, he'd picked the wrong time to try it, and the best thing for him to do right now was to acknowledge the error and move on.

In his defence, there would have been no right time, ever, and he knew in his heart the outcome would have been the same no matter when he tried to approach his father. The rift between them was uncrossable, and he'd known that when making his decision. He'd chosen to go through with it because the opportunity had presented itself, he'd had the time to fit it in, and it was a chance to get it over with.

"Who was that?" Brendan repeated.

"I'll explain later. Not right now, but I will later."

"That's okay, Kevin," Caitlyn said, shooting her brother a look.

Johnnie Walker had always been a terrible husband and father. Alcohol and an inflated sense of entitlement had dominated his personality from the beginning of their family life, when Estelle Stephens had married him after discovering she was pregnant. Her inability to have other children after Kevin's birth fuelled Johnnie's resentment of both mother and son, and after his promotion to foreman at the detergent factory, when Kevin was four, he'd focused more and more of his attention on the little cadre of followers, male and female, that he'd built up around him in his little fiefdom at work.

After shifts he went straight from the shop floor to his favourite bar downtown to begin his evening drinking, and from there he usually ended up in the bedroom of his latest girlfriend. His eventual arrival home had always been a nightmare for young Kevin, who found himself on the receiving end of his father's bad temper almost as often as his mother had.

Kevin glanced in the rear-view mirror. Joshua had dozed off to sleep, lulled by the sunshine coming in through the window. Caitlyn was staring at him, apprehensive, while Brendan was looking over his shoulder at the corner they'd just turned, trying to puzzle out what had happened.

Kevin felt his anger subside into a familiar feeling of guilt that had persisted in his heart over the years, like silt at the bottom of a water tank. It had always been his firm belief that he should have had more courage in facing his father's overarching unhappiness, that there must have been something he could have said or done to repair things, and that the no-man's land between them could have been crossed from his side just as well as from Johnnie's.

His mother had never stopped trying, not until Johnnie had finally moved out shortly after her cancer diagnosis. She'd had the courage Kevin believed he lacked, and he'd loved and admired her equally as much as he'd feared and despised his father. Only after Johnnie left them for good did she finally admit that her marriage was over, and as she'd battled through the cancer treatments, she'd focused what energy she had left on Kevin.

By this time he was in high school, a six-footer with an 85 per cent grade average who excelled at any sport he felt like playing. After classes he hurried home to do the housework and tend to whatever physical needs Estelle had that he was capable of helping her with, and on the weekends he would do the shopping and complete other errands, fitting them in around his extra-curricular sports activities.

Now that the physical and psychological violence had left their home, they became close, each other's best friend. Kevin would read to her from the books assigned in his English classes and she'd tell him stories about her childhood, which she'd spent growing up on a farm outside Athens with two older sisters and two younger brothers. All the while pretending that her body wasn't losing its fight against the cancer that gradually spread everywhere despite the treatments.

Johnnie had attended her funeral, having the common

sense to sit at the rear of the church and remain in the background as her coffin was lowered into her grave, but the next day he quietly moved back into the house on Hubbell Street, reclaiming it as his rightful property.

It was May, and the following month Kevin graduated from high school. He attended commencement alone, wishing his mother could have been there to share in his accomplishment. He got a summer job with a paving company that paid well. The work gave him a great suntan and kept him in shape. He continued to do the housework, cook the meals, serve his father, and ignore his complaints, never uttering a word until the last weekend in August when he announced, packed bags at the door, that he was leaving.

They fought bitterly, his father angry that he was being abandoned to fend for himself. Kevin said things he'd vowed he'd never say. After an eternity, his taxi arrived at the door and it was time to leave.

He refused to look back, but in those long nights that followed, years afterward, he always did. Inevitably, he wished he'd known at the time what he could have done differently.

"We should go," Caitlyn said, experimentally.

It took a moment for her words to penetrate the turbulence inside Kevin's head. He looked at her in the mirror. "Yes. You're right."

"It'll be okay, Kevin."

He bit his lip, nodding. He put his hands on the key in the ignition switch, but before he could start the engine it occurred to him where he was. The realization flashed through him like a jolt of energy, giving him something new and completely different to consider. The change of subject was definitely welcome, and he chewed the inside of his cheek for a moment before nodding and making the decision.

"One more stop," he said, starting the car and shifting into gear. "Just around the corner. This time, just me and nobody else."

"Are you sure? Maybe we should just go home."

"We will." Kevin looked at her in the mirror. "Right after this."

chapter FORTY-TWO

He drove up to the next corner and turned right, onto Havelock Street. The address listed on Warren Whitlock's driver's licence was halfway down the block, on the right-hand side. The lots were very narrow and the houses were mostly wartime bungalows, squat little red brick boxes with shingled roofs and tiny front porches, but the one that matched Whitlock's address was situated on a double lot with a separate garage next to it, close to the street. There was no sidewalk on this side, so the house and garage were very near the curb, only about eight feet in.

Kevin drove past the house and pulled over two doors down. He shut off the engine and turned around. "Two minutes," he told Caitlyn, "then we're out of here. I want you to sit tight."

"Is this guy going to yell at you, too?" Brendan asked.

"There shouldn't be anyone home," Kevin said. "Just a quick look-see, all right?" He waited for them both to nod, then unbuckled and got out.

He walked back down the sidewalk toward the Whitlock house. He wasn't sure what he was doing here, what he was looking for, but his brain had suddenly shifted into a different gear and he badly wanted to produce something, anything, that would deliver Warren Whitlock into their hands.

The place looked well cared for, neat and tidy. The curtains were drawn in all the windows. There was no sign of pets, either a dog or a cat, and no stray objects of any kind visible outside. He walked past the front of the house, seeing nothing out of the ordinary.

He stopped in front of the stubby paved strip between the garage and the curb. The garage was only large enough to hold one vehicle. There was a big wooden door in the front that swung up out of the way and another door on the side connected to the back door of the house by a well-worn path across the lawn. Both garage doors were padlocked. The front door had a window in it, a single pane about the size of a magazine.

Kevin hesitated, then took a step forward. Technically, he was still standing on city property, since there was an easement running along the front of each lot for sewage lines or whatever. It went in from the edge of the street at least six feet, perhaps eight. The garage might have been built right on the edge of the easement, or it might actually be encroaching on it by a foot or two. He took another step forward. Technically, he probably wouldn't be trespassing if he edged close enough to take a look through that little window.

"Plain view" evidence laws in Canada frowned on this sort of behaviour by the police. Going onto private property and looking into windows for evidence could be construed by the courts as a search, and without a warrant anything he found might not be admissible in a court case. Whether or not he was standing on city property, as opposed to private property, would probably be moot to a judge with one eye on the appeal process.

There was a clock ticking in his head right now, keeping track of how long he was leaving the kids by themselves in the car, and he knew he had to get moving. Making a sudden decision, he reversed himself and walked up to the front door of Whitlock's house. He knocked on the door and waited several beats, gambling that Whitlock was at work and no one else was in the house. When no one answered, he went back to the garage and banged on the big front door, as though hoping that someone might be out here instead of in the house.

He looked through the window and saw the back end of a Volvo parked inside.

He spun on his heel and strode quickly back to his car and the waiting children, suddenly understanding what was going on and how he could get a warrant to search the garage, the car, and likely Whitlock's house to boot.

chapter
FORTY-THREE

Energetic legwork produced two witnesses who knew that Warren Whitlock had been in a relationship with Andie Matheson several years ago. He had admitted to city manager Brenda Morton, somewhat reluctantly, that he was dating Andie when she asked him about it at the time, and when Andie broke it off he'd talked to city procurement clerk Sabrina Arliss about it at length. Apparently he and Arliss were friends who often took lunch breaks together.

Convinced that they were halfway to establishing reasonable grounds to believe that a search of Whitlock's house and garage would produce evidence connecting him to Andie Matheson's murder, Kevin then put Bishop in front of the CPIC terminal and instructed him to query Rita Whitlock, Warren's mother.

Bishop quickly found a driver's licence in her name that had been suspended six years ago as a result of a medical report filed by her physician. The report specified dementia as the reason for the suspension of her licence.

More importantly, he also found a vehicle registered in her name. The registration had recently been renewed and was still valid. The automobile was a 2004 Volvo XC sport utility vehicle with over two hundred thousand kilometres on it. The SUV fell within the likely candidates set out by Dave Martin as the vehicle used to dump Andie Matheson's body and the murder weapon.

Bishop shook his head at the screen and turned to look at Kevin over his shoulder. "Brilliant, absolutely brilliant. What gave you the idea of running his old lady's name?"

"I don't know," Kevin said. "Just a sudden inspiration, I guess."

They arrested Warren Whitlock that evening and brought him up to the detachment office for processing while his house and property were searched. Whitlock called his attorney, a local woman who'd represented him during his divorce nine years ago, and was then put into the interview room.

As they watched him fidget nervously on the monitor in the next room, Kevin took a call from Dave Martin. He put it on speaker so Ellie and Carty could listen in.

"We have a match on the car tires," Martin said. "This is the one we wanted to find."

"Now we have to put him inside it last Thursday morning," Kevin said.

"I don't know about last Thursday necessarily, but we're lifting prints from the interior and the back hatch that will likely match his. It's starting to add up."

"Yeah, we're getting there. Thanks, Dave."

"It's what they pay me the big bucks for."

As Kevin put his phone away, Ellie said, "I know you're tired, but this is the one you've been waiting for."

He put his hand on the door handle, nodding.

In the room, seated at the table across from Warren Whitlock, Kevin took care of the preliminaries regarding Whitlock's rights and then got down to business.

"Tell me about your relationship with Andrea

Matheson."

"We dated. Briefly." Whitlock ran his hand nervously through his short red hair.

"When was that?"

"The summer of 2016. We called it off the next spring."

"Was it a sexual relationship?"

Whitlock's eyes dropped to his hands. "Does it matter? I mean, I had a crush on her for a while, you know, I'd see her around city hall, so I asked her out a couple of times and finally she said yes. So we dated. It was a nice Christmas, for once. She went with me to see my mother. But it kind of tapered off after that, and eventually we both agreed to move on."

"I see." Kevin nodded. "It was an amicable split, is that what you're saying?"

"Yeah."

"You had sex with her before that? While you were dating?"

"Yeah."

"When was the last time you saw her?"

Whitlock removed his glasses and rubbed an eye. "I'm not sure, exactly. A year ago? Maybe a year and a half?"

"Where was that?"

"In the Walmart. Or the grocery store. I can't remember which. It was one of those things where you bump into each other, it's awkward, you make small talk, and then you excuse yourself and get out of there as fast as you can."

Kevin paused for a moment, opening his file folder and turning over a few pages. "You mentioned your mother. Tell me about her."

Whitlock folded his arms. "She's in long-term care."

"Here in the city?"

"Yes. At Birchmont Manor."

"What's her name?"

"Rita."

"How old is she, Warren?"

"Seventy-six. She suffers from dementia."

"I'm sorry to hear that. What about your father? Is he still alive?"

"Yeah."

"Where's he?"

"Napanee."

"Is that where you're originally from?"

Whitlock nodded. "I moved to Ottawa to go to Carleton when I was eighteen."

"And your mother moved up here to Brockville to live with you, is that right?"

"Yeah. After they split, I brought her up here. She rented the house on Havelock Street, and I moved in to look after her. After my divorce." He frowned. "Why are you asking me about my family?"

"I understand you were married to the niece of Peter Lambton."

Whitlock stuck his legs out, crossing them at the ankles. "I don't want to go through all that."

"What was her name?"

"Erica. I don't want to talk about her right now."

Kevin paused again, turning over another page. "What kind of car do you drive?"

"I don't own a car. I bike everywhere. I'm a believer in personal fitness and protecting the environment."

"I see," Kevin said.

"Actually, I own three bicycles. They're all registered with the Brockville police, by the way. Most people don't realize they have a free program for bikes."

"What about in wintertime? What do you do then?"

"I walk or bus or take a taxi. People give me a ride every now and again."

"We found a car in your garage. Who does it belong to?"

Whitlock closed his eyes for a moment. "My mother."

"Do you drive it?"

He grimaced. "Rarely. Occasionally."

"What sort of occasions?"

"When I have a lot of shopping to do."

"Do you ever let anyone else drive it?"

"No. Never. It's only insured for my mother and myself. Well, actually, I took Mom off the insurance when she went into long-term care; it took the cost of the premiums down quite a bit."

"I see. Did you drive it last week?"

Whitlock's eyes searched the ceiling. "Um, I don't think so."

"Did you drive it down to Peter Lambton's cottage on Hill Island last Wednesday night or early Thursday morning?"

"No. I didn't."

"We lifted tire tread marks from two different spots along the Parkway on Thursday morning. One set of tire prints from the place where the car stopped and the driver disposed of Andie Matheson's nude body in the ditch, and the other place where the driver realized he'd forgotten to get rid of the knife he used to kill her. He pulled over, got out, and threw the knife into the ditch."

Whitlock's eyes continued to avoid Kevin's.

"Both sets of tire tread marks match the tires on your mother's Volvo."

Whitlock ran a hand through his hair. "No, it can't be. You're wrong. It's a system error of some kind."

"There's no error," Kevin assured him. "Our forensic identification specialists are world-class at this sort of thing. Your mother's car was there. Both spots."

Whitlock shook his head. "You're wrong."

"We also lifted shoe prints from both scenes," Kevin added, "and we'll be comparing them to shoes we find in your house. They'll match too, won't they?"

Whitlock said nothing.

Kevin waited. Whitlock remained silent. Kevin turned another page in the folder. "Talk to me about Peter Lambton."

"I've already talked to the other two," Whitlock said, "the Chinese detective and the woman, about that. I don't have anything else to say about it."

"Were you aware that Andie had an affair with Lambton just before you two got together?"

"Yeah, I was aware of it."

"How did you feel about that?"

Whitlock sat up, pulling his feet in. "I don't know. The guy's a creep. I felt sorry for her."

"Did she help you with your investigation? While you were putting together your complaint against him?"

Whitlock folded his arms across his chest. "I have no comment on that at all."

"Did you discuss it with her? Maybe pillow talk or something?"

"I have nothing to say about that. Period."

"Was she your informant? The one who got you started on your complaint against the mayor?"

Whitlock said nothing.

"What time was it when you went down to Lambton's cottage after Andie?"

Silence.

"Was it last Wednesday night, or was it early morning."

"I didn't go down there. I've never been there."

Kevin placed a series of printouts on the table where Whitlock could see them. "These are fingerprints we lifted from Lambton's cottage after Andie was murdered, and this one," he tapped one of the photographs, "was found on blood-stained bedding thrown into the dumpster behind the Thousand Islands Mall. We're comparing them now to the prints you just gave us when you were booked. They're going to match as well, aren't they? They'll tell us you were at the cottage, you went into the kitchen and grabbed the knife that was used to kill her, you stabbed her fifteen times with it—fifteen times—and then you disposed of the bloody mess after she was dead."

Whitlock shook his head. "Systems errors," he said, stubbornly. "Faulty data. I wasn't there. I didn't do it."

Kevin didn't bother arguing with him. His lawyer could have the pleasure of explaining to him how miniscule the chances were that the physical evidence of Dave Martin's team would be thrown out at trial for faulty or improper procedures. He returned the photographs to the file folder and closed it.

"Warren, were you aware that Andie was pregnant when she was murdered?"

Whitlock froze. His eyes flicked to Kevin and away again.

"Were you? Did you know that the father was likely Peter Lambton?"

Whitlock said nothing, but his eyes searched the wall across from him.

"We're running DNA tests on the fetus to determine paternity. Did you know it didn't die right away, after Andie was attacked? She was stabbed a number of times in the abdomen, but somehow the killer missed her womb."

Whitlock's lower lip began to tremble.

"The pathologist told me during the post-mortem," Kevin continued, " that the fetus would have continued to live on the oxygen in the blood right around it for, I don't know, maybe a minute or two after her heart stopped."

Whitlock's hands curled into fists.

"We have photographs that were taken during the autopsy. Would you like to see them? In case you're lying and you had sex with her recently and the baby was yours?"

Warren Whitlock leaned forward suddenly and vomited across Kevin's shoes.

chapter
FORTY-FOUR

The house on Havelock Street was small and cramped. Downstairs there was an eat-in kitchen, a living room, a ten-by-ten bedroom, and the bathroom. Upstairs there were two bedrooms with slanting ceilings and a storage closet between them, at the top of the stairs. The basement was partially finished, with a cement floor and drywall on two sides. There was a washer and dryer down there, two of Whitlock's bicycles, a few spare pieces of furniture, and not much else.

Bishop was going through the stuff in the downstairs bedroom, which belonged to Whitlock. There was room in here for a double bed, a highboy dresser, and a closet holding Whitlock's spare suit, shirts, and winter sweaters. He'd just finished up the closet when Leung stuck his head in.

"How's it going?"

"This guy's life is depressing as hell," Bishop said. "How's it going upstairs?"

"We've finished his mother's bedroom. Looks like he left it more or less the way it was on the day she went into long-term care."

Bishop shuddered. "It's claustrophobic in here, man. Don't you feel it?"

"Yeah. There wasn't anything of interest in her room. We're just starting on the other one now." The second bedroom upstairs was being used by Whitlock as a home office, and Leung was hoping the desktop computer and filing cabinet might yield evidence that would be important to the investigation.

Bishop's cellphone rang. As he took it out and answered it, Leung hesitated in the doorway. If it was Kevin calling for an update, he might want to hear from Leung as well, so he decided to linger for a moment in order to be sure.

"No, it's the place on Havelock I told you about. It'll be a while."

Leung could tell from Bishop's tone that it was a personal call, probably his wife, but still he hesitated.

"That's too bad. I think you would have enjoyed getting out. What about the other thing I mentioned, did you think about it yet?"

As Leung watched Bishop listen to his wife's response, he saw Bishop's eyes widen as something occurred to him. He looked at Leung and held up a finger, asking him to wait.

"Yeah, I'm here with Dennis. You remember, Dennis Leung? Yeah, he's taking the upstairs and I'm taking the downstairs. Plus the basement. No, we did the garage first. So it's still going to be a couple of hours. I need to go for now, but I'll call you later. Okay? Love you. Bye."

Bishop slipped the phone into his pocket. "Can I ask you a question?"

"Sure," Leung said.

"Your wife, Lily. She works, right?"

"Yes. At a bank downtown."

"Right, she's a manager or something. Does she have

any hobbies? You know, stuff she likes to do in her off hours?"

"She does a lot of things with the kids," Leung said slowly, trying to figure out where Bishop was going with this.

"Yeah, but what about her own time? Does she like to do stuff like painting or scrapbooking or shit like that?"

"Not really. She used to do some pottery when we were first married, but she sold the kiln and the wheel when May was born."

"Perfect. That's perfect. Listen, she's met Jennifer, my wife, right? At the Christmas party. I remember them talking together."

Leung nodded.

"She's really nice. Lily is. Jenn suffers from severe depression and anxiety, I don't think I mentioned that to you before."

Leung shook his head.

"It's not something I talk about because she hates people knowing about it, thinking she's weak and a failure and all that stigma shit that people hang on other people who have to deal with this kind of thing every day."

"I understand," Leung said.

"Here's where I'm coming from. That woman, Freeland, the one who was a friend of Lambton's wife, she does that tabletop glassblowing. What the hell's it called? Lampwork? Something like that. Anyway, she gives beginner lessons and I thought Jenn might really like trying it out. She's very creative but it's like she doesn't have an outlet and I thought this might be the thing. She asked her friend at work, but she wasn't interested. I was wondering if Lily might go for it. Maybe try a lesson or two with Jenn, give her someone to go along with."

Leung pursed his lips, thinking about it.

"I know it's a lot to ask," Bishop added, "but she's really nice, and Jenn likes her. It'd be someone she could trust. Someone who wouldn't make her feel like an idiot if she didn't do well at it. If you know what I mean."

"I know exactly what you mean." The smile started at the corners of Leung's eyes and spread outward. "I tell you what, I can ask her about it. Okay?"

Bishop exhaled in relief. "That'd be great, Dennis. I really appreciate it. If she thinks she might, get her to call me first."

"Sure."

Bishop turned to the highboy dresser and opened the small drawer on the top left. "I can give her Jenn's cell number and she can call her to talk it over. Fuck me. Look what we have here."

Leung frowned in confusion as Bishop motioned him over for a look.

Inside the drawer, sitting on top of Whitlock's neatly folded white underwear, was a cellphone. It was an iPhone with a bright pink case.

"I think," Bishop grinned, "we just found Andie Matheson's damned cellphone."

chapter FORTY-FIVE

Kevin let himself into the house through the side door. He paused at the bottom of the stairs to listen. The house was quiet, other than the sound of water running in the bathroom—Janie, in the shower.

Garbage bag in hand, he went downstairs into the basement. He opened the lid on the washing machine, dropped in a detergent bud, and shook the contents of the bag into the washer.

It was the stuff he'd been wearing tonight during the Whitlock interrogation, including trousers, socks, underwear, and shirt. Thankfully, he always kept a complete change of clothing in his locker, and after a quick shower he'd dressed again, expecting to resume his interrogation of Warren Whitlock. Ellie, however, had decided to close it down for the night. She wanted Whitlock to have ample time to recover from his upset stomach and to think about the situation he was in.

Whether or not he confessed was hardly an

overwhelming concern. The physical evidence that was beginning to come in would be more than enough for the Crown to build a rock-solid case against Whitlock for the murder of Andie Matheson.

Kevin lowered the lid on the washer but didn't start it. The plumbing in their house was a little wonky, and turning on the hot water in one place would suddenly reduce it elsewhere. He knew Janie loved hot showers, and he didn't want to have her suddenly doused with cold water out of the blue.

He sat down on a stool and stared at the floor, thinking that Andie Matheson had been a very lonely, sad person. Her unfortunate habit of falling into relationships with older men had led to one unhappy outcome after another, from Peter Lambton to Leon Gracz, Derek Colter, and Warren Whitlock. When she finally thought she'd found happiness, discovering she was pregnant with Lambton's child, Whitlock's unbalanced jealousy had destroyed everything.

Kevin suspected that Whitlock's cellphone GPS data would likely tell the tale. He'd probably been stalking her for some time, sitting outside her apartment building in his mother's Volvo, following her when she left for work in the morning, and when she'd resumed her affair with Peter Lambton he'd no doubt found out about it. His hatred of Lambton was all-consuming, and when he saw that Andie had gone back to him it must have been overwhelming.

And yet it seemed he'd wavered for a long time, for weeks, unable to decide what to do about it. Kevin wondered if Lambton's statement to the press six days ago, accepting the failure of his recent court challenge but insisting on his innocence regarding the complaint brought against him by Whitlock, had been the trigger. Why Whitlock had attacked Andie rather than his nemesis, however, was more than Kevin could fathom. Perhaps it was connected in some way to his own abuse at the hands of his ex-wife, Lambton's niece.

Kevin sighed. He didn't want to think about it any more tonight.

Two women were dead, and two men were about to be held accountable to the fullest extent of the law. Lambton had loved his wife's money, but not her. Whitlock had loved Andie Matheson to an unhealthy extreme.

Lives lost, and relationships in ruins. Kevin thought of Kyle Baldwin, who could be said to have toppled the first domino when he'd carelessly misled Andie into moving to the city on the misconception that he'd made a romantic commitment to her. Kyle was alive, in a happy relationship, and Andie was dead.

He heard the shower quit in the bathroom above his head, and inevitably his thoughts turned to Janie.

The first time he met her was in the fall of 2012. The Sparrow Lake Police Service had disbanded that summer, and Kevin's request for a transfer into the OPP had been accepted. He'd just cleaned out his desk and was on his way to Smiths Falls to meet with Fisher and Patterson when he decided he needed a haircut first. A new beauty salon had opened up in the village a few weeks ago, and when he looked in the window he saw that all of the chairs were empty. He went in.

Janie was twenty-five, her divorce from her husband was in the works, and she was living alone in the little house on Queen Street with a four-year-old and a two-year-old. She'd started her own business and had just signed a lease to rent the storefront on Main Street at a rent she knew was low but she still wasn't sure she could afford. She'd been open for two weeks and while Kevin wasn't her first customer, he could tell from the determined way that she kept her face empty of emotion that she was relieved someone, anyone, had walked through the door.

He would never forget the feeling of her fingers on the back of his neck as she gave him the twelve-dollar businessman's trim. It was like his entire body was suddenly filled with electricity. He'd paid with a twenty and waved off the change. Outside in the car he felt like a fool, but he knew without a doubt he'd go back tomorrow to try to talk to her again.

He slowly stood up and started the washer, then went upstairs. Janie met him in the hallway, a towel wrapped around her body, another in her hand as she dried her shoulder-length hair.

"Hey there, big guy." She stood on her toes and kissed the side of his jaw. "Everybody's asleep. Let's hit the hay while we can."

He followed her into the bedroom. He watched her open her side of the closet. Dropping the towels on the floor, she took out a night dress and pulled it on, her back to him. He stripped, pulled on a pair of track pants, turned off the bedside light, and slipped under the covers.

She got in beside him, rolled over onto her side, and rested her chin on his bicep. "I'm exhausted. Those two women, I swear they yapped the whole way here. I couldn't get a word in edgewise."

Kevin reached over with his free hand and moved a strand of damp hair from the corner of her mouth.

"I'm glad you're home."

"Mmm."

"I was thinking."

"Mmm?"

"We should cancel the landline. Just go with our cells. Save some money."

"Mmm."

Kevin's mind began to drift as sleep approached.

"Caitlyn wants a cat," Janie murmured.

"I know."

"A kitten..."

"It's okay with me."

She began to snore, oblivious.

A cat. Another life in his life.

Half-conscious, he smiled at the darkness. A wife, children, a cat. He was surrounded by lives. Living beings pressed in around him on all sides.

It felt good. It felt warm and secure.

Home. Family. Love.

Things he'd always wanted and thought he'd probably never have.

Why was he so fortunate when so many others were not?

He fell asleep.

chapter FORTY-SIX

Jack Riley lived in a tumble-down farmhouse at the corner of Tamarack Lane and Lake Road, just above Sparrow Lake where Ellie lived in her four-season cottage on the waterfront. Riley was an old bachelor who'd taken a liking to her despite the fact that she was a cop, and he kept an eye on things when she was away. He kept an eye on things when she was there, as well, and would occasionally call her when a suspicious-looking vehicle turned down the lane toward her property.

Danny Merrick, assistant commissioner of special projects for the Royal Canadian Mounted Police, had encountered Riley's distant early warning system before. Riley would instantly spot his black Town Car as a dead giveaway, and he would be on the phone to Ellie before Merrick's driver reached the first bend in the road above her cottage.

Because it was consistent with his nature as a long-time investigator, Merrick had decided to do a little research on Riley and his side interests. As a result, before turning down Tamarack Lane on this particular evening, he told Sergeant Dominic Lambert to stop at Riley's house.

At the front door he introduced himself, explained that he was about to pay a social call on Ellie, and described what he wanted. At first, Riley insisted he had no idea what Merrick was talking about, but after a few minutes of affable coaxing and the sight of cash emerging from Merrick's wallet, the light began to dawn.

"Wait right here and I'll get it."

Merrick lounged inside Riley's kitchen door, thinking about nothing in particular, until the old man returned with a medium-sized paper bag, its top carefully rolled.

"You'd better start with one jar and see how you make out," Riley advised, shoving Merrick's payment into his pocket. "I know she likes it, but easy does it until you know what you're getting yourself into."

"Thanks." Merrick tucked the bag into the crook of his arm.

"She's a good person," Riley said, holding the door open for him.

Merrick stepped outside. "She is."

"I keep an eye on her." He looked at the paper bag. "Which you know, since you also know I'm into that stuff."

Merrick nodded, smiling.

"She's a city girl. She's still getting used to things out here."

Merrick reached into his suit jacket. "I'm kind of a caretaker with the federal government. I've worked with Ellie before, and I consider her a friend as well as a damned fine law enforcement colleague. I had two reasons for stopping tonight. One was for this," he moved the bag in his arm, "and the other was to give you this."

He held out a business card. "I keep an eye on her too, and I want you to have my personal number. It's written on the back. You see anything at all wrong down there, anything that seems off, call me. Any time. Day or night."

Riley eyed the card. "You're not with Excise, are you?"

Merrick laughed. "No, I'm not. But I may report you if this stuff doesn't measure up."

"Then I got nothing to worry about."

It was a given that Riley would call down to Ellie as soon as Merrick's ass was off his verandah.

As he got out of the Town Car in front of her cottage, Merrick retrieved his case of beer from the trunk and balanced the paper bag on top of it. Lambert slid down his window.

"Eleven o'clock, Dom," Merrick told him. "I'll call if there's any change."

"Yes, sir."

As the Town Car rolled back up the lane, Merrick turned around to find Ellie standing there with her arms folded, head tilted to one side.

"Riley called ahead," Merrick said.

"He did." She dropped her cigarette, stepped on it, and motioned him toward the kitchen door on the far side of the cottage. "Glad you could stop by."

"Sorry I can't stay long." He followed her around the corner and up the wooden stairs. "Thanks." He preceded her into the kitchen and put his gifts down on the counter next to the sink.

"Another crisis?" She closed the door and went to a kitchen cupboard for two whiskey glasses.

"The usual. 'Oh no, oh God, we're all going to die.' That sort of thing." He took the mason jar out of the paper bag and held it up to the light. The liquid inside the jar was clear and colourless. There were no particulates floating in suspension, no silt on the bottom of the jar, no nothing. "Is this stuff as good as it looks?"

"Better. But only in moderation." She winked at him as she took the jar and screwed off the lid. "Especially if you have to work tonight."

"Just a taste. So I can experience the legend that is Jack

Riley's moonshine."

Ellie opened his case of beer and put a few bottles in the fridge. She took two cold bottles of her own beer out and handed one to him. She poured two fingers of the potato vodka in each glass, and they sat down in her living room. It was still half an hour before sunset, and she'd opened the vertical blinds on the sliding doors leading onto her back deck because she knew he liked to look at the lake.

She took a drink first, so he could see whether or not it would kill her. She swallowed, wiped the tears from her eyes, and managed a faint smile. "Good."

He sniffed it cautiously, then downed a mouthful. He gasped, coughed, and barked a hoarse laugh. "God! Oh!"

"The beer's your chaser," she reminded him.

He swigged beer. After a moment, he laughed again. "Oh, yes. He definitely has skills."

"He does."

Ellie watched Merrick set his glass aside and cross his legs, his eyes on the sliding doors and the darkening water beyond. She marvelled that he always seemed comfortable in her presence, always natural around her, always calm and relaxed.

Their lives were very separate, and their careers often required them to withhold many things from each other, but nonetheless they'd become good friends over the past year. More than friends, a few times. It was exactly the kind of relationship she wanted. He was exactly the kind of friend she needed.

"Two homicides," he said, sipping his beer. The Kathryn Lambton and Andie Matheson murders were still front and centre in the news. "Leeds County's getting to be a very dangerous place."

After his arrest for the murder of Andie Matheson, Warren Whitlock continued to maintain his innocence. Ellie was confident, however, that the physical evidence results coming back from the lab was solidifying their case against him.

The Centre of Forensic Science had matched samples of blood traces lifted from the front passenger footwell and the rear cargo area of Mrs. Whitlock's Volvo to those sent by the pathologist, Dr. Burton, after Andie Matheson's autopsy, placing the victim and the knife in the vehicle after her murder. The tire treads on the Volvo were identical to those collected by Martin and his team from the Parkway dump sites, and no fingerprints other than Whitlock's had been found inside the vehicle.

Whitlock's cellphone records not only proved his involvement with Andie two years ago, but also that he'd unsuccessfully tried to rekindle the relationship over the past few weeks. As well, the phone's GPS data established a pattern of stalking during Whitlock's off hours and placed him in the immediate vicinity of Hill Island the night before and the morning of the murder.

The discovery of the victim's cellphone in his underwear drawer was the icing on the cake. Stubbornly insisting he was innocent, Whitlock refused to explain how it had gotten there, or why his prints were the only ones found on it other than those of the victim.

Early in the investigation, Ellie and Dave Martin had conjectured that their target could be profiled as a disorganized offender, and fingerprint evidence in particular had proven that theory correct.

Whitlock had gone to the cottage presumably to confront Andie Matheson and Peter Lambton, and had apparently not made advance preparations for murder. He hadn't brought gloves with him, and he hadn't taken the time to look for a pair in the cottage. He'd seized on the knife in the kitchen as a weapon of opportunity, leaving fingerprints on the walnut knife block and the island which he'd failed to wipe off afterward.

He'd grabbed the shower curtain from the bathroom and used it to wrap the victim's body before hauling it downstairs and outside to the Volvo, leaving bloody fingerprints all over it. He'd used towels from the bathroom to clean up after himself, but in hastily wiping down the staircase and front door, he missed several of his fingerprints on the underside of the banister.

He'd driven to his house and changed his bloodstained clothes, shoving them into the garbage bag with the victim's clothing, the bedding, the towels, and the shower curtain before disposing of everything in the dumpster behind the mall. In his panic he seemed to have overlooked the fact that not only would his fingerprints be found but also his DNA on his discarded, bloodstained clothing. Apparently he'd hoped that the dumpster would be hauled away without any of it ever being discovered.

Peter Lambton, on the other hand, had already informed his lawyer that he would be entering a guilty plea for the murder of his wife. Ellie had agreed with Kevin that Lambton had been trying to hide a guilty conscience from them, but she'd also suspected it was because he'd murdered Andie Matheson. All the while, however, it had been the guilty knowledge of having strangled his wife and dropped her to the bottom of the St. Lawrence River with a boat anchor tied to her ankle.

A veteran city councillor had been appointed interim mayor, and the city clerk had stepped into Warren Whitlock's job as director of corporate services. Marian Applewood, the supervisor of the procurement unit who was such a big fan of Ellie March, was named acting city clerk. Governance of the municipality had taken a serious hit over the past week, and council and city staff were closing ranks and reaching out to the people of Brockville to do whatever was necessary to calm the waters.

Meanwhile, the OPP's East Region issued a brief statement announcing the closure of the investigation of Peter Lambton for criminal wrongdoing in connection with city contracts. No charges would be laid. A second statement, issued with a similar lack of fanfare, announced that Inspector Todd Fisher had been placed on administrative leave pending an investigation of conflict of interest under the force's code of conduct. Fisher's replacement would be named in the coming days.

"Speaking of dangerous places," Ellie said, "I'd like to ask your advice on something."

Merrick nodded slowly.

Ellie finished her moonshine and chased it with beer. When she could speak again she said, "There are changes coming, and I have a couple of opportunities. They're both management positions. I'm not management material, but I think I should probably take one of them. You've got a lot of senior management experience and you obviously can handle internal politics. I'd like to pick your brain."

"Of course."

Without getting into details, she explained Fisher's situation and the opening it would create. "I could do it as a lateral transfer, since it's an equivalent rank. On a permanent basis, or just temporarily. Leanne's already hinted to me that she's going to offer it to me, so I'm thinking ahead. The only thing is, it means moving back to the region. I'm not sure I want to do that."

Merrick nodded. "Since it's not a promotion, it's a question of whether you prefer headquarters or field work."

"Exactly. Leeds is a good detachment, I know the staff, and I've got a good feel for the community. Not much of a learning curve, and Leanne is an excellent regional commander, so no problem there." She studied him. "But that doesn't answer the question. I just feel that moving back to the field at this point is a step backward for me. Not that it's inferior work in any way. It's just..."

"Been there, done that."

She nodded. "I like the flexibility of the CIB. There are fifteen detachments in this region, and my assignments send me to any one of them, depending on the availability of case managers. I love the responsibility. I love the challenges. I love the work."

"So what's the other opportunity?"

"Tony's getting an overseas assignment."

Merrick's eyes lit up. "Is he? Where?"

"In Africa. It's a training assignment. I'm not sure where." She watched him file the information away for future reference. Merrick knew Tony Agosta, having met him as a result of the Lane investigation into which he and the RCMP had been drawn last year. She wasn't worried that he'd spill the beans or use the information in an inappropriate way; she'd learned that Merrick was one of the most trustworthy persons she'd ever met. At the same time, she was amused to see how much interest he took in the internal machinations of someone else's law enforcement agency.

"So you've been offered the acting assignment to replace him?"

Ellie nodded.

"So it's a step up, but it's administrative and will take you out of the work that you like so much as a major case manager."

"Exactly."

"Serious internal politics. Fighting for your budget. Fighting off other senior managers for key people when they become available, and then fighting to keep them. Worrying about closure rates and results-driven policing policy issues, providing advice on corporate analysis frameworks and input into the yearly strategic plan, blah blah blah."

She sighed. "Yeah. All of that."

"Would you hate it? Would you be miserable every waking moment of your life if you took it?"

"I don't know." She stood up and walked over to the sliding doors. It was beginning to get dark outside. She looked at his reflection in the glass. "It's in Orillia. I couldn't do it from here."

"A four-and-a half hour drive from Ottawa. Three hundred and seventy-six kilometres."

"And you have that information in your head, just like

that."

"I do."

She waited for a few moments, her eyes travelling back out to the cold, still surface of the lake, but he offered no other comment. "All those things you listed, all that corporate junk, is stuff I should learn about."

"We all need to, at some point in our career." He set aside his beer and stood up. "Patience with organizational politics is a virtue," he said, coming over to stand beside her. "It's an area of weakness for you right now. It's a chance to work on it, turn it into a strength."

She looked at him. They were eye-to-eye; there was only about an inch difference in their height. "Or go nuts trying."

He smiled. "By the way, happy belated birthday."

"Thank you. I don't celebrate birthdays."

"*Au contraire*, I brought gifts. Beer and paint remover. That means we're celebrating right now. Even if it's, like, very late."

"And I appreciate it. Especially the paint remover."

He turned toward her, leaning against the frame of the sliding door. "Why don't you? Celebrate, I mean."

She looked away. These were things she didn't talk about. Not because they were painful or embarrassing, but because they weren't important to her. But she wanted him to understand. *That* was important to her.

"I've told you before that Paul and Mary were my adoptive parents. I don't know who my birth parents were." When he nodded, she continued. "April 20 was the day they brought me home. There was some confusion about my actual birth date. Mary told me years later that the DOB field had accidentally been left blank in my documentation with the agency, so they didn't have a clue. Every little girl is supposed to have a birthday, so they decided that the twentieth would be mine."

"I see."

"I didn't have a birth certificate. So when Mary sent

away for one, that's what she put on the form. April 20." She paused, a little embarrassed by the sadness she could see in his eyes. "So I never bother with birthday stuff. There isn't much point."

"Everyone should celebrate their birthday," Merrick said. "It's a celebration of ourselves, of who we are. Just for one day out of the year."

She shook her head. "No. Every little girl should have a birthday, for sure. My girls know their real birthdays and they celebrate them with Gareth and Suzie, and that's the way it should be. But I was always different. April 20 was important to Paul and Mary. It was the day they became parents, the day I joined their lives. So when I was a little girl, it was important to me because it was important to them. I tried to be happy about it, even after they explained to me that I was adopted, but once I left home it stopped being important at all. Mary still sent me a card with twenty dollars in it every April 20, and that was nice, but it was just a thing."

She put her hand flat on the window to feel its coldness. "She hasn't sent me one for three years, now. She doesn't remember any more."

"I'm sorry, Ellie."

She closed her eyes and leaned her shoulder into his chest. "Don't worry about it, Danny. It's just life. That's all. Just life."

He put his arm around her.

chapter
FORTY-SEVEN

Kevin had a meeting with his lawyer at the Brockville courthouse on Friday morning to sign some papers she had prepared for him in his child adoption case. The downtown area was congested, and he had to park a couple of blocks away and walk back. As he passed through the front entrance he noticed a number of journalists hanging around and remembered that Warren Whitlock was scheduled to make an appearance today.

When he located the lawyer-client meeting room that had been reserved for their use, the door was closed. Leaning against the wall, he took out his cellphone and checked the time. He was nearly fifteen minutes early.

He sent a text message to OPP Constable Mary Finn, who handled court case management duties for the Leeds County detachment here in the courthouse, asking about Whitlock's appearance. While he was waiting for a reply, he received a message from his lawyer.

Running 30 mins late. The rm's still ours.

No problem, he replied. *Here now. See you when I see you.*

As he put his phone away, he saw Finn walking toward the courtrooms at the back of the building. He caught up to her just as she was about to head into the washroom.

"What time's Whitlock's appearance?" he asked.

"In about ten minutes. Are you sitting in?"

"Might as well, I guess."

"See you in there." She banged open the washroom door and hurried inside.

Kevin strolled toward the courtrooms, looking at the notice boards that displayed their schedules for the day. When he found *R. v. Whitlock* he eased open the door and stepped inside.

Court was not yet in session, but the room was crowded. He caught the eye of the uniformed security officer down at the railing that separated the public seating area from the court proper. The man nodded and started up the aisle as Kevin found a spot against the wall just inside the door.

"Walker, isn't it?" The man shook Kevin's hand.

"Yeah. Sorry, I'm having a brain cramp at the moment."

"Rhamdani. Looks like a full house for this one."

Kevin nodded. Rhamdani was a uniformed special constable attached to the Court Services Bureau of the Brockville Police Service, which was mandated to provide courtroom security as well as other court- and prisoner-related duties in the city. Kevin didn't remember ever meeting him, but Rhamdani apparently knew him by sight.

They both looked up front as the court registrar and the court clerk entered through a side door. The two women made their way to a bench directly in front of the judge's podium where the registrar sat down and began sorting through documents in front of her.

"Excuse me." Rhamdani walked away and let himself through the little gate to talk to the clerk, who was looking over the registrar's shoulder at the documents on the bench.

The door opened behind Kevin, and Finn walked in.

"Hey," he said.

Finn smiled apologetically. She was a tall, willowy blonde for whom Kevin held enormous respect. Her intelligence was off the charts, and her ceiling was much higher than his, a fact he readily acknowledged without resentment.

As an OPP court case manager, she was responsible for all the files for the Leeds County detachment in the Brockville court location. She expedited all their cases through the system, worked closely with the Crown attorney's office, juggled schedules so that officers attended court during duty hours whenever possible, avoiding overtime, and she reviewed Crown briefs submitted by OPP officers to make sure they were on time and complete.

Kevin looked around for Mark Allore, who was responsible for the Crown briefs on the Whitlock case, but couldn't find him.

"He's just outside," Finn said, reading his mind.

"Everything set?"

Finn nodded. Whitlock had been arraigned and charged, and he'd entered a plea of not guilty. He'd had his bail hearing and had lost, the court deciding he posed a risk to the community and should remain in custody.

At that point his lawyer, who normally handled family law, stepped aside in favour of another attorney with criminal experience. Because he was from Kingston, the new lawyer was now filing a motion to change the venue to that city.

Allore came in, and he and Finn moved up to their spot behind the prosecution table. Moments later, Warren Whitlock was escorted into the courtroom by another security officer. He was seated in the enclosed bench in front of the railing that was reserved for the accused.

Whitlock stared with amusement at the three feet of

Plexiglas running along the top of the enclosure, as though he were sitting in a penalty box at a hockey game and the whole thing was a joke of some kind.

The judge entered and the court session began. As Kevin listened to the preliminaries, shifting for a more comfortable position against the back wall, he became aware that someone had slipped into the room and was standing just out of range of his peripheral vision.

Kevin scanned the benches and saw that it was indeed a full house, with no available spots for anyone else to sit down. He edged sideways and was about to turn around and invite them to take the spot next to him when the person suddenly began to move forward up the aisle.

She was small, not much more than five feet tall. She wore a pink windbreaker, jeans, and white sneakers. Her straight, sandy brown hair was pulled back in a ponytail.

Kevin watched as she moved steadily up the aisle. Her features looked familiar. As he struggled to place her, she reached the gate at the top of the aisle, just behind the accused's box.

Her hand darted under her windbreaker.

Before anyone could react, she jumped up on the railing behind Whitlock, reached a gun over the top of the Plexiglas, and shot him in the head.

Kevin lunged forward, pelting up the aisle as she fired a second shot. He was still several steps away when Rhamdani appeared from nowhere and dove along the railing, tackling her by the legs and driving her down across the laps of spectators in the front row.

Kevin reached the end of the row and began hauling people out of the way.

Rhamdani suddenly reared up and held the woman's pistol high in the air. "Gun!"

"Here!" Kevin shouted.

Rhamdani twisted around and reached out to him.

Kevin took the gun, dropped out the magazine, and cleared the chamber.

"Kevin, here!" It was Allore, behind him, holding out a plastic bag.

Kevin dropped the gun into the bag and turned back to see that the people in the front row were now standing up on the bench to give Rhamdani room to maneuver. He'd already secured the woman's hands behind her back with a plastic locking strap and was hauling her up.

Kevin stepped back so that Rhamdani could turn her around and bring her out into the aisle.

As the woman faced him, Kevin realized with a shock that she bore a very striking resemblance to Howie Burnside.

It was Erica Burnside, Warren Whitlock's ex-wife.

Peter Lambton's niece.

chapter
FORTY-EIGHT

It took Dennis Leung about thirty minutes to drive from his house in Brockville to Delta, a small village in the municipality of Rideau Lakes between Athens and Westport. It was a bright Saturday morning and there were other things he could be doing, but Tom Carty had asked him to run up to see him, and Leung had agreed.

When he arrived at the village he discovered that it was swamped with people and vehicles. Carty had mentioned something about a festival of some kind he was volunteering for, but he hadn't provided any details. Carty told him to come to the fairgrounds and to look him up in the main exhibition hall, and that was it.

Leung was a little disconcerted that it cost him two dollars to park in the exhibition grounds and another ten for admission into the festival, but only because it was his habit not to carry much cash on him at any given time. He preferred to pay for things with his debit card whenever he could. Fortunately, there was a toonie in the centre console ashtray that got him through the barrier and into a parking spot, and a couple of fives in his wallet that paid for his entrance into the building.

According to the signage plastered everywhere, the event was the village's annual maple syrup festival. The hall was filled with vendors selling bottles of maple syrup in all sizes, from little samplers to large jugs, plain containers and glass bottles shaped like maple leaves, bears, sugar shacks, and hockey goaltenders. There were packages of maple syrup candy and confections, and countless other products associated with maple syrup, cottage life, and whatever else could be loosely connected to the overall theme of the festival. Leung wondered if he might go into diabetic shock just from breathing the air in the room.

The odour of syrup was quickly overpowered by the smell of cooking food as he walked through the door into the big room in which the pancake breakfast was being held. Carty had said he would be working one of the grills, and Leung headed toward the far side through the rows of tables crowded with people eating breakfast. He passed a big pile of fifty-pound sacks of pancake mix and an industrial size mixer being operated by a teenager in a black T-shirt and an apron. He continued down the line of volunteers tending to grills covered with half-cooked pancakes until he spotted Carty turning over sausages with tongs. He wore a white apron over a long-sleeved henley T-shirt with the OPP logo on it, and when he saw Leung he motioned with the tongs for him to come over.

"Thanks for coming, Dennis." Carty turned over a sausage that was blackening nicely on the underside. "Have you had breakfast yet?"

"Yes. So this is a maple syrup festival, is it?"

"Yeah." Carty looked at the man standing next to him. "Have you met Derek?"

The man put down the spatula he'd been using to flip pancakes and stuck out his hand. "Derek Flood."

"Dennis Leung."

Flood was a few inches shorter than Carty but around the same age. His straight brown hair stuck out all over the place but his face was clean-shaven, his eyes were friendly, and his grip was firm.

"Derek's area chief for the Rideau Lakes Fire Department." Carty handed his tongs to an elderly woman standing behind him and took off his apron. "Let's just step outside for a moment."

"Sure." Leung waited for Carty to grab his windbreaker from the top of a mini-fridge, and then followed him down the row of grills and out a side door into a parking lot at the rear of the hall.

"My truck's just over here." Shrugging into his windbreaker, Carty led the way to a black Dodge Ram parked in the second row of vehicles. He unlocked it and motioned Leung into the passenger seat. Carty climbed behind the wheel and shut the door.

"Thanks for coming up on your day off," he said.

"No problem."

"Look, this probably could have waited until Monday, but I wanted to talk to you about it today."

"Okay."

"Your work on the Lambton cases was exemplary. That's what my reports say, that's what I've told RHQ, and that's what I'm telling you now."

"Thank you."

"I've assigned Mark Allore to the Erica Burnside case. He'll handle everything, not only the Whitlock shooting but also trying to establish the link to Lambton."

"Okay." Leung was aware that although the murder of Warren Whitlock had occurred within the jurisdiction of the Brockville Police Service, a joint forces operation had been set up including the BPS and the OPP to investigate what exactly had happened. Ellie March and Kevin Walker believed that Peter Lambton had been behind his niece's actions, that he'd convinced her to take a gun into the courthouse and shoot her ex-husband, and that Lambton's probable motive was to avenge Whitlock's murder of his lover, Andie Matheson.

"Obviously there's a connection to the Matheson and Kathryn Lambton cases, and senior management would really like to nail Lambton's ass for this one as well as for his wife."

"I agree," Leung said.

Carty nodded. "I want Allore on it because Bishop's going to be carrying the lion's share of the unit caseload for the next while, and I need you to split the work with him."

"All right. No problem."

"The other thing about this is the lack of security at the courthouse. The shit's really going to hit the fan on that, and Allore's the kind of guy who can handle it."

"Understood." Leung was aware that many courthouses in Ontario still hadn't implemented adequate security measures despite the passage of legislation in 2014 by the Ontario government that would provide the legal authority to do so. The Ottawa courthouse, for example, had gone ahead and created a single public access point with metal detectors and ongoing scrutiny of people entering the building by security officers, but many smaller courthouses in the province, Brockville included, had not yet taken similar steps. The Whitlock shooting was already well on its way to becoming a major political problem involving unions, multiple levels of government, and other opinionated stakeholders.

"Not that you couldn't handle it either, Dennis, under normal circumstances."

Leung said nothing.

Carty studied him for a moment. "I got a call last night from Jim Cherry with the DEU. He was calling to thank me for your assistance in an ongoing investigation in our jurisdiction. He wanted to know whether you'd be available for more work. I told him I'd get back to him. Is this something you want, Dennis?"

"Uh, not exactly." Leung stared out the windshield.

Beth Sanderson must have spread the word within the Drug Enforcement Unit that he'd been sitting surveillance on Howie Burnside and Paul Whiteman, and that he'd provided solid information contributing to their investigation of the outlaw motorcycle gang members who were actively moving drugs in Leeds County.

"The question that's in my mind," Carty said, rubbing his chin, "is whether or not you've got a thing for Burnside and his crew."

Leung looked out the side window of the truck.

"The punk, Whiteman, said something about you harassing them at their yard office and hassling him in a restaurant downtown. We've already got the straight story on both incidents, so his bullshit doesn't cut it with anyone."

Leung said nothing.

"Now, I wouldn't blame you for looking for a little payback, but that's not what we do, is it?"

"No, sir."

"So I won't ask the question. I'll proceed on the assumption you don't have a thing for Burnside and his punks, but that Allore is the guy to handle all the upcoming work related to them, Erica Burnside, and Lambton going forward."

"That's fine," Leung said.

Carty turned in his seat and held out his hand. "You're a helluva cop, Dennis. I haven't had a chance to say this yet, but I'm damned glad to have you in the unit. I hope you'll stick around."

Leung shook his hand. "That's the plan, sir."

"Glad to hear it."

chapter
FORTY-NINE

Sharon Lawson and her son Ray lived in a small frame house on Old River Road on the edge of Rockport. Through the trees in their backyard they could see the Thousand Islands Parkway at a spot about a kilometre west from where Andie Matheson's body had been found nine days ago. There was an antenna tower bolted to one side of the house with nothing on the top of it, and an oil tank next to it that looked like it needed to be replaced very soon.

Kevin pulled into the gravel driveway beside a grey passenger van and got out. He didn't really want to be here, but this was his case to finish up and his responsibility to handle. The sort of thing he was paid to do.

The woman who answered the door was a small, tired-looking brunette in jeans and a black T-shirt. She pushed hair from her eyes and looked up at him. "Yes?"

Kevin showed her his badge and identified himself. "Are you Mrs. Lawson?"

"Yes, I am. Is there something wrong at work?"

"Is your son at home, ma'am? Ray Lawson?"

Kevin had waited until today to follow up on the break-and-enter at Willard's Convenience Store because it was a Saturday and the boy would not be at school. Sharon Lawson worked evenings as a manager of a large trucking company's border office at the Lansdowne port of entry, and he needed to have them both at home when he talked to her son.

"Oh, god." Her hand flew to her mouth. "Yes, he's in the backyard, but..."

Kevin always dreaded the sudden look of fear and panic in the faces of parents whose children came to his attention in a negative way. "May I come in?"

She stepped aside. "Yes, of course. What's wrong? I don't understand why you need to see him."

"Could you bring him inside, Mrs. Lawson, so we can talk?"

"Yes, of course." She closed the door behind him and led the way down a hallway into the kitchen. "He's just in back. I'll go get him." She went down a short flight of stairs and outside through a side door.

Kevin stood in front of a window over the sink that gave him a view of the backyard. Ray Lawson was bent over a bicycle that was turned upside down on its seat and handlebars. He was struggling with a wrench, trying to loosen something. His mother walked up to him and gestured toward the house. Ray straightened abruptly and avoided her eyes as she continued to speak.

When Kevin saw the boy's shoulders slump and the wrench drop from his fingers, he thought he might have a chance to steer this thing in a positive direction after all.

The boy reluctantly followed his mother across the lawn. Kevin stepped into the dining room. The house as a whole seemed very neat and tidy. He went through the dining room into the living room and sat down on a couch. He took out his pen and notebook and opened it on his knee. He rehearsed in his head the order in which he wanted to cover things. How it turned out would depend in large part on the boy's responses to Kevin's questions.

He heard them enter the kitchen. Mrs. Lawson looked into the dining room and saw him sitting on the couch in the living room. She took her son by the sleeve of his jacket and towed him into Kevin's presence. "This is Ray."

"Sit down." Kevin pointed at a chair in the corner. "Mrs. Lawson, please have a seat as well."

As the boy lowered himself into the armchair, Kevin took out his badge. "I'm Detective Constable Walker of the Ontario Provincial Police. I'm here to ask you some questions about a very serious matter I'm investigating." He looked at Ray's mother. "Mrs. Lawson, I want you to remain present at all times, but when I ask Ray a direct question I want him to answer it and not you. Do you understand? He needs to speak for himself."

"All right." She folded her arms, upset.

"Before we begin, Ray, I need to explain what's happening. You're not under arrest right now, okay? We're going to discuss the situation you're in, and we're going to talk about the options you and your mom have, and see where it goes. You can talk to a lawyer right now if you want. I can help you get in touch with one. Do you want to do that?"

"We can't afford a lawyer," Mrs. Lawson said, her voice rising.

"Duty counsel can be—"

"No." The boy's head was down and his fists were pinned between his knees. "This is bullshit. I don't need a lawyer."

Kevin made a quick note in his notebook and then studied the boy for a moment. He was small and thin for his age, pale, and he looked very much like his mother. He would be in the first throes of puberty, Kevin realized, and would be suffering the moodiness, lack of confidence, and self-absorption common to kids that age.

"How old are you, Ray?"

"Thirteen."

"Where do you go to school?"

"Crestvale. In Gan." It was a public school in the nearby village of Gananoque.

"Grade eight?"

Ray nodded, head still down.

"Ray, ten days ago, a week last Wednesday evening, you went into Willard's Convenience Store on the Parkway and tried to buy cigarettes. Is that correct?"

Ray said nothing.

Kevin glanced at Mrs. Lawson, who was watching her son intently. "I spoke to Mr. Haddad, the owner. He told me about it. He also told me, Ray, that you took a chocolate bar and didn't pay for it."

"Oh, Ray." Mrs. Lawson's shoulders sagged. "Not again."

"That night, after Mr. Haddad closed the store and went home, someone broke in and stole six cartons of cigarettes. Do you know anything about that, Ray?"

He shook his head.

"Someone dragged a garbage can around to the bathroom window at the side of the building and broke in that way. They had to be fairly small to get through such a narrow opening, so we're not looking at an adult. You sure you don't know anything about it?"

He said nothing, his eyes down.

Kevin leaned back and crossed his legs. "Here's the thing, Ray. We had a scenes-of-crime officer process the store the next morning. Do you know what that means? They went in and took photographs, they lifted fingerprints, searched for hairs or threads from the burglar's clothing, maybe traces of DNA from sweat or spit, and then they took it all back to the lab for analysis. So when we arrest someone, we'll take their fingerprints and whatnot and match everything to the evidence collected from the scene and, boom. We've got our thief."

"Ray," Mrs. Lawson groaned, "you didn't. Tell me you

didn't."

The boy said nothing.

"I'm prepared to arrest you," Kevin went on. "Right now, this morning. I'm pretty certain the evidence will prove you were the one who broke into Mr. Haddad's store." He waited, but Ray remained silent. "Break-and-enter's a pretty serious crime. As police officers we take it very seriously, and so do the courts. When a kid like you is convicted of B-and-E, the judge can sentence you to custody, which means you're sent to a detention facility like the ones in Kingston or Ottawa. The average sentence for a kid on a B-and-E conviction is ninety days. Three months."

"Surely to God there's some mistake," Mrs. Lawson said, wringing her hands. "It can't be Ray. He wouldn't do something like that. Would you, Ray?"

The boy glanced at her and looked away again. Kevin watched his lower lip move slowly between his teeth. It was a sign that Ray was beginning to succumb to the stress of the situation. Hopefully, he'd soon begin to talk about it.

"More than half of the kids ordered into custody are at least sixteen," Kevin said. "You'd be one of the youngest. It can be pretty rough."

Mrs. Lawson began to cry.

"I'm not going to juvie." He looked at his mother. "I'm *not!*"

"Did you do it, Ray? What he's saying?"

"This is bullshit."

"Oh, Ray." Mrs. Lawson put her face in her hands. "I've worked so hard. Ever since your father died, I've tried so hard. But I never seem to do the right thing."

"It's not my *fault.*"

"When I make a mistake, Ray, it's my fault and nobody else's. It's the same for you, for this police officer, for everybody. When we do something wrong, we have to own it."

"It's bullshit."

"Did you do it, Ray? Did you break into that store and steal cigarettes?"

"It's bullshit."

"Stop using that word."

"Judges are less inclined to send young offenders into custody these days," Kevin said to Mrs. Lawson. "That's a good thing. In almost three-quarters of break-and-enter convictions, someone like your son, with no prior convictions, will be sentenced to probation. On average for one year."

"Instead of jail?"

"Yes." He looked at Ray. "So that would mean you'd have to meet with a probation officer on a regular basis. They'd set a bunch of objectives for you that you'd have to achieve, and if you screwed up at any step along the way, the court would get involved again and then for sure you'd be looking at a detention centre."

Ray shook his head. "A probation officer."

"That's right." Kevin tried to make his voice sound tough. "The lesser of two evils. But it depends on you, Ray. How you handle all this. Whether or not you tell the truth. To me, right now, and your mother. Or whether you give us the gears, play games with us, and try the gangsta routine."

The boy continued to shake his head, eyes down.

He turned to Mrs. Lawson. "How does he do in school?"

"His grades are excellent," she replied, wiping tears from her face with the back of her hand. "I can't believe this is happening."

"I haven't arrested him yet," Kevin reminded her. "There are ways in which we can avoid Ray going through the court system and ending up with a criminal record."

"Oh my god, is it possible? What do we have to do?" She rubbed at her tears with a finger.

Kevin spotted a box of tissues on a side table next to

the television set. He got up and handed it to her. "Yes it's possible," he said, sitting down again, "but it depends entirely on Ray's attitude. And yours, as well."

"I don't understand." She pulled out tissues and pressed them to her eyes.

"First, he needs to admit what he did. Rather than force me to arrest him and go through the whole process of matching his fingerprints and all the rest of it, he needs to tell me what he did. That's step one. Then there's a victim, don't forget. Mr. Haddad. Ray needs to find a way to make it up to him."

"Ray could return the cigarettes. I could pay for the broken window."

Kevin shook his head. "It needs to go far beyond that. There's been a history of shoplifting that Mr. Haddad tells me you've been trying to make up for," he glanced at Ray, who was avoiding his mother's eyes, "and there's a history of disrespect and a lack of consideration that needs to be corrected. Not just personally to Mr. Haddad but generally to adults in authority at whatever level."

He looked at Ray directly now. "You haven't given me any serious lip so far. I've dealt with some hard cases, but I'm not really seeing that from you yet, other than the coarse language, so there's that in your favour at the moment."

"He's never been in trouble with the police before," Mrs. Lawson said, squeezing the tissues in her hand. "Have you, Ray?"

"No."

"So let me put all the cards on the table, Ray." Kevin leaned forward. "What you did is very serious. A break-and-enter is too serious for me to let you off with just a warning. If we were just talking about the chocolate bar, then it would be different. But you broke a window, unlawfully entered the store, and stole items worth more than five hundred dollars. We can't just turn our backs on that. Do you understand?"

His chin was down and his eyes were on his fists in his

lap, but he nodded.

"Victory! Kevin hid his pleasure behind a stern expression. "The law allows me to use what's called an extrajudicial sanction." He turned to Mrs. Lawson. "It'll avoid arresting and charging him, and it'll keep him out of the court system. In Ray's case, it would involve completing a community program for kids that'll steer him in the right direction."

"All right." Mrs. Lawson nodded vigorously, wiping her cheeks. "All right. What do we need to do?"

"It's what Ray needs to do." Kevin took the toughness out of his voice. "Tell me about the cigarettes, Ray."

The boy opened and closed his fists several times. Finally, his eyes still down, he said, "They're in my room. I can get them if you want."

"Later. First, tell me what happened."

"He's such a dickhead. All I wanted—"

"Ray!" His mother pointed a finger at him. "Do *not* start that up!"

"Sorry." He finally looked up and made eye contact with Kevin. "I did what you said. Went through the window and into the bathroom. I could've taken everything he had, but I didn't. I got a couple of bags and filled them with cartons and went back out through the window again."

"How did you open the storage cabinet?"

"With a little crowbar. You know." He glanced at his mother. "From the van. I put it back."

"Oh, Ray."

"Was there anyone else with you when you broke in?"

"No."

"You acted entirely on your own?"

"Yes."

"Did you sell the cigarettes to anyone?"

"No. I opened one of the cartons and had a few from one of the packs. The rest are still okay."

"Do you want to talk to a lawyer now?" Kevin asked.

He looked at his mother. "Do I need to?"

"You have every right to," Kevin said, "and I can help you contact a lawyer who can assist you at no cost to your mother."

"I don't know," Ray said.

Kevin waited. The boy shrugged. Kevin waited a few moments longer, then took a folded sheet of paper from his inside jacket pocket. "This form is a request for referral to the community program I mentioned." He unfolded it and handed it to Ray. "If you agree to go through with it, it means you won't have to go to court and you won't need a lawyer. But you can always talk to a lawyer first if you want to. Right now or later."

The boy frowned at the form for a moment and then gave it to his mother.

"I've filled out part of it already." He looked at Mrs. Lawson. "You and he will complete the rest of it, sign it, and contact the agency I've put down on the back of the form. As you can see, I'm giving you four days to contact them and set up an appointment. They have Saturday hours, so you can call them today, but if by next Wednesday you haven't made an appointment I'll come back and arrest Ray and we'll go from there."

"We'll call them today." She looked at her watch. "This morning."

"Complete and sign this form now, before I leave, and take it with you to the appointment."

"Okay. Ray?" She stood up. "Let's do this at the table." She started for the dining room.

"Just a moment." Kevin stood up as well. "Ray. Take your mother in to your bedroom and get the cigarettes, and bring them back out here to me."

"Yes, sir."

"One other thing. As I said before, there's the prior shoplifting from Mr. Haddad's store and a history of disrespect toward him and other adults. Isn't that right?"

He nodded.

"I talked to Mr. Haddad before I came over here. For

almost an hour, actually. I explained to him how I wanted to approach things and what I was hoping you'd say and do this morning. You can understand he was a little upset at first."

Ray looked down. His mother folded her arms.

"I explained to him that the *Youth Criminal Justice Act*, which is the law that covers young people who commit crimes, actively encourages police officers to deal with these situations the way we're going to deal with yours. He finally calmed down."

Ray said nothing, his eyes still lowered.

"We're very sorry," Mrs. Lawson said. "He's always been polite to me. Even though..." She looked at Ray.

"I made a suggestion to him, and after some thought he agreed to it. As soon as you start this program, Ray, Mr. Haddad will expect you at his store every Saturday morning. You're going to work for him. You'll stock shelves, clean up, whatever he tells you to do. You're going to do it for free. I'm putting it into my report as one of the conditions you have to meet, along with the agency program."

Ray looked at his mother, his eyes wide.

"Now, bring those cigarettes out here and we'll get this form done."

Ray's bedroom turned out to be in the basement. Kevin listened to them walk through the kitchen and go down the stairs. He went into the dining room and sat down at the table. Mrs. Lawson had left the referral form on it on her way through. He moved it over in front of the empty seat at the head of the table.

He closed his eyes and rubbed his forehead.

Sometimes when he dealt with minors and their parents, there was a lot of yelling and screaming and sometimes there was denial and stubborn silence, but this morning he'd managed to find the middle road between the two extremes. Mrs. Lawson was clearly a loving parent who was trying her best to balance a career as the sole wage-earner in the family with being a single parent. Ray likely missed his father and was entering a phase in which his emotions were easily confused, and right and wrong were becoming much more difficult to sort out. Given his own family background, Kevin understood the position in which they both found themselves.

At that moment, just for a moment as he looked around the Lawson dining room while waiting for a chance to help a young boy take an important step toward finding a better path through his life, Kevin thought about his own mother and how much he missed her.

He heard their footsteps coming up the basement stairs.

Ray walked into the dining room with two plastic bags in his hand. He put them down on the table. "Here they are."

"Will you give them back to Mr. Haddad?" Mrs. Lawson asked, looking over the top of her son's head.

"No. Not right away. At the moment they're evidence. Sit down, Ray. Mrs. Lawson? Fill out the rest of the form with Ray and then sign it."

She picked up the chair at the head of the table and brought it around next to her son. She sat down, accepted Kevin's pen, and moved the form over to where both she and Ray could read it.

Kevin watched her study the form. Then she handed the pen to Ray, pointed, and said, "Check that off. Check them all off."

The boy nodded and applied pen to paper.

Kevin smiled.

Finally, a difference made.

Acknowledgments

This book is a work of fiction. Although the Ontario Provincial Police, the Leeds County Crime Unit, and most of the locales, including the city of Brockville, actually exist, all people and events in this novel are entirely the invention of the author, and any resemblance to actual people or events is strictly coincidental.

The author wishes to thank Detective Inspector Randy Millar of the Ontario Provincial Police, Retired. Any errors in fact, procedures, legal practices, or other errors or omissions are entirely the responsibility of the author or are the result of creative licence. Thanks go out as well to Margaret Leroux for superb copy editing and unwavering support.

The author referred to the following publications while writing this novel: Frederick A. Jaffe, *A Guide to Pathological Evidence* (Toronto: Carswell, 1976); Zoran Miladinovic, "Youth court statistics in Canada, 2014/2015," *Juristat*, Vol. 36, No. 1 (Ottawa: Statistics Canada, 2016); and John Warui Kiringe, "A Survey of Traditional Health Remedies Used by the Maasi of Southern Kaijiado District, Kenya," *Ethnobotany Research and Applications*, Vol. 4, pp, 61-74, Dec. 2006.

Most importantly, thanks once again to Lynn L. Clark for your editing, your patience, your partnership, and your love.

About the Author

Michael J. McCann lives in Oxford Station, Ontario, Canada. A graduate of Trent University in Peterborough, ON, and Queen's University in Kingston, ON, he worked for Carswell Legal Publications (Western) as Production Editor of *Criminal Reports (Third Series)* before spending fifteen years with the Canada Border Services Agency as a training specialist, project officer, and program manager at national headquarters in Ottawa. He's married and has one son.

In addition to the March and Walker Crime Novel series, he's also the author of the Donaghue and Stainer Crime Novel series, including *Blood Passage, Marcie's Murder, The Fregoli Delusion,* and *The Rainy Day Killer,* as well as *The Ghost Man,* a supernatural thriller.

If you enjoyed

PERSISTENT GUILT

you won't want to miss the exciting
debut of Ellie March and Kevin Walker in

Ask your local independent bookstore
to order it today!

Sorrow Lake
Michael J. McCann
ISBN: 978-1-927884-02-7

Follow Ellie March and Kevin Walker in

BURN COUNTRY

The second March & Walker Crime Novel

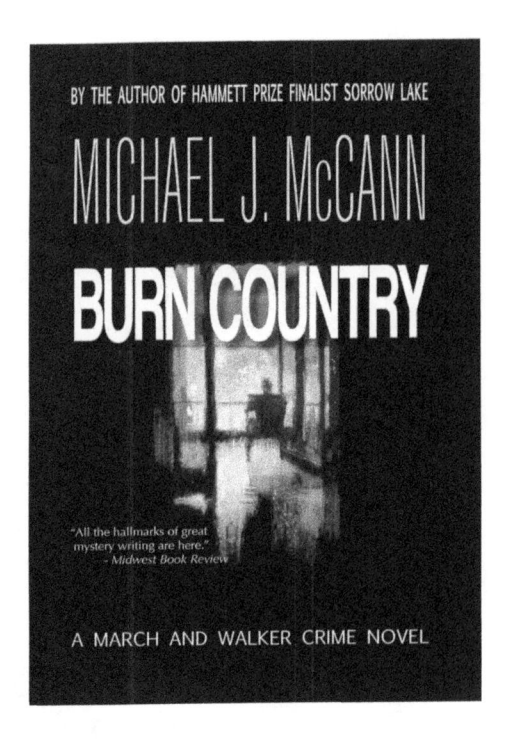

Ask your local independent bookstore
to order it today!

Burn Country
Michael J. McCann
ISBN: 978-1-927884-09-6

Also by Michael J. McCann
THE
DONAGHUE AND STAINER CRIME NOVEL SERIES

Blood Passage　　　　　ISBN: 978-0-9877087-0-0
by Michael J. McCann　　eBook ISBN: 978-0-9877087-1-7

Would you believe a small boy who claims he was murdered in his previous life? The first Donaghue and Stainer Crime Novel.

Marcie's Murder　　　　ISBN: 978-0-9877087-2-4
by Michael J. McCann　　eBook ISBN: 978-0-9877087-3-1

Donaghue's on vacation when he's jailed on suspicion of murder. Can Stainer get him out in time to find the real killer before it's too late?

The Fregoli Delusion　　ISBN: 978-0-9877087-4-8
by Michael J. McCann　　eBook ISBN: 978-0-9877087-5-5

Their only witness has a rare disorder that renders his testimony useless. Is Stainer wrong to believe he may actually know who the real killer is?

The Rainy Day Killer　　ISBN: 978-0-9877087-8-6
by Michael J. McCann　　eBook ISBN: 978-0-9877087-9-3

A serial killer preys on unsuspecting women — when it rains. Will Stainer's impending wedding end in murder, or will she survive to say her vows?

Also from the

PLAID RACCOON PRESS

THE PORTAL & THE EXPERIMENT
TWO NOVELLAS OF SUSPENSE

BY

LYNN L. CLARK

Ask your local independent bookstore
to order it today!

ISBN: 978-1-927884-11-9

BW
NOV - - 2019

AUG - - 2025 MB

DISCARD

AUG - - 2025

CPSIA information can be obtained
at www.ICGtesting.com
Printed in the USA
LVHW031510221019
634989LV00001B/127/P

9 781927 884133